PENGUIN BOOKS

HILDA LESSWAYS

Arnold Bennett was born in 1867 in the 'Potteries'—the region of England about which almost all his best novels were written. After studying art for a time, he began to prepare for his father's profession, that of solicitor; and at twenty-one he left Staffordshire to work in the office of a London firm.

He wrote a novel called *A Man from the North*, having meanwhile become assistant editor of a woman's weekly. Later he edited this paper, and noticed that the serial stories which were offered to him by a literary syndicate were not as good as they should be. He wrote a serial and sold it to the syndicate for £75. This sale encouraged him to write another, which became famous. It was *The Grand Babylon Hotel*.

He also wrote much serious criticism, and a serious novel, *Anna of the Five Towns;* and at last decided to give up his editorship and devote himself wholly to writing. This decision took him to Paris, where in the course of the next eight years he wrote a number of novels, several plays, and, at length, *The Old Wives' Tale*, which was an immediate success throughout the English-speaking world.

Subsequently Bennett wrote many other books, ranging from the farce of *The Card* to the elaborate documentation of *Imperial Palace. Clayhanger*, which was published in 1910, is the first novel of a trilogy: it was followed by *Hilda Lessways* (1911), and *These Twain*, which appeared during the First World War. Arnold Bennett died, a much-loved figure, in 1931.

Also available in Penguins are *Anna of the Five Towns, The Grand Babylon Hotel, The Card, Clayhanger* and *These Twain*. (*The Grand Babylon Hotel, Clayhanger,* and *These Twain* are available in Penguins in the United States.)

ARNOLD BENNETT

HILDA LESSWAYS

PENGUIN BOOKS

Penguin Books Ltd, Harmondsworth, Middlesex, England
Penguin Books Inc, 7110 Ambassador Road,
Baltimore, Maryland 21207, U.S.A.
Penguin Books Australia Ltd, Ringwood, Victoria, Australia
Penguin Books Canada Ltd, 41 Steelcase Road West,
Markham, Ontario, Canada
Penguin Books (N.Z.) Ltd, 182–190 Wairau Road,
Auckland 10, New Zealand

———

First published in Great Britain by Methuen & Co. 1911
Published in Penguin Books 1975
Reprinted 1976

———

Published by Penguin Books Inc by arrangement with
Doubleday & Company, Inc., New York

———

Copyright 1911 by George H. Doran Company

———

Printed in the United States of America
by The Colonial Press, Inc.,
Clinton, Massachusetts 01510
Set in Linotype Times

CONTENTS

BOOK I

HER START IN LIFE

CHAPTER 1

AN EVENT IN MR SKELLORN'S LIFE

I

THE Lessways household, consisting of Hilda and her widowed mother, was temporarily without a servant. Hilda hated domestic work, and because she hated it she often did it passionately and thoroughly. That afternoon, as she emerged from the kitchen, her dark, defiant face was full of grim satisfaction in the fact that she had left a kitchen polished and irreproachable, a kitchen without the slightest indication that it ever had been or ever would be used for preparing human nature's daily food; a show kitchen. Even the apron which she had worn was hung in concealment behind the scullery door. The lobby clock, which stood over six feet high and had to be wound up every night by hauling on a rope, was noisily getting ready to strike two. But for Mrs Lessways's disorderly and undesired assistance, Hilda's task might have been finished a quarter of an hour earlier. She passed quietly up the stairs. When she was near the top, her mother's voice, at once querulous and amiable, came from the sitting-room:

'Where are you going to?'

There was a pause, dramatic for both of them, and in that minute pause the very life itself of the house seemed for an instant to be suspended, and then the waves of the hostile love that united these two women resumed their beating, and Hilda's lips hardened.

'Upstairs,' she answered callously.

No reply from the sitting-room!

At two o'clock on the last Wednesday of every month, old Mr Skellorn, employed by Mrs Lessways to collect her cottage-rents, called with a statement of account, and cash in a linen bag. He was now due. During his previous visit Hilda had sought to instil some commonsense into her mother on the subject of repairs, and there had ensued an altercation which had never been settled.

'If I stayed down, she wouldn't like it,' Hilda complained
fiercely within herself, 'and if I keep away she doesn't like that
either! That's mother all over!'

She went to her bedroom. And into the soft, controlled shutting
of the door she put more exasperated vehemence than would have
sufficed to bang it off its hinges.

II

At this date, late October in 1878, Hilda was within a few weeks
of twenty-one. She was a woman, but she could not realize that
she was a woman. She remembered that when she first went to
school at the age of eight, an assistant teacher aged nineteen had
seemed to her to be unquestionably and absolutely a woman, had
seemed to belong definitely to a previous generation. The years
had passed, and Hilda was now older than that mature woman
was then; and yet she could not feel adult though her childhood
gleamed dimly afar off, and though the intervening expanse of
ten years stretched out like a hundred years, like eternity. She
was in trouble; the trouble grew daily more and more tragic; and
the trouble was that she wanted she knew not what. If her mother
had said to her squarely, 'Tell me what it is will make you a bit
more contented, and you shall have it even if it kills me!' Hilda
could only have answered with the fervour of despair, 'I don't
know! I don't know!'

Her mother was a creature contented enough. And why not –
with a sufficient income, a comfortable home, and fair health?
At the end of a day devoted partly to sheer vacuous idleness and
partly to the monotonous simple machinery of physical existence
– everlasting cookery, everlasting cleanliness, everlasting stit-
chery – her mother did not with a yearning sigh demand, 'Must
this sort of thing continue for ever, or will a new era dawn?'
Not a bit! Mrs Lessways went to bed in the placid expectancy of a
very similar day on the morrow, and of an interminable succession
of such days. The which was incomprehensible and offensive to
Hilda.

She was in a prison with her mother, and saw no method of
escape, saw not so much as a locked door, saw nothing but blank
walls. Even could she by a miracle break prison, where should she

look for the unknown object of her desire, and for what should she look? Enigmas! It is true that she read, occasionally with feverish enjoyment, especially verse. But she did not and could not read enough. Of the shelf-ful of books which in thirty years had drifted by one accident or another into the Lessways household, she had read every volume, except Cruden's *Concordance*. A heterogeneous and forlorn assemblage! Lavater's *Physiognomy*, in a translation and in full calf! Thomson's *Seasons*, which had thrilled her by its romantic beauty! Mrs Henry Wood's *Danesbury House*, and one or two novels by Charlotte M. Yonge and Dinah Maria Craik, which she had gulped eagerly down for the mere interest of their stories. Disraeli's *Ixion*, which she had admired without understanding it. A *History of the North American Indians*! These were the more exciting items of the set. The most exciting of all was a green volume of Tennyson's containing *Maud*. She knew *Maud* by heart. By simple unpleasant obstinacy she had forced her mother to give her this volume for a birthday present, having seen a quotation from it in a ladies' magazine. At that date in Turnhill, as in many other towns of England, the poem had not yet lived down a reputation for immorality; but fortunately Mrs Lessways had only the vaguest notion of its dangerousness, and was indeed a negligent kind of woman. Dangerous the book was! Once in reciting it aloud in her room, Hilda had come so near to fainting that she had had to stop and lie down on the bed, until she could convince herself that she was not the male lover crying to his beloved. An astounding and fearful experience, and not to be too lightly renewed! For Hilda, *Maud* was a source of lovely and exquisite pain.

Why had she not used her force of character to obtain more books? One reason lay in the excessive difficulty to be faced. Birthdays are infrequent; and besides, the enterprise of purchasing *Maud* had proved so complicated and tedious that Mrs Lessways, with that curious stiffness which marked her sometimes, had sworn never to attempt to buy another book. Turnhill, a town of fifteen thousand persons, had no bookseller; the only bookseller that Mrs Lessways had ever heard of did business at Oldcastle. Mrs Lessways had journeyed twice over the Hillport ridge to Oldcastle, in the odd quest of a book called *Maud* by 'Tennyson

– the poet laureate'; the book had had to be sent from London;
and on her second excursion to Oldcastle Mrs Lessways had been
caught by the rain in the middle of Hillport Marsh. No! Hilda
could not easily demand the gift of another book, when all sorts
of nice, really useful presents could be bought in the High Street.
Nor was there in Turnhill a Municipal Library, nor any public
lending library.

Yet possibly Hilda's terrific egoism might have got fresh books
somehow from somewhere, had she really believed in the virtue of
books. Thus far, however, books had not furnished her with what
she wanted, and her faith in their promise was insecure.

Books failing, might she not have escaped into some vocation?
The sole vocation conceivable for her was that of teaching, and
she knew, without having tried it, that she abhorred teaching.
Further, there was no economical reason why she should work.
In 1878, unless pushed by necessity, no girl might dream of a
vocation: the idea was monstrous; it was almost unmentionable.
Still further, she had no wish to work for work's sake. Marriage
remained. But she felt herself a child, ages short of marriage.
And she never met a man. It was literally a fact that, except Mr
Skellorn, a few tradesmen, the vicar, the curate, and a sidesman
or so, she never even spoke to a man from one month's end to
the next. The Church choir had its annual dance, to which she
was invited; but the perverse creature cared not for dancing. Her
mother did not seek society, did not appear to require it. Nor
did Hilda acutely feel the lack of it. She could not define her
need. All she knew was that youth, moment by moment, was
dropping down inexorably behind her. And, still a child in heart
and soul, she saw herself ageing, and then aged, and then
withered. Her twenty-first birthday was well above the horizon.
Soon, soon, she would be 'over twenty-one'! And she was not
yet born! That was it! She was not yet born! If the passionate
strength of desire could have done the miracle, time would have
stood still in the heavens while Hilda sought the way of life.

And withal she was not wholly unhappy. Just as her attitude to
her mother was self-contradictory, so was her attitude towards
existence. Sometimes this profound infelicity of hers changed its
hues for an instant, and lo! it was bliss that she was bathed in.
A phenomenon which disconcerted her! She did not know that

she had the most precious of all faculties, the power to feel intensely.

III

Mr Skellorn did not come; he was most definitely late.

From the window of her bedroom, at the front of the house, Hilda looked westwards up towards the slopes of Chatterley Wood, where as a child she used to go with other children to pick the sparse bluebells that thrived on smoke. The bailiwick of Turnhill lay behind her; and all the murky district of the Five Towns, of which Turnhill is the northern outpost, lay to the south. At the foot of Chatterley Wood the canal wound in large curves on its way towards the undefiled plains of Cheshire and the sea. On the canal-side, exactly opposite to Hilda's window, was a flour-mill, that sometimes made nearly as much smoke as the kilns and chimneys closing the prospect on either hand. From the flour-mill a bricked path, which separated a considerable row of new cottages from their appurtenant gardens, led straight into Lessways Street, in front of Mrs Lessways's house. By this path Mr Skellorn should have arrived, for he inhabited the farthest of the cottages.

Hilda held Mr Skellorn in disdain, as she held the row of cottages in disdain. It seemd to her that Mr Skellorn and the cottages mysteriously resembled each other in their primness, their smugness, their detestable self-complacency. Yet those cottages, perhaps thirty in all, had stood for a great deal until Hilda, glancing at them, shattered them with her scorn. The row was called Freehold Villas: a consciously proud name in a district where much of the land was copyhold and could only change owners subject to the payment of 'fines' and to the feudal consent of a 'court' presided over by the agent of a lord of the manor. Most of the dwellings were owned by their occupiers, who, each an absolute monarch of the soil, niggled in his sooty garden of an evening amid the flutter of drying shirts and towels. Freehold Villas symbolized the final triumph of Victorian economics, the apotheosis of the prudent and industrious artisan. It corresponded with a Building Society Secretary's dream of paradise. And indeed it was a very real achievement. Nevertheless Hilda's irrational contempt would not admit this. She saw in Freehold Villas nothing but narrowness (what long narrow strips of gardens, and what narrow homes all flattened together!), and uniformity, and brickiness, and polished brassiness, and righteousness, and an eternal laundry.

From the upper floor of her own home she gazed destructively down upon all that, and into the chill, crimson eye of the descending sun. Her own home was not ideal, but it was better than all that. It was one of the two middle houses of a detached terrace of four houses built by her grandfather Lessways, the teapot manufacturer; it was the chief of the four, obviously the habitation of the proprietor of the terrace. One of the corner houses comprised a grocer's shop, and this house had been robbed of its just proportion of garden so that the seigneurial garden-plot might be triflingly larger than the others. The terrace was not a terrace of cottages, but of houses rated at from twenty-six to thirty-six pounds a year; beyond the means of artisans and petty insurance agents and rent-collectors. And further, it was well built, generously built; and its architecture, though debased, showed some faint traces of Georgian amenity. It was admittedly the best row of houses in that newly settled quarter of the town. In coming to it out of Freehold Villas Mr Skellorn obviously came to something superior, wider, more liberal.

Suddenly Hilda heard her mother's voice, in a rather startled conversational tone, and then another woman speaking; then the voices died away. Mrs Lessways had evidently opened the back door to somebody, and taken her at once into the sitting-room. The occurrence was unusual. Hilda went softly out on to the landing and listened, but she could catch nothing more than a faint, irregular murmur. Scarcely had she stationed herself on the landing when her mother burst out of the sitting-room, and called loudly:

'Hilda!' And again in an instant, very impatiently and excitedly, long before Hilda could possibly have appeared in response, had she been in her bedroom, as her mother supposed her to be: 'Hilda!'

Hilda could see without being seen. Mrs Lessways's thin, wrinkled face, bordered by her untidy but still black and glossy hair, was upturned from below in an expression of tragic fretfulness. It was the uncontrolled face, shamelessly expressive, of one who thinks himself unwatched. Hilda moved silently to descend, and then demanded in a low tone whose harsh self-possession was a reproof to that volatile creature, her mother:

'What's the matter?'

Mrs Lessways gave a surprised 'Oh!' and like a flash her features changed in the attempt to appear calm and collected.

'I was just coming downstairs,' said Hilda. And to herself: 'She's always trying to pretend I'm nobody, but when the least thing happens out of the way, she runs to me for all the world like a child.' And as Mrs Lessways offered no reply, but simply stood at the foot of the stairs, she asked again: 'What is it?'

'Well,' said her mother lamentably. 'It's Mr Skellorn. Here's Mrs Grant –'

'Who's Mrs Grant?' Hilda inquired, with a touch of scorn, although she knew perfectly well that Mr Skellorn had a married daughter of that name.

'Hsh! Hsh!' Mrs Lessways protested, indicating the open door of the sitting-room. 'You know Mrs Grant! It seems Mr Skellorn has had a paralytic stroke. Isn't it terrible?'

Hilda continued smoothly to descend the stairs, and followed her mother into the sitting-room.

CHAPTER 2
THE END OF THE SCENE

I

THE linen money-bag and the account-book, proper to the last Wednesday in the month, lay on the green damask cloth of the round table where Hilda and her mother took their meals. A paralytic stroke had not been drastic enough to mar Mr Skellorn's most precious reputation for probity and reliability. His statement of receipts and expenditure, together with the corresponding cash, had been due at two o'clock, and despite the paralytic stroke it was less than a quarter of an hour late. On one side of the bag and the book were ranged the older women – Mrs Lessways, thin and vivacious; and Mrs Grant, large and solemn; and on the other side, as it were in opposition, the young, dark, slim girl with her rather wiry black hair, and her straight, prominent eyebrows, and her extraordinary expression of uncompromising aloofness.

'She's just enjoying it, that's what she's doing!' said Hilda to herself, of Mrs Grant.

And the fact was that Mrs Grant, quite unconsciously, did appear to be savouring the catastrophe with pleasure. Although paralytic strokes were more prevalent at that period than now, they constituted even then a striking dramatic event. Moreover, they were considered as direct visitations of God. Also there was something mysteriously and agreeably impressive in the word 'paralytic', which people would repeat for the pleasure of repeating it. Mrs Grant, over whose mighty breast flowed a black mantle suited to the occasion, used the word again and again as she narrated afresh for Hilda the history of the stroke.

'Yes,' she said, 'they came and fetched me out of my bed at three o'clock this morning; and would you believe me, though he couldn't hardly speak, the money and this here book was all waiting in his desk, and he would have me come with it! And him sixty-seven! He always was like that. And I do believe if he'd been paralysed on both sides instead of only all down his right side, and speechless too, he'd ha' made me understand as I must come here at two o'clock. If I'm a bit late it's because I was kept at home with my son Enoch; he's got a whitlow that's worrying the life out of him, our Enoch has.'

Mrs Lessways warmly deprecated any apology for inexactitude, and wiped her sympathetic eyes.

'It's all over with father,' Mrs Grant resumed. 'Doctor hinted to me quiet-like as he'd never leave his bed again. He's laid himself down for the rest of his days . . . And he'd been warned! He'd had warnings. But there! . . .'

Mrs Grant contemplated with solemn gleeful satisfaction the overwhelming grandeur of the disaster that had happened to her father. The active old man, a continual figure of the streets, had been cut off in a moment from the world and condemned for life to a mattress. She sincerely imagined herself to be filled with proper grief; but an aesthetic appreciation of the theatrical effectiveness of the misfortune was certainly stronger in her than any other feeling. Observing that Mrs Lessways wept, she also drew out a handkerchief.

'I'm wishful for you to count the money,' said Mrs Grant. 'I wouldn't like there to be any –'

'Nay, that I'll not!' protested Mrs Lessways.

Mrs Grant's pressing duties necessitated her immediate departure. Mrs Lessways ceremoniously insisted on her leaving by the front door.

'I don't know where you'll find another rent-collector that's worth his salt – in this town,' observed Mrs Grant, on the doorstep. 'I can't think *what* you'll do, Mrs Lessways!'

'I shall collect my rents myself,' was the answer.

When Mrs Grant had crossed the road and taken the bricked path leading to the paralytic's house, Mrs Lessways slowly shut the door and bolted it, and then said to Hilda:

'Well, my girl, I do think you might have tried to show just a little more feeling!'

They were close together in the narrow lobby, of which the heavy pulse was the clock's ticking.

Hilda replied:

'You surely aren't serious about collecting those rents your-self, are you, mother?'

'Serious? Of course I'm serious!' said Mrs Lessways.

II

'Why shouldn't I collect the rents myself?' asked Mrs Less-ways.

This half-defiant question was put about two hours later. In the meantime no remark had been made about the rents. Mother and daughter were now at tea in the sitting-room. Hilda had passed the greater part of those two hours upstairs in her bedroom, pondering on her mother's preposterous notion of collecting the rents herself. Alone, she would invent conversations with her mother, silencing the foolish woman with unanswerable sarcastic phrases that utterly destroyed her illogical arguments. She would repeat these phrases, repeat even entire conversations, with pleasure; and, dwelling also with pleasure upon her grievances against her mother, would gradually arrive at a state of dull-glowing resentment. She could, if she chose, easily free her brain from the obsession either by reading or by a sharp jerk of volition; but often she preferred not to do so, saying to herself volup-tuously: 'No, I *will* nurse my grievance; I'll nurse it and nurse it and nurse it! It is mine, and it is just, and anybody with any sense at all would admit instantly that I am absolutely right.' Thus it was on this afternoon. When she came to tea her face was for-midably expressive, nor would she attempt to modify the rancour of those uncompromising features. On the contrary, as soon as she saw that her mother had noticed her condition, she deliber-ately intensified it.

Mrs Lessways, who was incapable of sustained thought, and who had completely forgotten and recalled the subject of the cottage-rents several times since the departure of Mrs Grant, nevertheless at once diagnosed the cause of the trouble; and with her usual precipitancy began to repulse an attack which had not even been opened. Mrs Lessways was not good at strategy, especially in conflicts with her daughter. She was an ingenuous, hasty thing, and much too candidly human. And not only was she deficient in practical common sense and most absurdly unable to learn from experience, but she had not even the wit to cover her shortcomings by resorting to the traditional authoritativeness of the mother. Her brief, rare efforts to play the mother were ludicrous. She was too simply honest to acquire stature by standing on her maternal dignity. By a profound instinct she wistfully treated everybody as an equal, as a fellow-creature; even her own daughter. It was not the way to come with credit out of the threatened altercation about rent-collecting.

As Hilda offered no reply, Mrs Lessways said reproachfully:

'Hilda, you're too bad sometimes!' And then, after a further silence: 'Anyhow, I'm quite decided.'

'Then what's the good of talking about it?' said the merciless child.

'But *why* shouldn't I collect the rents myself? I'm not asking you to collect them. And I shall save the five per cent, and goodness knows we need it.'

'You're more likely to lose twenty-five per cent,' said Hilda. 'I'll have some more tea, please.'

Mrs Lessways was quite genuinely scandalized. 'You needn't think I shall be easy with those Calder Street tenants, because I shan't! Not me! I'm more likely to be too hard!'

'You'll be too hard, and you'll be too easy, too,' said Hilda savagely. 'You'll lose the good tenants and you'll keep the bad ones, and the houses will all go to rack and ruin, and then you'll sell all the property at a loss. That's how it will be. And what shall you do if you're not feeling well, and if it rains on Monday mornings?'

Hilda could conceive her mother forgetting all about the rents on Monday morning, or putting them off till Monday afternoon on some grotesque excuse. Her fancy heard the interminable complainings, devisings, futile resolvings, of the self-appointed rent-collector. It was impossible to imagine a woman less fitted by nature than her mother to collect rents from unthrifty artisans such as inhabited Calder Street. The project sickened her. It would render the domestic existence an inferno.

As for Mrs Lessways, she was shocked, for her project had seemed very beautiful to her, and for the moment she was perfectly convinced that she could collect rents and manage property

as well as anyone. She was convinced that her habits were regular,
her temper firm and tactful, and her judgement excellent. She
was more than shocked; she was wounded. She wept, as she
pushed forward Hilda's replenished cup.

'You ought to take shame!' she murmured weakly, yet with
certitude.

'Why?' said Hilda, feigning simplicity. 'What have I said? *I*
didn't begin. You asked me. I can't help what I think.'

'It's your tone,' said Mrs Lessways grievously.

III

Despite all Hilda's terrible wisdom and sagacity, this remark of
the foolish mother's was the truest word spoken in the discussion.
It was Hilda's tone that was at the root of the evil. If Hilda, with
the intelligence as to which she was secretly so complacent, did
not amicably rule her mother, the unavoidable inference was that
she was either a clumsy or a wicked girl, or both. She indeed felt
dimly that she was a little of both. But she did not mind. Sitting
there in the small, familiar room, close to the sewing-machine, the
steel fender, the tarnished chandelier, and all the other daily
objects which she at once detested and loved, sitting close to her
silly mother who angered her, and yet in whom she recognized a
quality that was mysteriously precious and admirable, staring
through the small window at the brown, tattered garden-plot
where blackened rhododendrons were swaying in the October
blast, she wilfully bathed herself in grim gloom and in an affectation of despair.

Somehow she enjoyed the experience. She had only to tighten
her lips – and she became oblivious of her clumsiness and her
cruelty, savouring with pleasure the pain of the situation, clasping
it to her! Now and then a thought of Mr Skellorn's tragedy shot
through her brain, and the tenderness of pity welled up from somewhere within her and mingled exquisitely with her dark melancholy. And she found delight in reading her poor mother like an
open book, as she supposed. And all the while her mother was
dreaming upon the first year of Hilda's life, before she had discovered that her husband's health was as unstable as his character, and comparing the reality of the present with her early

illusions. But the clever girl was not clever enough to read just that page.

'We ought to be everything to each other,' said Mrs Lessways, pursuing her reflections aloud.

Hilda hated sentimentalism. She could not stand such talk.

'And you know,' said Hilda, speaking very frigidly and with even more than her usual incisive clearness of articulation, 'it's not your property. It's only yours for life. It's my property.'

The mother's mood changed in a moment.

'How do you know? You've never seen your father's will.' She spoke in harsh challenge.

'No; because you've never let me see it.'

'You ought to have more confidence in your mother. Your father had. And I'm trustee and executor.' Mrs Lessways was exceeding jealous of her legal position, whose importance she never forgot nor would consent to minimize.

'That's all very well, for you,' said Hilda, 'but if the property isn't managed right, I may find myself slaving when I'm your age, mother. And whose fault will it be? ... However, I shall –,

'You will what?'

'Nothing.'

'I suppose her ladyship will be consulting her own lawyer next!' said Mrs Lessways bitterly.

They looked at each other. Hilda's face flushed to a sombre red. Mrs Lessways brusquely left the room. Then Hilda could hear her rattling fussily at the kitchen range. After a few minutes Hilda followed her to the kitchen, which was now nearly in darkness. The figure of Mrs Lessways, still doing nothing whatever with great vigour at the range, was dimly visible. Hilda approached her, and awkwardly touched her shoulder.

'Mother!' she demanded sharply; and she was astonished by her awkwardness and her sharpness.

'Is that you?' her mother asked, in a queer, foolish tone.

They kissed. Such a candid peacemaking had never occurred between them before. Mrs Lessways, as simple in forgiveness as in wrath, did not disguise her pleasure in the remarkable fact that it was Hilda who had made the overture. Hilda thought: 'How strange I am! What is coming over me?' She glanced at the range in which was a pale gleam of red, and that gleam, in the heavy twilight, seemed to her to be inexpressibly, enchantingly mournful. And she herself was mournful about the future — very mournful. She saw no hope. Yet her sadness was beautiful to her. And she was proud.

CHAPTER 3

MR CANNON

I

A LITTLE later Hilda came downstairs dressed to go out. Her mother was lighting a glimmer of gas in the lobby. Ere Mrs Lessways could descend from her tiptoes to her heels and turn round Hilda said quickly, forestalling curiosity.

'I'm going to get that thread you want. Just give me some money, will you?'

Nobody could have guessed from her placid tone and indifferent demeanour that she was in a state of extreme agitation. But so it was. Suddenly, after kissing her mother in the kitchen, she had formed a tremendous resolve And in a moment the resolve had possessed her, sending her flying upstairs, and burning her into a fever, as with the assured movements of familiarity she put on her bonnet, mantle, 'fall', and gloves in the darkness of the chamber. She held herself in leash while her mother lifted a skirt and found a large loaded pocket within and a purse in the pocket and a sixpence in the purse. But when she had shut the door on all that interior haunted by her mother's restlessness, when she was safe in the porch and in the windy obscurity of the street, she yielded with voluptuous apprehension to a thrill that shook her.

'I might have tidied my hair,' she thought. 'Pooh! What does my hair matter?'

Her mind was full of an adventure through which she had passed seven years previously, when she was thirteen and a little girl at school. For several days, then, she had been ruthlessly mortifying her mother by complaints about the meals. Her fastidious appetite could not be suited. At last, one noon when the child had refused the whole of a plenteous dinner, Mrs Lessways had burst into tears and, slapping four pennies down on the table, had cried, 'Here! I fairly give you up! Go out and buy your own dinner! Then perhaps you'll get what you want!' And the

child, without an instant's hesitation, had seized the coins and
gone out, hatless, and bought food at a little tripe-shop that was
also an eating-house, and consumed it there; and then in grim
silence returned home. Both mother and daughter had been
stupefied and frightened by the boldness of the daughter's initiative, by her amazing, flaunting disregard of filial decency. Mrs
Lessways would not having related the episode to anybody upon
any consideration whatever. It was a shameful secret, never even
referred to. But Mrs Lessways had unmistakably though indirectly referred to it when in anger she had said to her daughter
aged twenty: 'I suppose her ladyship will be consulting her own
lawyer next!' Hilda had understood, and that was why she had
blushed.

And now, as she turned from Lessways Street into the Oldcastle Road, on her way to the centre of the town, she experienced
almost exactly the intense excitement of the reckless and supercilious child in quest of its dinner. The only difference was that
the recent reconciliation had inspired her with a certain negligent
compassion for her mother, with a curious tenderness that caused
her to wonder at herself.

II

The Market Square of Turnhill was very large for the size of the
town. The diminutive Town Hall, which in reality was nothing
but a watch-house, seemed to be a mere incident on its irregular
expanse, to which the two-storey shops and dwellings made a
low border. Behind this crimson, blue-slated border rose the
loftier forms of a church and a large chapel, situate in adjacent
streets. The square was calm and almost deserted in the gloom.
It typified the slow tranquillity of the bailiwick, which was
removed from the central life of the Five Towns, and unconnected therewith by even a tram or an omnibus. Only within
recent years had Turnhill got so much as a railway station – rail-
head of a branch line. Turnhill was the extremity of civilization
in those parts. Go northwards out of this Market Square, and
you would soon find yourself amid the wild and hilly moorlands,
sprinkled with iron-and-coal villages whose red-flaming furnaces
illustrated the eternal damnation which was the chief article of

their devout religious belief. And in the Market Square not even the late edition of the *Staffordshire Signal* was cried, though it was discreetly on sale with its excellent sporting news in a few shops. In the hot and malodorous candle-lit factories, where the real strenuous life of the town would remain cooped up for another half-hour of the evening, men and women had yet scarcely taken to horse-racing; they would gamble upon rabbits, cocks, pigeons, and their own fists, without the mediation of the *Signal*. The one noise in the Market Square was the bell of a hawker selling warm pikelets at a penny each for the high tea of the tradesmen. The hawker was a deathless institution, a living proof that withdrawn Turnhill would continue always to be exactly what it always had been. Still, to the east of the Square, across the High Street, a vast space was being cleared of hovels for the erection of a new Town Hall daringly magnificent.

Hilda crossed the Square, scorning it.

She said to herself: 'I'd better get the thing over before I buy the thread. I should never be able to stand Miss Dayson's finicking! I should scream out!' But the next instant, with her passion for proving to herself how strong she could be, she added: 'Well, I just *will* buy the thread first!' And she went straight into Dayson's little fancy shop, which was full of counter and cardboard boxes and Miss Dayson, and stayed therein for at least five minutes, emerging with a miraculously achieved leisureliness. A few doors away was a somewhat new building, of three storeys – the highest in the Square. The ground floor was an ironmongery; it comprised also a side entrance, of which the door was always open. This side entrance showed a brass-plate, 'Q. Karkeek, Solicitor'. And the wire-blinds of the two windows of the first floor also bore the words: 'Q. Karkeek, Solicitor. Q. Karkeek, Solicitor'. The queerness of the name had attracted Hilda's attention several years earlier, when the signs were fresh. It was an accident that she had noticed it; she had not noticed the door-plates or the wire-blinds of other solicitors. She did not know Mr Q. Karkeek by sight, nor even whether he was old or young, married or single, agreeable or repulsive.

The side entrance gave directly on to a long flight of naked stairs, and up these stairs Hilda climbed into the unknown, towards the redoubtable and the perilous. 'I'm bound to be

seen,' she said to herself, 'but I don't care, and I *don't* care!'
At the top of the stairs was a passage, at right angles, and then a
glazed door with the legend in black letters, 'Q. Karkeek,
Solicitor', and two other doors mysteriously labelled 'Private'.
She opened the glazed door, and saw a dirty middle-aged man on
a stool, and she said at once to him, in a harsh, clear, deliberate
voice, without giving herself time to reflect.

'I want to see Mr Karkeek.'

The man stared at her sourly, as if bewildered.

She said to herself: 'I shan't be able to stand this excitement
much longer.'

'You can't see Mr Karkeek,' said the man. 'Mr Karkeek's
detained at Hanbridge County Court. But if you're in such a
hurry like, you'd better see Mr Cannon. It's Mr Cannon as they
generally do see. Who d'ye come from, miss?'

'Come from?' Hilda repeated, unnerved.

'What name?'

She had not expected this. 'I suppose I shall have to tell him!'
she said to herself, and aloud: 'Lessways.'

'Oh! Ah!' exclaimed the man. 'Bless us! Yes!' It was as if he
had said: 'Of course it's Lessways! And don't I know all about
you!' And Hilda was overwhelmed by the sense of the enormity
of the folly which she was committing.

The man swung half round on his stool, and seized the end of
an india-rubber tube which hung at the side of the battered and
littered desk, just under a gas-jet. He spoke low, like a conspirator,
into the mouthpiece of the tube. 'Miss Lessways – to see you, sir.'
Then very quickly he clapped the tube to his ear and listened.
And then he put it to his mouth again and repeated: 'Lessways.'
Hilda was agonized.

'I'll ask ye to step this way, miss,' said the man, slipping off
his stool. At the same time he put a long inky penholder, which
he had been holding in his wrinkled right hand, between his
teeth.

'Never,' thought Hilda as she followed the clerk, in a whirl
of horrible misgivings, 'never have I done anything as mad as
this before! I'm under twenty-one!'

III

There she was at last, seated in front of a lawyer in a lawyer's office – her ladyship consulting her own lawyer! It seemed incredible! A few minutes ago she had been at home, and now she was in a world unfamiliar and alarming. Perhaps it was a pity that her mother had unsuspectingly put the scheme into her head! However, the deed was done. Hilda generally acted first and reflected afterwards. She was frightened, but rather by the unknown than by anything she could define.

'You've come about the property?' said Mr Cannon amiably, in a matter-of-fact tone.

He had deep black eyes, and black hair, like Hilda's; good, regular teeth, and a clear complexion; perhaps his nose was rather large, but it was straight. With his large pale hands he occasionally stroked his long soft moustache; the chin was blue. He was smartly dressed in dark blue; he had a beautiful necktie, and the genuine whiteness of his wristbands was remarkable in a district where starched linen was usually either grey or bluish. He was not a dandy, but he respected his person; he evidently gave careful attention to his body; and this trait alone set him apart among the citizens of Turnhill.

'Yes,' said Hilda. She thought: 'He's a very handsome man! How strange I don't remember seeing him in the streets!' She was in awe of him. He was indefinitely older than herself; and she felt like a child, out of place in the easy-chair.

'I suppose it's about the rent-collecting?' he pursued.

'Yes – it is,' she answered, astonished that he could thus divine her purpose. 'I mean –'

'What does your mother want to do?'

'Oh!' said Hilda, speaking low. 'It's not mother. I've come to consult you myself. Mother doesn't know. I'm nearly twenty-one, and it's really my property, you know!' She blushed with shame.

'Ah!' he exclaimed. He tried to disguise his astonishment in an easy, friendly smile. But he was most obviously startled. He looked at Hilda in a different way, with a much intensified curiosity.

'Yes,' she resumed. He now seemed to her more like a fellow-creature, and less like a member of the inimical older generation.

'So you're nearly twenty-one?'

'In December,' she said. 'And I think under my father's will –' She stopped, at a loss. 'The fact is, I don't think mother will be quite able to look after the property properly, and I'm afraid – you see, now that Mr Skellorn has had this stroke –'

'Yes,' said Mr Cannon, 'I heard about that, and I was thinking perhaps Mrs Lessways had sent you ... We collect rents, you know.'

'I see!' Hilda murmured. 'Well, the truth is, mother hasn't the slightest idea I'm here. Not the slightest! And I wouldn't hurt her feelings for anything.' He nodded sympathetically. 'But I thought something ought to be done. She's decided to collect our Calder Street rents herself, and she isn't fitted to do it. And then there's the question of the repairs ... I know the rents are going down. I expect it's all mother's for life, but I want there to be something left for me when she's gone, you see! And if – I've never seen the will. I suppose there's no way of seeing a copy of it, somewhere? ... I can't very well ask mother again.'

'I know all about the will,' said Mr Cannon.

'You do?'

Wondrous, magical man!

'Yes,' he explained. 'I used to be at Toms and Scoles's. I was there when it was made. I copied it.'

'Really!' She felt that he would save her, not only from any possible unpleasant consequences of her escapade, but also from suffering ultimate loss by reason of her mother's foolishness.

'You're quite right,' he continued. 'I remember it perfectly. Your mother is what we call tenant-for-life; everything goes to you in the end.'

'Well?' Hilda asked abruptly. 'All I want to know is, what I can do.'

'Of course, without upsetting your mother?'

He glanced at her. She blushed again.

'Naturally,' she said coldly.

'You say you think the property is going down – it *is*, everybody knows that – and your mother thinks of collecting the rents herself ... Well, young lady, it's very difficult, very difficult, your mother being the trustee and executor.'

'Yes, that's what she's always saying – she's the trustee and executor.'

'You'd better let me think it over for a day or two.'

'And shall I call in again?'

'You might slip in if you're passing. I'll see what can be done. Of course it would never do for you to have any difficulty with your mother.'

'Oh no!' she concurred vehemently. 'Anything would be better than that. But I thought there was no harm in me –'

'Certainly not.'

She had a profound confidence in him. And she was very content so far with the result of her adventure.

'I hope nobody will find out I've been here,' she said timidly. 'Because if it *did* get to mother's ears –'

'Nobody will find out,' he reassured her.

Assuredly his influence was tranquillizing. Even while he insisted on the difficulties of the situation, he seemed to be smoothing them away. She was convinced that he would devise some means of changing her mother's absurd purpose and of strengthening her own position. But when, at the end of the interview, he came round the large table which separated them, and she rose and looked up at him, close, she was suddenly very afraid of him. He was a tall and muscular man, and he stood like a monarch, and she stood like a child. And his gesture seemed to say: 'Yes, I know you are afraid. And I rather like you to be afraid. But I am benevolent in the exercise of my power.' Under his gaze, her gaze fastened on the wire-blind and the dark window, and she read off the reversed letters on the blind.

Like a mouse she escaped to the stairs. She was happy and fearful and expectant ... It was done! She had consulted a lawyer! She was astounded at herself.

In the Market Square it was now black night. She looked shyly up at the lighted wire-blinds over the ironmongery. 'I was there!' she said. 'He is still there.' The whole town, the whole future, seemed to be drenched now in romance. Nevertheless, the causes of her immense discontent had not apparently been removed nor in any way modified.

CHAPTER 4
DOMESTICITY INVADED

I

EARLY in the afternoon, two days later, Hilda came, with an air of reproach, into her mother's empty bedroom. Mrs Lessways had contracted a severe cold in the head, a malady to which she was subject and which she accepted with fatalistic submission, even pleasurably giving herself up to it, as a martyr to the rack. Mrs Lessways's colds annoyed Hilda, who out of her wisdom could always point to the precise indiscretion which had caused them, and to whom the spectacle of a head wrapped day and night in flannel was offensively ridiculous. Moreover, Hilda in these crises was further and still more acutely exasperated by the pillage of her handkerchiefs. Although she possessed a supply of handkerchiefs far beyond her own needs, she really hated to lend to her mother in the hour of necessity. She did lend, and she lent without spoken protest, but with frigid bitterness. Her youthful passion for order and efficiency was aggrieved by her mother's negligent and inadequate arrangements for coping with the inevitable plague. She now made a police-visit to the bedroom because she considered that her mother had been demanding handkerchiefs at a stage too early in the progress of the disease. Impossible that her mother should have come to the end of her own handkerchiefs! She knew with all the certitude of her omniscience that numerous clean handkerchiefs must be concealed somewhere in the untidiness of her mother's wardrobe.

See her as she enters the bedroom, the principal bedroom of the house, whose wide bed and large wardrobe recall the past when she had a father as well as a mother, and when that bedroom awed her footsteps! A thin, brown-frocked girl, wearing a detested but enforced small black apron; with fine, pale, determined features, rather unfeminine hair, and glowering, challenging black eyes. She had a very decided way of putting down her uncoquettishly shod feet. Absurdly young, of course; wistfully

young! She was undeveloped, and did not even look nearly
twenty-one. You are at liberty to smile at her airs; at that careless critical glance which pityingly said: 'Ah! if this were my
room, it would be different from what it is'; at that serious,
worried expression, as if the anxiety of the whole world's de-
ficiencies oppressed the heart within; and at that supreme
conviction of wisdom, which after all was little but an exaggerated perception of folly and inconsistency in others! . . . She
is not to be comprehended on an acquaintance of three days.
Years must go to the understanding of her. She did not understand herself. She was not even acquainted with herself. Why!
She was naïve enough to be puzzled because she felt older than
her mother and younger than her beautiful girlish complexion,
simultaneously!

She opened the central mirrored door of the once formidable
wardrobe, and as she did so the image of the bed and of half the
room shot across the swinging glass, taking the place of her own
reflection. And instantly, when she inserted herself between the
exposed face of the wardrobe and its door, she was precipitated
into the most secret intimacy of her mother's existence. There
was the familiar odour of old kid gloves . . . She was more intimate with her mother now than she could ever be in talking to her.
The lower part of this section of the wardrobe consisted of three
deep drawers with inset brass handles, an exquisitely exact piece
of mahogany cabinet-work. From one of the drawers a bit of
white linen untidily protruded. Her mother! The upper part was
filled with sliding trays, each having a raised edge to keep the
contents from falling out. These trays were heaped pell-mell with
her mother's personal belongings – small garments, odd in-
determinate trifles, a muff, a bundle of whalebone, veils, bags, and
especially cardboard boxes. Quantities of various cardboard
boxes! Her mother kept everything, could not bear that anything
which had once been useful should be abandoned or destroyed;
whereas Hilda's propensity was to throw away with an impatient
gesture whatever threatened to be an encumbrance. Sighing, she
began to arrange the contents of the trays in some kind of
method. Incompetent and careless mother! Hilda wondered how
the old thing managed to conduct her life from day to day with
even a semblance of the decency of order. It did not occur to her

that for twenty-five years before she was born, and for a long time afterwards, Mrs Lessways had contrived to struggle along through the world, without her daughter's aid, to the general satisfaction of herself and some others. At length, ferreting on the highest shelf but one, she had the deep, proud satisfaction of the philosopher who has correctly deduced consequences from character. Underneath a Paisley shawl she discovered a lost treasure of clean handkerchiefs. One, two, three, four – there were eleven! And among them was of one her own, appropriated by her mother through sheer inexcusable inadvertence. They had probably been lying under the shawl for weeks, months!

Still, she did not allow herself to be vexed. Since the singular hysterical embrace in the twilight of the kitchen, she had felt for her mother a curious, kind, forbearing, fatalistic indulgence. 'Mother is like that, and there you are!' And further, her mood had been so changed and uplifted by excitement and expectation that she could not be genuinely harsh. She had been thrilled by the audacity of the visit to Mr Cannon. And though she hoped from it little but a negative advantage, she was experiencing the rare happiness of adventure. She had slipped out for a moment from the confined and stifling circle of domestic dailiness. She had scented the feverish perfume of the world. And she owed all this to herself alone! She meant on the morrow, while her mother was marketing, to pursue the enterprise; the consciousness of this intention was sweet, but she knew not why it was sweet. She only knew that she lived in the preoccupation of a dream.

Having taken two of the handkerchiefs, she shut the wardrobe and turned the key. She went first to her own small, prim room to restore stolen property to its rightful place, and then she descended towards the kitchen with the other handkerchief. Giving it to her mother, and concealing her triumph beneath a mask of wise, long-suffering benevolence, she would say: 'I've found ten of your handkerchiefs, mother. Here's one!' And her mother, ingenuously startled and pleased, would exclaim: 'Where, child?' And she, still controlling herself, as befitted a superior being, would reply casually: 'In your wardrobe, of course! You stuck to it there weren't any; but I was sure there were.'

II

The dialogue which actually did accompany the presentation of the handkerchief, though roughly corresponding to her rehearsal of it, was lacking in the dramatic pungency necessary for a really effective triumph; the reason being that the thoughts of both mother and daughter were diverted in different ways from the handkerchief by the presence of Florrie in the kitchen.

Florrie was the new servant, and she had come into the house that morning. Sponsored by an aunt who was one of the best of the Calder Street tenants, Florrie had been accepted rather unwillingly, the objection to her being that she was too young – thirteen and a half. Mrs Lessways had a vague humanitarian sentiment against the employment of children; as for Hilda's feeling, it was at one moment more compassionate even than her mother's, and at another almost cynically indifferent. The aunt, however, a person of powerful common sense, had persuaded Mrs Lessways that the truest kindness would be to give Florrie a trial. Florrie was very strong, and she had been brought up to work hard, and she enjoyed working hard. 'Don't you, Florrie?' 'Yes, aunt,' with a delightful smiling, whispering timidity. She was the eldest of a family of ten, and had always assisted her mother in the management of a half-crown house and the nurture of a regiment of infants. But at thirteen and a half a girl ought to be earning money for her parents. Bless you! She knew what a pawnshop was, her father being often out of a job owing to potter's asthma; and she had some knowledge of cookery, and was in particular very good at boiling potatoes. To take her would be a real kindness on the part of Mrs Lessways, for the 'place' was not merely an easy place, it was a 'good' place. Supposing that Mrs Lessways refused to have her – well Florrie might go on to a 'potbank' and come to harm, or she might engage herself with tradespeople, where notoriously the work was never finished, or she might even be forced into a public-house. Her aunt knew that they wanted a servant at the Queen Adelaide, where the wages would be pretty high. But no! No niece of hers should ever go into service at a public-house if she could help it! What with hot rum and coffee to be ready for customers at half-past five of a morning, and cleaning up at nights after closing, a poor girl would

never see her bed! Whereas at Mrs Lessways's . . . ! So Mrs Lessways took Florrie in order to save her from slavery.

The slim child was pretty, with graceful and eager movements,
and certainly a rapid comprehension. Her grey eyes sparkled, and
her brown hair was coquettishly tied up, rather in the manner of
a horse's tail on May Day. She had arrived all by herself in the
morning, with a tiny bundle, and she made a remarkably neat
appearance – if you did not look at her boots, which had evidently been somebody else's a long time before. Hilda had been
clearly aware of a feeling of pleasure at the prospect of this young
girl's presence in the house.

Hilda now saw her in another aspect. She wore a large foul
apron of sacking, which made her elegant body quite shapeless,
and she was kneeling on the red-and-black tiled floor of the
kitchen, with her enormous cracked boots sticking out behind
her. At one side of her was a pail full of steaming brown water,
and in her red coarse little hands, which did not seem to belong
to those gracile arms, she held a dripping clout. In front of her,
on a half-dried space of clean, shining floor, stood Mrs Lessways,
her head wrapped in a flannel petticoat. Nearer to the child
stretched a small semi-circle of liquid mud; to the rear was the
untouched dirty floor. Florrie was looking up at her mistress with
respectful, strained attention. She could not proceed with her
work because Mrs Lessways had chosen this moment to instruct
her, with much snuffling, in the duties and responsibilities of her
position.

'Yes, mum,' Florrie whispered. She seemed to be incapable of
speaking beyond a whisper. But the whisper was delicate and
agreeable; and perhaps it was a mysterious sign of her alleged
unusual physical strength.

'You'll have to be down at half past six. Then you'll light your
kitchen fire, but of course you'll get your coal up first. And then
you'll do your boots. Now the bacon – but never mind that –
either Miss Hilda or me will be down tomorrow morning to
show you.'

'Yes, mum.' Florrie's whisper was grateful.

'When you've got things going a bit like, you'll do your
parlour – I've told you all about that, though. But I didn't tell
you – except on Wednesdays. On Wednesdays you give your par-

lour a thorough turn-out *after* breakfast, and mind it's got to be all straight for dinner at half-past twelve.'

'Yes, mum.'

'I shall show you about your fire-irons –' Mrs Lessways was continuing to make everything in the house the private property of Florrie, when Hilda interrupted her about the handkerchief, and afterwards with an exhortation to beware of the dampness of the floor, which exhortation Mrs Lessways faintly resented; whereupon Hilda left the kitchen; it was always imprudent to come between Mrs Lessways and a new servant.

Hilda remained listening in the lobby to the interminable and rambling instruction. At length Mrs Lessways said benevolently.

'There's no reason why you shouldn't go to bed at half past eight, or nine at the latest. No reason whatever. And if you're quick and handy – and I'm sure you are – you'll have plenty of time in the afternoon for plain sewing and darning. I shall see how you can darn,' Mrs Lessways added encouragingly.

'Yes, mum.'

Hilda's heart revolted, less against her mother's defects as an organizer than against the odious mess of the whole business of domesticity. She knew that, with her mother in the house, Florrie would never get to bed at half past eight and very seldom at nine, and that she would never be free in the afternoons. She knew that if her mother would only consent to sit still and not interfere, the housework could be accomplished with half the labour that at present went to it. There were three women in the place or at any rate a woman, a young woman, and a girl – and in theory the main preoccupation of all of them was this business of domesticity. It was, of course, ridiculous, and she would never be able to make anyone see that it was ridiculous. But that was not all. The very business itself absolutely disgusted her. It disgusted her to such a point that she would have preferred to do it with her own hands in secret rather than see others do it openly in all its squalor. The business might be more efficiently organized – for example, there was no reason why the sitting-room should be made uninhabitable between breakfast and dinner once a week – but it could never be other than odious. The kitchen floor must inevitably be washed every day by a girl on her knees in sackcloth

with terrible hands. She was witnessing now the first stage in the
progress of a victim of the business of domesticity. Today Florrie
was a charming young creature, full of slender grace. Soon she
would be a dehumanized drudge. And Hilda could not stop it!
All over the town, in every street of the town, behind all the nice
curtains and blinds, the same hidden shame was being enacted:
a vast, sloppy, steaming, greasy, social horror – inevitable! It
amounted to barbarism, Hilda thought in her revolt. She turned
from it with loathing. And yet nobody else seemed to turn from
it with loathing. Nobody else seemed to perceive that this business
of domesticity was not life itself, was at best the clumsy external
machinery of life. On the contrary, about half the adult population worshipped it as an exercise sacred and paramount,
enlarging its importance and with positive gusto permitting it to
monopolize their existence. Nine-tenths of her mother's conversation was concerned with the business of domesticity –
and withal Mrs Lessways took the business more lightly than
most!

III

There was an impatient knock at the front door – rare phenomenon, but not unknown.

Mrs Lessways cried out thickly from the folds of her flannel
petticoat:

'Hilda, just see who that is, will you? . . . knocking like that!
Florrie can't come.'

And just as Hilda reached the front door, her mother opened
the kitchen door wide, to view the troublesome disturber and to
inform him, if as was probable he was exceeding his rights, that
he would have done better to try the back door.

It was Mr Cannon at the front door.

Hilda heard the kitchen door slammed to behind her but the
noise was like a hallucination in her brain. She was staggered by
the apparition of Mr Cannon in the porch. She had vaguely
wondered what he might do to execute his promise of aid; she had
felt that time was running short if her mother was to be prevented
from commencing rent-collector on the Monday; she had perhaps ingenuously expected from him some kind of miracle; but of

a surety she had never dreamed that he would call in person at her home. 'He must be mad!' she would have exclaimed to herself, if the grandeur of his image in her heart had not made any such accusation impossible to her. He was not mad; he was merely inscrutable, terrifyingly so. It was as if her adventurous audacity, personified, had doubled back on her, and was exquisitely threatening her.

'Good afternoon!' said Mr Cannon, smiling confidently and yet with ceremoniousness. 'Is your mother about?'

'Yes.' Hilda did not know it, but she was whispering quite in the manner of Florrie.

'Shall I come in?'

'Oh! Please do!' The words jumped out of her mouth all at once, so anxious was she to destroy any impression conceivably made that she did not desire him to come in.

He crossed the step and took her hand with one gesture. She shut the door. He waited in suave silence. There was barely space for them together in the narrow lobby, and she scarce dared look up at him. He easily dominated her. His bigness subdued her, and the handsomeness of his face and his attire was like a moral intimidation. He had a large physical splendour that was well set off and illustrated by the brilliance of his linen and his broadcloth. She was as modest as a mouse beside him. The superior young woman, the stern and yet indulgent philosopher, had utterly vanished, and only a poor little mouse remained.

'Will you please come into the drawing-room?' she murmured when, after an immense effort to keep full control of her faculties, she had decided where he must be put.

'Thanks,' he said.

As she diminished herself, with beautiful shy curves of her body, against the wall so that he could manoeuvre his bigness through the drawing-room doorway, he gave her a glance half benign and half politely malicious, which seemed to say again: 'I know you're afraid, and I rather like it. But you know you needn't be.'

'Please take a seat,' she implored. And then quickly, as he seemed to have no intention of speaking to her confidentially, 'I'll tell mother.'

Leaving the room, she saw him sink smoothly into a seat, his rich-piled hat in one gloved hand and an ebony walking-stick in the other. His presence had a disastrous effect on the chill, unfrequented drawing-room, reducing it instantly to a condition of paltry shabbiness.

The kitchen door was still shut. Yes, all the squalor of the business of domesticity must be hidden from this splendid being! Hilda went as a criminal into the kitchen. Mrs Lessways with violent movements signalled her to close the door before speaking. Florrie gazed spellbound upwards at both of them. The household was in a high fever.

'You don't mean to tell me that's Mr Cannon!' Mrs Lessways excitedly whispered.

'Do – do – you know him?' Hilda faltered.

'Do I know him! . . . What does he want?'

'He wants to see you.'

'What about?'

'I suppose it's about property or something,' Hilda replied, blushing. Never had she felt so abject in front of her mother.

Mrs Lessways rapidly unpinned the flannel petticoat and then threw it, with a desperate gesture of sacrifice, on to the deal table. The situation had to be met. The resplendent male awaited her in the death-cold room. The resplendent male had his overcoat, but she, suffering, must face the rigour and the risk unprotected. No matter if she caught bronchitis! The thing had to be done. Even Hilda did not think of accusing her mother of folly. Mrs Lessways, having patted her hair, emptied several handkerchiefs from the twin pockets of her embroidered black apron, and, snatching at the clean handkerchief furnished by Hilda, departed to her fate. She was certainly startled and puzzled, but she was not a whit intimidated, and the perception of this fact inspired Hilda with a new, reluctant respect for her mother.

Hilda, from the kitchen, heard the greetings in the drawing-room, and then the reverberations of the sufferer's nose. She desired to go into the drawing-room. Her mother probably expected her to go in. But she dared not. She was afraid.

'I was wondering,' said the voice of Mr Cannon, 'whether

you've ever thought of selling your Calder Street property, Mrs Lessways.' And then the drawing-room door was closed, and the ticking of the grandfather's clock resumed possession of the lobby.

CHAPTER 5
MRS LESSWAYS'S SHREWDNESS

I

WAITING irresolute in the kitchen doorway, Hilda passed the most thrillingly agreeable moments that destiny had ever vouchsafed to her. She dwelt on the mysterious, attractive quality of Mr Cannon's voice – she was sure that, though in speaking to her mother he was softly persuasive, he had used to herself a tone even more intimate and ingratiating. He and she had a secret; they were conspirators together: which fact was both disconcerting and delicious. She recalled their propinquity in the lobby; the remembered syllables which he had uttered mingled with the faint scent of his broadcloth, the whiteness of his wristbands, the gleams of his studs, the droop of his moustaches, the downward ray of his glance, and the proud, nimble carriage of his great limbs, – and formed in her mind the image of an ideal. An image regarded not with any tenderness, but with naïve admiration and unquestioning respect! And yet also with more than that, for when she dwelt on his glance, she had a slight transient feeling of faintness which came and went in a second, and which she did not analyse – and could not have analysed.

Clouds of fear sailed in swift capriciousness across the sky of her dreaming, obscuring it: fear of Mr Cannon's breath-taking initiative, fear of the upshot of her adventure, and a fear without a name. Nevertheless she exulted. She exulted because she was in the very midst of her wondrous adventure and tingling with a thousand apprehensions.

After a long time the latch of the drawing-room door cracked warningly. Hilda retired within the kitchen out of sight of the lobby. She knew that the child in her would compel her to wait like a child until the visitor was gone, instead of issuing forth boldly like a young woman. But to Florrie the young mistress with her stern dark mask and formidable eyebrows and air of superb disdain was as august as a goddess. Florrie, moving

backwards, had now got nearly to the scullery door with her
wringing and splashing and wiping; and she had dirtied even her
face. As Hilda absently looked at her, she thought somehow of
Mr Cannon's white wristbands. She saw the washing and the
ironing of those wristbands, and a slatternly woman or two
sighing and grumbling amid wreaths of steam, and a background
of cinders and suds and sloppiness . . . All that, so that the grand
creature might have a rim of pure white to his coat-sleeves for a
day! It was inevitable. But the grand creature must never know.
The shame necessary to his splendour must be concealed from
him, lest he might be offended. And this was woman's loyalty!
Her ideas concerning the business of domesticity were now mixed
and opposing and irreconcilable, and she began to suspect that
the bases of society might be more complex and confusing than
in her youthful downrightness she had imagined.

II

'Well, you've got your way!' said Mrs Lessways, with a certain
grim, disdainful cheerfulness, from which benevolence was not
quite absent. The drastic treatment accorded to her cold seemed
to have done it good. At any rate she had not resumed the
flannel petticoat, and the nasal symptoms were much less pronounced.

'Got my way?' Hilda repeated, at a loss and newly apprehensive.

Mother and daughter were setting tea. Florrie had been doing
very well, but she was not yet quite equal to her situation, and
the mistresses were now performing her lighter duties while she
changed from the offensive drudge to the neat parlour-maid.
Throughout the afternoon Hilda had avoided her mother's sight;
partly because she wanted to be alone (without knowing why),
and partly because she was afraid lest Mr Cannon, as a member
of the older generation, might have betrayed her to her mother.
This fear was not very genuine, though she pretended that it was
and enjoyed playing with it: as if she really desired a catastrophe
for the outcome of her adventure. She had only come downstairs
in response to her mother's direct summons, and instantly on
seeing her she had known that Mr Cannon was not a traitor.

Which knowledge somehow rendered her gay in spite of herself. So that, what with this gaiety, and the stimulation produced in Mrs Lessways by the visit of Mr Cannon, and the general household relief at the obvious fact that Florrie would rather more than 'do', the atmosphere around the tinkling tea-table in the half-light was decidedly pleasant.

Nevertheless the singular turn of Mrs Lessways's phrase – 'You've got your way,' – had startled the guilty Hilda.

'Mr Cannon's going to see to the collecting of the Calder Street rents,' explained Mrs Lessways. 'So I hope you're satisfied, miss.'

Hilda was aware of self-consciousness.

'Yes, you may well colour up!' Mrs Lessways pursued, genial but malicious. 'You're as pleased as Punch, and you're saying to yourself you've made your old mother give way to ye again! And so you needn't tell me!'

'I thought,' said Hilda, with all possible prim worldliness – 'I thought I heard him saying something about buying the property?'

Mrs Lessways laughed, sceptically, confidently, as one who could not be deceived. 'Pooh!' she said. 'That was only a try-on. That was only so that he could begin his palaver! Don't tell me! I may be a simpleton, but I'm not such a simpleton as he thinks for, nor as some other folks think for, either!' (At this point Hilda had to admit that in truth her mother was not completely a simpleton. In her mother was a vein of perceptive shrewdness that occasionally cropped out and made all Hilda's critical philosophy seem schoolgirlish.) 'Do you think I don't know George Cannon? He came here o' purpose to get that rent-collecting. Well, he's got it, and he's welcome to it, for I doubt not he'll do it a sight better than poor Mr Skellorn! But he needn't hug himself that he's been too clever for me, because he hasn't. I gave him the rent-collecting because I thought I would! . . . Buy! He's no more got a good customer for Calder Street than he's got a good customer for this slop-bowl!'

Hilda resented this casual detraction of a being who had so deeply impressed her. And moreover she was convinced that her mother, secretly very flattered and delighted by the visit, was adopting a derisive attitude in order to 'show off' before her daughter. Parents are thus ingenuous! But she was so shocked and sneaped that she found it more convenient to say nothing.

'George Cannon could talk the hind leg off a horse,' Mrs Lessways continued quite happily. 'And yet it isn't as if he said a great deal. He doesn't. I'll say this for him. He's always the gentleman. And I couldn't say as much for his sister being a lady, and I'm sorry for it. He's the most gentlemanly man in Turnhill, and always so spruce, too!'

'His sister?'

'Well, his half-sister, since you're so particular, Miss Precise!'

'Not Miss Gailey?' said Hilda, who began faintly to recall a forgotten fact of which she thought she had once been cognizant.

'Yes, Miss Gailey,' Mrs Lessways snapped, still very genial and content. 'I did hear she's quarrelled out and out with *him*, too, at last!' She tightened her lips. 'Draw the blind down.'

Miss Gailey, a spinster of superior breeding and a teacher of dancing, had in the distant past been an intimate friend of Mrs Lessways. The friendship was legendary in the house, and the grand quarrel which had finally put an end to it dated in Hilda's early memories like a historical event. For many years the two had not exchanged a word.

Mrs Lessways lit the gas, and the china and the white cloth and the coloured fruit-jelly and the silver spoons caught the light and threw it off again, with gaiety.

'Has she swept the hearth? Yes, she has,' said Mrs Lessways, glancing round at the red fire.

Hilda sat down to wait, folding her hands as it were in meekness. In a few moments Florrie entered with the teapot and the hot-water jug. The child wore proudly a new white apron that was a little too long for her, and she smiled happily at Mrs Lessways's brief compliment on her appearance and her briskness. She might have been in paradise.

'Come in for your cup in three minutes,' said Mrs Lessways; and to Hilda, when Florrie had whispered and gone; 'Now we shall see if she can make tea. I told her very particularly this morning, and she seems quick enough.'

And when three minutes had expired Mrs Lessways tasted the tea. Yes, it was good. It was quite good. Undeniably the water had boiled within five seconds of being poured on the leaves.

There was something *in* this Florrie. Already she was exhibiting the mysterious quality of efficiency. The first day, being the first day, had of course not been without its discouraging moments, but on the whole Florrie had proved that she could be trusted to understand, and to do things.

'Here's an extra piece of sugar for you,' said Mrs Lessways, beaming, as Florrie left the parlour with her big breakfast-cup full of steaming tea, to drink with the thick bread-and-butter on the scrubbed kitchen-table, all by herself. 'And don't touch the gas in the kitchen – it's quite high enough for young eyes,' Mrs Lessways cried out after her.

'Little poppet!' she murmured to herself, maternally reflecting upon Florence's tender youth.

III

She was happy, was Mrs Lessways, in her domesticity. She foresaw an immediate future that would be tranquil. She was preparing herself to lean upon the reliability of Florrie as upon a cushion. She liked the little poppet. And she liked well-made tea and pure jelly. And she had settled the Calder Street problem; and incidentally Hilda was thereby placated. Why should she not be happy? She wished for nothing else. And she was not a woman to meet trouble half-way. One of her greatest qualities was that she did not unduly worry. (Hilda might say that she did not worry enough, letting things go.) In spite of her cold, she yielded with more gusto than usual to the meal, and even said that if Florrie 'continued to shape' they would have hot toast again. Hot toast had long since been dropped from the menu, as an item too troublesome. As a rule the meals were taken hurriedly and negligently, like a religious formality which has lost its meaning but which custom insists on.

Hilda could not but share her mother's satisfaction. She could not entirely escape the soft influence of the tranquillity in which the household was newly bathed. The domestic existence of unmated women together, though it is full of secret exasperations, also has its hours of charm – a charm honied, perverse and unique. Hilda felt the charm. But she was suddenly sad, and she again found pleasure in her sadness. She was sad because her adventure was over – over too soon and too easily. She thought, now, that really she would have preferred a catastrophe as the end of it. She had got what she desired; but she was no better off than she had been before the paralytic stroke of Mr Skellorn. Domesticity had closed in on her once more. Her secret adventure had become sterile. Its risks were destroyed, and nothing could spring from it. Nevertheless it lived in her heart. After all it had been tremendous! And the virtue of audacious initiative was miraculous! . . . Yes, her mother was shrewd enough – that could not be denied – but she was not so shrewd as she imagined; for it had never occurred to her, and it never would occur to her, even in the absurdest dream – that the author of Mr Cannon's visit was the girl sitting opposite to her and delicately pecking at jelly!

'How is he Miss Gailey's half-brother?' Hilda demanded half-way through the meal.

'Why! Mrs Gailey – Sarah Gailey's mother, that is – married a foreigner after her first husband died.'

'But Mr Cannon isn't a foreigner?'

'He's half a foreigner. Look at his eyes. Surely you knew all about that, child! . . . No, it was before your time.'

Hilda then learnt that Mrs Gailey had married a French modeller named Canonges, who had been brought over from Limoges (or some such sounding place) by Peels at Bursley, the great rivals of Mintons and of Copelands. And that in course of time the modeller had informally changed the name to Cannon, because no one in the Five Towns could pronounce the true name rightly. And that George Cannon, the son of the union, had been left early an orphan.

'How did he come to be a solicitor?' Hilda questioned eagerly.

'They say he isn't really a solicitor,' said Mrs Lessways. 'That is, he hasn't passed his examinations like. But I dare say he knows as much law as a lot of 'em, *and* more! And he has that Mr Karkeek to cover him like. That's what they *say* . . . He used to be a lawyer's clerk – at Toms and Scoles's, I think it was. Then he left the district for a year or two – or it might be several. And then his lordship comes back all of a sudden, and sets up with Mr Karkeek, just like that.'

'Can he talk French?'

'Who? Mr Cannon? He can talk *English*! My word, he can that! Eh, he's a "customer", he is – a regular "customer"!'

Hilda, instead of being seated at the table, was away in far realms of romance.

The startling thought occurred to her:

'Of course, he'll expect me to go and see him! He's done what I asked him, and he'll expect me to go and see him and talk it over. And I suppose I shall have to pay him something. I'd forgotten that, and I ought not to have forgotten it.'

CHAPTER 6
VICTOR HUGO AND ISAAC PITMAN

I

THE next morning, Saturday, Hilda ran no risk in visiting Mr Cannon. Her mother's cold, after a fictitious improvement, had assumed an aggravated form in order to prove that not with impunity may nature be flouted in unheated October drawing-rooms; and Hilda had been requested to go to market alone. She was free. And even supposing that the visit should be observed by the curious, nobody would attach any importance to it, because everybody would soon be aware that Mr Cannon had assumed charge of the Calder Street property.

Past the brass plates of Mr Q. Karkeek, out of the straw-littered hubbub of the market-place, she climbed the long flight of stairs leading to the offices on the first floor. In one worsted-gloved hand she held a market-basket of multi-coloured wicker, which dangled a little below the frilled and flounced edge of her blue jacket. Secure in the pocket of her valanced brown skirt – for at that time and in that place it had not yet occurred to any woman that pockets were a superfluity – a private half-sovereign lay in the inmost compartment of her purse; this coin was destined to recompense Mr Cannon. Her free hand went up to the heavy chignon that hung uncertainly beneath her bonnet – a gesture of coquetry which she told herself she despised.

Her face was a prim and rather forbidding mask, assuredly a mysterious mask. She could not have explained her own feelings. She was still in the adventure, but the end of it was immediate. She had nothing to hope from the future. Her essential infelicity was as profound and as enigmatic as ever. She might have said with deliberate and vehement sincerity that she was not happy. Wise, experienced observers, studying her as she walked her ways in the streets, might have said of her with sympathetically sad conviction, 'That girl is not happy! What a pity!' It was so. And yet, in her unhappiness she was blest. She

savoured her unhappiness. She drank it down passionately, as
though it were the very water of life – which it was. She lived to
the utmost in every moment. The recondite romance of existence
was not hidden from her. The sudden creation – her creation – of
the link with Mr Cannon seemed to her surpassingly strange and
romantic; and in so regarding it she had no ulterior thought
whatever: she looked on it with the single-mindedness of an
artist looking on his work. And was it not indeed astounding
that by a swift caprice and stroke of audacity she should have
changed and tranquillized the ominous future for her unsus-
pecting mother and herself? Was it not absolutely disconcerting
that she and this Mr Cannon, whom she had never known before
and in whom she had no other interest, should bear between them
this singular secret, at once innocent and guilty, in the midst of
the whole town so deaf and blind?

II

A somewhat shabby-genteel, youngish man appeared at the head
of the stairs; he was wearing a silk hat and a too-ample frock-
coat. And immediately, from the hidden corridor at the top, she
heard the voice of Mr Cannon, imperious:

'Karkeek!'

The shabby-genteel man stopped. Hilda wanted to escape, but
she could not, chiefly because her pride would not allow. She
had to go on. She went on, frowning.

The man vanished back into the corridor. She could hear that
Mr Cannon had joined him in conversation. She arrived at the
corridor.

'How-d'ye-do, Miss Lessways?' Mr Cannon greeted her with
calm politeness, turning from Mr Karkeek, who raised his hat.
'Will you come this way? One moment, Mr Karkeek.'

Through a door marked 'Private' Mr Cannon introduced
Hilda straight into his own room; then shut the door on her.
He held in one hand a large calf-bound volume, from which
evidently he was expounding something to Mr Karkeek. The
contrast between the expensive informality of Mr Cannon's new
suit and the battered ceremoniousness of Mr Karkeek's struck
her just as much as the contrast between their demeanours; and

she felt, vaguely, the oddness of the fact that the name of the deferential Mr Karkeek, and not the name of the commanding Mr Cannon, should be upon the door-plates and the wire-blinds of the establishment. But of course she was not in a position to estimate the full significance of this remarkable phenomenon. Further, though she perfectly remembered her mother's observations upon Mr Cannon's status, they did not in the slightest degree damage him in her eyes – when once those eyes had been set on him again. They seemed to her inessential. The essential, for her, was the incontestable natural authority and dignity of his bearing.

She sat down, self-consciously, in the chair – opposite the owner's chair – which she had occupied at her first visit, and thus surveyed, across the large flat desk, all the ranged documents and bundles with the writing thereon upside down. There also was his blotting-pad, and his vast inkstand, and his pens, and his thick diary. The disposition of the things on the desk seemed to indicate, sharply and incontrovertibly, that orderliness, that inexorable efficiency, which more than aught else she admired in the external conduct of life. The spectacle satisfied her, soothed her, and seemed to explain the attractiveness of Mr Cannon.

Immediately to her left was an open bookcase almost filled with heavy volumes. The last of a uniform row of Law Reports was absent from its place – being at that moment in the corridor, in the hands of Mr Cannon. The next book, a thin one, had toppled over sideways and was bridging the vacancy at an angle; several other similar thin books filled up the remainder of the shelf. She stared, with the factitious interest of one who is very nervously awaiting an encounter, at the titles, and presently deciphered the words, 'Victor Hugo', on each of the thin volumes. Her interest instantly became real. Characteristically abrupt and unreflecting, she deposited her basket on the floor and, going to the bookcase, took out the slanting volume. Its title was *Les Rayons et Les Ombres*. She opened it by hazard at the following poem, which had no heading and which stood, a small triptych of print, rather solitary in the lower half of a large white page:

> *Dieu qui sourit et qui donne*
> *Et qui vient vers qui l'attend*
> *Pourvu que vous soyez bonne,*
> > *Sera content.*

Le monde où tout étincelle,
Mais où rien n'est enflammé,
Pourvu que vous soyez belle,
Sera charmé.

Mon cœur, dans l'ombre amoureuse,
Où l'énivrent deux beaux yeux,
Pourvu que tu sois heureuse,
Sera joyeux.

That was all. But she shook as though a miracle had been enacted. Hilda, owing partly to the fondness of an otherwise stern grandfather and partly to the vanity of her unimportant father, had finally been sent to a school attended by girls who on the average were a little above herself in station – Chetwynd's, in the valley between Turnhill and Bursley. (It was still called Chetwynd's though it had changed hands.) Among the staff was a mistress who was known as Miss Miranda – she seemed to have no surname. One of Miss Miranda's duties had been to teach optional French, and one of Miss Miranda's delights had been to dictate this very poem of Victor Hugo's to her pupils for learning by heart. It was Miss Miranda's sole French poem, and she imposed it with unfading delight on the successive generations whom she 'grounded' in French. Hilda had apparently forgotten most of her French, but as she now read the poem (for the first time in print), it re-established itself in her memory as the most lovely verse that she had ever known, and the recitations of it in Miss Miranda's small class-room came back to her with an effect beautiful and tragic. And also there was the name of Victor Hugo, which Miss Miranda's insistent enthusiasm had rendered sublime and legendary to a sensitive child! Hilda now saw the sacred name stamped in gold on a whole set of elegant volumes! It was marvellous that she should have turned the page containing just that poem! It was equally marvellous that she should have discovered the works of Victor Hugo in the matter-of-fact office of Mr Cannon! But was it? Was he not half-French, and were not these books precisely a corroboration of what her mother had told her? Mr Cannon's origin at once assumed for her the strange seductive hues of romance; he shared the glory of Victor Hugo. Then the voices in the corridor ceased, and with a decisive movement he unlatched the door. She relinquished the book and calmly sat down as he entered.

III

'Of course, your mother's told you?'

'Yes.'

'I had no difficulty at all. I just asked her what she was going to do about the rent-collecting.'

Standing up in front of Hilda, but on his own side of the desk, Mr Cannon smiled as a conqueror who can recount a triumph with pride, but without conceit. She looked at him with naïve admiration. To admire him was agreeable to her; and she liked also to feel unimportant in his presence. But she fought, unsuccessfully, against the humiliating idea that his personal smartness convicted her of being shabby – of being even inefficient in one department of her existence; and she could have wished to be magnificently dressed.

'Mrs Lessways is a very shrewd lady – very shrewd indeed!' said Mr Cannon, with a smile, this time, to indicate humorously that Mrs Lessways was not so easy to handle as might be imagined, and that even the cleverest must mind their p's and q's with such a lady.

'Oh yes, she *is*!' Hilda agreed, with an exaggerated emphasis that showed a lack of conviction. Indeed, she had never thought of her mother as a *very* shrewd lady.

Mr Cannon continued to smile in silence upon the shrewdness of Mrs Lessways, giving little appreciative movements of the diaphragm, drawing in his lips and by consequence pushing out his cheeks like a child's; and his eyes were all the time saying lightly: 'Still, I managed her!' And while this pleasant intimate silence persisted, the noises of the market-place made themselves prominent, quite agreeably – in particular the hard metallic stamping and slipping, on the bricked pavement under the window, of a team of cart-horses that were being turned in a space too small for their grand, free movements, and the good-humoured cracking of a whip. Again Hilda was impressed, mystically, by the strangeness of the secret relation between herself and this splendid effective man. There they were, safe within the room, almost on a footing of familiar friendship! The atmosphere was different from that of the first interview. And none knew! And she alone had brought it all about by a simple caprice!

'I was fine and startled when I saw you at our door, Mr Cannon!' she said.

He might have said, 'Were you? You didn't show it.' She was half expecting him to say some such thing. But he became reflective, and began: 'Well, you see –' and then hesitated.

'You didn't tell me you thought of calling.'

'Well,' he proceeded at last – and she could not be sure whether he was replying to her or not – 'I was pretty nearly ready to buy that Calder Street property. And I thought I'd talk *that* over with your mother first! It just happened to make a good beginning, you see.' He spoke with all the flattering charm of the confidential.

Hilda flushed. Under her mother's suggestion, she had been misjudging him. He had not been guilty of mere scheming. She was profoundly glad. The act of apology to him, performed in her own mind, gave her a curious delight.

'I wish she would sell,' said Hilda, to whom the ownership of a slum was obnoxious.

'Very soon your consent would be necessary to any sale.'

'Really!' she exclaimed, agreeably flattered, but scarcely surprised by this information. 'I should consent quick enough! I can't bear to walk down the street!'

He laughed condescendingly. 'Well, I don't think your mother *would* care to sell, if you ask me.' He sat down.

Hilda frowned, regretting her confession and resenting his laughter.

'What will your charges be, please, Mr Cannon?' she demanded abruptly, and yet girlishly timid. And at the same moment she drew forth her purse, which she had been holding ready in her hand.

For a second he thought she was referring to the price of rent-collecting, but the appearance of the purse explained her meaning. 'Oh! There's no charge!' he said, in a low voice, seizing a penholder

'But I must pay you something! I can't –'

'No, you mustn't!'

Their glances met in conflict across the table. She had known that he would say exactly that. And she had been determined to insist on paying a fee – utterly determined! But she could not, now, withstand the force of his will. Her glance failed her. She was disconcerted by the sudden demonstration of her inferiority. She was distressed. And then a feeling of faintness, and the gathering of a mist in the air, positively frightened her. The mist cleared. His glance seemed to say, with kindness: 'You see how much stronger I am than you! But you can trust me!' The sense of adventure grew even more acute in her. She marvelled at what life was, and hid the purse like a shame.

'It's very kind of you,' she murmured.

'Not a bit!' he said. 'I've got a job through this. Don't forget that. We don't collect rents for nothing, you know – especially Calder Street sort of rents!'

She picked up her basket and rose. He also rose.

'So you've been looking at my Victor Hugo,' he remarked, putting his right hand negligently into his pocket instead of holding it forth in adieu.

IV

So overset was she by the dramatic surprise of his challenging remark, and so enlightened by the sudden perception of it being perfectly characteristic of him, that her manner changed in an instant to a delicate, startled timidity. All the complex sensitiveness of her nature was expressed simultaneously in the changing tints of her face, the confusion of her eyes and her gestures, the exquisite hesitations of her voice as she told him about the coincidence which had brought back to her in his office the poem of her schooldays.

He came to the bookcase and, taking out the volume, handled it carelessly.

'I only brought these things here because they're nicely bound and fill up the shelf,' he said. 'Not much use in a lawyer's office, you know!' He glanced from the volume to her, and from her to the volume. 'Ah, Miss Miranda! Yes! Well! It isn't so wonderful as all that. My father used to give her lessons in French. This Hugo was his. He thought a great deal of it.' Mr Cannon's pose exhibited pride, but it was obvious that he did not share his father's taste. His tone rather patronized his father, and Hugo too. As he let the pages of the book slip by under his thumb, he stopped, and with a very good French accent, quite different from Hilda's memory of Miss Miranda's, murmured in a sort of chanting – '*Dieu qui sourit et qui donne*'.

'That's the very one!' cried Hilda.

'Ah! There you are then! You see – the bookmark was at that page. Hilda had not noticed the thin ribbon almost concealed in the jointure of the pages. 'I wouldn't be a bit astonished if my father had lent her this very book! Curious, isn't it?'

It was. Nevertheless, Hilda felt that his sense of the miraculousness of life was not so keen as her own; and she was disappointed.

'I suppose you're very fond of reading?' he said.

'No, I'm not,' she replied. Her spirit lifted a little courageously, to meet his with defiance, like a ship lifting its prow above the threatening billow. Her eyes wavered, but did not fall before his.

'Really! Now, I should have said you were a great reader. What do you do with yourself?' He now spoke like a brother, confident of a truthful response.

'I just waste my time,' she answered coldly. She saw that he was puzzled, interested, and piqued, and that he was examining her quite afresh.

'Well,' he said shortly, after a pause, adopting the benevolent tone of an uncle or even a great-uncle, 'you'll be getting married one of these days.'

'I don't want to get married,' she retorted obstinately, and with a harder glance.

'Then what do you want?'

'I don't know.' She discovered great relief, even pleasure, in thus callously exposing her mind to a stranger.

Tapping his teeth with one thumb, he gazed at her, apparently in meditation upon her peculiar case. At last he said:

'I tell you what you ought to do. You ought to go in for phonography.'

'Phonography?' She was at a loss.

'Yes; Pitman's shorthand, you know.'

'Oh! shorthand – yes. I've heard of it. But why?'

'Why? It's going to be the great thing of the future. There never was anything like it!' His voice grew warm and his glance scintillated. And now Hilda understood her mother's account of his persuasiveness; she felt the truth of that odd remark that he could talk the hind leg off a horse.

'But does it lead to anything?' she inquired, with her strong sense of intrinsic values.

'I should say it did!' he answered. 'It leads to everything! There's nothing it won't lead to! It's the key of the future. You'll see. Look at Dayson. He's taken it up, and now he's giving lessons in it. He's got a room over his aunt's. I can tell you he staggered me. He wrote in shorthand as fast as ever I could read to him, and then he read out what he'd written, without a single slip. I'm having one of my chaps taught. I'm paying for the lessons. I thought of learning myself – yes, really! Oh! It's a thing that'll revolutionize all business and secretarial work and so on – revolutionize it! And it's spreading. It'll be the Open Sesame to everything. Anybody that can write a hundred and twenty words a minute 'll be able to walk into any situation he wants – straight *into* it! There's never been anything like it. Look! Here it is!'

He snatched up a pale-green booklet from the desk and opened it before her. She saw the cryptic characters for the first time. And then she saw them with his glowing eyes. In their mysterious strokes and curves and dots she saw romance, and the key of the future; she saw the philosopher's stone. She saw a new religion that had already begun to work like leaven in the town. The revelation was deliciously intoxicating. She was converted, as by lightning. She yielded to the ecstasy of discipleship. Here – somehow, inexplicably, incomprehensibly – here was the answer to the enigma of her long desire. And it was an answer original, strange, distinguished, unexpected, unique; yes, and divine! How lovely, how beatific, to be the master of this enchanted key!

'It must be very interesting!' she said, low, with the venturesome shyness of a deer that is reassured.

'I don't mind telling you this,' Mr Cannon went on, with the fire of the prophet. 'I've got something coming along pretty soon' – he repeated more slowly – 'I've got something coming along pretty soon, where there'll be scope for a young lady that can write shorthand *well*. I can't tell you what it is, but it's something different from anything there's ever been in this town; *and* better.'

His eyes masterfully held hers, seeming to say: 'I'm vague.

But I was vague when I told you I'd see what could be done about
your mother – and look at what I did, and how quickly and easily
I did it! When I'm vague, it means a lot.' And she entirely
understood that his vagueness was calculated – out of pride.

They talked about Mr Dayson a little.

'I must go now,' said Hilda awkwardly.

'I'd like you to take that Hugo,' he said. 'I dare say it would
interest you . . . Remind you of old times.'

'Oh no!'

'You can return it when you like.'

Her features became apologetic. She had too hastily assumed
that he wished to force a gift on her.

'Please!' he ejaculated. No abuse this time of moral authority!
But an appeal, boyish, wistful, supplicating. It was irresistible,
completely irresistible. It gave her an extraordinary sense of
personal power.

He wrapped up the book for her in a sheet of blue 'draft' paper
that noisily crackled. While he was doing so, a tiny part of her
brain was, as it were, automatically exploring a box of old books
in the attic at home and searching therein for a Gasc's French–
English Dictionary which she had used at school and never
thought of since.

'My compliments to your mother,' he said at parting.

She gazed at him questioningly.

'Oh! I was forgetting,' he corrected himself, with an avuncular,
ironic smile. 'You're not supposed to have seen me, are you?'

Then she was outside in the din; and from thrilling altitudes she
had to bring her mind to marketing. She hid under apples the
flat blue parcel in the basket.

CHAPTER 7
THE EDITORIAL SECRETARY

I

ARTHUR DAYSON, though a very good shorthand writer, and not without experience as a newspaper reporter and sub-editor, was a nincompoop. There could be no other explanation of his bland, complacent indifference as he sat poking at a coke stove one cold night of January 1880, in full view of a most marvellous and ravishing spectacle. The stove was in a room on the floor above the offices labelled as Mr Q. Karkeek's; its pipe, supported by wire stays, went straight up nearly to the grimy ceiling, and then turned horizontally and disappeared through a clumsy hole in the scorched wall. It was a shabby stove, but not more so than the other few articles of furniture – a large table, a small desk, three deteriorated cane-chairs, two gas brackets, and an old copying press on its rickety stand. The sole object that could emerge brightly from the ordeal of the gas-flare was a splendid freshly printed blue poster gummed with stamp-paper to the wall: which poster bore the words, in vast capitals of two sizes: '*The Five Towns Chronicle and Turnhill Guardian*'. Copies of this poster had also been fixed face outwards, on the two curtainless black windows, to announce to the Market Square what was afoot in the top storey over the ironmonger's.

A young woman, very soberly attired, was straining at the double iron-handles of the copying-press. Some copying-presses have a screw so accurately turned and so well oiled, and handles so massively like a fly-wheel, that a touch will send the handles whizzing round and round till they stop suddenly, and then one slight wrench more, and the letters are duly copied! But this was not such a press. It had been outworn in Mr Karkeek's office; rust had intensified its original defects of design, and it produced the minimum of result with the maximum of means. Nevertheless, the young woman loved it. She clenched her hands and her teeth, and she frowned, as though she loved it. And when she had sufficiently crushed the letter-book in the press, she lovingly un-screwed and drew forth the book; and with solicitude she opened the book on the smaller table, and tenderly detached the blotting-paper from the damp tissue paper, and at last extracted the copied letter and examined its surface.

'Smudged!' she murmured, tragic.

And the excellent ass Dayson, always facetiously cheerful, and without a grain of humour, remarked:

'Copiousness with the H_2O, Miss Lessways, is the father of smudged epistles. I'm ready to go through these proofs with you as soon as you are.'

He was over thirty. He had had affairs with young women. He reckoned that there remained little for him to learn. He had deliberately watched this young woman at the press. He had clearly seen her staring under the gas-jet at the copied letter. And yet in her fierce muscular movements, and in her bendings and straightenings, and in her delicate caressings, and in her savage scowlings and wrinklings, and in her rapt gazings, and in all her awful absorption, he had quite failed to perceive the terrible eager outpouring of a human soul, mighty, passionate, and wistful. He had kept his eyes on her slim bust and tight-girded waist that sprung suddenly neat and smooth out of the curving skirt-folds, and it had not occurred to him to exclaim even in his own heart: 'With your girlishness and your ferocity, your inti-midating seriousness, and your delicious absurdity, I would give a week's wages just to take hold of you and shake you!' No! The dolt had seen absolutely naught but a conscientious female beginner learning the duties of the post which he himself had baptized as that of 'editorial secretary'.

II

Hilda was no longer in a nameless trouble. She no longer wanted she knew not what. She knew beyond all questioning that she had found that which she had wanted. For nearly a year she had had lessons in phonography from Miss Dayson's nephew, often as a member of a varying night-class, and sometimes alone during the day. She could not write shorthand as well as Mr Dayson, and she never would, for Mr Dayson had the shorthand soul; but, as the result of sustained and terrific effort, she could write it pretty well. She had grappled with Isaac Pitman as with Apollyon and had not been worsted. She could scarcely believe that in class she had taken down at the rate of ninety words a minute Mr Dayson's purposely difficult political speechifyings (which always contained the phrase 'capital punishment', because 'capital punishment' was a famous grammalogue); but it was so, Mr Dayson's watch proved it.

About half-way through the period of study, she had learnt from Mr Cannon, on one of his rare visits to her mother's, something about his long-matured scheme for a new local paper. She had at once divined that he meant to offer her some kind of a situation in the enterprise, and she was right. Gratitude filled her. Mrs Lessways, being one of your happy-go-lucky, broad-minded women, with an experimental disposition – a disposition to let things alone and see how they will turn out – had made little objection, though she was not encouraging.

Instantly the newspaper had become the chief article of Hilda's faith. She accepted the idea of it as a nun accepts the sacred wafer, in ecstasy. Yet she knew little about it. She was aware that Mr Cannon meant to establish it first as a weekly, and then, when it had grown, to transform it into a daily and wage war with that powerful monopolist, *The Staffordshire Signal*, which from its offices at Hanbridge covered the entire district. The original title had been *The Turnhill Guardian and Five Towns General Chronicle*, and she had approved it; but when Mr Cannon, with a view to the intended development, had inverted the title to *The Five Towns Chronicle and Turnhill Guardian*, she had enthusiastically applauded his deep wisdom. Also she had applauded his project of moving, later on, to Hanbridge, the natural centre of the Five Towns. This was nearly the limit of her knowledge. She neither knew nor cared anything about the resources or the politics or the programme or the prospects of the paper. To her all newspapers were much alike. She did not even explore, in meditation, the extraordinary psychology of Mr Cannon – the man whose original energy and restless love of initiative was leading him to found a newspaper on the top of a successful but audaciously irregular practice as a lawyer. She incuriously and with religious admiration accepted Mr Cannon as she accepted the idea of the paper. And being, of course, entirely ignorant of journalism, she was not in a position to criticize the organizing arrangements of the newspaper. Not that these would have seemed excessively peculiar to anybody familiar with the haphazard improvisations of minor journalism in the provinces! She had indeed, in her innocence, imagined that the basic fact of a newspaper enterprise would be a printing-press; but when Mr Dayson, who had been on *The Signal* and on sundry country papers in Shropshire, assured her that the majority of weekly sheets were printed on jobbing presses in private hands, she corrected her foolish notion.

Her sole interest – but it was tremendous! – lay in what she herself had to do – namely, take down from dictation, transcribe, copy, classify, and keep letters and documents, and occasionally correct proofs. All beyond this was misty for her, and she never adjusted her sight in order to pierce the mist.

Save for her desire to perfect herself in her duties, she had no desire. She was content. In the dismal, dirty, untidy, untidiable, uncomfortable office, arctic near the windows, and tropic near the stove, with dust on her dress and ink on her fingers and the fumes of gas in her quivering nostrils, and her mind strained and racked by an exaggerated sense of her responsibilities, she was in heaven! She who so vehemently objected to the squalid mess of the business of domesticity, revelled in the squalid mess of this business. She whose heart would revolt because Florrie's work was never done, was delighted to wait to all hours on the convenience of men who seemed to be the very incarnation of incalculable change and caprice. And what was she? Nothing but a clerk, at a commencing salary of fifteen shillings per week! Ah! but she was a priestess! She had a vocation which was unsoiled by the economic excuse. She was a pioneer. No young woman had ever done what she was doing. She was the only girl in the Five Towns who knew shorthand. And in a fortnight (they said) the paper was to come out!

III

At the large table which was laden with prodigious, heterogeneous masses of paper and general litter, she bent over the proofs by Mr Dayson's side. He had one proof; she had a duplicate; the copy lay between them. It was the rough galley of a circular to the burgesses that they were correcting together. Reading and explaining aloud, he inscribed the cabalistic signs of correction in the margin of his proof, and she faithfully copied them in the margin of hers, for practice.

'l.c.,' he intoned.

'What does that mean?'

'Lower case,' he explained grandiosely, in the naïve vanity of his knowledge. 'Small letter; not a capital.'

'Thank you,' she said, and, writing 'l.c.', noted in her striving brain that 'lower case' meant a small letter instead of a capital; but she knew not why, and she did not ask; the reason did not trouble her.

'I think we'll put "enlightened" there, before "public". Ring it, will you.'

'Ring it? Oh! I see!'

'Yes, put a ring round the word in the margin. That's to show it isn't the intelligent compositor's mistake, you see!'

Then there was a familiar and masterful footstep on the stairs, and the attention of both of them wavered.

IV

Arthur Dayson and his proof-correcting lost all interest and all importance for Hilda as Mr Cannon came into the room. The unconscious, expressive gesture, scornful and abrupt, with which she neglected them might have been terribly wounding to a young man more sensitive than Dayson. But Dayson, in his self-sufficient, good-natured mediocrity, had the hide of an alligator. He even judged her movement quite natural, for he was a flunkey born. Hilda gazed at her master with anxiety as he deposited his black walking-stick in the corner behind the door and loosed his white muffler and large overcoat (which Dayson called an 'immensikoff'). She thought the master looked tired and worried. Supposing he fell ill at this supreme juncture! The whole enterprise would be scotched, and not forty Daysons could keep it going! The master was doing too much – law by day and journalism by night. They were perhaps all doing too much, but the others did not matter. Nevertheless, Mr Cannon advanced to the table buoyant and faintly smiling, straightening his shoulders back, proudly proving to himself and to them that his individual force was inexhaustible. That straightening of the shoulders always affected Hilda as something wistful, as almost pathetic in its confident boyishness. It made her feel maternal and say to herself (but not in words) with a sort of maternal superiority: 'How brave he is, poor thing!' Yes, in her heart she would apply the epithet 'poor thing' to this grand creature whose superiority she acknowledged with more fervour than anybody. As for the undaunted straightening of the shoulders, she adopted it, and after a time it grew to be a characteristic gesture with her.

'Well?' Mr Cannon greeted them.

'Well,' said Arthur Dayson, with a factitious air of treating him as an equal, 'I've been round to Bennion's and made it clear to him that if he can't guarantee to run off a maximum of two thousand of an eight-page sheet we shall have to try Clayhanger at Bursley, even if it's the last minute.'

'What did he say?'

'Grunted.'

'I shall risk two thousand, any way.'

'Paper delivered, governor?' Dayson asked in a low voice, leering pawkily, as though to indicate that he was a man who could be trusted to think of everything.

'Will be tomorrow, I think,' said Mr Cannon. 'Got that letter ready, Miss Lessways?'

Hilda sprang into life.

'Yes,' she said, handing it diffidently. 'But if you'd like me to do it again – you see it's –'

'Plethora of H_2O,' Dayson put in, indulgent.

'Oh no!' Mr Cannon decided. Having read the letter, he gave it to Dayson. 'It doesn't matter, but you ought to have signed it before it was copied in the letter-book.'

'Gemini! Miss!' murmured Dayson, glancing at Hilda with uplifted brows.

The fact was that both of them had forgotten this formality. Dayson took a pen, and after describing a few flourishes in the air, about a quarter of an inch above the level of the paper, he magnificently signed: 'Dayson & Co.' Such was the title of the proprietorship. Just as Karkeek was Mr Cannon's dummy in the law, so was Dayson in the newspaper business. But whereas Karkeek was privately ashamed, Dayson was proud of his role, which gave him the illusion of power and glory.

'Just take this down, will you,' said Mr Cannon.

Hilda grasped at her notebook and seized a pencil, and then held herself tense to receive the message, staring downwards at the blank page. Dayson lolled in his chair, throwing his head back. He knew that the presence of himself, the great shorthand expert, made Hilda nervous when she had to write from dictation; and this flattered his simple vanity. Hilda hated and condemned her nervousness, but she could not conquer it.

Mr Cannon, standing over the table, pushed his hat away from his broad, shining forehead, and then, meditative, absently lifted higher his carefully tended hand and lowered the singing gas-jet, only to raise it again.

'Mr Ezra Brunt. Dear Sir, *Re* advertisement. With reference to your letter replying to ours, in which you inquire as to the circulation of the above newspaper, we beg to state that it is our intention to print four thousand of –'

'Two thousand,' Hilda interrupted confidently.

Unruffled, Mr Cannon went on politely: 'No – four thousand of the first number. Our representative would be pleased to call upon you by appointment. Respectfully yours. – You might sign that, Dayson, and get it off tonight. Is Sowter here?'

For answer, Dayson jerked his head towards an inner door. Sowter was the old clerk who had first received Hilda into the offices of Mr Q. Karkeek. He was earning a little extra money by clerical work at nights in connection with the advertisement department of the new organ.

Mr Cannon marched to the inner door and opened it. Then he turned and called:

'Dayson – a moment.'

'Certainly,' said Dayson, jumping up. He planted his hat doggishly at the back of his head, stuck his hands into his pockets, and swaggered after his employer.

The inner door closed on the three men. Hilda, staring at the notebook, blushing and nibbling at the pencil, was left alone under the gas. She could feel her heart beating violently.

CHAPTER 8

JANET ORGREAVE

I

'OUR friend is waiting for that letter to Brunt,' said Arthur Dayson, emerging from the inner room a little later.

'In one moment,' Hilda replied coldly, though she had not begun to write the letter.

Dayson disappeared, nodding.

She resented his referring to Mr Cannon as 'our friend', but she did not know why, unless it was that she vaguely regarded it as presumptuous, or, in the alternative, if he meant to be facetious, as ill-bred, on the part of Arthur Dayson. She chose a sheet of paper, and wrote the letter in longhand, as quickly as she could, but with arduous care in the formation of every character; she wrote with the whole of her faculties fully applied. Even in the smallest task she could not economize herself; she had to give all or nothing. When she came to the figures – 4,000 – she intensified her ardour, lavishing enormous unnecessary force: it was like a steam-hammer cracking a nut. Her conscience had instantly and finally decided against her. But she ignored her conscience. She knew and owned that she was wrong to abet Mr Cannon's deception. And she abetted it. She would have abetted it if she had believed that the act would involve her in everlasting damnation – not solely out of loyalty to Mr Cannon; only a little out of loyalty; chiefly out of mere unreasoning pride and obstinate adherence to a decision.

The letter finished, she took it into the inner room, where the three men sat in mysterious conclave. Mr Cannon read it over, and then Arthur Dayson borrowed the old clerk's vile pen, and, with the ceremonious delays due to his sense of his own importance, flourishingly added the signature.

When she came forth she heard a knock at the outer door.

'Come in,' she commanded defiantly, for she was still un-

consciously in the defiant mood in which she had offered the
lying letter to Mr Cannon.

II

A well-dressed, kind-featured, and almost beautiful young
woman, of about the same age as Hilda, opened the door with a
charming gesture of diffidence.

For a second the two gazed at each other astounded.

'Well, Hilda, of all the –!'

'Janet!'

It was an old schoolfellow, Janet Orgreave, daughter of
Osmond Orgreave, a successful architect at Bursley. Janet had
passed part of her schooldays at Chetwynd's; and with her
brother Charlie she had also attended Sarah Gailey's private
dancing-class (famous throughout Turnhill, Bursley, and Hanbridge) at the same time as Hilda. She was known, she was almost notorious, as a universal favourite. By instinct, without
taking thought, she pleased everybody, great and small. Nature
had spoiled her, endowing her with some beauty, and undeniable
elegance, and abundant sincere kindliness. She had only to
smile, and she made a friend; it cost her nothing. She smiled
now, and produced the illusion, not merely in Hilda but in herself also, that her pleasure in this very astonishing encounter was
quite peculiarly poignant.

They shook hands, as women of the world.

'Did you know I was here?' Hilda questioned, characteristically on her guard, with a nervous girlish movement of the
leg that perhaps sinned against the code of authentic worldliness.

'No indeed!' exclaimed Janet.

'Well, I am! I'm engaged here.'

'How splendid of you!' said Janet enthusiastically, with no
suggestion whatever in her tone that Hilda's situation was odd,
or of dubious propriety, or aught but enviable.

But Hilda surveyed her with secret envy, transient yet real.
In the half-dozen years that had passed since the days of the
dancing-class, Janet had matured. She was now the finished
product. She had the charm of her sex, and she depended on it.
She had grace and an overflowing goodness. She had a smooth

ease of manner. She was dignified. And, with her furs, and her
expensive veil protecting those bright apple-red cheeks, and all
the studied minor details of her costume, she was admirably
and luxuriously attired. She was the usual, as distinguished from
the unusual, woman, brought to perfection. She represented no
revolt against established custom. Doubts and longings did not
beset her. She was content within her sphere: a destined queen of
the home. And yet she could not be accused of being old-
fashioned. None would dare to despise her. She was what Hilda
could never be, had never long desired to be. She was what Hilda
had definitely renounced being. And there stood Hilda, im-
mature, graceless, harsh, inelegant, dowdy, holding the letter
between her inky fingers, in the midst of all that hard masculine
mess – and a part of it, the blindly devoted subaltern, who could
expect none of the ritual of homage given to women, who must
sit and work and stand and strain and say 'yes', and pretend
stiffly that she was a sound, serviceable, thick-skinned imitation
man among men! If Hilda had been a valkyrie or a saint she
might have felt no envy and no pang. But she was a woman.
Self-pity shot through her tremendous pride; and the lancinating
stab made her inattentive even to her curiosity concerning the
purpose of Janet's visit.

III

'I came to see Mr Cannon,' said Janet. 'The housekeeper downstairs told me he was here somewhere.'

'He's engaged,' answered Hilda in a low voice, with the
devotee's instinct to surround her superior with mystery.

'Oh!' murmured Janet, checked.

Hilda wondered furiously what she could be wanting with Mr
Cannon.

Janet recommenced: 'It's really about Miss Gailey, you know.'

'Yes – what?'

Hilda nodded eagerly, speaking in a tone still lower and more
careful.

Janet dropped her voice accordingly: 'She's Mr Cannon's
sister, of course?'

'Half-sister.'

'I mean. I've just come away from seeing her.' She hesitated. 'I only heard by accident. So I came over with father. He had to come to a meeting of the Guardians here, or something. They've quarrelled, haven't they?'

'Who? Miss Gailey and Mr Cannon? Well, you see, she quarrels with everyone.' Hilda appeared to defend Mr Cannon.

'I'm afraid she does, poor thing!'

'She quarrelled with mother.'

'Really! When was that?'

'Oh! Years and years ago! I don't know when. I was always surprised mother let me go to the class.'

'It was very nice of your mother,' said Janet, appreciative.

'Is she in trouble?' Hilda asked bluntly.

'I'm afraid she is.'

'What?'

Janet suddenly gave a gesture of intimacy. 'I believe she's starving!'

'Starving!' Hilda repeated in a blank whisper.

'Yes, I do! I do really believe she hasn't got enough to eat. She's quarrelled with just about everybody there was to quarrel with. She suffers fearfully with rheumatism. She never goes out – or scarcely ever. You know her dancing-classes have all fallen away to nothing. I fancy she tried taking lodgers –'

'Yes, she did. I understand she was very good at house-keeping.'

'She hasn't got any lodgers now. There she is, all alone in that house, and –'

'But she can't be *starving*!' Hilda protested. At intervals she glanced at the inner door, alarmed.

'I really think she is,' Janet persisted, softly persuasive.

'But what's to be done?'

'That's the point. I've just seen her. I went on purpose, because I'd heard ... But I had to pretend all sorts of things to make an excuse for myself. I couldn't offer her anything, could I? Isn't it dreadful?'

They were much worried, these two young maids, full of health and vigour and faith, and pride and simplicity, by this startling first glimpse into one of the nether realities of existence. And they loyally tried to feel more worried than they actually

were; they did their best, out of sympathy, to moderate the
leaping, joyous vitality that was in them – and did not succeed
very well. They were fine, they were touching – but they were also
rather deliciously amusing – as they concentrated all their
resources of solemnity and of worldly experience on the tragic
case of the woman whom life had defeated. Hilda's memory
rushed strangely to Victor Hugo. She was experiencing the same
utter desolation – but somehow less noble – as had gripped her
when she first realized the eternal picture, in *Oceana Nox*, of the
pale-fronted widows who, tired of waiting for those whose barque
had never returned out of the tempest, talked quietly among
themselves of the lost – stirring the cinders in the fireplace and in
their hearts . . . Yet Sarah Gailey was not even a widow. She was
an ageing dancing-mistress. She had once taught the grace of
rhythmic movement to young limbs; and now she was rheumatic.

'Nobody but Mr Cannon can do anything,' Janet murmured.

'I'm sure he hasn't the slightest idea – not the slightest! said
Hilda half defensively. But she was saying to herself: 'This man
made me write a lie, and now I hear that his sister is starving –
in the same town!' And she thought of his glossy opulence. 'I'm
quite sure of *that*!' she repeated to Janet.

'Oh! So am I!' Janet eagerly concurred. 'That's why I came . . .
Somebody had to give him a hint . . . I never dreamt of finding
you, dear!'

'It is strange, isn't it?' said Hilda, the wondrous romance of
things seizing her. Seen afresh, through the eyes of this charming,
sympathetic acquaintance, was not Mr Cannon's originality in
engaging her positively astounding?

'I suppose *you* couldn't give him a hint?'

'Yes, I'll tell him,' said Hilda. 'Of course!' In spite of herself
she was assuming a certain proprietorship in Mr Cannon.

'I'm so glad!' Janet replied. 'It is good of you!'

'It seems to me it's you that's good, Janet,' Hilda said grimly.
She thought: 'Should *I*, out of simple kindliness and charity,
have deliberately come to tell a man I didn't know . . . that his
sister was starving? Never!'

'He's bound to see after it!' said Janet, content.

'Why, of course!' said Hilda, clinching the affair, in an intimate, confidential murmur.

'You'll tell him tonight?'

Hilda nodded.

They exchanged a grave glance of mutual appreciation and understanding. Each was sure of the other's high esteem. Each was glad that chance had brought about the meeting between them. Then they lifted away their apprehensive solicitude for Sarah Gailey, and Janet, having sighed relief, began to talk about old times. And their voices grew louder and more free.

'Can you tell me what time it is?' Janet asked, later. 'I've broken the spring of my watch, and I have to meet father at the station at ten-fifteen.'

'I haven't a notion!' said Hilda, rather ashamed.

'I hope it isn't ten o'clock.'

'I could ask,' said Hilda hesitatingly. The hour, for aught she knew, was nine, eleven, or even midnight. She was oblivious of time.

'I'll run,' said Janet, preparing to go. 'I shall tell Charlie I've seen you, next time I write to him. I'm sure he'll be glad. And you must come to see us. You really must, now! Mother and father will be delighted. Do you still recite, like you used to?'

Hilda shook her head, blushing.

She made no definite response to the invitation, which surprised, agitated, and flattered her. She wanted to accept it, but she was convinced that she never would accept it. Before departing, Janet lifted her veil, with a beautiful gesture, and offered her lips to kiss. They embraced affectionately. The next moment Hilda, at the top of the dim, naked, resounding stair was watching Janet descend – a figure infinitely stylish and agreeable to the eye.

CHAPTER 9
IN THE STREET

I

A FEW minutes later, just as Hilda had sealed up the last of the letters, Mr Cannon issued somewhat hurriedly out of the inner room, buttoning his overcoat at the neck.

'Good night,' he said, and took his stick from the corner where he had placed it.

'Mr Cannon!'

'Well?'

'I wanted to speak to you.'

'What is it? I'm in a hurry.'

She glanced at the inner door, which he had left open. From beyond that door came the voices of Arthur Dayson and the old clerk; Hilda lacked the courage to cross the length of the room and deliberately close it, and though Mr Cannon did not seem inclined to move, his eyes followed the direction of hers and he must have divined her embarrassment. She knew not what to do. A crisis seemed to rise up monstrous between them, in an instant. She was trembling, and in acute trouble.

'It's rather important,' she said timidly, but not without an unintentional violence.

'Well, tomorrow afternoon.'

He, too, was apparently in a fractious state. The situation was perhaps perilous. But she could not allow her conduct to be influenced by danger or difficulty, which indeed nearly always had the effect of confirming her purpose. If something had to be done, it had to be done – and let that suffice! He waited, impatient, for her to agree and allow him to go.

'No,' she answered, with positive resentment in her clear voice. 'I must speak to you tonight. It's very important.'

He made with his tongue an inarticulate noise of controlled exasperation.

'If you've finished, put your things on and walk along with me,' he said.

She hurried to obey, and overtook him as he slowly descended the lower flight of stairs. She had buttoned her jacket and knotted her thick scarf, and now, with the letters pressed tightly under her arm lest they should fall, she was pulling on her gloves.

'I have an appointment at the Saracen's,' he said mildly, meaning the Saracen's Head – the central rendezvous of the town, where Conservative and Liberal met on neutral ground.

II

He turned to the left, towards the High Street and the great cleared space out of which the cellarage of the new Town Hall had already been scooped. He carried his thick gloves in his white and elegant hand, as one who did not feel the frost. She stepped after him. Their breaths whitened the keen air. She was extremely afraid, and considered herself an abject coward, but she was determined to the point of desperation. He ought to know the truth, and he ought to know it at once: nothing else mattered. She reflected in her terror: 'If I don't begin right off, he will be asking me to begin, and that will be worse than ever.' She was like one who, having boastfully undertaken to plunge into deep, cold water from a height, has climbed to the height, and measured the fearful distance, and is sick, and dares not leap, but knows that he must leap.

'I suppose you know Miss Gailey is practically starving,' she said abruptly, harshly, staring at the gutter.

She had leapt. Life seemed to leave her. She had not intended to use such words, nor such a tone. She certainly did not suppose that he knew about Miss Gailey's condition. She had affirmed to Janet Orgreave her absolute assurance that he did not know. As for the tone, it was accusing, it was brutal, it was full of the unconscious and terrible clumsy cruelty of youth.

'What?' His head moved sharply sideways, to look at her.

'Miss Gailey – she's starving, it seems!' Hilda said timidly now, almost apologetically. 'I felt sure you didn't know. I thought *some*one should tell you.'

'What do you mean – starving?' he asked gruffly.

'Not enough to eat,' she replied, with the direct simplicity of a child.

'And how did this tale get about?'

'It's true,' she said. 'I was told tonight.'

'Who told you?'

'A friend of mine – who's seen her!'

'But who?'

'It wouldn't be right for me to tell you who.'

They walked on in an appalling silence to the corner of the Square and the High Street.

'Here's the letter-box,' he said, stopping.

She dropped the letters with nervous haste into the box. Then she looked up at him appealingly. In the brightness of the starry night she saw that his face had a sardonic, meditative smile. The middle part of the lower lip was pushed out, while the corners were pulled down – an expression of scornful disgust. She burst out:

'Of course, I know very well it's not your fault. I know, if you'd *known* ... but what with her never seeing you, and perhaps people not caring to –'

'I'm very obliged to you,' he interrupted her quietly, still meditative. He was evidently sincere. His attitude was dignified. Many men would have been ashamed, humiliated, even though aware of innocence. But he contrived to rise above such weakness. She was glad; she admired him. And she was very glad also that he did not deign to asseverate that he had been ignorant of his half-sister's plight. Naturally he had been ignorant!

III

She was suddenly happy; she was inspired by an unreasoning joy. She was happy because she was so young and fragile and inexperienced, and he so much older, and more powerful, and more capable. She was happy because she was a mere girl and he a mature and important male. She thought their relation in that moment exquisitely beautiful. She was happy because she had been exceedingly afraid and the fear had gone. The dark Square and far-stretching streets lay placid and void under the night, surrounding their silence in a larger silence: and because of that also she was happy. A policeman with his arms hidden under his cloak marched unhasting downwards from the direction of the Bank.

'Fine night, officer,' said Mr Cannon cordially.

'Yes, sir. Good night, sir,' the policeman responded with respect and sturdy self-respect, his footsteps ringing onwards.

And the sight and bearing of this hardy, frost-defying policeman watching over the town, and the greetings between him and Mr Cannon – these too seemed strangely beautiful to Hilda. And then a train reverberated along its embankment in the distance, and the gliding procession of yellow windows was divided at regular intervals by the black silhouettes of the scaffolding-poles of the new Town Hall. Beautiful! She was filled with a delicious sadness. It was Janet's train. In some first-class compartment Janet and her father were shut together, side by side, intimate, mutually understanding. Again, a beautiful relation! From the summit of a high kiln in the middle distance, flames shot intermittently forth, formidable. Crockery was being fired in the night: and unseen the fireman somewhere flitted about the mouths of the kiln. And here and there in the dim faces of the streets a window shone golden . . . there were living people behind the blind! It was all beautiful, joy-giving. The thought of her mother fidgeting for her return home was delightful. The thought of Mr Cannon and Miss Gailey, separated during many years, and now destined to some kind of reconciliation, was indescribably touching, and beautiful in a way that she could not define.

'I was only thinking the other day,' said Mr Cannon, treating her as an equal in years and wisdom – 'I was only thinking I'd got the very thing for my half-sister – the very opening for her – a chance in a thousand, if only she'd . . .' It was unnecessary for him to finish the sentence.

'And is it too late now?' Hilda asked eagerly.

'No,' he said. 'It isn't too late. I shall go round and see her tomorrow morning first thing. It wouldn't do for me to go to-night – you see – might seem too odd.'

'Yes,' Hilda murmured. 'Well, good night.'

They separated. She knew that he was profoundly stirred. Nevertheless, he had inquired for no further details concerning

Miss Gailey. He was too proud, and beneath his inflexibility too
sensitive, to do so. He meant to discover the truth for himself.
He had believed – that was the essential. His behaviour had been
superb. The lying letter to Ezra Brunt was a mere peccadillo,
even if it was that, even if it was not actually virtuous.

She walked off rapidly, trying to imitate the fine, free, calmly
defiant bearing of Mr Cannon and the policeman.

IV

'Florrie gone to bed?' she asked briskly of her mother, who was
fussing about her in the parlour, pretending to be fretful, but
secretly enchanted to welcome her, with a warm fire and plenteous food, back again into the house. And Hilda, too, was enchanted at her reception.

'Florrie gone to bed? I should just think Florrie has gone to
bed. Half past ten and after! Eh my! This going out after tea.
I never heard of such doings. Now do warm your feet.'

'I should have been home sooner, only something happened,'
said Hilda.

'Oh!' Mrs Lessways exclaimed indifferently. She had in fact
no curiosity as to the affairs of Dayson and Company. The sole
thing that interested her was Hilda's daily absence and daily
return. She seemed quite content to remain in ignorance of what
Hilda did in the mysterious office. Her conversation, profuse
when she was in good spirits, rarely went beyond the trifling
separate events of existence personal and domestic – the life of
the house hour by hour and minute by minute. It was often
astounding to Hilda that her mother never showed any sign of
being weary of these topics, nor any desire to discover other
topics.

'Yes,' said Hilda. 'Miss Gailey –'

Mrs Lessways became instantly a different creature.

'And does he know?' she asked blankly, when Hilda had
informed her of Janet's visit and news.

'Yes. I told him – of course.'

'You?'

'Well, somebody had to tell him,' said Hilda, with an affectation of carelessness. 'So I told him myself.'

'And how did he take it?'

'Well, how should he take it?' Hilda retorted largely. 'He *had* to take it! He was much obliged, and he said so.'

Mrs Lessways began to weep.

'What ever's the matter?'

'I was only thinking of poor Sarah!' Mrs Lessways answered the implied rebuke of Hilda's brusque question. 'I shall go and see her tomorrow morning.'

'But, mother, don't you think you'd better wait?'

Mrs Lessways spoke up resolutely: 'I shall go and see Sarah Gailey tomorrow morning, and let that be understood! I don't need my daughter to teach me when I ought to go and see my friends and when I oughtn't . . . I knew Sarah Gailey before your Mr Cannon was born.'

'Oh, very well! Very well!' Hilda soothed her lightly.

'I shall tell Sarah Gailey she's got to reckon with me, whether she wants to or not! That's what I shall tell Sarah Gailey!' Mrs Lessways wiped her eyes.

'Mother,' Hilda asked, when they had gone upstairs, 'did you wind the clock?'

'I don't think I did,' answered the culprit uncertainly from her bedroom door.

'Mother, how tiresome you are! Night before last you wouldn't let me touch it. You said you preferred to do it yourself. And now I shall be waiting for it to strike tomorrow morning, to get up – lend me that candle, do!'

She tripped down to the lobby gladly, and opened the big door of the clock, and put her hand into the dark cavity and, grimacing, hauled up the heavy weights. This forgetfulness of her mother's somehow increased her extraordinary satisfaction with life. She remounted the shadowy stairs on the wings of a pure and ingenuous elation.

CHAPTER 10
MISS GAILEY IN DECLENSION

I

KNOWING whom she was to meet, Hilda came home to tea, on the next day but one, with a demeanour whose characteristics were heightened by nervousness. The weather was still colder, and she had tied the broad ribbons of her small bonnet rather closely under her chin, the double bow a little to the left. A knitted bodice over the dress and under the jacket made the latter tighter than usual, so that the fur edges of it curved away somewhat between the buttons, and all the upper part of the figure seemed to be too strictly confined, while the petticoats surged out freely beneath. A muff, brightly coloured to match the skirt and the bonnet and her cheeks, completed the costume. She went into the house through the garden and delicately stamped her feet on the lobby tiles, partly to warm them and shake off a few bits of snow, and partly to announce clearly her arrival. Then, just as she was, hands in muff, she entered the parlour. She was tingling with keen, rosy life, and with the sense of youthful power. She had the deep, unconscious conviction of the superiority of youth to age. And there were the two older women, waiting for her, as it were on the defensive, and as nervous as she!

'Good afternoon, Miss Gailey,' she said, with a kind and even very cordial smile, and heartily shook the flaccid, rheumatic hand that was primly held out to her. And yet in spite of herself, perhaps unknown to herself, there was in her tone and her smile and her vigorous clasp something which meant, 'Poor old thing!' pityingly, indulgently, scornfully.

She had not spoken to Miss Gailey, and she had scarcely seen her, since the days of the dancing-class. A woman who is in process of losing everything but her pride can disappear from view as easily in a small town as in a great city; her acquaintances will say to each other, 'I haven't met So-and-so lately. I wonder . . .' And curiosity will go no further. And in a short time her invisibility will cease to excite any remark, except, 'She keeps herself to herself nowadays.' To Hilda Miss Gailey appeared no older; her brown hair had very little grey in it, and her skin was fairly smooth and well-preserved. But she seemed curiously smaller, and less significant, this woman who, with a certain pedagogic air, used to instruct girls in grace and boys in gallantry, this woman who was regarded by all her pupils as the authoritative source of correctness and ease in deportment. 'Now, Master Charles,' Hilda could remember her saying, 'will you ask me for the next polka all over again, and try not to look as if you were doing me a favour and were rather ashamed of yourself?' She had a tongue for the sneaping of too casual boys, and girls also.

And she spoke so correctly – as correctly as she performed the figures of a dance! Hilda, who also spoke without the local peculiarities, had been deprived of her Five Towns accent at Chetwynd's School, where the purest Kensingtonian was inculcated; but Miss Gailey had lost hers in Kensington itself – so rumour said – many years before. And now, in her declension, she was still perfect of speech. But the authority and the importance were gone in substance: only the shadow of them remained. She had now, indeed, a manner half apologetic and half defiant, but timorously and weakly defiant. Her head was restless with little nervous movements; her watery eyes seemed to say: 'Do not suppose that I am not as proud and independent as ever I was, because I *am*. Look at my silk dress, and my polished boots, and my smooth hair, and my hands! Can anyone find any trace of shabbiness in *me*?' But beneath all this desperate bravery was the wistful acknowledgement, continually peeping out, that she had after all come down in the world, albeit with a special personal dignity that none save she could have kept.

II

The two women were seated at a splendid fire. Hilda, whose nervousness was quickly vanishing, came between them to warm her hands that were shining with cold, despite muff and gloves. 'Here, mother!' she said teasingly, putting the muff and gloves in her mother's lap.

Sarah Gailey rose with slow stiffness from her chair.

'Now don't let this child disturb you, Sarah!' Mrs Lessways protested.

'Oh no, Caroline!' said Miss Gailey composedly. 'I was only getting my apron.'

From a reticule on the table she drew forth a small black satin apron on which was embroidered in filoselle a spray of moss-roses. It was extremely elegant – much more so than Mrs Less-ways's – though not in quite the latest style of fashionable aprons; not being edible, it had probably been long preserved in a ward-robe, on the chance of just such an occasion as this. She adjusted the elastic round her thin waist, and sat down again. The apron was a sign that she had come definitely to spend the whole evening. It was a proof of the completeness of the reconciliation between the former friends.

As the conversation shifted from the immediate topic of the weather to the great general question of cures for chilblains, Hilda wondered what had passed between her mother and Miss Gailey, and whether her mother had overcome by mere breezy force or by guile: which details she never learnt, for Mrs Less-ways was very loyal to her former crony, and moreover she had necessarily to support the honour of the older generation against the younger. It seemed incredible to Hilda that this woman who sat with such dignity and such gentility by her mother's fire was she who the day before yesterday had been starving in the pride-imposed prison of her own house. Could Miss Gailey have known that Hilda knew! . . . But Hilda knew that Miss Gailey knew that she knew – and that others guessed! Such, however, was the sublime force of convention that the universal pretence of ignorance securely triumphed.

Then Florrie – changed, grown, budded, practised in the technicalities of parlours, but timid because of 'company' – came in to set the tea. And Miss Gailey inspected her with the calm and omniscient detachment of a deity, and said to Caroline when she was gone that Florrie seemed a promising little thing – with the 'makings of a good servant' in her. Afterwards the mistress recounted this judgement to Florrie, who was thereby apparently much impressed and encouraged in well-doing.

III

'And so you're thinking of going to London, Miss Gailey?' said Hilda, during tea. The meal was progressing satisfactorily, though Caroline could not persuade Sarah to eat enough.

Miss Gailey flushed slightly, with the characteristic nervous movement of the head. Evidently her sensitiveness was extreme.

'And what do you know about it, you inquisitive little puss?' Mrs Lessways intervened hastily, though it was she who had informed Hilda of the vague project. Somehow, in presence of her old friend, Mrs Lessways seemed to feel herself under an obligation to play the assertive and crushing mother.

'Has Mr Cannon mentioned it?' said Miss Gailey politely. Miss Gailey, at any rate, recognized in the most scrupulous way that Hilda was an adult, and no longer a foal-legged pupil for dancing. 'Well, he seems so set on it. He came round to see me about it yesterday morning, without any warning. And he was full of it! I told you how full he was of it, didn't I, Caroline? You know how he is when anything takes him.'

'Do I know how he is?' murmured Caroline, arching her eyebrows. She spoke much more broadly than either of the others.

Miss Gailey continued to Hilda, with seriousness: 'It's a boarding-house that he's got control of up there. Something about a bill of sale on the furniture, I think. But perhaps you know?'

'No, I don't,' said Hilda.

'Oh!' said Miss Gailey, relieved. 'Well, anyhow he's bent on me taking charge of this boarding-house. He will have it it's just the thing for me. But – but I don't know!' She finished weakly.

'Everyone knows you're a splendid housekeeper,' said Mrs Lessways. 'Always were.'

'I remember the refreshments at your annual dances,' said Hilda, politely enthusiastic.

'I always attended to those myself,' Miss Gailey judicially observed.

'I don't know anything about refreshments at dances,' said Mrs Lessways, 'but I do know what your housekeeping is, Sarah!'

'Well, that's what George says!' Sarah simpered. 'He says he never had such meals and such attention as that year he lived with me.'

'I'm sure he's been sorry many a time he ever left you!' exclaimed Caroline. 'Many and many a time!'

'Oh, well ... Relatives, you know ...' Sarah murmured vaguely. This was the only reference to the estrangement. She went on with more vivacity. 'And then Mr Cannon has always had ideas about boarding-houses and furnished rooms and so on. He always did say there was lots of money to be made out of them if only they were managed properly; only they never are ... He ought to know; he's been a bachelor long enough, and he's tried enough of them! He says he isn't at all comfortable where he is,' she added, as it were aside to Caroline. 'It's some people who used to let lodgings to theatre people at Hanbridge.'

'Oh! *Them!*' cried Caroline.

The talk meandered into a maze of reminiscences, and Hilda had to realize her youthfulness and the very inferior range of her experience. Sarah and Caroline recalled to each other dozens of persons and events, opening up historical vistas in a manner that filled the young girl with envious respect, in spite of herself.

'Do you remember Hanbridge Theatre being built, Sarah?' questioned Caroline. 'My grandfather – Hilda's great-grandfather – tendered for it – not that he got the job – but he was very old.'

'Did he now? No I don't. But I dare say I was in London then.'

'I dare say that would be it.'

'Yes,' said Sarah, turning to Hilda once more, 'that's just what Mr Cannon says. He says it isn't as if I didn't know what London is ... But it's such a long time ago!' She glanced at Caroline as if for sympathy.

'Come, come, Sarah!' Caroline protested stoutly, and yet with a care for Sarah's sensitiveness. 'It isn't so long ago as all that!'

'It seems so long,' said Sarah, reflective; and her mouth worked uneasily. Then, after a pause: 'He's so set on it!'

'Set on what? On you going to London?'

'Yes.'

'And why not?'

'Well, I don't know whether I could –'

'Paw!' scoffed Caroline lightly and flatteringly. 'You're younger than I am, and I'm not going to have anyone making out that I'm getting old. Now do finish that bit of cake.'

'No, thank you, Caroline. I really couldn't.'

'Not but what I should be sorry enough to lose you,' Caroline concluded. 'There's no friends like the old friends.'

'Ah! No!' Sarah thickly muttered, gazing with her watery eyes at a spot on the white diaper.

'Hilda, do turn down that there gas a bit,' said Mrs Lessways sharply and self-consciously. 'It's fizzing.' And she changed the subject.

IV

With a nervous exaggeration of solicitude Hilda sprang to the gas-jet. Suddenly she was drenched in the most desolating sadness. She could not bear to look at Miss Gailey; and further, Miss Gailey seemed unreal to her, not an actual woman, but an abstract figure of sorrow that fancy had created. A few minutes previously Hilda had been taking pride in the tact and the enterprise of George Cannon, who possessed a mysterious gift of finding an opportunity for everybody who needed it. He had set Hilda on her feet; and he was doing the same for his half-sister, and with such skilful diplomacy that Miss Gailey was able to pretend to herself and to others that George Cannon, and not Sarah Gailey, was the obliged person. But now Hilda saw Sarah Gailey afraid to go to London, and George Cannon pushing her forward with all the ruthless strength of his enterprising spirit. And the sight was extraordinarily, incomprehensibly tragic. Sarah Gailey's timorous glance seemed to be saying: 'I am terrified to go. It isn't beyond my strength – it's beyond my spirit. But I shall have to go, and I shall have to seem glad to go. And nobody can save me!'

And Miss Gailey's excellent silk dress, and her fine apron, and her primness and dignified manners, and her superb pretence of being undamaged struck Hilda as intolerably pathetic – so that she was obliged to look away lest she might weep at the sight of that pathos. Yes, it was a fact that she could not bear to look!

Nor could she bear to let her imagination roam into Miss Gailey's immediate past! She said to herself: 'Only yesterday morning perhaps she didn't know where her next meal was coming from. He must have managed somehow to give her some money. Only yesterday morning perhaps she didn't know where her next meal – If I say that to myself once more I shall burst out crying!' She balanced her spoon on her teacup and let it fall.

'Now, Miss Fidgety!' her mother commented, with good humour. And then they all heard a knock at the front door.

'Will Florrie have heard it?' Mrs Lessways asked nervously. What she meant was: 'Who on earth can this be?' But such questions cannot be put in the presence of a newly reconciled old friend. It was necessary to behave as though knocks at the front door were a regular accompaniment of tea.

CHAPTER 11
DISILLUSION

I

THE entrance of George Cannon into the parlour produced a tumult greatly stimulating the vitality and the self-consciousness of all three women. Sarah Gailey's excitement was expressed in flushing, and in characteristic small futile movements of the head and hands, and in monosyllables that conveyed naught except a vague but keen apprehension. Mrs Lessways was perturbed and somewhat apprehensive also; but she was flattered and pleased. Hilda was frankly suspicious during the first moments. She guessed that Mr Cannon was aware of his sister's visit, and that he had come to further his own purposes. He confirmed her idea by greeting his sister without apparent surprise; but as, in response to Mrs Lessways's insistence, he took off his great overcoat, with those large, powerful gestures which impress susceptible women and give pleasure even to the indifferent, he said casually to Sarah Gailey, 'I didn't expect to meet you here, Sally. I've come to have a private word with Mrs Lessways about putting one of her Calder Street tenants onto the pavement.' Sarah laughed nervously and said that she would retire, and Mrs Lessways said that Sarah would do no such thing, and that she was very welcome to hear all that Mr Cannon might have to say concerning the Calder Street property.

In a minute Mr Cannon was resplendently sitting down to the table with them, and rubbing his friendly hands, and admitting that he should not refuse a cup of tea if pressed. And Hilda received her mother's sharp instructions to get a cup and saucer from the sideboard and a spoon from the drawer. She bore these to the table like a handmaid, but like a delicate and superior handmaid, and it pleased her to constitute herself a delicate and superior handmaid. Mr Cannon sat next to her mother, and Hilda put down the tinkling cup and saucer on the white cloth between them; and as she did so Mr Cannon turned and thanked her with a confidential smile, to which she responded. They were not now employer and employee, but exclusively in the social world; nevertheless, their business relations made an intimacy which it was piquant to feel in the home. Moreover, Sarah Gailey was opposite to them, and Hilda could not keep out of her dark eyes the intelligence: 'If she is here, if you are all amicable together, it is due to me.' Delicious and somehow perilous secret! ... Going back to her seat, she arranged more safely the vast over-coat which he had thrown carelessly down on her mother's rocking-chair. It was inordinately heavy, and would have out-weighed a dozen of her skimpy little jackets; she, who would have been lost in it like à cat in a rug, enjoyed the thought of the force of the creature capable of wearing it lightly for a garment. Withal the rough, soft surface of it was agreeable to the hand. Out of one of the immense pockets hung the end of a coloured silk muffler, filmy as anything that she herself wore.

Then they were all definitely seated, and Mr Cannon accepted his tea from the hand of Mrs Lessways. The whiteness of his linen, the new smartness of his suit the elegance and gallantry of his gestures – these phenomena incited the women to a responsive emulation; they were something which it was a feminine duty to live up to. Archness reigned, especially between the hostess and the caller. Hilda answered to the mood. And Sarah Gailey, though she said little and never finished a sentence, did her best to answer to it by noddings and nervous appreciative smiles, and swift turnings of the head from one to another. When Mr Cannon and Mrs Lessways, in half a dozen serious words interjected among the archness, had adversely settled the fate of a whole family in Calder Street, there remained scarcely a trace, in the company's demeanour, of the shamed consciousness that only two days before its members had been divided by disastrous enmities and that one of them had lacked the means of life.

II

'Oh no! my dear girl! You're too modest – that's what's the matter with you,' said George Cannon eagerly to his half-sister.

The epithet flattered but did not allay her timidity. To Hilda it seemed mysteriously romantic.

The supreme topic had worked its way into the conversation. Uppermost in the minds of all, it seemed to have forced itself out by its own intrinsic energy, against the will of the company. Impossible to decide who first had let it forth! But George Cannon had now fairly seized it and run off with it. He was almost boyishly excited over it. The Latin strain in him animated his features and his speech. He was a poet as he talked of the boarding-house that awaited a mistress. He had pulled out of his pocket the cutting of an advertisement of it from the London *Daily Telegraph*, a paper that was never seen in Turnhill. And this bit of paper, describing in four lines the advantages of the boarding-house, had the effect of giving the actual house a symbolic reality. 'There it is!' he exclaimed, slapping down the paper. And there it appeared really to be. The bit of paper was extraordinarily persuasive. It compelled everybody to realize, now for the first time, that the house did in fact exist. George Cannon had an overwhelming answer to all timorous objections. The boarding-house was remunerative; boarders were at that very moment in it. The nominal proprietor was not leaving it because he was losing money on the boarding-house, but because he had lost money in another enterprise quite foreign to it, and had pledged all the contents of the boarding-house as security. The occasion was one in a thousand, one in a million. He, George Cannon, through a client, had the entire marvellous affair between his finger and thumb, and most obviously Sarah Gailey was the woman of all women for the vacant post at his disposition. Chance was waiting on her. She had nothing whatever to do but walk into the house as a regent into a kingdom, and rule. Only, delay was impossible. All was possible except delay. She would inevitably succeed; she could not fail. And it would be a family affair . . .

Tea was finished and forgotten.

'For your own sake!' he wound up a peroration. 'It really doesn't matter to me . . . Don't you agree with me, Mrs Lessways?' His glance was a homage.

'Oh, you!' exclaimed Mrs Lessways, smiling happily. 'You've

only got to open your mouth, and you'd talk anybody into the middle of next week.'

'Mother!' Hilda mildly reproved. She was convinced now that Mr Cannon had come on purpose to clinch the affair.

He laughed appreciatively.

'But really! Seriously!' he insisted.

And Mrs Lessways, straightening her face, said, with slight self-consciousness: 'Oh, *I* think it's worth while considering!'

'There you are!' cried Mr Cannon to Miss Gailey.

'I should be all alone up there!' said Miss Gailey, as cheerfully as she could.

'I'll go up with you and see you into the place. I should have to come back the same night – I'm so tremendously busy just now – what with the paper and so on.'

'Yes, but – I quite admit all you say, George – but –'

'Here's another idea,' he broke out. 'Why don't you ask Mrs Lessways to go up with you and stay a week or two? It would be a rare change for her, and company for you.'

Miss Gailey looked quickly at her old friend.

'Oh! Bless you!' said Mrs Lessways. 'I've only been to London once, and that was only for two days – before Hilda was born. I should be no use in London, at my time of life. I'm one of your home-stayers.' Nevertheless, it was plain that the notion appealed to her fancy, and that she would enjoy flirting with it.

'Nonsense, Mrs Lessways!' said George Cannon. 'It would do you a world of good, and it would make all the difference to Sally.'

'That it would!' Sarah agreed, still questioning Caroline with her watery, appealing eyes. In Caroline, Sarah saw her salvation, and snatched at it. Caroline could do nothing well; she had no excellence; all that Caroline could do Sarah could do better. And yet Caroline, by the mysterious virtue of her dry and yet genial shrewdness, and of the unstable but reliable equilibrium of her temperament, was the skilled Sarah's superior. They both knew it and felt it. The lofty Hilda admitted it. Caroline herself negligently admitted it by a peculiar, brusque, unaffected geniality of condescension towards Sarah.

'Do go, mother!' said Hilda. To herself she had been saying:

'Another of his wonderful ideas!' The prospect of being alone in the house with Florrie, of being free for a space to live her own life untrammelled and throw all her ardour into her work, was inexpressibly attractive to Hilda. It promised the most delicious experience that she had ever had.

'Yes,' retorted Mrs Lessways. 'And leave you here by yourself! A nice thing!'

'I shall be all right,' said Hilda confidently and joyously. She was sure that the excursion to London had appealed to her mother's latent love of the unexpected, and that her faculty for accepting placidly whatever fate offered would prevent her from resisting the pressure that Sarah Gailey and Mr Cannon would obviously exert.

'Shall you!' Mrs Lessways muttered.

'Why not take your daughter with you, too?' Mr Cannon suggested.

'Oh!' cried Hilda, shocked. 'I couldn't possibly leave my work just now ... The paper just coming out ... You couldn't spare me.' She spoke with pride, using phrases similar to those which he had used to explain to Sarah Gailey why he could not remain with her in London even for a night.

'Oh yes, I could,' he answered kindly, lightly, carelessly, shattering – in his preoccupation with one idea – all her fine, loyal pretensions. 'We should manage all right.'

III

She was hurt. She was mortally pierced. The blow was too cruel. She lowered her glance before his, and fixed it on the table-cloth. Her brow darkened. Her lower lip bulged out. She was the child again. He had with atrocious inhumanity reduced her to the un-importance of a child. She had bestowed on him and his interests the gift of her whole soul, and he had said that it was negligible. And the worst was that he was perfectly unaware of what he had done. He had not even observed the symptoms of her face. He had turned at once to the older women and was continuing the conversation. He had ridden over her, and ridden on without a look behind. The conversation moved, after a pause, back to the plausible excuse for his call. He desired to see some old rent-

book which would show how the doomed tenant in Calder Street
had originally fallen into arrears.

'Where is that old book of Mr Skellorn's, Hilda?' her mother
asked.

She could not speak. The sob was at her throat. If she had
spoken it would have burst through, and she would have been not
merely the child, but the disgraced child.

'Hilda!' repeated her mother.

Her singular silence drew the attention of all. She blushed a
sombre scarlet. No! She could not speak. She cursed herself.
'What a little fool I am! Surely I can . . .' Useless! She could not
speak. She took the one desperate course open to her, and ran
out of the room, to the astonishment of three puzzled and rather
frightened adults. Her shame was now notorious. 'Baby! Great
baby!' she gnashed at her own inconceivable silliness. Had she
no pride? . . . And now she was in the gloom of the lobby, and
she could hear Florrie in the kitchen softly whistling . . . She was
out in the dark lobby exactly like a foolish, passionate child . . .
She knew all the time that she could easily persuade her mother
to leave her alone with Florrie in the house; she had levers to
move her mother . . . But of what use, now, to do that?

CHAPTER 12

THE TELEGRAM

I

IT was the end of February 1880. A day resembling spring had
come, illusive, but exquisite. Hilda, having started out too hurriedly for the office after the midday dinner, had had to return
home for a proof which she had forgotten.

She now had the house to herself, as a kingdom over which she
reigned; for, amid all her humiliation and pensive dejection, she
had been able to exert sufficient harsh force to drive her mother to
London in company with Miss Gailey. She was alone, free; and
she tasted her freedom to the point of ecstasy. She conned corrected proofs at her meals: this was life. When Florrie came in
with another dish, Hilda looked up impatiently from printed
matter, as if disturbed out of a dream, and Florrie put on an
apologetic air, to invoke pardon. It was largely pretence on
Hilda's part, but it was life. Then she had the delicious anxiety of
being responsible for Florrie. 'Now, Florrie, I'm going out tonight, to see Miss Orgreave at Bleakridge. I shall rely on you to go
to bed not later than nine. I've got the key. *I may not be back till
the last train.*' 'Yes, miss!' And what with Hilda's solemnity and
Florrie's impressed eyes, the ten-forty-five was transformed into a
train that circulated in the dark and mysterious hour just before
cockcrow. Hilda, alone, was always appealing to Florrie's
loyalty. Sometimes when discreetly abolishing some old-fashioned,
work-increasing method of her mother's, she would speak to
Florrie in a tone of sudden, transient intimacy, raising her for a
moment to the rank of an intellectual equal as her voice hinted
that her mother after all belonged to the effete generation.

Awkwardly, with her gloved hands, turning over the pages of a
book in which the slip-proof had been carelessly left hidden,
Hilda, from her bedroom, heard Florrie come whistling down the
attic stairs. Florrie had certainly heard nothing of her young
mistress since the door-bang which had signalled her departure for

the office. In the delusion that she was utterly solitary in the house,
Florrie was whistling, not at all like a modest young woman, but
like a carter. Hilda knew that she could whistle, and had several
times indicated to her indirectly that whistling was undesirable;
but she had never heard her whistling as she whistled now. Her
first impulse was to rush out of the bedroom and 'catch' Florrie
and make her look foolish, but a sense of honour restrained her
from a triumph so mean, and she kept perfectly still. She heard
Florrie run into her mother's bedroom; and then she heard that
voice, usually so timid, saying loudly, exultantly, and even
coarsely: 'Oh! How beautiful I am! How beautiful I am! Shan't I
just mash the men! Shan't I just mash 'em!' This new and vulgar
word 'mash' offended Hilda.

II

She crept noiselessly to the door, which was ajar, and looked forth
like a thief. The door of her mother's room was wide open, and
across the landing she could see Florrie posturing in front of the
large mirror of the wardrobe. The sight shocked her in a most
peculiar manner. It was Florrie's afternoon out, and the child was
wearing, for the first time, an old brown skirt that Hilda had
abandoned to her. But in this long skirt she was no more a child.
Although scarcely yet fifteen years old, she was a grown woman.
She had astoundingly developed during her service with Mrs
Lessways. She was scarcely less tall than Hilda, and she possessed
a sturdy, rounded figure which put Hilda's to shame. It was
uncanny – the precocity of the children of the poor! It was
disturbing! On a chair lay Florrie's new 'serviceable' cloak, and a
cheap but sound bonnet: both articles the fruit of a special
journey with her aunt to Baines's drapery shop at Bursley, where
there was a small special sober department for servants who were
wise enough not to yield to the temptation of 'finery'. Florrie,
who at thirteen and a half had never been able to rattle one
penny against another, had since then earned some two thousand
five hundred pennies, and had clothed herself and put money
aside and also poured a shower of silver upon her clamorous
family. Amazing feat! Amazing growth! She seized the 'good'
warm cloak and hid her poor old bodice beneath it, and drew out

her thick pigtail, and shook it into position with a free gesture of the head; and on the head she poised the bonnet, and tied the ribbons under the delightful chin. And then, after a moment of hard scrutiny, danced and whistled, and cried again: 'How beautiful I am! How pretty I am!'

She was. She positively did not look a bit like a drudge. She was not the Florrie of the kitchen and of the sack-apron, but a young, fledged creature with bursting bosom who could trouble any man by the capricious modesty of a gaze downcast. The miraculous skirt, odious on Hilda, had the brightness of a new skirt. Her hands and arms were red and chapped, but her face had bloomed perfect in the kitchen like a flower in a marl-pit. It was a face that an ambitious girl could rely on. Its charms and the fluid charm of her movements atoned a thousand times for all her barbaric ignorance and crudity; the grime on her neck was naught.

Hilda watched, intensely ashamed of this spying, but she could not bring herself to withdraw. She was angry with Florrie; she was outraged. Then she thought: 'Why should I be angry? The fact is I'm being mother all over again. After all, why shouldn't Florrie . . .?' And she was a little jealous of Florrie, and a little envious of her, because Florrie had the naturalness of a savage or of an animal, unsophisticated by ideals of primness. Hilda was disconcerted at the discovery of Florrie as an authentic young woman. Florrie, more than seven years her junior! She felt experienced, and indulgent as the old are indulgent. For the first time in her life she did honestly feel old. And she asked herself – half in dismay: 'Florrie has got thus far. Where am *I*? What am *I* doing?' It was upsetting.

At length Florrie took off the bonnet and ran upstairs, and shut the door of her attic. Apparently she meant to improve the bonnet by some touch. After waiting nervously a few moments, the aged Hilda slipped silently downstairs, and through the kitchen, and so by the garden, where with their feet in mire the bare trees were giving signs of hope under the soft blue sky, into the street. Florrie would never know that she had been watched.

III

Ten minutes later, when she went into the office of Dayson & Co.,
Hilda was younger than ever. It was a young, fragile girl, despite
the dark frown of her intense seriousness, who with accustomed
gestures poked the stove, and hung bonnet and jacket on a nail
and then sat down to the loaded desk; it was an ingenuous girl
absurdly but fiercely anxious to shoulder the world's weight. She
had passed a whole night in revolt against George Cannon's
indignity; she had called it, furiously, an insult. She had said to
herself: 'Well, if I'm so useless as all that, I'll never go near his
office again.' But the next afternoon she had appeared as usual at
the office, meek, modest, with a smile, fatigued and exquisitely
resigned, and a soft voice. And she had worked with even
increased energy and devotion. This kissing of the rod, this
irrational instinctive humility, was a strange and sweet experience
for her. Such was the Hilda of the office; but Hilda at home,
cantankerous, obstinate, and rude, had offered a remarkable
contrast to her until the moment when it was decided that her
mother should accompany Miss Gailey to London. From that
moment Hilda at home had been an angel, and the Hilda of the
office had shown some return of sturdy pride.

Today the first number of *The Five Towns Chronicle* was to go
to press . . . The delays had been inexplicable and exasperating to
Hilda, though she had not criticized them, even to herself; they
were now over. The town had no air of being excited about the
appearance of its new paper. But the office was excited. The very
room itself looked feverish. It was changed; more tables had been
brought into it, and papers and litter had accumulated enormously; it was a room humanized by habitation, with a physiognomy
that was individual and sympathetic

From beyond the closed door of the inner room came the
sound of men's rapid voices. Hilda could distinguish Mr Cannon's
and Arthur Dayson's; there was a third, unfamiliar to her. Having
nothing to do, she began to make work, re-arranging the contents
of her table, fingering with a factitious hurry the thick bundles of
proofs of correspondence from the villages (so energetically
organized by the great Dayson), and the now useless 'copy', and
the innumerable letters, that Dayson was always disturbing, and

the samples of encaustic tiles brought in by an inventor who desired the powerful aid of the press, and the catalogues, and Dayson's cuttings from the Manchester, Birmingham, and London papers, and the notepaper and envelopes and cards, and Veale Chifferiel & Co.'s almanac that had somehow come up with other matters from Mr Karkeek's office below. And then she dusted, with pursed lips that blamed the disgraceful and yet excusable untidiness of men; and then she examined, with despair and with pride, her dirty little hands, whose finger-tips all clustered together (they were now like the hands of a nice, careless school-boy), and lightly dusted one against the other. Then she found a galley-proof under the table. It was a duplicate proof of *The Five Towns Chronicle*'s leading article, dictated to her by a prodigious Arthur Dayson, in Mr Cannon's presence, on the previous day, and dealing faithfully with 'The Calder Street Scandal' and with Mr Enville, a member of the Local Board – implicated in the said scandal. The proof was useless now, for the leader-page was made up. Nevertheless, Hilda carefully classified it 'in case . . .'

IV

On a chair was the *Daily Telegraph*, which Dayson had evidently been reading, for it was blue pencilled. Hilda too must read it; her duty was to read it: Dayson had told her that she ought never to neglect the chance of reading any newspaper whatever, and that a young woman in her responsible situation could not possibly know too much. Which advice, though it came from a person ridiculous to her, seemed sound enough, and was in fact rather flattering. In the *Telegraph* she saw, between Dayson's blue lines, an account of a terrible military disaster. She was moved by it in different ways. It produced in her a grievous, horror-struck desolation; but it also gave her an extraordinary sensation of fervid pleasure. It was an item of news that would have to appear in the *Chronicle*, and this would mean changes in the make-up, and work at express speed, and similar delights. Already the paper was supposed to be on the machine, though in fact, as she well knew, it was not. No doubt the subject of discussion in the inner room was the disaster! . . . Yes, she was acutely and happily excited. And always afterwards, when she heard or saw the sinister word

'Majuba' (whose political associations never in the least interested her), she would recall her contradictory, delicious feelings on that dramatic afternoon.

While she was busily cutting out the news from the *Telegraph* to be ready for Arthur Dayson, there was a very timid knock at the door, and Florrie entered, as into some formidable cabinet of tyrannic rulers.

'If ye please, miss –' she began to whisper.

'Why, Florrie,' Hilda exclaimed, 'what have you put that old skirt on for, when I've given you mine? I told you –'

'I did put it on, miss. But there came a telegram. I told the boy you were here, but he said that wasn't no affair of his, so I brought it myself, and I thought you wouldn't care for to see me in your skirt, miss, not while on duty, miss, 'specially here like! So I up quick and changed it back.'

'Telegram?' Hilda repeated the word.

Florrie, breathless after running and all this whispering, advanced in the prettiest confusion towards the throne, and Hilda took the telegram with a gesture as casual as she could manage. Florrie's abashed mien, and the arrival of the telegram, stiffened her back and steadied her hand. Imagine that infant being afraid of her, Hilda! This too was life! And the murmur of the men in the inner room was thrilling to Hilda's ears.

She brusquely opened the telegram and read. 'Lessways, Lessways Street, Turnhill. Mother ill. Can you come? – Gailey.'

CHAPTER 13
HILDA'S WORLD

I

THE conversation in the inner room promised to be interminable.
Hilda could not decide what to do. She felt no real alarm on her
mother's account. Mrs Lessways, often slightly indisposed, was
never seriously ill; she possessed one of those constitutions which
do not go to extremes of disease; if a malady overtook her, she
invariably 'had' it in a mild form. Doubtless Sarah Gailey, preoccupied and worried by new responsibilities, desired to avoid the
added care of nursing the sick. Hence the telegram. Moreover, if
the case had been grave, she would not have put the telegram in
the interrogative; she would have written, 'Please come at once'.
No, Hilda was not unduly disturbed. Nevertheless, she had an odd
idea that she ought to rush to the station and catch the next train,
which left Knype at five minutes to four; this idea did not spring
from her own conscience, but rather from the old-fashioned
collective family conscience. But at a quarter to four, when it was
already too late to catch the local train at Turnhill, the men had
not emerged from the inner room; nor had Hilda come to any
decision. As the departure of her mother and Miss Gailey had
involved much solemn poring over time-tables, it happened that
she knew the times of all the trains to London; to catch the next
and last she would have to leave Turnhill at 5.55. She said that she
would wait and see. Her work for the first number of the paper
was practically done, but there was this mysterious conclave
which fretted her curiosity and threatened exciting developments;
also the Majuba disaster would mean trouble for somebody. And
in any event she hated the very thought of quitting Turnhill
before the *Chronicle* was definitely out. She had lived for the
moment of its publication, and she could not bear to miss it. She
was almost angry with her mother; she was certainly angry with
Miss Gailey. All the egotism of the devotee in her was aroused
and irate.

Then the men came forth from the inner room, with a rather unexpected suddenness. Mr Cannon appeared first; and after him Mr Enville; lastly Arthur Dayson, papers in hand. Intimidated by the presence of the stranger, Hilda affected to be busy at her table. Mr Enville shook hands very amicably with George Cannon, and instantly departed. As he passed down the stairs she caught sight of him; he was a grizzled man of fifty, lean and shabby, despite his reputation for riches. She knew that he was a candidate for the supreme position of Chief Bailiff at the end of the year, and he did not accord with her spectacular ideal of a Chief Bailiff; the actual Chief Bailiff was a beautiful and picturesque old man, with perfectly tended white whiskers, and always a flower in his coat. Further, she could not reconcile this nearly effusive friendliness between Mr Enville and Mr Cannon with the animadversions of the leading article which Arthur Dayson had composed, and Mr Cannon had approved, only twenty-four hours earlier.

As Mr Cannon shut the door at the head of the stairs, she saw him give a discreet, disdainful wink to Dayson. Then he turned sharply to Hilda, and said, thoughtful and stern:

'Your notebook, please.'

Bracing herself, and still full of pride in her ability to write this mysterious shorthand, she opened her notebook, and waited with poised pencil. The mien of the two men had communicated to her an excitement far surpassing their own, in degree and in felicity. The whole of her vital force was concentrated at the point of her pencil, and she seemed to be saying to herself: 'I'm very sorry, mother, but see how important this is! I shall consider what I can do for you the very moment I am free.'

Arthur Dayson coughed and plumped heavily on a chair.

II

It was in such moments as this that Dayson really lived, with all the force of his mediocrity. George Cannon was not a journalist; he could compose a letter, but he had not the trick of composing an article. He felt, indeed, a negligent disdain for the people who possessed this trick, as for performers in a circus; he certainly did not envy them, for he knew that he could buy them, as a carpenter buys tools. His attitude was that of the genuine bourgeois towards the artist: possessive, incurious, and contemptuous. Dayson, however, ignored George Cannon's attitude, perhaps did not even perceive what it was. He gloried in his performance. Accustomed to dictate extempore speeches on any subject whatever to his shorthand pupils, he was quite at his ease, quite master of his faculties, and self-satisfaction seemed to stand out on his brow like genial sweat while the banal phrases poured glibly from the cavern behind his jagged teeth; and each phrase was a perfect model of provincial journalese. George Cannon had to sit and listen – to approve, or at worst to make tentative suggestions.

The first phrase which penetrated through the outer brain of the shorthand writer to the secret fastness where Hilda sat in judgement on the world was this:

'The campaign of vulgar vilification inaugurated yesterday by our contemporary *The Staffordshire Signal* against our esteemed fellow-townsman Mr Richard Enville . . .'

This phrase came soon after such phrases as 'Our first bow to the public' . . . 'Our solemn and bounden duty to the district which it is our highest ambition to serve . . .' etc. Phrases which had already occurred in the leading article dictated on the previous day.

Hilda soon comprehended that in twenty-four hours Mr Enville, from being an unscrupulous speculator who had used his official position to make illicit profits out of the sale of land to the town for town improvements, had become the very mirror of honesty and high fidelity to the noblest traditions of local government. Without understanding the situation, and before even she had formulated to herself any criticism of the persons concerned, she felt suddenly sick. She dared not look at George Cannon, but once when she raised her head to await the flow of a period that had been arrested at a laudatory superlative, she caught Dayson winking coarsely at him. She hated Dayson for that; George Cannon might wink at Dayson (though she regretted the condescending familiarity), but Dayson had no right to presume to wink at George Cannon. She hoped that Mr Cannon had silently snubbed him.

As the article proceeded there arose a crying from the Square

below. A *Signal* boy, one of the earliest to break the silent habit
of the Square, was bawling a fresh edition of Arthur Dayson's
contemporary, and across the web of the dictator's verbiage she
could hear the words: 'South Africa – Details –' Mr Cannon
glanced at his watch impatiently. Hilda could see, under her bent
and frowning brow, his white hand moving on the dark expanse
of his waistcoat.

Immediately afterwards Mr Cannon, interrupting, said:

'That'll be all right. Finish it. I must be off.'

'Right you are!' said Dayson grandly. 'I'll run down with it to
the printer's myself – soon as it's copied.'

Mr Cannon nodded. 'And tell him we've got to be on the railway bookstalls first thing tomorrow morning.'

'He'll never do it.'

'He must do it. I don't care if he works all night.'

'But –'

'There hasn't got to be any "buts", Dayson. There's been a
damned sight too much delay as it is.'

'All right! All right!' Dayson placated him hastily.

Mr Cannon departed.

It seemed to Hilda that she shivered, but whether with pain or
pleasure she knew not. Never before had Mr Cannon sworn in her
presence. All day his manner had been peculiar, as though the
strain of mysterious anxieties was changing his spirit. And now
he was gone, and she had said naught to him about the telegram
from Miss Gailey!

Arthur Dayson rolled oratorically on in defence of the man
whom yesterday he had attacked.

And then Sowter, the old clerk, entered.

'What is it? Don't interrupt me!' snapped Dayson.

'There's the *Signal* . . . Latest details . . . This here Majuba
business!'

'What do I care about your Majuba?' Dayson retorted. 'I've
got something more important than your Majuba.'

'It was the governor as told me to give it you,' said Sowter,
restive.

'Well, give it me, then; and don't waste my time!' Dayson held
out an imperial hand for the sheet. He looked at Hilda as if for
moral support and added, to her, in a martyred tone: 'I suppose I

shall have to dash off a few lines about Sowter's Majuba while you're copying out my article.'

'And the governor said to remind you that Mr Enville wants a proof of his advertisement,' Sowter called out sulkily as he was disappearing down the stairs.

Hilda blushed, as she had blushed in writing George Cannon's first lie about the printing of the first issue. She had accustomed herself to lies, and really without any difficulty or hesitation. Yes! She had even reached the level of being religiously proud of them! But now her bullied and crushed conscience leaped up again, and in the swift alarm of the shock her heart was once again more violently beating. Yet amid the wild confusion of her feelings, a mechanical intelligence guided her hand to follow Arthur Dayson's final sentences. And there shone out from her soul a contempt for the miserable hack, so dazzling that it would have blinded him – had he not been already blind.

III

That evening she sat alone in the office. The first number of *The Five Towns Chronicle*, after the most astounding adventures, had miraculously gone to press. Dayson and Sowter had departed. There was no reason why Hilda should remain – burning gas to no purpose. She had telegraphed, by favour of a Karkeek office-boy, to Miss Gailey, saying that she would come by the first train on the morrow – Saturday, and she had therefore much to do at home. Nevertheless, she sat idle in the office, unable to leave. Her whole life was in that office, and it was just when she was most weary of the environment that she would vacillate longest before quitting it. She was unhappy and apprehensive, much less about her mother than about the attitude of her conscience towards the morals of this new world of hers. The dramatic Enville incident had spoiled the pleasure which she had felt in sacrificing her formal duty as a daughter to her duty as a clerk. She had been disillusioned. She foresaw the future with alarm.

And yet, strangely, the disillusion and the fear were a source of pleasure. She savoured them with her loyalty, that loyalty which had survived even the frightful blow of George Cannon's casual disdain at her mother's tea-table! Whatever this new world might be, it was hers, and it was precious. She would no more think of abandoning it than a young mother would think of abandoning a baby obviously imperfect ... Nay, she would cling to it the tighter!

George Cannon came up the stairs with his decisive and rapid step. She rose from her chair at the table as he entered. He was wearing a new overcoat, that she had never seen before, with a fine velvet collar.

'You're going?' he asked, a little breathless.

'I *was* going,' she replied in her clear, timid voice implying that she was ready to stay.

'Everything all right?'

'Mr Dayson said so.'

'He's gone?'

'Yes. Mr Sowter's gone too.'

'Good!' he murmured. And he straightened his shoulders, and, putting his hands in the pockets of his trousers, began to walk about the room.

Hilda moved to get her bonnet and jacket. She moved very quietly and delicately, and, because he was there, she put on her bonnet and jacket with gestures of an almost apologetic modesty. He seemed to ignore her, so that she was able to glance surreptitiously at his face. He was now apparently less worried. Still, it was an enigmatic face. She had no notion of what he had been doing since his hurried exit in the afternoon. He might have been attending to his legal practice, or he might have been abroad on mysterious errands.

'Funny business, this newspaper business is, isn't it?' he remarked, after a moment. 'Just imagine Enville, now! Upon my soul I didn't think he had it in him! . . . Of course,' – he threw his head up with a careless laugh – 'of course, it would have been madness for us to miss such a chance! He's one of the men of the future, in this town.'

'Yes,' she agreed, in an eager whisper.

In an instant George Cannon had completely changed the attitude of her conscience – by less than a phrase, by a mere intonation. In an instant he had reassured her into perfect security. It was plain, from every accent of his voice, that he had done nothing of which he thought he ought to be ashamed. Business

was business, and newspapers were newspapers; and the simple
truth was that her absurd conscience had been in the wrong. Her
duty was to accept the standards of her new world. Who was she?
Nobody! She did accept the standards of her new world, with
fervour. Sh e was proud of them, actually proud of their apparent
wickedness. She had accomplished an act of faith. Her joy became
intense, and shot glinting from her eyes as she put on her gloves.
Her life became grand to her. She knew she was known in the
town as 'the girl who could write shorthand'. Her situation was not
ordinary; it was unique. Again, the irregularity of the hours, and
the fact that the work never commenced till the afternoon,
seemed to her romantic and beautiful. Here she was, at nine
o'clock, alone with George Cannon on the second floor of the
house! And who, gazing from the Square at the lighted window,
would guess that she and he were there alone?

All the activities of newspaper production were poetized by her
fervour. The *Chronicle* was not a poor little weekly sheet,
struggling into existence anyhow, at haphazard, dependent on
other newspapers for all except purely local items of news. It was
an organ! It was the courageous rival of the ineffable *Signal*, its
natural enemy! One day it would trample on the *Signal*! And
though her role was humble, though she understood scarcely
anything of the enterprise beyond her own duties, yet she was very
proud of her role too. And she was glad that the men were
seemingly so careless, so disorderly, so forgetful of details, so – in
a word – childish! For it was part of her role to remind them, to
set them right, to watch over their carelessness, to restore order
where they had left disorder. In so far as her role affected them,
she condescended to them.

She informed George Cannon of her mother's indisposition,
and that she meant to go to London the next morning, and to
return most probably in a few days. He stopped in his walk, near
her. Like herself, he was not seriously concerned about Mrs
Lessways, but he showed a courteous sympathy.

'It's a good thing you didn't go to London when your mother
went,' he said, after a little conversation.

He did not add: 'You've been indispensable.' He had no air of
apologizing for his insult at the tea-table. But he looked firmly at
her, with a peculiar expression.

Suddenly she felt all her slimness and fragility; she felt all the girl in herself and all the dominant man in him, and all the empty space around them. She went hot. Her sight became dim. She was ecstatically blissful; she was deeply ashamed. She desired the experience to last for ever, and him and herself to be eternally moveless; and at the same time she desired to fly. Or rather, she had no desire to fly, but her voice and limbs acted of themselves, against her volition.

'Good night, then.'

'But I say! Your wages. Shall I pay you now?'

'No, no! It doesn't matter in the least, thanks.'

He shook hands, with a careless, good-natured smile which seemed to be saying: 'Foolish creature! You can't defend yourself, and these airs are amusing. But I am benevolent.' And she was ashamed of her shame, and furious against the childishness that made her frown, and lower her eyes, and escape out of the room like a mouse.

CHAPTER 14
TO LONDON

I

In the middle of the night Hilda woke up, and within a few seconds she convinced herself that her attitude to Miss Gailey's telegram had been simply monstrous. She saw it, in the darkness, as an enormity. She ought to have responded to the telegram at once; she ought to have gone to London by the afternoon train. What had there been to prevent her from knocking at the door of the inner room, and saying to Mr Cannon, in the presence of no matter whom: 'I am very sorry, Mr Cannon, but I've just had a telegram that mother is ill in London, and I must leave by the next train'? There had been nothing to prevent her! At latest she should have caught the evening train. Business was of no account in such a crisis. Her mother might be very ill, might be dying, might be dead. It was not for trifles that people sent such telegrams. The astounding thing was that she should have been so blind to her obvious duty . . . And she said to herself, thinking with a mysterious and beautiful remorse of the last minute of her talk with Mr Cannon: 'If I had done as I ought to have done, I should have been in London, or on my way to London, instead of in the room with him there; and *that* would not have occurred!' But what 'that' was, she could not have explained. Nevertheless, Mr Cannon's phrase, 'It's a good thing you didn't go to London', still gave her a pleasure, though the pleasure was dulled.

Then she tried to reassure herself. Sarah Gailey was nervous and easily frightened. Her mother had an excellent constitution. The notion of her mother being seriously ill was silly. In a few hours she would be with her mother, and would be laughing at these absurd night-fears. In any case there would assuredly be a letter from Sarah Gailey by the first post, so that before starting she would have exact information. She succeeded, partially, in reassuring herself for a brief space; but soon she was more unhappy than ever in the clear conviction of her wrongdoing.

Again and again she formulated, in her fancy, scenes of the immediate future, as for example at her mother's dying bed, and she imagined conversations and repeated the actual words used by herself and others, interminably. And then she returned to the previous day, and hundreds of times she went into the inner room and said to Mr Cannon: 'I'm very sorry, Mr Cannon, but I've just had a telegram –' etc. Why had she not said it? . . . Thus worked the shuttles of her mind, with ruthless, insane insistence, until she knew not whether she was awake or asleep, and the very tissues of her physical brain seemed raw.

She thought feebly: 'If I got up and lighted the candle and walked about, I should end this.' But she could not rise. She was netted down to the bed. And when she tried to soothe herself with other images – images of delight – she found that they had lost their power. Undressing, a few hours earlier, she had lived again, in exquisite and delicious alarm, through the last minute of her talk with Mr Cannon; she had gone to sleep while reconstituting those instants. But now their memory left her indifferent, even inspired repugnance. And her remorse little by little lost its mysterious beauty.

She clung to the idea of the reassuring letter which she would receive. That was her sole glint of consolation.

II

At six she was abroad in the house, intensely alive, intensely conscious of every particle of her body, and of every tiniest operation of her mind. In less than two hours the letter would drop into the lobby! At half-past six both she and Florrie were dressed, and Florrie, stern with the solemnity and importance of her mission, was setting forth to the Saracen's Head to order a cab to be at the door at eight o'clock.

Hilda had much to do, for it was of course necessary to shut up the house, and the packing of her trunk had to be finished, and the trunk locked and corded, and a label found; and there was breakfast to cook. Mrs Lessways would have easily passed a couple of days in preparing the house for closure. Nevertheless, time, instead of flying, lagged. At seven-thirty Hilda, in the partially dismantled parlour, and Florrie in the kitchen, were sitting down to breakfast. 'In a quarter of an hour', said Hilda to herself, 'the post will be here.' But in four minutes she had eaten the bacon and drunk the scalding tea, and in five she had carried all the breakfast-things into the kitchen, where Florrie was loudly munching over the sloppy deal table. She told Florrie sharply that there would be ample time to wash up. Then she went to her bedroom, and, dragging out her trunk, slid it unaided down the stairs. Back again in the bedroom, she carelessly glanced at the money in her purse, and then put on her things for the journey. Waiting, she stood at the window to look for the postman. Presently she saw him in the distance; he approached quickly, but spent an unendurable minute out of sight in the shop next door. When he emerged Hilda was in anguish. Had he a letter for her? Had he not? He seemed to waver at the gateway, and to decide to enter . . . She heard the double blow of his drumstick baton . . . Now in a few seconds she would know about her mother.

Proudly restraining herself, she walked with composure to the stairs. She was astonished to see Florrie bending down to pick up the letter. Florrie must have been waiting ready to rush to the front door. As she raised her body and caught sight of Hilda, Florrie blushed.

The stairs were blocked by the trunk which Hilda had left on the stair-mat for the cabman to deal with. Standing behind the trunk, Hilda held forth her hand for the letter.

'Please, miss, it's for me,' Florrie whispered, like a criminal.

'For you?' Hilda cried, startled.

In proof Florrie timidly exposed the envelope, on which Hilda plainly saw, in a coarse, scrawling masculine hand, the words 'Miss Florrie Bagster'. Florrie's face was a burning peony.

Hilda turned superciliously away, too proud to demand any explanations. All her alarms were refreshed by the failure of a letter from Miss Gailey. In vain she urged to herself that Miss Gailey had thought it unnecessary to write, expecting to see her; or that the illness having passed, Miss Gailey, busy, had put off writing. She could not dismiss a vision of a boarding-house in London upset from top to bottom by the grave illness of one person in it, and a distracted landlady who had not a moment even to scribble a post card. And all the time, as this vision tore and desolated her, she was thinking: 'Fancy that child having a follower at her age! She's certainly got a follower!'

The cab came five minutes before it was due.

III

As the cab rolled through Market Square, where the Saturday stalls were being busily set up, the ironmongery building was framed for an instant by the oblong of the rattling window. Hilda seemed to see the place anew – for the first time. A man was taking down the shutters of the shop. Above that were the wire-blinds with the name of 'Q. Karkeek'; and above the blinds the blue posters of the *Five Towns Chronicle*. No outward sign of Mr Cannon! And yet Mr Cannon ... She had an extremely disconcerting sensation of the mysteriousness of Mr Cannon, and of the mysteriousness of all existence. Mr Cannon existed some-where at that moment, engaged in some activity. In a house afar off, unknown to her, her mother existed – if she was not dead! Florrie, with a bundle of personal goods on her lap, and doubt-less the letter in her bosom, sat impressed and subdued, opposite to her in the shifting universe of the cab, which was moving away from the empty and silent home. Florrie was being thrown back out of luxury into her original hovel, and was accepting the stroke with the fatalism of the young and of the poor. And one day Hilda and her mother and Florrie would be united again in the home now deserted, whose heavy key was in the traveller's satchell . . . But would they?

At the station there was a quarter of an hour to wait. Hilda dismissed Florrie, with final injunctions, and followed her trunk to the bleak platform. The old porter was very kind. She went to the little yellow bookstall. There, under her hand, was a low pile of *The Five Towns Chronicle*. Miracle! Miraculous George Cannon! She flushed with pride, with a sense of ownership, as she took a penny from her purse to pay for a copy.

'It's th' new peeper,' drawled the bookstall lad, with a most foolish condescension towards the new paper.

'Lout!' she addressed him in her heart. 'If you knew whom you were talking to –!'

With what pride, masked by careful indifference, she would hand the copy of the *Chronicle* to her mother! Her mother would exclaim 'Bless us!' and spend a day or two in conning the thing, making singular discoveries in it at short intervals.

IV

It was not until she had reached Euston, and driven through a tumultuous and shabby thoroughfare to King's Cross, and taken another ticket, and installed herself in another train, that Hilda began to feel suddenly, like an abyss opening beneath her strength, the lack of food. Meticulous in her clerical duties, and in many minor mechanical details of her personal daily existence, she was capable of singular negligences concerning matters which the heroic part of her despised and which did not immediately bear on a great purpose in hand. Thus, in her carelessness, she found herself with less than two shillings in her pocket after paying for the ticket to Hornsey. She thought, grimly resigned: 'Never heed! I shall manage. In half an hour I shall be there, and my anxiety will be at an end.'

The train, almost empty, waited forlornly in a forlorn and empty part of the huge, resounding ochreish station. Then, without warning or signal, it slipped off, as though casually, towards an undetermined goal. Often it ran level with the roofs of vague, far-stretching acres of houses – houses vile and frowsy, and smoking like pyres in the dank air. And always it travelled on a platform of brick arches. Now and then the walled road received a tributary that rounded subtly into it, and this tributary could be seen curving away, on innumerable brick arches, through the chimneypots, and losing itself in a dim horizon of gloom. At intervals a large, lifeless station brought the train to a halt for a moment, and the march was resumed. A clock at one of these stations said a quarter to two.

Then the name of Hornsey quickened her apprehensive heart. As she descended nervously from the train, her trunk was shot out from the guard's van behind. She went and stood over it, until the last of a series of kindly porters came along and touched his cap. When she asked for a cab, he seemed doubtful whether a cab was available, and looked uncertainly along the immense empty

platform and across at other platforms. The train had wandered
away. She strove momentarily to understand the reason of these
great sleeping stations; but fatigue, emotional and physical, had
robbed her of all intelligent curiosity in the phenomena of the
mysterious and formidable city.

Presently the porter threw the trunk on his shoulder and she
trudged after him up steps and over an iron bridge and down
steps; and an express whizzed like a flying shell through the
station and vanished. And at a wicket, in a ragged road, there
actually stood a cab and a skeleton of a horse between the shafts.
The driver bounced up, enheartened at sight of the trunk and the
inexperienced, timid girl; but the horse did not stir in its crooked
coma.

'What address, miss?' asked the cabman.

'Cedars House, Harringay Park Road.'

The cabman paused in intense thought, and after a few seconds
responded cheerfully: 'Yes, miss.'

The porter touched his cap for threepence. The lashed horse
plunged forward. Hilda leaned back in the creaking and depraved
vehicle, and sighed, 'So this is their London!'

She found herself travelling in the direction from which she had
come, parallel to the railway, down the longest street that she had
ever seen. On her left were ten thousand small new houses, all
alike. On her right were broken patches of similar houses, inter-
spersed with fragments of green field and views of the arches of
the railway; the conception of the horrible patience which had
gone to the construction of these endless, endless arches made her
feel sick.

The cab turned into another road, and another; and then
stopped. She saw the words 'Cedars House' on a gateway. She
could not open the door of the cab. The cabman opened it.

'Blinds down here, miss!' he said, with appropriate mournful-
ness.

It seemed a rather large house; and every blind was drawn.
Had the incredible occurred, then? Had this disaster befallen just
her, of all the young women in the world?

She saw the figure of Sarah Gailey.

'Good afternoon,' she called out calmly. 'Here I am. Only I'm
afraid I haven't got enough to pay the cabman.'

But while she was speaking she knew from Sarah Gailey's face that the worst and the most ridiculous of her night-fears had been justified by destiny.

Three days previously Mrs Lessways had been suddenly taken ill in the street. A doctor passing in his carriage had come to her assistance and driven her home. Food eaten on the previous evening had 'disagreed' with her. At first the case was not regarded as very serious. But as the patient did not improve in the night Miss Gailey telegraphed to Hilda. Immediately afterwards, the doctor, summoned in alarm, diagnosed peritonitis caused by a perforating cancer. Mrs Lessways had died on the third day at eleven in the morning, while Hilda was in the train. Useless to protest that these catastrophes were unthinkable, that Mrs Lessways had never been ill in her life! The catastrophe had happened. And upstairs a corpse lay in proof.

BOOK II
HER RECOVERY

CHAPTER 1
SIN

I

FROM her bed Hilda could see the trees waving in the wind. Every morning she had thus watched them, without interest. At first the branches had been utterly bare, and beyond their reticulation had been visible the rosy façade of a new Board-school. But now the branches were rich with leafage, hiding most of the Board-school, so that only a large upper window of it could be seen. This window, upon which the sun glinted dazzlingly, threw back the rays on to Hilda's bed, giving her for a few moments the illusion of direct sunlight. The hour was eleven o'clock. On the night-table lay a tea-tray in disorder, and on the turned-down sheet some crumbs of toast. A low, nervous tap at the door caused Hilda to stir in the bed. Sarah Gailey entered hurriedly. In her bony yellowed hand she held a collection of tradesmen's account-books.

'Good morning, dear, how are you?' she asked, bending awkwardly over the bed. In the same instant she looked askance at the tray.

'I'm all right, thanks,' said Hilda lazily, observing the ceiling.

'You haven't been too cold without the eiderdown? I forgot to ask you before. You know I only took it off because I thought the weather was getting too warm . . . I didn't want it for another bed. I assure you it's in the chest of drawers in my room.' Sarah Gailey added the last words as if supplicating to be believed.

'You needn't tell me that,' said Hilda. She was not angry, but bored, by this characteristic remark of Miss Gailey's. In three months she had learnt a great deal about the new landlady of the Cedars, that strange neurotic compound of ability, devotion, thin-skinned vanity, and sheer, narrow stupidity. 'I've been quite warm enough,' Hilda added as quickly as she could, lest Miss Gailey might have time to convince herself to the contrary.

'And the toast? I do hope – after all I've said to that Hettie about –'

'You see I've eaten it all,' Hilda interrupted her, pointing to the plate.

Their faces were close together; they exchanged a sad smile. Miss Gailey was still bending over her, anxiously, as over a child. Yet neither the ageing and worn woman nor the flaccid girl felt the difference between them in age. Nor was Hilda in any ordinary sense ill. The explanation of Miss Gailey's yearning attitude lay in an exaggerated idea of her duty to Hilda, whose mother's death had been the result of an act of friendliness to her. If Mrs Lessways had not come to London in order to keep company with Sarah, she might – she would, under Providence – have been alive and well that day; such was Sarah's reasoning which by the way ignored certain statements of the doctor. Sarah would never forgive herself. But she sought, by an infatuated devotion, to earn the forgiveness of Caroline's daughter. Her attentions might have infuriated an earlier Hilda, or at least have been met with disdain only half concealed. But on the present actual Hilda they produced simply no effect of any kind. The actual Hilda, living far within the mysterious fastness of her own being, was too solitary, too preoccupied, and too fatigued, to be touched even by the noble beauty that distinguished the expiatory and protective gesture of the spinster, otherwise somewhat ludicrous, as she leaned across the bed and cut off the sunshine.

II

On the morning of her mother's funeral, Hilda had gone to Hornsey Station to meet an uncle of Mrs Lessways, who was coming down from Scotland by the night-train. She scarcely knew him, but he was to be recognizable by his hat and his muffler, and she was to await him at the ticket-gate. An entirely foolish and unnecessary arrangement, contrived by a peculiar old man: the only possible course was to accept it.

She had waited over half an hour, between eight and nine, and in that time she had had full opportunity to understand why those suburban stations had been built so large. A dark torrent of human beings, chiefly men, gathered out of all the streets of the vicinity, had dashed unceasingly into the enclosure and covered the long platforms with tramping feet. Every few minutes a train rolled in, as if from some inexhaustible magazine of trains beyond the horizon, and, sucking into itself a multitude and departing again, left one platform for one moment empty – and the next moment the platform was once more filled by the quenchless stream. Less frequently, but still often, other trains thundered through the station on a line removed from platforms, and these trains too were crammed with dark human beings, frowning in study over white newspapers. For even in 1880 the descent upon London from the suburbs was a formidable phenomenon. Train after train fled downwards with its freight towards the hidden city, and the torrent still surged, more rapid than ever, through the narrow gullet of the station. It was like the flight of some enormous and excited population from a country menaced with disaster.

Borne on and buffeted by the torrent, Hilda had seen a well-dressed epileptic youth, in charge of an elderly woman, approaching the station. He had passed slowly close by her, as she modestly waited in her hasty mourning, and she had a fearful vision of his idiotic greenish face supported somehow like a mask at the summit of that shaky structure of limbs. He had indeed stared at her with his apelike eyes. She had watched him, almost shuddering, till he was lost amid the heedless crowd within. Then, without waiting longer for her relative, without reflecting upon what she did, she had walked trembling back to the Cedars, checked by tributaries of the torrent at every street corner . . .

She had known nothing of the funeral. She had not had speech with the relative. She was in bed, somehow. The day had elapsed. And in the following night, when she was alone and quite awake, she had become aware that she, she herself, was that epileptic shape; that that epileptic shape was lying in her bed and that there was none other in the bed. Nor was this a fancy of madness! She knew that she was not mad, that she was utterly sane; and the conviction of sanity only intensified her awful discovery. She passed a trembling hand over her face, and felt the skin corrupt and green. Gazing into the darkness, she knew that her stare was apelike. She had felt, then, the fullest significance of horror. In the morning she had ceased to be the epileptic shape, but the risk of re-transformation had hovered near her, and the intimidation of it was such that she had wept, aghast and broken as much by the future as by the past. She had been discovered weeping . . .

Later, the phrase 'nervous breakdown' had lodged in her confused memory. The doctor had been very matter-of-fact, logical, and soothing. Overwork, strain, loss of sleep, the journey, anxiety, lack of food, the supreme shock, the obstinate refusal of youth to succumb and then the sudden sight of the epileptic (with whom the doctor was acquainted): thus had run the medical reasoning, after a discreet but thorough cross-examination of her; and it had seemed so plausible and so convincing that the doctor's pride in it was plain on his optimistic face as he gave the command: 'Absolute repose.' But to Hilda the reasoning and the resultant phrase, 'nervous breakdown', had meant nothing at all. Words! Empty words! She knew, profoundly and fatally, the evil principle which had conquered her so completely that she had no power left with which to fight it. This evil principle was Sin; it was not the force of sins, however multifarious; it was Sin itself. She was the Sinner, convicted and self-convicted. One of the last intelligent victims of a malady which has now almost passed away from the civilized earth, she existed in the chill and stricken desolation of incommutable doom.

III

She had sinned against her mother, and she could not make amends. The mere thought of her mother, so vivacious, cheerful, life-loving, even-tempered, charitable, disorderly, incompetent, foolish and yet shrewd, caused pain of such intensity that it ceased to be pain. She ought to have seen her mother before she died; she might have seen her, had she done what was obviously her duty. It was inconceivable to her, now, that she should have hesitated to fly instantly to London on receipt of the telegram. But she had hesitated, and her mother had expired without having sight of her. All exculpatory arguments were futile against the fact itself. In vain she blamed the wording of the telegram! In vain she tried to reason that chance, and not herself, was the evil-doer! In vain she invoked the aid of simple common sense against senti-mental fancy! In vain she went over the events of the afternoon preceding the death, in order to prove that at no moment had she been aware of not acting in accordance with her conscience! The whole of her conduct had been against her conscience, but pride and selfishness had made her deaf to conscience. She was the Sinner.

Her despair, except when at intervals she became the loathed epileptic shape, had been calm. Its symptoms had been, and remained, a complete lack of energy and a most extraordinary black indifference to the surrounding world. Save in the deep centre of her soul, where she agonized, she seemed to have lost all capacity for emotion. Nothing moved her, or even interested her. She sat in the house, and ate a little, and talked a little, like an automaton. She walked about the streets like a bored exile, but an exile who has forgotten his home. Her spirit never responded to the stimulus of environment. Suggestions at once lost their tonic force in the woolly cushion of her apathy. If she continued to live, it was by inertia; to cease from life would have required an effort. She did not regret the vocation which she had abandoned; she felt no curiosity about the fortunes of the newspaper. A tragic nonchalance held her.

After several weeks she had naturally begun to think of religion; for the malady alone was proof enough that she had a profoundly religious nature. Miss Gailey could rarely go to church, but one Sunday morning – doubtless with intent – she asked Hilda if they should go together, and Hilda agreed. As they approached the large, high-spired church Hilda had vague prickings of hope, and was thereby much astonished. But the service in no way responded to her expectations. 'How silly I am!' she thought disdainfully. 'This sort of thing has never moved me before. Why should it move me now?' The sermon, evangelical, was upon the Creed, and the preacher explained the emotional quality of real belief. It was a goodish sermon. But the preacher had effectually stopped the very last of those exquisite vague prickings of hope. Hilda agreed with his definition of real belief, and she knew that real belief was impossible for her. She could never say, with joyous fervour: 'I believe!' At best she could only assert that she did not disbelieve – and was she so sure even of that? No! Belief had been denied to her; and to dream of conso-lation from religion was sentimentally womanish; even in her indifference she preferred straightforward, honest damnation to the soft self-deceptions of feminine religiosity. Ah! If she could have been a Roman Catholic, genuine and convinced – with what ardour would she have cast herself down before the confessional, and whispered her sinfulness to the mysterious face within; and with what ecstasy would she have received the absolution – that cleansing bath of the soul! Then – she could have recommenced! . . . But she was not a Roman Catholic. She could no more become a Roman Catholic than she could become the queen of some romantic Latin country of palaces and cathedrals. She was a young provincial girl staying in a boarding-house at Hornsey, on the Great Northern line out of London, and she was suffering from nervous breakdown. Such was the exterior common sense of the situation.

Occasionally the memory of some verse of Victor Hugo, sounding the beat of one of his vast melancholies, would float through her mind and cause it to vibrate for an instant with a mournful sensation that resembled pleasure.

IV

'Are you thinking of getting up, dear?' asked Sarah Gailey, as she arranged more securely the contents of the tray and found space on it for her weekly books.

'Yes, I suppose I may as well,' Hilda murmured. 'It'll be lunch-time soon.' The days were long, yet somehow they seemed short too. Already before getting up, she would begin to think of the evening and of going to bed; and Saturday night followed quickly on Monday morning. It was scarcely credible that sixteen weeks had passed, thus, since her mother's death – sixteen weeks whose retrospect showed no achievement of any kind, and hardly a desire.

'I've given those Boutwoods notice,' said Sarah Gailey suddenly, the tray in her hands ready to lift.

'Not really?'

'They were shockingly late for breakfast again, this morning, both of them. And Mr Boutwood had the face to ask for another egg. Hettie came and told me, so I went in myself. I told him breakfast was served in my house at nine o'clock, and there was a notice to that effect in the bedrooms, not to mention the dining-room. And as good a breakfast as they'd get in any of their hotels, I lay! If the eggs are cold at ten o'clock and after, that's not my fault. They're both of them perfectly healthy, and yet they're bone-idle. They never want to go to bed and they never want to get up. It isn't as if they went to theatres and got home late and so on. I could make excuses for that – now and then. No! It's just idleness and carelessness. And if you saw their bedroom! Oh, my! A nice example to servants! Well, he was very insulting – most insulting. He said he paid me to give him not what I wanted, but what *he* wanted! He said if I went into a shop, and they began to tell me what I ought to want and when I ought to want it, I should be annoyed. I said I didn't need anyone to tell me that, I said! And my house wasn't a shop. He said it was a shop, and if it wasn't, it ought to be! Can you imagine it?'

Hilda tried to exhibit a tepid sympathy. Miss Gailey's nostrils were twitching, and the tears stood in those watery eyes. She could manage the house. By the exertion of all her powers and her force she had made of herself an exceptionally efficient mistress. But she could not manage the boarders, because she had not sufficient imagination to put herself in their place. Presiding over all her secret thoughts was the axiom that the Cedars was a perfect machine, and that the least that a grateful boarder could do was to fit into the machine.

'And so you said they could go?'

'That I did! And I'll tell you another thing, my dear, I –'

There was a knock at the door. Sarah Gailey stopped in her confidences like a caught conspirator, and opened the door. Hettie stood on the mat – the Hettie who despite frequent protests would leave Hilda's toast to cool into leather on the landing somewhere between the kitchen and the bedroom. In Hettie's hand was a telegram, which Miss Gailey accepted.

'Here, take the tray, Hettie,' said she, nervously tearing at the envelope. 'Put these books in my desk,' she added.

'And I wonder what *he'll* say!' she observed, staring absently at the opened telegram, after Hettie had gone.

'Who?'

'George. He says he'll be up here for lunch. He's bound to be vexed about the Boutwoods. But he doesn't understand. Men don't, you know! They don't understand the strain it is on you.' The appeal of her eyes was strangely pathetic.

Hilda said:

'I don't think I shall get up for lunch today.'

Sarah Gailey moved to the bed, forgetting her own trouble.

'You aren't so well, then, after all!' she muttered, with mournful commiseration. 'But, you know, he'll have to see you *this* time. He wants to.'

'But why?'

'Your affairs, I suppose. He says so. "Coming lunch one. Must see Hilda – George."'

Sarah Gailey offered the telegram. But Hilda could not bear to take it. This telegram was the first she had set eyes on since the telegram handed to her by Florrie in George Cannon's office. The mere sight of the salmon-tinted paper agitated her. 'Is it possible that I can be so silly,' she thought, 'over a bit of paper?' But so it was.

On a previous visit of George Cannon's to Hornsey she had kept her bed throughout the day, afraid to meet him, ashamed to meet him, inexplicably convinced that to meet him would be a crime against filial piety. There were obscure grottoes in her soul which she had not had the courage to explore candidly.

'I think,' said Sarah Gailey, reflective and anxious, 'I think if you *could* get up, it would be nicer than him seeing you here in bed.'

Hilda perceived that at last she would be compelled to face George Cannon.

CHAPTER 2
THE LITTLE ROOM

I

AFTER lunch Sarah Gailey left Hilda and Mr Cannon in 'the little room' together.

'The little room' – about eight feet square – had no other name; it was always spoken of affectionately by the boarders, and by the landlady with pride in its cosiness. Situated on the first floor, over the front part of the hall, it lay between the two principal bedrooms. Old boarders would discover the little room to new boarders, or new boarders would discover it for themselves, with immense satisfaction. It was the chamber of intimacy and of confidences; it was a refuge from the public life of the Cedars, and, to a certain extent, from the piano. Two women, newly acquainted, and feeling a mutual attraction, would say to each other: 'Shall we go up to the little room?' 'Oh yes, do let us!' And they would climb the stairs in a fever of anticipation. 'Quite the most charming room in the house, dear Miss Gailey!' another simpering spinster would say. Yet it contained nothing but an old carpet, two wicker arm-chairs, a small chair, a nearly empty dwarf bookcase, an engraving of Marie Antoinette regally facing the revolutionary mob, and a couple of photographs of the Cedars.

Hilda sat down in one of the arm-chairs, and George Cannon in the other; he had a small black bag which he placed on the floor by his side. Hilda's diffidence was extreme. Throughout lunch she had scarcely spoken; but as there had been eight people at the table, and George Cannon had chatted with all of them, her taciturnity had passed inconspicuous. Now she would be obliged to talk. And the sensations which she had experienced on first meeting George Cannon in the dining-room were renewed in a form even more acute.

She had, in the first place, the self-consciousness due to her mourning attire, which drew attention to herself; it might have been a compromising uniform; and the mere fact of her mother's death – quite apart from the question of her conduct in relation thereto – gave her, in an interview with a person whom she had not seen since before the death, a feeling akin to guiltiness – guiltiness of some misdemeanour of taste, some infraction of the social law against notoriety. She felt, in her mourning, like one who is being led publicly by policemen to the police-station. In her fancy she could hear people saying: 'Look at that girl in deep mourning', and she could see herself blushing, as it were apologetic.

But much worse than this general mortification in presence of an acquaintance seen after a long interval was the special constraint due to the identity of the acquaintance. It was with George Cannon that she had first deceived and plotted against her ingenuous mother's hasty plans. It was her loyalty to George Cannon that had been the cause of her inexplicable disloyalty to her mother. She could not recall her peculiar and delicious agitations during the final moments of her previous interview with Cannon – that night of February in the newspaper office, while her mother was dying in London – without a profound unreasoning shame which intensified most painfully her natural grief as an orphan.

There was this to be said: she was now disturbed out of her torpid indifference to her environment. As she fidgeted there, pale and frowning, in the noisy basket-chair, beneath George Cannon's eyes, she actually perceived again that romantic quality of existence which had always so powerfully presented itself to her in the past. She reflected: 'How strange that the dreaded scene has now actually begun! He has come to London, and here we are together, in this house, which at the beginning of the year was nothing but a name to me! And mother is away there in the churchyard, and I am in black! And it is all due to him. He sent Miss Gailey and mother to London. He willed it! . . . No! It is all due to me! I went to see him one late afternoon. I sought him out. He didn't seek me out. And just because I went to see him one afternoon, mother is dead, and I am here! Strange!' These reflections were dimly beautiful to her, even in her sadness and in her acute distress. The coma had assuredly passed, if only for a space.

II

'Well, now,' he said, after a few inanities had been succeeded by an awkward pause. 'I've got to talk business with you, so I suppose we may as well begin, eh?' His tone was fairly blithe, but it was that of a man who was throwing off with powerful ease the weariness of somewhat exasperating annoyances. Since lunch he had had a brief interview with Sarah Gailey.

'Yes,' she agreed glumly.

'Have you decided what you're going to do?' He began to smile sympathetically as he spoke.

'I'm not going back to the paper,' she curtly answered, cutting short the smile with fierceness, almost with ferocity. Beyond question she was rude in her bitterness. She asked herself: 'Why do I talk like this? Why can't I talk naturally and gently and cheerfully? I've really got nothing against him.' But she could not talk otherwise than she did talk. It was by this symptom of biting acrimony that her agitation showed itself. She knew that she was scowling as she looked at the opposite wall, but she could not smooth away the scowl.

'No, I suppose not,' he said quietly. 'But are you thinking of coming back to Turnhill?'

She remained mute for some seconds. A feeling of desolation came over her, and it seemed to her that she welcomed it, trying to intensify it, and yielding her features to it. 'How do I know?' she muttered at length, shrugging her shoulders.

'Because if you aren't,' he resumed, 'it's no use you keeping that house of yours empty. You must remember it's just as you left it; and the things in it aren't taking any good, either.'

She shrugged her shoulders again.

'I don't see that it matters to anybody but me,' she said, after another pause, with a sort of frigid and disdainful nonchalance. And once more she reflected: 'Is it possible that I can behave so odiously?'

He stood up suddenly.

'I don't know what you and Sarah have been plotting together,' he said, wounded and contemptuous, yet with lightness. 'But I'm sure I don't want to interfere in your affairs. With Sarah's I've got to interfere, unfortunately, and a famous time I'm having!' His nostrils grew fastidious. 'But not yours! I only promised your uncle . . . Your uncle told me you wanted me to –' He broke off.

In an instant she grew confused, alarmed and extremely ashamed. Her mood had changed in a flash. It seemed to her that she was in presence of a disgraceful disaster, which she herself had brought about by wicked and irresponsible temerity. She was like a child who, having naughtily trifled with danger, stands aghast at the calamity which his perverseness has caused. She was positively affrighted. She reflected in her terror: 'I asked for this, and I've got it!'

George Cannon stooped and picked up his little bag. There he towered, high and massive, above her! And she felt acutely her slightness, her girlishness, and her need of his help. She could not afford to transform sympathy into antipathy. She was alone in the world. Never before had she realized, as she realized then, the lurking terror of her loneliness. The moment was critical. In another moment he might be gone from the room, and she left solitary to irremediable humiliation and self-disgust.

'Please!' she whispered appealingly. The whole of her being became an appeal – the glance, the gesture, the curve of the slim and fragile body. She was like a slave. She had no pride, no secret reserve of thought. She was an instinct. Tears showed in her eyes and affected her voice.

He gave the twisted, difficult, rather foolish smile of one who is cursing the mortification of a predicament into which he has been cast through no fault of his own.

'Please what?'

'Please sit down.'

He waved a hand, deprecatingly, and obeyed.

'It's all right,' he said. 'All right! I ought to have known –' Then he smiled generously.

'Known what?' Her voice was now weak and liquid with woe.

'You'd be likely to be upset.'

Not furtively, but openly, she wiped her eyes.

'No, no!' she protested honestly. 'It's not that. It's – but – I'm very sorry.'

'I reckon I know a bit what worry is, myself!' he added, with a brief, almost harsh, laugh.

These strange words struck her with pity.

III

'Well, now,' – he seemed to be beginning again – let's leave Lessways Street for a minute . . . I can sell the Calder Street property for you, if you like. And at a pretty good price. Sooner or later the town will have to buy up all that side of the street. You remember I told your mother last year but one I could get a customer for it? but she wasn't having any.'

'Yes,' said Hilda eagerly; 'I remember.'

In her heart she apologized to George Cannon, once more, for having allowed her mother to persuade her, even for a day, that that attempt to buy was merely a trick on his part invented to open negotiations for the rent-collecting.

'You know what the net rents are,' he went on, 'as you've had 'em every month. I dare say the purchase money if it's carefully invested will bring you in as much. But even if it doesn't bring in quite as much, you mustn't forget that Calder Street's going down – it's getting more and more of a slum. And there'll always be a lot of bother with tenants of that class.'

'I wish I could sell everything – everything!' she exclaimed passionately. 'Lessways Street as well! Then I should be absolutely free!'

'You can!' he said, with dramatic emphasis. 'And let me tell you that ten years hence those Lessways Street houses won't be worth what they are now!'

'Is that property going down, too?' she asked. 'I thought they were building all round there.'

'So they are,' he answered. 'But cheap cottages. Your houses are too good for that part of the town; that's what's the matter with them. People who can afford £25 a year – and over – for rent won't care to live there much longer. You know the end house is empty.'

All houses seemed to her to be a singularly insecure and even perilous form of property. And the sale of everything she possessed presented itself to her fancy as a transaction which would enfranchise her from the past. It symbolized the starting-point of a new life, of a recommencement unhampered by the vestiges of grief and error. She could go anywhere, do what she chose. The entire world would lie before her.

'Please do sell it all for me!' she pleaded wistfully. 'Supposing you could, about how much should I have – I mean income?'

He glanced about, and then, taking a pencil from his waistcoat pocket, scribbled a few figures on his cuff.

'Quite three pounds a week,' he said.

IV

After a perfunctory discussion, which was somewhat self-consciously prolonged by both of them in order to avoid an appearance of hastiness in an important decision, George Cannon opened his black bag and then looked round for ink. The little room, having no table, had no inkpot, and the lawyer took from his pocket an Eagle indelible pencil – the fountain-pen of those simple days. It needed some adjustment; he stepped closer to the window, and held the pointed end of the case up to the light, while screwing the lower end; he was very fastidious in these mechanical details of his vocation. Hilda watched him from behind, with an intentness that fascinated herself.

'And how's the *Chronicle* getting on?' she asked, in a tone of friendly curiosity which gave an exaggerated impression of her actual feeling. She was more and more ashamed that during lunch she had not troubled to put a question about the paper. She was even ashamed of her social indifference. That Sarah Gailey, narrow and preoccupied, should be indifferent, should never once in three months have referred to her brother's organ, was not surprising; but it was monstrous that she, Hilda, the secretary, the priestess, should share this uncivil apathy; and it was unjust to mark the newspaper, as somehow she had been doing, with the stigma of her mother's death. She actually began to characterize her recent mental attitude to her past life as morbid.

'Oh!' he murmured absently, with gloomy hesitation, as he manipulated the pencil.

She went on still more persuasively:

'I suppose you've got a new secretary?'

'No,' he said, as though it fatigued and annoyed him to dwell on the subject. 'I told 'em they must manage without . . . It's no fun starting a new paper in a God-forsaken hole like the Five Towns, I can tell you.'

Plainly his high exuberant hopes had been dashed, had perhaps been destroyed.

She did not reply. She could not. She became suddenly sad with sympathy, and this sadness was beautiful to her. Already, when he was scribbling on it, she had noticed that his wristband was frayed. Now, silhouetted against the window, the edge of the wristband caught her attention again, and grew strangely significant. This man was passing through adversity! It seemed tragic and shocking to her that he should have to pass through adversity, that he could not remain for ever triumphant, brilliant, cocksure in all his grand schemes, and masculinely scatheless. It seemed wrong to her that he should suffer, and desirable that anybody should suffer rather than he. George Cannon with faulty linen! By what error of destiny had this heart-rending phenomenon of discord been caused? (Yes, heart-rending!) Was it due to weary carelessness, or to actual, horrible financial straits? Either explanation was very painful to her. She had a vision of a whole sisterhood of women toiling amid steam and soapsuds in secret, and in secret denying themselves, to provide him with all that he lacked so that he might always emerge into the world unblemished and glitteringly perfect. She would have sacrificed the happiness of multitudes to her sense of fitness.

V

There being no table, George Cannon removed a grotesque ornament from the dwarf bookcase, and used the top of the bookcase as a writing-board. Hilda was called upon to sign two papers. He explained exactly what these papers were, but she did not understand, nor did she desire to understand. One was an informal salenote and the other was an authority; but which was which, and to what each had reference, she superbly and wilfully ignored. She could, by a religious effort of volition, make of herself an excellent clerk, eagerly imitative and mechanical, but she had an instinctive antipathy to the higher forms of business. Moreover, she wanted to trust herself to him, if only as a mystic reparation of her odious rudeness at the beginning of the interview. And she thought also: 'These transactions will result in profit to him. It is by such transactions that he lives. I am helping him in his adversity.'

When he gave her the Eagle pencil, and pointed to the places where she was to sign, she took the pencil with fervour, more and more anxious to atone to him. For a moment she stood bewildered, in a dream, staring at the scratched mahogany top of the bookcase. And the bookcase seemed to her to be something sentient, patient and helpful, that had always been waiting there in the corner to aid George Cannon in this crisis – something human like herself. She loved the bookcase, and the Eagle pencil, and the papers, and the pattern on the wall. George Cannon was standing behind her. She felt his presence like a delicious danger. She signed the papers, in that large scrawling hand which for a few brief weeks she had by force cramped down to the submissive caligraphy of a clerk. As she signed, she saw the name 'Karkeek' in the midst of one of the documents, and remembered, with joyous nonchalance, that George Cannon's own name never appeared in George Cannon's affairs.

He took her place in front of the little bookcase, and folded the documents. There he was, beside her, in all his masculinity – his moustache, his blue chin, his wide white hands, his broadcloth – there he was planted on his massive feet as on a pedestal! She did not see him; she was aware of him. And she was aware of the closed door behind them. One of the basket-chairs, though empty, continued to creak, like a thing alive. Faintly, very faintly, she could hear the piano – Mrs Boutwood playing! Overhead were the footsteps of Sarah Gailey and Hettie – they were checking the linen from the laundry, as usual on Saturday afternoon. And she was aware of herself, thin, throbbing, fragile, mournful, somehow insignificant!

He looked round at her, with a half-turn of the head. In his glance was good humour, good nature, protectiveness, and rectitude; and, more than these, some of the old serenely smiling triumphant quality. He was not ruined! He was not really in adversity! He remained the conqueror! She thrilled with her relief.

'You're in my hands now – no mistake!' he murmured roguishly, picking up the documents, and bending over the bag.

Hilda could hear a heavy footstep on the stairs, ascending.

In the same instant she had an extraordinary and disconcerting impulse to seize his hand – she knew not why, whether it was to thank him, to express her sympathy, or to express her submission.

She struggled against this impulse, but the impulse was part of herself and of her inmost self. She was afraid, but her fear was pleasurable. She was ashamed, but her shame was pleasurable. She wanted to move away from where she stood. She thought: 'If only I willed to move away, I could move away. But, no! I shall not will it. I like remaining just here, in this fear, this shame, and this agitation.' She had a clear, dazzling perception of the splendour and the fineness of sin; but she did not know what sin! And all the time the muscles of her arm were tense in the combat between the weakening desire to keep her arms still and the growing desire to let her hand seize the hand of George Cannon. And all the time the heavy footstep was ascending the interminable staircase. And all the time George Cannon, with averted head, was fumbling in the bag. And then, in a flash, she was really afraid; the fear was no longer pleasurable, and her shame had become a curse. She said to herself: 'I cannot move, now. In a minute I shall do this horrible thing. Nothing can save me.' Despairing, she found a dark and tumultuous joy in despair. The trance endured for ages, while disaster approached nearer and nearer.

Then, after the heavy footstep had been climbing the staircase since earth began, the door was brusquely opened, and the jovial fat face of Mr Boutwood appeared, letting in the louder sound of the piano.

'Oh, I beg pardon!' he muttered, pretending that he had assumed the little room to be empty. The fact was that he was in search of George Cannon, in whom he had recognized a fraternal spirit.

'Come in, Mr Boutwood,' said Hilda, with an easy, disdainful calm which absolutely astounded herself. 'That's all, then?' she added, to George Cannon, glancing at him indifferently. She departed without waiting for an answer.

VI

Putting on a bonnet, and taking an umbrella to occupy her hands, she went out into the remedial freedom of the streets. And after turning the first corner she saw coming towards her the figure of a woman whom she seemed to know, elegant, even stately, in youthful grace. It was Janet Orgreave, wearing a fashionable fawn-coloured summer costume. As they recognized each other the girls blushed slightly. Janet hastened forward. Hilda stood still. She was amazed at the chance which had sent her two unexpected visitors in the same day. They shook hands and kissed.

'So I've found you!' said Janet. 'How are you, you poor dear? Why didn't you answer my letter?'

'Letter?' Hilda repeated, wondering. Then she remembered that she had indeed received a letter from Janet, but in her comatose dejection had neglected to answer it.

'I'm up in London with father for the week-end. We want you to come with us to the Abbey tomorrow. And you must come back with us to Bursley on Monday. You *must*! We're quite set on it. I've left father all alone this afternoon, to come up here and find you out. Not that he minds! What a way it is! But how are you, Hilda?'

Hilda was so touched by Janet's affectionate solicitude that her eyes filled with tears. She looked at that radiating and innocent goodness, and thought: 'How different I am from her! She hasn't the least idea how different I am!'

For a moment, Janet seemed to her to be a sort of angel – modish, but exquisitely genuine. She saw in the invitation to the Five Towns a miraculous defence against a peril the prospect of which was already alarming her. She would be compelled to go to Turnhill in order to visit Lessways Street and decide what of her mother's goods she must keep. She would of course take Janet with her. In all the Turnhill affairs Janet should accompany her. Her new life should begin under the protection of Janet's society. And her heart turned from the old life towards the new with hope and a vague brightening expectation of happiness.

At the Cedars, she led Janet to her bedroom, and then came out of the bedroom to bid good-bye to George Cannon. The extreme complexity of existence and of her sensations baffled and intimidated her.

CHAPTER 3
JOURNEY TO BLEAKRIDGE

I

HILDA and Janet were mounting the precipitous Sytch Bank together on their way from Turnhill into Bursley. It was dark; they had missed one train at Turnhill and had preferred not to wait for the next. Although they had been very busy in Hilda's house throughout all the afternoon and a part of the evening, and had eaten only a picnic meal, neither of them was aware of fatigue, and the two miles to Bursley seemed a trifle.

Going slowly up the steep slope, they did not converse. Janet said that the weather was changing, and Hilda, without replying, peered at the black, baffling sky. The air had, almost suddenly, grown warmer. Above, in the regions unseen, mysterious activities were in movement, as if marshalling vast forces. The stars had vanished. A gentle but equivocal wind on the cheek presaged rain, and seemed to be bearing downwards into the homeliness of the earth some strange vibration out of infinite space. The primeval elements of the summer night encouraged and intensified Hilda's mood, half joyous, half apprehensive. She thought: 'A few days ago, I was in Hornsey, with the prospect of the visit to Turnhill before me. Now the visit is behind me. I said that Janet should be my companion, and she has been my companion. I said that I would cut myself free, and I have cut myself free. I need never go to Turnhill again, unless I like. The two trunks will be sent for tomorrow; and all the rest will be sold – even the clock. The thing is done. I have absolute liberty, and an income, and the intimacy of this splendid affectionate Janet . . . How fortunate it was that Mr Cannon was not at his office when we called! Of course I was obliged to call . . . And yet would it not be more satisfactory if I had seen him? . . . I must have been in a horribly morbid state up at Hornsey . . . Soon I must decide about my future. Soon I shall actually have decided! . . . Life is very queer!' She had as yet no notion whatever of what she would do with her liberty and her income and the future; but she thought vaguely of something heroic, grandiose, and unusual.

II

In her hand she carried a small shabby book, bound in blue and gold, with gilt edges a little irregular. She had found this book while sorting out the multitudinous contents of her mother's wardrobe, and at the last moment, perceiving that it had been overlooked, and being somehow ashamed to leave it to the auctioneers, she had brought it away, not knowing how she would ultimately dispose of it. The book had possibly been dear to her mother, but she could not embarrass her freedom by conserving everything that had possibly been dear to her mother. It was entitled *The Girl's Week-day Book*, by Mrs Copley, and it had been published by the Religious Tract Society, no doubt in her mother's girlhood. The frontispiece, a steel engraving, showed a group of girls feeding some swans by the terraced margin of an ornamental water, and it bore the legend, 'Feeding the Swans'. And on the title page was the text: 'That our daughters may be as corner-stones, polished after the similitude of a palace. Psalm cxliv. 12'. In the table of contents were such phrases as: 'One thing at a time. Darkness and Light. Respect for Ministers. The Drowning Fly. Trifling with words of Scripture. Goose and Swan. Delicate Health. Conscientious Regard to Truth. Sensibility and Gentleness contrasted with Affectation. Curiosity and Tattling. Instability of Worldly Possessions.' A book representing, for Hilda, all that was most grotesque in an age that was now definitely finished and closed! A silly book!

During the picnic meal she had idly read extracts from it to Janet, amusing sentences; and though the book had once been held sacred by her who was dead, and though they were engaged in stirring the scarce-cold ashes of a tragedy, the girls had nevertheless permitted themselves a kindly, moderate mirth. Hilda had quoted from a conversation in it: 'Well, I would rather sit quietly round this cheerful fire, and talk with dear mamma, than go to the grandest ball that ever was known!' and Janet had plumply commented: 'What a dreadful lie!' And then they had both laughed openly, perhaps to relieve the spiritual tension caused by the day's task and the surroundings. After that, Hilda had continued to dip into the book, but silently. And Janet had imagined that Hilda was merely bored by the monotonous absurdity of the sentiments expressed.

Janet was wrong. Hilda had read the following: 'One word more. Do not rest in your religious impressions. You have, perhaps, been the subject of terror on account of sin; your mind has been solemnized by some event in Providence; by an alarming fit of sickness, or the death of a relative or a companion . . . This is indeed to be reckoned a great mercy; but then the danger is, lest you should rest here; lest those tears, and terrors, and resolutions, should be the only evidences on which you venture to conclude on the safety of your immortal state. What is your present condition ? . . .'

Which words intimidated Hilda in spite of herself. In vain she repeated that the book was a silly book. She really believed that it was silly, but she knew also that there was an aspect of it which was not silly. She was reminded by it that she had found no solution of the problem which had distracted her in Hornsey. 'What is your present condition ?' Her present condition was still that of a weakling and a coward who had sunk down inertly before the great problem of sin. And now, in the growing strength of her moral convalescence, she was raising her eyes again to meet the problem. Her future seemed to be bound up with the problem. As she breasted the top of the Sytch under the invisible lowering clouds, with her new, adored friend by her side, and the despised but powerful book in her hand, she mused in an ambiguous reverie upon her situation, dogged by the problem which alone was accompanying her out of the past into the future. Her reverie was shot through by piercing needles of regret for her mother; and even with the touch of Janet's arm against her own in the darkness she had sharp realizations of her extreme solitude in the world. Withal, the sense of life was precious and beautiful. She was not happy; but she was filled with the mysterious vital elation which surpasses happiness.

III

They descended gently into Bursley, crossing the top of St Luke's Square and turning eastwards into Market Square, ruled by the sombre and massive Town Hall in whose high tower an illuminated dial shone like a topaz. To Hilda, this nocturnal entry into Bursley had the romance of an entry into a town friendly but strange and recondite. During the few days of her stay with the Orgreaves in the suburb of Bleakridge, she had scarcely gone into the town once. She had never seen it at night. In the old Turnhill days she had come over to Bursley occasionally with her mother; but to shoppers from Turnhill, Bursley meant St Luke's Square and not a yard beyond.

Now the girls arrived at the commencement of the steam-car track, where a huge engine and tram were waiting, and as they turned another corner, the long perspective of Trafalgar Road, rising with its double row of lamps towards fashionable Bleakridge, was revealed to Hilda. She thought, naturally, that every other part of the Five Towns was more impressive and more important than the poor little outskirt, Turnhill, of her birth. In Turnhill there was no thoroughfare to compare with Trafalgar Road, and no fashionable suburb whatever. She had almost the feeling of being in a metropolis, if a local metropolis.

'It's beginning to rain, I think,' said Janet.

'Who's that?' Hilda questioned abruptly, ignoring the remark in the swift, unreflecting excitement of a sensibility surprised.

'Where?'

'There!'

They were going down Duck Bank into the hollow. On the right, opposite the lighted Dragon Hotel, lay Duck Square in obscure somnolence; at the corner of Duck Square and Trafalgar Road was a double-fronted shop, of which all the shutters were up except two or three in the centre of the doorway. Framed thus in the aperture, a young man stood within the shop under a bright central gas-jet; he was gazing intently at a large sheet of paper which he held in his outstretched hands, and the girls saw him in profile: tall, rather lanky, fair, with hair dishevelled, and a serious, studious, and magnanimous face; quite unconscious that he made a picture for unseen observers.

'That?' said Janet, in a confidential and interested tone. 'That's young Clayhanger – Edwin Clayhanger.* His father's the printer, you know. Came from Turnhill, originally.'

'I never knew,' said Hilda. 'But I seem to have heard the name.'

'Oh! It must have been a long time ago. He's got the best business in Bursley now. Father says it's one of the best in the Five Towns. He's built that new house just close to ours. Don't you remember I pointed it out to you? Father's the architect. They're going to move into it next week or the week after. I expect that's why the son and heir's working so late tonight, packing and so on, perhaps.'

The young man moved out of sight. But his face had made in those few thrilling seconds a deep impression on Hilda; so that in her mind she still saw it, with an almost physical particularity of detail. It presented itself to her, in some mysterious way, as a romantic visage, wistful, full of sad subtleties, of the unknown and the seductive, and of a latent benevolence. It was as recondite and as sympathetic as the town in which she had discovered it.

She said nothing.

'Old Mr Clayhanger is a regular character,' Janet eagerly went on, to Hilda's great content. 'Some people don't like him. But I rather do like him.' She was always thus kind. 'Grandmother once told me he sprang from simply nothing at all – worked on a pot-bank when he was quite a child.'

'Who? The father, you mean?'

'Yes, the father. Now, goodness knows how much he isn't worth! Father is always saying he could buy *us* up, lock, stock, and barrel.' Janet laughed. 'People often call him a miser, but he can't be so much of a miser, seeing that he's built this new house.'

'And I suppose the son's in the business?'

'Yes. He wanted to be an architect. That was how father got to know him. But old Mr Clayhanger wouldn't have it. And so he's a printer, and one day he'll be one of the principal men in the town.'

'Oh! So you know him?'

'Well, we do and we don't. I go into the shop sometimes; and then I've seen him once or twice up at the new house. We've asked him to come in and see us. But he's never come, and I don't

* See the author's novel, *Clayhanger*.

think he ever will. I believe his father *does* keep him grinding away rather hard. I'm sure he's frightfully clever.'

'How can you tell?'

'Oh! From bits of things he says. And he's read everything, it seems! And once he saved a great heavy printing-machine from going through the floor of the printing-shop into the basement. If it hadn't been for him there'd have been a dreadful accident. Everybody was talking about that. He doesn't look it, does he?'

They were now passing the corner at which stood the shop. Hilda peered within the narrowing, unshuttered slit, but she could see no more of Edwin Clayhanger.

'No, he doesn't,' she agreed, while thinking nevertheless that he did look precisely that. 'And so he lives all alone with his father. No mother?'

'No mother. But there are two sisters. The youngest is married, and just going to have a baby, poor thing! The other one keeps house. I believe she's a splendid girl, but neither of them is a bit like Edwin. Not a bit. He's –'

'What?'

'I don't know. Look here, miss! What about this rain? I vote we take the car up the hill.'

IV

The steam-car was rumbling after them down Duck Bank. It stopped, huge above them, and they climbed into it through an odour of warm grease that trailed from the engine. The conductor touched his hat to Janet, who smiled like a sister upon this fellow-being. Two middle-aged men were the only other occupants of the interior of the car; both raised their hats to Janet. The girls sat down in opposite corners next to the door. Then, with a deafening continuous clatter of loose glass-panes and throbbing of its filthy floor, the vehicle started again, elephantine.

It was impossible to talk in that unique din. Hilda had no desire to talk. She watched Janet pay the fares as in a dream, without even offering her own penny, though as a rule she was touchily punctilious in sharing expenses with the sumptuous Janet. Without being in the least aware of it, and quite innocently, Janet had painted a picture of the young man, Edwin Clayhanger, which intensified a hundredfold the strong romantic piquancy of Hilda's brief vision of him. In an instant Hilda saw her ideal future – that future which had loomed grandiose, indefinite, and strange – she saw it quite precise and simple as the wife of such a creature as Edwin Clayhanger. The change was astounding in its abruptness. She saw all the delightful and pure vistas of love with a man, subtle, baffling, and benevolent, and above all superior; with a man who would be respected by a whole town as a pillar of society, while bringing to his intimacy with herself an exotic and wistful quality which neither she nor anyone could possibly define. She asked: 'What attracts me in him? I don't know. *I like him*.' She who had never spoken to him! She who never before had vividly seen herself as married to a man! He was clever; he was sincere; he was kind; he was trustworthy; he would have wealth and importance and reputation. All this was good; but all this would have been indifferent to her, had there not been an enigmatic and inscrutable and unprecedented something in his face, in his bearing, which challenged and inflamed her imagination.

It did not occur to her to think of Janet as in the future a married woman. But of herself she thought, with new agitations: 'I am innocent now! I am ignorant now! I am a girl now! But one day I shall be so no longer. One day I shall be a woman. One day I shall be in the power and possession of some man – if not this man, then some other. Everything happens; and this will happen!' And the hazardous strangeness of life enchanted her.

CHAPTER 4
WITH THE ORGREAVES

I

THE Orgreave family was holding its nightly session in the large drawing-room of Lane End House when Hilda and Janet arrived. The bow windows stood generously open in three different places, and the heavy outer curtains as well as the lace inner ones were moving gently in the capricious breeze that came across the oval lawn. The multitudinous sound of rain on leaves entered also with the wind; and a steam-car could be heard thundering down Trafalgar Road, from which the house was separated by only a few intervening minor roofs.

Mrs Orgreave, the plump, faded image of goodness, with Janet's full red lips and Janet's kindly eyes, sat as usual, whether in winter or in summer, near the fireplace, surveying with placidity the theatre where the innumerable dramas of her motherhood had been enacted. Tom, her eldest, the thin, spectacled lawyer had, as a boy of seven, rampaged on that identical Turkey hearthrug, when it was new, a quarter of a century earlier. He was now seated at the grand piano with the youngest child, Alicia, a gawky little treasure, always alternating between pertness and timidity, aged twelve. Jimmie and Johnnie, young bloods of nineteen and eighteen, were only present in their mother's heart, being in process of establishing, by practice, the right to go forth into the world of an evening and return when they chose without suffering too much from family curiosity. Two other children – Marian, eldest daughter and sole furnisher of grandchildren to the family, and Charlie, a young doctor – were permanently away in London. Osmond Orgreave, the elegant and faintly mocking father of the brood, a handsome grizzled man of between fifty and sixty, was walking to and fro between the grand piano and the small upright piano in the farther half of the room.

'Well, my dear?' said Mrs Orgreave to Hilda. 'You aren't wet?' She drew Hilda towards her and stroked her shoulder, and then kissed her. The embrace was to convey the mother's sympathy with Hilda in the ordeal of the visit to Turnhill, and her satisfaction that the ordeal was now over. The ageing lady seemed to kiss her on behalf of the entire friendly family; all the others, appreciating the delicacy of the situation, refrained from the peril of clumsy speech.

'Oh no, mother!' Janet exclaimed reassuringly. 'We came up by car. And I had my umbrella. And it only began to rain in earnest just as we got to the gate.'

'Very thoughtful of it, I'm sure!' piped the pigtailed Alicia from the piano. She could talk, in her pert moments, exactly like her brothers.

'Alicia, darling,' said Janet coaxingly, as she sat on the sofa flanked by the hat, gloves, and jacket which she had just taken off, 'will you run upstairs with these things, and take Hilda's too? I'm quite exhausted. Father will swoon if I leave them here. I suppose he's walking about because he's so proud of his new birthday slippers.'

'But I'm just playing the symphony with Tom!' Alicia protested.

'I'll run up – I was just going to,' said Hilda.

'You'll do no such thing!' Mrs Orgreave announced sharply. 'Alicia, I'm surprised at you! Here Janet and Hilda have been out since noon, and you –'

'And so on and so on,' said Alicia, jumping up from the piano in obedience.

'We didn't wait supper,' Mrs Orgreave went on. 'But I told Martha to leave –'

'Mother, dearest,' Janet stopped her. 'Please don't mention food. We've stuffed ourselves, haven't we, Hilda? Anyone been?'

'Swetnam,' said Alicia, as she left the room with her arms full.

'*Mr* Swetnam,' corrected Mrs Orgreave.

'Which one? The Ineffable?'

'The Ineffable,' replied Mr Orgreave, who had wandered, smilingly enigmatically, to the sofa. His legs, like the whole of his person, had a distinguished air; and he held up first one slippered foot and then the other to the silent, sham-ecstatic inspection of the girls. 'He may look in again, later on. It's evidently Hilda he wants to see.' This said, Mr Orgreave lazily sank into an easy chair, opposite the sofa, and lighted a cigarette. He was one of the most industrious men in the Five Towns, and assuredly the most industrious architect; but into an idle hour he could pack more indolence than even Johnnie and Jimmie, alleged wastrels, could accomplish in a week.

'I say, Janet,' Tom sang out from the piano, 'you aren't really exhausted, are you?'

'I'm getting better.'

'Well, let's dash through the scherzo before the infant comes back. She can't take it half fast enough.'

'And do you think I can?' said Janet, rising. In theory, Janet was not a pianist, and she never played solos, nor accompanied songs; but in the actual practice of duet-playing her sympathetic presence of mind at difficult crises of the music caused her to be esteemed by Tom, the expert and enthusiast, as superior to all other performers in the family.

II

Hilda listened with pleasure and with exaltation to the scherzo. Beyond a little part-singing at school she had no practical acquaintance with music; there had never been a piano at home. But she knew that this music was Beethoven's; and from the mere intonation of that name, as it was uttered in her presence in the house of the Orgreaves, she was aware of its greatness, and the religious faculty in her had enabled her at once to accept its supremacy as an article of genuine belief; so that, though she understood it not, she felt it, and was uplifted by it. Whenever she heard Beethoven – and she heard it often, because Tom, in the words of the family, had for the moment got Beethoven on the brain – her thoughts and her aspirations were ennobled.

She was singularly content with this existence amid the intimacy of the Orgreaves. The largeness and prodigality and culture of the family life, so different from anything she had ever known, and in particular so different from the desolating atmosphere of the Cedars, soothed and flattered her in a manner subtly agreeable. At the same time she was but little irked by it, for the reason that her spirit was not one to be unduly affected by exterior social, intellectual, and physical conditions. Moreover, the Orgreaves, though obviously of a class superior to her own, had the facile and yet aristocratic unceremoniousness which, unconsciously, repudiates such distinctions until circumstances arise that compel their acknowledgement. To live among the Orgreaves was like living in a small private republic that throbbed with a hundred activities and interests. Each member of it was a centre of various energy. And from each, Hilda drew something that was precious: from Mrs Orgreave, sheer love and calm wisdom; from Janet, sheer love and the spectacle of elegance; from little Alicia, candour and admiration; from Tom, knowledge, artistic enthusiasm, and shy, curt sympathy; from Johnnie and Jimmie, the homage of their proud and naïve mannishness: as for Mr Orgreave, she admired him perhaps as much as she admired even Janet, and once when he and she had taken a walk together up to Toft End, she had thought him quite exquisite in his attitude to her, quizzical, worldly, and yet sensitively understanding and humane. And withal they never worried her by interferences and criticisms; they never presumed on their hospitality, but left her as free as though her age had been twice what it was. Undoubtedly, in the ardour of her gratitude she idealized every one of them. The sole reproach which in secret she would formulate against them had reference to their quasi-cynical levity in conversation. They would never treat a serious topic seriously for more than a few minutes. Either one or another would yield to the temptation of clever facetiousness, and clever facetiousness would always carry off the honours in a discussion. This did not apply to Mrs Orgreave, who was incapable of humour; but it applied a little even to Janet.

The thought continually arising in Hilda's mind was: 'Why do they care for me? What can they see in me? Why are they so good to me? I was never good to them.' She did not guess that, at her very first visit to Lane End House, the force and mystery of her character had powerfully attracted these rather experienced amateurs of human nature. She was unaware that she had made her mark upon Janet and Charlie so far back as the days of the dancing-classes. And she under-estimated the appeal of her situation as an orphan and a solitary whose mother's death, in its swiftness, had amounted to a tragedy.

The scherzo was finished, and Alicia had not returned to the drawing-room. The two pianists sat hesitant.

'Where is that infant?' Tom demanded. 'If I finish it all without her she'll be vexed.'

'I can tell you where she ought to be,' said Mrs Orgreave placidly. 'She ought to be in bed. No wonder she looks pale, stopping up till this time of night!'

Then there were unusual and startling movements behind the door, accompanied by giggling. And Alicia entered, followed by Charlie – Charlie, who was supposed at that precise instant to be in London!

'Hello, mater!' said the curly-headed Charlie, with a sublime affectation of calmness, as though he had slipped out of the next room. He produced an effect fully equal to his desires.

III

In a little while, Charlie, on the sofa, was seated at a small table covered with viands and fruit; the white cloth spread on the table made a curiously charming patch amid the sombre colours of the drawing-room. He had protested that, having consumed much food *en route*, he was not hungry; but in vain. Mrs Orgreave demolished such arguments by the power of her notorious theory, which admitted no exceptions, that any person coming off an express train must be in need of sustenance. The odd thing was that all the others discovered mysterious appetites and began to eat and drink with gusto, sitting, standing, or walking about, while Charlie, munching, related how he had miraculously got three days' leave from the hospital, and how he had impulsively 'cabbed it' to Euston, and how, having arrived at Knype, he had also 'cabbed it' from Knype to Bleakridge instead of waiting for the Loop Line train. The blot on his advent, in the eyes of Mrs Orgreave, was that he had no fresh news of Marian and her children.

'You don't seem very surprised to find Hilda here,' said Alicia.

'It's not my business to be surprised at anything, kid,' Charlie retorted, smiling at Hilda, who sat beside him on the sofa. 'Moreover, don't I get ten columns of news every three days? I know far more about this town than you do, I bet!'

Everybody laughed at Mrs Orgreave, the great letter-writer and universal disseminator of information.

'Now, Alicia, you must go to bed,' said Mrs Orgreave. And Alicia regretted that she had been so indiscreet as to draw attention to herself.

'The kid can stay up if she will say her piece,' said Charlie mockingly. He knew that he could play the autocrat, for that evening at any rate.

'What piece?' the child demanded, blushing and defiant.

'Her "Abou Ben Adhem",' said Charlie. 'Do you think I don't know all about that too?'

'Oh, mother, you are a bore!' Alicia exclaimed, pouting. 'Why did you tell him that? . . . Well, I'll say it if Hilda will recite something as well.'

'Me!' murmured Hilda, staggered. 'I never recite!'

'I've always understood you recite beautifully,' said Mrs Orgreave.

'You know you do, Hilda!' said Janet.

'Of course you do,' said Charlie.

'*You*'ve never heard me, anyhow!' she replied to him obstinately. How could they have got it fixed into their heads that she was a reciter? This renown was most disconcerting.

'Now, Hilda!' Mr Orgreave soothingly admonished her from the back of the sofa. She turned her head and looked up at him, smiling in her distress.

'Go ahead, then, kid! It's agreed,' said Charlie.

And Alicia galloped through Leigh Hunt's moral poem, which she was preparing for an imminent speech-day, in an extraordinarily short space of time.

'But I can't remember anything. I haven't recited for years and years,' Hilda pleaded, when the child burst out, 'Now, Hilda!'

'*Stuff!*' Charlie pronounced.

'Some Tennyson?' Mrs Orgreave suggested. 'Don't you know any Tennyson? We must have something, now.' And Alicia, exulting in the fact that she had paid the penalty imposed, cried that there could be no drawing back.

Hilda was lost. Mrs Orgreave's tone, with all its softness, was a command. 'Tennyson? I've forgotten "Maud",' she muttered.

'I'll prompt you,' said Charlie. 'Thomas!'

Everybody looked at Tom, expert in literature as well as in music; Tom, the collector, the owner of books and bookcases.

Tom went to a bookcase and drew forth a green volume, familiar and sacred throughout all England.

'Oh, dear! ' Hilda moaned.

'Where do you mean to begin?' Charlie sternly inquired. 'It just happens that I'm reading "In Memoriam", myself. I read ten stanzas a day.'

Hilda bent over the book with him.

'But I must stand up,' she said, with sudden fire. 'I can't recite sitting down.'

They all cried 'Bravo!' and made a circle for her. And she stood up.

The utterance of the first lines was a martyrdom for her. But after that she surrendered herself frankly to the mood of the poem and forgot to suffer shame, speaking in a loud, clear, dramatic voice which she accompanied by glances and even by gestures. After about thirty lines she stopped, and, regaining her ordinary senses, perceived that the entire family was staring at her with an extreme intentness.

'I can't do any more,' she murmured weakly, and dropped on to the sofa.

Everybody clapped very heartily.

'It's wonderful!' said Janet in a low tone.

'I should just say it was!' said Tom seriously, and Hilda was saturated with delicious joy.

'You ought to go on the stage; that's what you ought to do!' said Charlie.

For a fraction of a second, Hilda dreamt of the stage, and then Mrs Orgreave said softly, like a mother:

'I'm quite sure Hilda would never dream of any such thing!'

IV

There was an irruption of Jimmie and Johnnie, and three of the Swetnam brothers, including him known as the Ineffable. Jimmie and Johnnie played the role of the absolutely imperturbable with a skill equal to Charlie's own; and only a series of calm 'How-dos?' marked the greetings of these relatives. The Swetnams were more rollickingly demonstrative. Now that the drawing-room was quite thickly populated, Hilda, made nervous by Mr Orgreave's jocular insinuation that she herself was the object of the Swetnams' call, took refuge, first with Janet, and then, as Janet was drawn into the general crowd, with Charlie, who was absently turning over the pages of 'In Memoriam'.

'Know this?' he inquired, friendly, indicating the poem.

'I don't,' she said. 'It's splendid, isn't it?'

'Well,' he answered, 'it's rather on the religious tack, you know. That's why I'm reading it.' He smiled oddly.

'Really?'

He hesitated, and then nodded. It was the strangest avowal from this young dandy of twenty-three with the airy and cynical tongue. Hilda thought: 'Here, then, is another!' And her own most secret troubles recurred to her mind.

'What's that about Teddy Clayhanger?' Charlie cried out, suddenly looking up. He had caught the name in a distant conversation.

Janet explained how they had seen Edwin, and went on to say that it was impossible to persuade him to call.

'What rot!' said Charlie. 'I bet you what you like I get him here tomorrow night.' He added to Hilda: 'Went to school with him!' Hilda's face burned.

'I bet you don't,' said Janet stoutly, from across the room.

'I'll bet you a shilling I do,' said Charlie.

'Haven't a penny left,' Janet smiled. 'Father, will you lend me a shilling?'

'That's what I'm here for,' said Mr Orgreave.

'Mr Orgreave,' the youngest Swetnam put in, 'you talk exactly like the dad talks.'

The bet was made, and according to a singular but long-established family custom, Tom had to be stakeholder.

Hilda became troubled and apprehensive. She hoped that Charlie would lose, and then she hoped that he would win. Looking forward to the intimate bedroom chat with Janet which brought each evening to a heavenly close, she said to herself: 'If he *does* come, I shall make Janet promise that I'm not to be asked to recite or anything. In fact, I shall get her to see that I'm not discussed.'

CHAPTER 5
EDWIN CLAYHANGER

I

THE next evening, Mr and Mrs Orgreave, Hilda, Janet, and Alicia were in the dining-room of the Orgreaves awaiting the advent at the supper-table of sundry young men whose voices could be heard through open doors in the distance of the drawing-room.

Charlie Orgreave had won his bet: and Edwin Clayhanger was among those young men who had remained behind in the drawing-room to exchange, according to the practice of young men, ideas upon life and the world. Hilda had been introduced to him, but owing to the performance of another Beethoven symphony there had been almost no conversation before supper, and she had not heard him talk. She had stationed herself behind the grand piano, on the plea of turning over the pages for the musicians (though it was only with great uncertainty, and in peril of missing the exact instant for turning, that she followed the music on the page), and from this security she had furtively glanced at Edwin when her task allowed. 'Perhaps I was quite mistaken last night,' she said to herself. 'Perhaps he is perfectly ordinary.' The strange thing was that she could not decide whether he was ordinary or not. At one moment his face presented no interest; at another she saw it just as she had seen it, framed in the illuminated aperture of the shop-shutters, on the previous night. Or she fancied that she saw it thus. The more she tried to distinguish between Edwin's reality and her fancies concerning Edwin, the less she succeeded. She would pronounce positively that her fancies were absurd and even despicable. But this abrupt positiveness did not convince. Supposing that he was after all marvellous among men! During the day she had taken advantage of the mention of his name to ascertain discreetly some details of the legendary feat by which as a boy he had saved his father's printing-shop from destruction. The details were vague, and not very comprehensible, but they seemed to indicate on his part an astounding presence of mind, a heroic promptitude in action. Assuredly, the Orgreaves regarded him as a creature out of the common run. And at the same time they all had the air of feeling rather sorry for him.

Standing near the supper-table, Hilda listened intently for the sound of his voice among the other voices in the drawing-room. But she could not separate it from the rest. Perhaps he was keeping silence. She said to herself: 'Yet what do I care whether he is keeping silence or not?'

Mr Orgreave remarked, in the suspense, glancing ironically at his wife:

'I think I'll go upstairs and do an hour's planning. They aren't likely to be more than an hour, I expect?'

'Hilda,' said Mrs Orgreave, quite calm, but taking her husband quite seriously, 'will you please go and tell those young men from me that supper is waiting.'

II

Of course Hilda obeyed, though it appeared strange to her that Mrs Orgreave had not sent Alicia on such an errand. Passing out of the bright dining-room where the gas was lit, she hesitated a moment in the dark broad corridor that led to the drawing-room. The mission, she felt, would make her rather prominent in front of Edwin Clayhanger, the stranger, and she had an objection to being prominent in front of him; she had, indeed, taken every possible precaution against such a danger. 'How silly I am to loiter here!' she thought. 'I might be Alicia!'

The boys, she could now hear, were discussing French literature, and in particular Victor Hugo. When she caught the name of Victor Hugo she lifted her chin, and moved forward a little. She worshipped Victor Hugo with a passion unreflecting and intense, simply because certain detached lines from his poems were the most splendid occupants of her memory, dignifying every painful or sordid souvenir. At last Charlie's clear, gay voice said:

'It's all very well, and Victor Hugo is Victor Hugo, but you can say what you like – there's a lot of this that'll bear skipping, your worships.'

Already she was at the doorway. In the dusk of the unlighted chamber the faces of the four Orgreaves and Clayhanger showed like pale patches on the gloom.

'Not a line!' she said fiercely, with her extremely clear articulation. She had no right to make such a statement, for she had not read the twentieth part of Victor Hugo's work; she did not even know what book they were discussing – Charlie held the volume lightly in his hand – but she was incensed against the mere levity of Charlie's tone.

She saw Edwin Clayhanger jump at the startling interruption. And all five looked round. She could feel her face burning.

Charlie quizzed her with a word, and then turned to Edwin Clayhanger for support. 'Don't *you* think that some of it's dullish, Teddy?'

Edwin Clayhanger, shamefaced, looked at Hilda wistfully, as if in apology, as if appealing to her clemency against her fierceness; and said slowly:

'Well – yes.'

He had agreed with Charlie; but while disagreeing with Hilda he had mysteriously proved to her that she had been right in saying to herself on the previous evening: '*I like him.*'

The incident appeared to her to be enormous and dramatic. She moved away, as it were breathless under emotion, and then, remembering her errand, threw over her shoulder:

'Mrs Orgreave wants to know when you're coming to supper.'

III

The supper-table was noisy and joyous – more than usually so on account of the presence of Charlie, the gayest member of the family. At either end of the long, white-spread board sat Mr and Mrs Orgreave; Alicia stood by Mr Orgreave, who accepted her caresses with the negligence of a handsome father. Along one side sat Hilda, next to Janet, and these two were flanked by Jimmie and Johnnie, tall, unbending, apparently determined to prove by a politely supercilious demeanour that to pass a whole evening thus in the home circle was considered by them to be a concession on their part rather than a privilege. Edwin Clayhanger sat exactly opposite to Hilda, with Charlie for sponsor; and Tom's spectacles gleamed close by.

Hilda, while still constrained, was conscious of pleasure in the scene, and of a certain pride in forming part of it. These prodigal and splendid persons respected and liked her, even loved her. Her recitation on the previous evening had been a triumph. She was glad that she had shown them that she could at any rate do one thing rather well; but she was equally glad that she had obtained Janet's promise to avoid any discussion of her qualities or her situation. After all, with her self-conscious restraint and her pitiful assured income of three pounds a week, she was a poor little creature compared with the easy, luxurious beings of this household, whose upkeep could not cost less than three pounds a day. Janet, in rich and complicated white, and glistening with jewels at hand and neck, was a princess beside her. She hated her spare black frock, and for the second time in her life desired expensive clothes markedly feminine. She felt that she was at a grave disadvantage, and that to remedy this disadvantage would be necessary, not only dresses and precious stones, but an instinctive faculty of soft allurement which she had not. Each gesture of Janet's showed seductive grace, while her own rare gestures were stiffened by a kind of masculine harshness. Every time that the sad-eyed and modest Edwin Clayhanger glanced at Janet, and included herself in the glance, she fancied that he was unjustly but inevitably misprizing herself. And at length she thought: 'Why did I make Janet promise that I shouldn't be talked about? Why shouldn't he know all about my mourning, and that I'm the only girl in the Five Towns that can write shorthand? Why should I be afraid to recite again? However much I might have suffered through nervousness if I'd recited, I should have shown I'm not such a poor little thing as all that! Why am I such a baby?' She wilted under her own disdain.

It was strange to think that Edwin Clayhanger, scarcely older than the irresponsible Charlie, was the heir to an important business, was potentially a rich and influential man. Had not Mr Orgreaves said that old Mr Clayhanger could buy up all the Orgreaves if he chose? It was strange to think that this wistful and apparently timid young man, this nice boy, would one day be the head of a household, and of a table such as this! Yes, it would assuredly arrive! Everything happened. And the mother of that household? Would it be she? Her imagination leaped far into the future, as she exchanged a quiet, furtive smile with Mrs Orgreave, and she tried to see herself as another Mrs Orgreave, a strenuous and passionate past behind her, honoured, beloved, teased, adored. But she could not quite see herself thus. Impossible that she, with her temperament so feverish, restive, and peculiar should ever reach such a haven! It was fantastically too much to expect! And yet, one day, if not with Edwin Clayhanger, then with another, with some mysterious being whom she had never seen! . . . Did not everything happen? . . . But then, equally, strange and terrible misfortunes might be lying in wait for her! . . . The indescribable sharp savour of life was in her nostrils.

IV

The conversation had turned upon Bradlaugh, the shameless free-thinker, the man who had known how to make himself the centre of discussion in every house in England. This was the Bradlaugh year, the apogee of his notoriety. Dozens of times at the Cedars' meal-table had she heard the shocking name of Bradlaugh on outraged tongues, but never once had a word been uttered in his favour. The public opinion of the boarding-house was absolutely unanimous in reckoning him a scoundrel. In the dining-room of the Orgreaves the attitude towards him was different. His free-thought was not precisely defended, but champions of his right to sit in the House of Commons were numerous. Hilda grew excited, and even more self-conscious. It was as if she were in momentary expectation of being challenged by these hardy debaters: 'Are not *you* a free-thinker?' Her interest was personal; the interest of one in peril. Compared with the discussions at the Cedars, this discussion was as the open, tossing, windy sea to a weed-choked canal. The talk veered into mere profane politics, and Mr Orgreave, entrenching himself behind an assumption of careless disdain, was severely attacked by all his sons except Jimmie, who, above Hilda's left shoulder, pretended to share the paternal scorn. The indifference of Hilda to politics was complete. She began to feel less disturbed; she began to dream. Then she suddenly heard, through her dream, the name of Bradlaugh again; and Edwin Clayhanger, in response to a direct question from Mr Orgreave, was saying:

'You can't help what you believe. You can't make yourself believe anything. And I don't see why you should, either. There's no virtue in believing.'

And Tom was crying 'Hooray!'

Hilda was thunderstruck. She was blinded as though by a mystic revelation. She wanted to exult, and to exult with all the ardour of her soul. This truth which Edwin Clayhanger had enunciated she had indeed always been vaguely aware of; but now in a flash she felt it, she faced it, she throbbed to its authenticity, and was free. It solved every difficulty, and loosed the load that for months past had wearied her back. 'There's no virtue in believing.' It was fundamental. It was the gift of life and of peace. Her soul shouted, as she realized that just there, in that instant, at that table, a new epoch had dawned for her. Never would she forget the instant and the scene – scene of her re-birth!

Mrs Orgreave remonstrated with mild sadness:

'No virtue in believing! Eh, Mr Edwin!'

And Hilda, under the ageing lady's grieved glance, tried to quench the exultation on her face, somewhat like a child trapped. But she could not. Tom again cried 'Hooray!' His tone, however, grated on her sensibility. It lacked emotion. It was the tone of a pugilist's backer. And Janet permitted herself some pleasantry. And Charlie became frankly facetious. Was it conceivable that Charlie could be interested in religion? She liked him very much, partly because he and she had learnt to understand each other at the dancing-classes, and partly because his curly hair and his candid smile compelled sympathy. But her esteem for him had limits. It was astonishing that a family otherwise simply perfect should be content with jocosity when jocosity was so obviously out of place. Were they, then, afraid of being serious? . . . Edwin Clayhanger was not laughing; he had blushed. Her eyes were fixed on him with the extremest intensity, studying him, careless of the danger that his gaze might catch hers. She was lost in him. And then, he caught her; and, burning with honest shame, she looked downwards.

CHAPTER 6
IN THE GARDEN

I

THAT evening Janet did not stay long in Hilda's bedroom, having perceived that Hilda was in one of her dark, dreamy moods.

As soon as she was gone, Hilda lowered the gas a little, and then went to the window, and opened it wider, and, drawing aside the blind, looked forth. The night was obscure and warm; and a wet wind moved furtively about in the elm-trees of the garden, The window was at the side of the house; it gave on the west, and commanded the new house just finished by Mr Orgreave for the Clayhanger family. The block of this generously planned dwelling rose massively at a distance of perhaps forty feet, dwarfing a whole row of cottages in the small street behind Lane End House; its various chimney-pots stood out a deeper black against the enigmatic sky. Beyond the Clayhanger garden-plot, as yet uncultivated, and its high boundary wall, ran the great silent thoroughfare, Trafalgar Road, whose gas-lamps reigned in the nocturnal silence that the last steam-car had left in its wake.

Hilda gazed at the house; and it seemed strange to her that the house, which but a short time ago had no existence whatever, and was yet cold and soulless was destined to be the living home of a family, with history in its walls and memories clinging about it. The formidable magic of life was always thus discovering itself to her, so that she could not look upon even an untenanted, terra-cotta-faced villa without a secret thrill; and the impenetrable sky above was not more charmed and enchanted than those brick walls. When she reflected that one day the wistful, boyish Edwin Clayhanger would be the master of that house, that in that house his will would be stronger than any other will, the mystery that hides beneath the surface of all things surged up and overwhelmed thought. And although scarcely a couple of hours had elapsed since the key of the new life had been put into her hands, she could not make an answer when she asked herself: 'Am I happy or unhappy?'

II

The sound of young men's voices came round the corner of the house from the lawn: Some of the brothers Orgreave were saying good night to Edwin Clayhanger in the porch. She knew that they had been chatting a long time in the hall, after Clayhanger had bidden adieu to the rest of the family. She wondered what they had been talking about, and what young men did in general talk about when they were by themselves and confidential. In her fancy she endowed their conversations with the inexplicable attractiveness of masculinity, as masculinity is understood by women alone. She had an intense desire to overhear such a conversation, and she felt that she would affront the unguessed perils of it with delight, drinking it up eagerly, every drop, even were the draught deadly. Meanwhile, the mere inarticulate sound of those distant voices pleased her, and she was glad that she was listening and that the boys knew it not.

Silence succeeded the banging of the front door. And then, after a pause, she was startled to hear the crunching of gravel almost under her window. In alarm she dropped the blind, but continued to peer between the edge of the blind and the window-frame. At one point the contiguous demesnes of the Orgreaves and the Clayhangers were separated only by a poor, sparse hedge, a few yards in length. Somebody was pushing his way through this hedge. It was Edwin Clayhanger. Despite the darkness of the night she could be sure that the dim figure was Edwin Clayhanger's by the peculiar, exaggerated swing of the loose arms. He passed the hedge, carelessly brushed his clothes with his hands, and walked slowly up the Clayhanger garden towards the new house, and in the deep shadow of the house was lost. Still, she could catch vague noises of movement. In a state of extreme excitation she wondered what he could be doing. It seemed to her that he and she were sharing the night together.

III

She thought:

'I would give anything to be able to speak to him privately and ask him a little more about what he said tonight. I ought to. I may never see him again. At any rate, I may never have another chance. He may have meant something else. He may not have been serious . . .' The skin of her face prickled, and a physical wave of emotion seemed to sweep downwards through her whole body. The thrill was exquisite, but it was intimidating.

She whispered to herself:

'I could go downstairs and outside, and find him, and just ask him.'

The next instant she was opening the door of her bedroom . . . No, all the household had not yet retired, for a light was still burning in the corridor. Nevertheless she might go. She descended the stairs, asking herself aghast: 'Why am I doing this?' Another light was burning in the hall, and through the slit of the half-shut door of the breakfast-room she could see light. She stood hesitant. Then she heard the striking of a match in the breakfast-room, and she boldly pushed the door open. Tom, with a book before him, was lighting his pipe.

'Hello!' he said. 'What's the matter?'

'Oh, nothing!' she replied. 'Only, I'm just going to walk about in the garden a minute. I shan't go to sleep unless I do.' She spoke quite easily.

'All serene!' he agreed. 'So long as you keep off the grass! It's bound to be damp. I'll unchain the door for you, shall I?'

She said that she could unfasten the door for herself, and he did not insist. The hospitality of the Orgreaves was never irksome. Tom had scarcely half-risen from his chair.

'I shan't be long,' she added casually.

'That's all right, Hilda,' he said. 'I'm not going to bed just yet.'

'All the others gone?'

He nodded. She pulled the door to, tripped delicately through the hall, and unchained the heavy front door as quietly as she could.

IV

She was outside, amid all the influences of the night. Gradually her eyes accustomed themselves again to the gloom. She passed along the façade of the house until she came to the corner, where the breeze surprised her, and whence she could discern the other house and, across the indistinct hedge, the other garden. Where was Edwin Clayhanger? Was he wandering in the other garden, or had he entered the house? Then a brief flare lit up a lower window of the dark mass for a few instants. He was within. She hesitated. Should she go forward, or should she go back? At length she went forward, and, finding in the hedge the gap which Clayhanger had made, forced her way through it. Her skirt was torn by an obstinate twig. Quite calmly she bent down and with her fingers examined the rent; it was not important. She was now in the garden of the Clayhangers, and he whom she sought was moving somewhere in the house. 'Supposing I *do* meet him,' she thought, 'what shall I say to him?' She did not know what she should say to him, nor why she had entered upon this singular adventure. But the consciousness of self, the fine, disturbing sense of being alive in every vein and nerve, was a rich reward for her audacity. She wished that that tense moment of expectation might endure for ever.

She approached the house, trembling. It was not by volition that she walked over the uneven clayey ground, but by instinct. She was in front of the garden-porch, and here she hesitated again, apparently waiting for a sign from the house. She glanced timidly about her, as though in fear of marauders that might spring out upon her from the shadow. Just over the boundary wall the placid flame of a gas-lamp peeped. Then, feeling with her feet for the steps, she ascended into the shelter of the porch. Almost at the same moment there was another flare behind the glass of the door; she heard the sound of unlatching; the flare expired. She was absolutely terror-struck now.

The door opened, grating on some dirt or gravel.

'Who's there?' demanded a queer, shaking voice.

She could see his form.

'Me!' she answered, in a harsh tone which was the expression of her dismay.

The deed was done, irretrievably. In her bedroom she had said that she would try to speak with him, and lo! they were face to face, in the dark, in secret! Her terror was now, at any rate, desperately calm. She had plunged; she was falling into the deep sea; she was hopelessly cut off from the past.

'Oh!' came the uncertain voice weakly. 'Did you want me? Did anyone want me?'

She heard the door being closed behind him.

She told him, with peculiar curtness, how she had seen him from her window, and how she wished to ask him an important question.

'I dare say you think it's very queer of me,' she added.

'Not at all,' he said, with an insincerity that annoyed her.

'Yes, you do!' she sharply insisted. 'But I want to know' – what did she want to know? – 'I want to know – did you mean it when you said – you know, at supper – that there's no virtue in believing?'

He stammered: 'Did I say there was no virtue in believing?'

She cried out, irritated: 'Of course you did! Do you mean to say you can say a thing like that and then forget about it? If it's true, it's one of the most wonderful things that were ever said. And that's why I wanted to know if you meant it, or whether you were only saying it because it sounded clever.'

She stopped momentarily, wondering why she was thus imply-ing an untruth; for the fact was that she had never doubted that he had been in earnest.

'That's what they're always doing in that house, you know – being clever!' she went on, in a tone apparently inimical to 'that house'.

'Yes,' came the voice. 'I meant it. Why?'

And the voice was so simple and so sincere that it pierced straight to her heart and changed her secret mood swiftly to the religious, so that she really was occupied by the thoughts with which, a moment previously, she had only pretended to be occu-pied; and the splendour of the revelation was renewed. Neverthe-less, some impulse, perverse or defensive, compelled her to assume a doubt of his assurance. She suspected that, had she not adopted this tactic, she might have melted before him in gratitude.

'You did?' she murmured.

She thanked him, after that, rather coldly; and they talked a little about the mere worry of these religious questions. He protested that they never worried him, and reaffirmed his original proposition.

'I hope you are right,' she said softly, in a thrilled voice. She was thinking that this was the most wonderful, miraculous experience that she had ever had.

V

Silence.

'Now,' she thought, 'I must go back.' Inwardly she gave a delicious sigh.

But just as she was about to take her prim leave, the scarce-discerned figure of her companion stepped out into the garden.

'By Jove!' said Edwin Clayhanger. 'It's beginning to rain, I do believe.'

The wind blew, and she felt rain on her cheek. Clayhanger advised her to stand against the other wall of the porch for better protection. She obeyed. He re-entered the porch, but was still exposed to the rain. She called him to her side. Already he was so close that she could have touched his shoulder by outstretching her arm.

'Oh! I'm all right!' he said lightly, and did not move.

'You needn't be afraid of me!' She was hurt that he had refused her invitation to approach her. The next instant she would have given her tongue not to have uttered those words. But she was in such a tingling state of extreme sensitiveness as rendered it impossible for her to exercise a normal self-control.

Scarcely conscious of what she did, she asked him the time. He struck a match to look at his watch. The wind blew the match out, but she saw his wistful face, with his disordered hair under the hat. It had the quality of a vision.

He offered to get a light in the house, but abruptly she said good night.

Then they were shaking hands – she knew not how or why. She could not loose his hand. She thought: 'Never have I held a hand so honest as this hand.' At last she dropped it. They stood silent while a trap rattled up Trafalgar Road. It was as if she was

bound to remain moveless until the sounds of the trap had died
away.

She walked proudly out into the rain. He called to her: 'I say,
Miss Lessways!' But she did not stop.

In a minute she was back again in Lane End House.

'That you?' Tom's voice from the breakfast-room!

'Yes,' she answered clearly. 'I've put the chain on. Good night.'

'Good night. Thanks.'

She ascended the stairs, smiling to herself, with the raindrops
fresh on her cheek. In her mind were no distinct thoughts, either
concerning the non-virtue of belief, or the new epoch, or Edwin
Clayhanger, or even the strangeness of her behaviour. But all her
being vibrated to the mysterious and beautiful romance of
existence.

CHAPTER 7
THE NEXT MEETING

I

FOR several days the town of Bursley was to Hilda simply a place made perilous and redoubtable by the apprehension of meeting Edwin Clayhanger accidentally in the streets thereof. And the burden of her meditations was: 'What can he have thought of me?' She had said nothing to anybody of the deliberately sought adventure in the garden. And with the strangest ingenuous confidence she assumed that Edwin Clayhanger, too, would keep an absolute silence about it. She had therefore naught to fear, except in the privacy of his own mind. She did not blame herself – it never occurred to her to do so – but she rather wondered at herself, inimically, prophesying that one day her impulsiveness would throw her into some serious difficulty. The memory of the night beautifully coloured her whole daily existence. In spite of her avoidance of the town, due to her dread of seeing Clayhanger, she was constantly thinking: 'But this cannot continue for ever. One day I am bound to meet him again.' And she seemed to be waiting for that day.

It came with inevitable quickness. The last day but one of June was appointed throughout the country for the celebration of the Centenary of Sunday Schools. Neither Hilda nor any of the Orgreave children had ever seen the inside of a Sunday School; and the tendency up at Lane End House was to condescend towards the festival as towards a rejoicing of the proletariat. But in face of the magnitude of the affair, looming more enormous as it approached, this attitude could not be maintained. The preparations for the Centenary filled newspapers and changed the physiognomy of towns. And on the morning of the ceremonial service, gloriously flattered by the sun, there was candid excitement at the breakfast-table of the Orgreaves. Mr Orgreaves regretted that pressure of work would prevent him from seeing the fun. Tom was going to see the fun at Hanbridge. Jimmie and Johnnie were going to see the fun, but they would not say where. The servants were going to see the fun. Charlie had returned to London. Alicia wanted to go and see the fun, but as she was flushed and feverish, Mrs Orgreave forbade and decided to remain at home with Alicia. Otherwise, even Mrs Orgreave would have gone to see the fun. Hilda and Janet apparently hesitated about going, but Mr Orgreave, pointing out that there could not under the most favourable circumstance be another Centenary of Sunday Schools for at least a hundred years, sarcastically urged them to set forth. The fact was, as Janet teasingly told him while she hung on his neck, that he wished to accentuate as much as possible his own martyrdom to industry. Were not all the shops and offices of the Five Towns closed? Did not every member of his family, save those detained by illness, attend the historic spectacle of the Centenary? He alone had sacrificed pleasure to work. Thus Janet's loving, ironic smiles foretold, would the father of the brood discourse during the next few days.

II

Hilda and Janet accordingly went down a beflagged and sunlit Trafalgar Road together. Janet was wearing still another white dress, and Hilda, to her marked relief, had abandoned black for a slate-coloured frock made by a dressmaker in Bleakridge. It was Mrs Orgreave herself who had first counselled Hilda, if she hated black, as she said she did, to abandon black. The entire family chorus had approved.

The risk of encountering Edwin Clayhanger on that day of multitudes was surely infinitesimal. Nevertheless, in six minutes the improbable had occurred. At the corner of Trafalgar Road and Duck Square Janet, attracted by the sight of banners in the distance, turned to the left along Wedgwood Street and past the front of Clayhanger's shop. Theoretically shops were closed, but one shutter of Clayhanger's was down, and in its place stood Edwin Clayhanger. Hilda felt her features stiffening into a sort of wilful and insincere hostility as she shook hands. Within the darkness of the shop she saw the figures of two dowdy women – doubtless the sisters of whom Janet had told her; they disappeared before Janet and Hilda entered.

'It has happened! I have seen him again!' Hilda said to herself as she sat in the shop listening to Janet and to Edwin Clayhanger. It appeared likely that Edwin Clayhanger would join them in the enterprise of witnessing the historic spectacle.

A few minutes later everybody was startled by the gay apparition of Osmond Orgreave swinging his cane. Curiosity had been too much for industriousness, and Osmond Orgreave had yielded to the general interest.

'Oh! Father!' cried Janet. 'What a deceitful thing you are!'

'Only a day or two ago,' Hilda was thinking, 'I had never even heard of him. And his shop seemed so strange and romantic to me. And now I am sitting in his shop like an old friend. And nobody suspects that he and I have had a secret meeting!' The shop itself seemed to be important and prosperous.

Mr Orgreave, having decided for pleasure, was anxious to find it at once, and, under his impatience, they left the shop. Janet went out first with her gay father. Edwin Clayhanger waited respectfully for Hilda to pass. But just as she was about to step forth she caught sight of George Cannon coming along the opposite side of Wedgwood Street in the direction of Trafalgar Road; he was in close conversation with another man. She kept within the shelter of the shop until the two had gone by. She did not want to meet George Cannon, with whom she had not had speech since the interview at the Cedars; he had written to her about the property sales, and she had replied. There was no reason why she should hesitate to meet him. But she wished not to complicate the situation. She thought: 'If he saw me, he'd come across and speak to me, and I might have to introduce him to all these people, and goodness knows what!' The contretemps caused her heart to beat.

When they emerged from the shop Janet, a few yards ahead with Mr Orgreave, was beckoning.

III

Hilda stood on a barrel by the side of Edwin Clayhanger on another barrel. There, from the top of St Luke's Square, they surveyed a vast rectangular carpet of upturned faces that made a pattern of pale dots on a coloured and black groundwork. Nearly all the children of Bursley, thousands upon thousands, were

massed in the Square, wedged in tight together, so that there
seemed not to be an inch of space anywhere between the shuttered
shop fronts on the east of the Square and the shuttered shop fronts
on the west of the Square. At the bottom of the Square a row of
railway lorries were crammed with tiny babes – or such they
appeared – toddlers too weak to walk in processions. At the top
of the Square a large platform full of bearded adults rose like an
island out of the unconscious sea of infants. And from every
window of every house adults looked down in safe ease upon that
wavy ocean over which banners gleamed in the dazzling and fierce
sunshine.

She might have put up her sunshade. But she would not do so.
She thought: 'If all those children can stand the sun without
fainting, I can!' She was extraordinarily affected by the mere sight
of the immense multitude of children; they were as helpless and as
fatalistic as sheep, utterly at the mercy of the adults who had
herded them. There was about them a collective wistfulness that
cut the heart; to dwell on the idea of it would have brought her to
tears. And when the multitude sang, so lustily, so willingly, so
bravely, pouring forth with the brass instruments a volume of
tone enormous and majestic, she had a tightness of the throat that
was excruciating. The Centenary of Sunday Schools was quite
other than she had expected; she had not bargained for these
emotions.

It was after the hymn 'There is a fountain filled with blood',
during the quietude of a speech, that Edwin Clayhanger, taking up
an evangelistic phrase in the speech, whispered to her:

'More blood!'

'What?' she asked, amazed by his ironical accent, which jarred
on her mood, and also by his familiar manner of leaning towards
her and dropping the words in her ear.

'Well,' he said. 'Look at it! It only wants the Ganges at the
bottom of the Square!'

Evidently for Edwin Clayhanger all religions were equally
heathenish! She was quite startled out of her amazement, and her
response was an almost humble entreaty not to make fun. The
next moment she regretted that she had not answered him with
sharp firmness. She was somewhat out of humour with him. He
had begun by losing sight of Mr Orgreave and Janet – and of

course it was hopeless to seek for them in those thronging streets around St Luke's Square. Then he had said to her, in a most peculiar tone: 'I hope you didn't catch cold in the rain the other night,' and she had not liked that. She had regarded it as a fault in tact, almost as a sexual disloyalty on his part to refer at all to the scene in the garden. Finally, his way of negotiating with the barrel man for the use of two barrels had been lacking, for Hilda, in the qualities of largeness and masterfulness; any one of the Orgreave boys would, she was sure, have carried the thing off in a more worldly manner.

The climax of the service came with the singing of 'When I survey the wondrous Cross'. The physical effect of it on Hilda was nearly overwhelming. The terrible and sublime words seemed to surge upon her charged with all the multitudinous significance of the crowd. She was profoundly stirred, and to prevent an outburst of tears she shook her head.

'What's the matter?' said Edwin Clayhanger.

'Clumsy dolt!' she thought. 'Haven't you got enough sense to leave me alone?' And she said aloud, passionately transforming her weakness into ferocity: 'That's the most splendid religious verse ever written! You can say what you like. It's worth while believing anything, if you can sing words like that and mean them!'

He agreed that the hymn was fine.

'Do you know who wrote it?' she demanded threateningly.

He did not. She was delighted.

'Dr Watts, of course!' she said, with a scornful sneer. What did Janet mean by saying that he had read simply everything?

IV

An episode which supervened close to their barrels did a great deal to intensify the hostility of her mood. On the edge of the crowd an old man, who had been trying to force his way through it, was being guyed by a gang of louts who had surrounded an ice-cream barrow. Suddenly she recognized this old man. His name was Shushions; he was a familiar figure of the streets of Turnhill, and he had the reputation of being the oldest Sunday School teacher in the Five Towns. He was indeed exceedingly old, foolish and undignified in senility; and the louts were odiously jeering at his defenceless dotage, and a young policeman was obviously with the louts and against the aged, fatuous victim.

Hilda gave an exclamation of revolt, and called upon Edwin Clayhanger to go to the rescue of Mr Shushions. Not he, however, but she, jumped down first and pushed towards the barrow. She made the path, and he followed. She protested to the policeman, and he too modestly seconded her. Yet the policeman, ignoring her, addressed himself to Edwin Clayhanger. Hilda was infuriated. It appeared that old Mr Shusions had had a ticket for the platform, but had lost it.

'He must be got on to the platform somehow!' she decided, with a fiery glance.

But Edwin Clayhanger seemed to be incapable of a heroic action. He hesitated. The policeman hesitated. Fortunately, the plight of the doting oldest Sunday School teacher in the Five Towns had been observed from the platform, and two fussy, rosetted officials bustled up and offered to take charge of him. And Hilda, dissolving in painful pity, bent over him softly and arranged his disordered clothes; she was weeping.

'Shall we go back to our barrels?' Edwin Clayhanger rather sheepishly suggested after Mr Shushions had been dragged away. But she would not go back to the barrels.

'I think it's time we set about to find Janet and Mr Orgreave,' she replied coldly, and they drew out of the crowd. She was profoundly deceived in Edwin Clayhanger, so famous for his presence of mind in saving printing-shops from destruction! She did not know what he ought to have done; she made no attempt to conceive what he ought to have done. But that he ought to have done something – something decisive and grandly masculine – she was sure.

V

Later, after sundry adventures, and having found Mr Orgreave and Janet, they stood at the tail of the steam-car, which Janet had decided should carry her up to Bleakridge; and Edwin shook hands. Yes, Hilda was profoundly deceived in him. Nevertheless, his wistful and honest glance, as he parted from her, had its effect.

If he had not one quality, he had another. She tried hard to maintain her scorn of him, but it was exceedingly difficult to do so.

Mr Orgreave wiped his brow as the car jolted them out of the tumult of the Centenary. It was hot, but he did not seem to be in the slightest degree fatigued or dispirited, whereas Janet put back her head and shut her eyes.

'Caught sight of a friend of yours this morning, Hilda!' he said pleasantly.

'Oh!'

'Yes. Mr Cannon. By the way, I forget to tell you yesterday that his famous newspaper – *yours* – has come to an end.' He spoke, as it were, with calm sympathy. 'Yes! Well, it's not surprising, not surprising! Nothing's ever stood up against the *Signal* yet!'

Hilda was saddened. When they reached Lane End House, a few seconds in front of the hurrying and apologetic servants, Mrs Orgreave told her that Mr George Cannon had called to see her, and had left a note for her. She ran up to her room with the note. It said merely that the writer wished to have an interview with her at once.

BOOK III

HER BURDEN

CHAPTER 1
HILDA INDISPENSABLE

I

HILDA made no response of any kind to George Cannon's request for an immediate interview, allowing day after day to pass in inactivity, and wondering the while how she might excuse or explain her singular conduct when circumstances should bring the situation to a head. She knew that she ought either to go over to Turnhill, or write him with an appointment to see her at Lane End House; but she did nothing; nor did she say a word of the matter to Janet in the bedroom at nights. All that she could tell herself was that she did not want to see George Cannon; she was not honestly persuaded that she feared to see him. In the meantime, Edwin Clayhanger was invisible, though the removal of the Clayhanger household to the new residence at Bleakridge had made a considerable stir of straw and litter in Trafalgar Road.

On Tuesday in the following week she received a letter from Sarah Gailey. It was brought up to her room early in the morning by a half-dressed Alicia Orgreave, and she read it as she lay in bed. Sarah Gailey, struggling with the complexities of the Cedars, away in Hornsey, was unwell and gloomily desolate. She wrote that she suffered from terrible headaches on waking, and that she was often feverish, and that she had no energy whatever. 'I am at a very trying age for a woman,' she said. 'I don't know whether you understand, but I've come to a time of life that really upsets one above a bit, and I'm fit for nothing.' Hilda understood; she was flattered, even touched, by this confidence; it made her feel older, and more important in the world, and a whole generation away from Alicia, who was drawing up the blind with the cries and awkward gestures of a prattling infant. To the letter there was a postscript: 'Has George been to see you yet about me? He wrote me he should, but I haven't heard since. In fact, I've been waiting to hear. I'll say nothing about that yet. I'm ashamed you should be bothered. It's so important for you

to have a good holiday. Again, much love, S. G.' The prim handwriting got smaller and smaller towards the end of the postscript
and the end of the page, and the last lines were perfectly parallel
with the lower edge of the paper; all the others sloped feebly
downwards from left to right.

'Oh!' piped Alicia from the window. 'Maggie Clayhanger has
got her curtains up in the drawing-room! Oh! Aren't they proud
things! *Oh!* – I do believe she's caught me staring at her!' And
Alicia withdrew abruptly into the room, blushing for her detected
sin of ungenteel curiosity. She bumped down on the bed. 'Three
days more,' she said. 'Not counting today. Four, counting
today.'

'School?'

Alicia nodded, her finger in her mouth. 'Isn't it horrid, going
to school on a day like this? I hear you and Janet are off up to
Hillport this afternoon again, to play tennis. You do have
times!'

'No,' said Hilda. 'I've got to go to Turnhill this afternoon.'

'But Janet told me you were –' Her glance fell on the letter. 'Is
it business?'

'Yes.'

The child was impressed, and her change of tone, her frank
awe, gave pleasure to Hilda's vanity. 'Shall I go and tell Jan?
She isn't near dressed.'

'Yes, do.'

Off scampered Alicia, leaving the door unlatched behind her.

Hilda gazed at the letter, holding it limply in her left hand
amid the soft disorder of the counterpane. It had come to her,
an intolerably pathetic messenger and accuser, out of the
exacerbating frowsiness of the Cedars. Yesterday afternoon care-
ridden Sarah Gailey was writing it, with sighs, at the desk in her
stuffy, uncomfortable bedroom. As Hilda gazed at the formation
of the words, she could see the unhappy Sarah Gailey writing
them, and the letter was like a bit of Sarah Gailey's self, magically
and disconcertingly projected into the spacious, laughing home
of the Orgreaves, and into the mysterious new happiness that
was forming around Hilda. The Orgreaves, so far as Hilda could
discover, had no real anxieties. They were a joyous lot, favoured
alike by temperament and by fortune. And she, Hilda – what real

anxieties had she? None! She was sure of a small but adequate income. Her grief for her mother was assuaged. The problem of her soul no longer troubled: in part it had been solved, and in part it had faded imperceptibly away. Nor was she exercised about the future, about the 'new life'. Instead of rushing ardently to meet the future, she felt content to wait for its coming. Why disturb oneself? She was free. She was enjoying existence with the Orgreaves. Yes, she was happy in this roseate passivity.

The letter shook her, arousing as it did the sharp sense of her indebtedness to Sarah Gailey, who alone had succoured her in her long period of despairing infelicity. Had she guessed that it was Sarah Gailey's affair upon which George Cannon had desired to see her, she would not have delayed an hour; no reluctance to meet George Cannon would have caused her to tarry. But she had not guessed; the idea had never occurred to her.

She rose, picked up the envelope from the carpet, carefully replaced the letter in it, and laid it with love on the glittering dressing-table. Through the unlatched door she heard a tramping of unshod masculine feet in the passage, and the delightful curt greeting of Osmond Orgreave and his sleepy son Jimmie – splendid powerful males. She glanced at the garden, and at the garden of the Clayhangers, swimming in fresh sunshine. She glanced in the mirror, and saw the deshabille of her black hair and of her insecure nightgown, and thought: 'Truly, I am not so bad-looking! And how well I feel! How fond they all are of me! I'm just at the right age. I'm young, but I'm mature. I've had a lot of experience, and I'm not a fool. I'm strong – I could stand anything!' She put her shoulders back, with a challenging gesture. The pride of life was hers.

And then, this disturbing vision of Sarah Gailey, alone, unhappy, unattractive, enfeebled, ageing – ageing! It seemed to her inexpressibly cruel that people must grow old and weak and desolate; it seemed monstrous. A pang, momentary, but excruciating, smote her. She said to herself: 'Sarah Gailey has nothing to look forward to, except worry. Sarah Gailey is at the end, instead of at the beginning!'

II

When she got off the train at Turnhill station, early that afternoon, she had no qualm at the thought of meeting George Cannon; she was not even concerned to invent a decent excuse for her silence in relation to his urgent letter. She went to see him for the sake of Sarah Gailey, and because she apparently might be of use in some affair of Sarah's – she knew not what. She was proud that either Sarah or he thought that she could be of use, or that it was worth while consulting her. She had a grave air, as of one to whom esteem has brought responsibilities.

In Child Street, leading to High Street, she passed the office of Godlimans, the auctioneers. And there, among a group of white posters covering the large window, was a poster of the sale of 'valuable household furniture and effects removed from No. 15 Lessways Street'. And on the poster, in a very black line by itself, stood out saliently the phrase: 'Massive Bedroom Suite'. Her mother's! Hers! She had to stop and read the poster through, though she was curiously afraid of being caught in the act. All the principal items were mentioned by the faithful auctioneers; and the furniture, thus described, had a strange aspect of special importance, as if it had been subtly better, more solid, more desirable, than any other houseful of furniture in the town – Lessways's furniture! She sought for the date. The sale had taken place on the previous night, at the very hour when she was lolling and laughing in the drawing-room of Lane End House with the Orgreaves! The furniture was sold, dispersed, gone! The house was empty! The past was irremediably closed! The realization of this naturally affected her, raising phantoms of her mother, and of the face of the cab-driver as he remarked on the drawn blinds at the Cedars. But she was still more affected by the thought that the poster was on the window, and the furniture scattered, solely because she had willed it. She had said: 'Please sell all the furniture, and you needn't consult me about the sale. I don't want to know. I prefer not to know. Just get it done.' And it had been done! How mysteriously romantic! Some girls would not have sold the furniture, would not have dared to sell it, would have accepted the furniture and the house as a solemn charge, and gone on living among those relics, obedient to a tradition

But she had dared! She had willed – and the solid furniture had vanished away! And she was adventurously free!

She went forward. At the corner of Child Street and High Street the new Town Hall was rising to the skies. Already its walls were higher than the highest house in the vicinity. And workmen were crawling over it, amid dust, and a load of crimson bricks was trembling and revolving upwards on a thin rope that hung down from the blue. Glimpses of London had modified old estimates of her native town. Nevertheless, the new Town Hall still appeared extraordinarily large and important to her.

She saw the detested Arthur Dayson in the distance of the street, and crossed hurriedly to the Square, looking fixedly at the storeys above the ironmonger's so that Arthur Dayson could not possibly catch her eye. There was no sign of the *Five Towns Chronicle* in the bare windows of the second storey. This did not surprise her; but she was startled by the absence of the Karkeek wire-blinds from the first-floor windows, equally bare with those of the second. When she got to the entrance she was still more startled to observe that the Karkeek brass-plate had been removed. She climbed the long stairs apprehensively.

III

'Anybody here?' she called out timidly. She was in the clerks' office, which was empty; but she could hear movements in another room. The place seemed in process of being dismantled.

Suddenly George Cannon appeared in a doorway frowning.

'Good afternoon, Mr Cannon!'

'Good afternoon, Miss Lessways.' He spoke with stiff politeness. His face looked weary.

After a slight hesitation he advanced, and they shook hands. Hilda was nervous. Her neglect of his letter now presented itself to her as inexcusable. She thought: 'If he is vexed about it I shall have to humour him. I really can't blame him. He must think me very queer.'

'I was wondering what had become of you,' he said, amply polite, but not cordial.

'Well,' she said, 'every day I was expecting you to call again, or to send me a note or something . . . And what with one thing and another –'

'I dare say your time's been fully occupied,' he filled up her pause. And she fancied that he spoke in a peculiar tone. She absurdly fancied that he was referring to the time which she had publicly spent with Edwin Clayhanger at the Centenary. She conceived that he might have seen her and Edwin Clayhanger together.

'I had a letter from Miss Gailey this morning,' she said. 'And it seems that it's about her that you wanted –'

'Yes.'

'I do wish I'd known. If I'd had the slightest idea I should have come over instantly.' She spoke with eager seriousness, and then added, smiling as if in appeal to be favourably understand: 'I thought it was only about *my* affairs – sale or what not. And as I'd asked you to manage all these things exactly as you thought best, I didn't trouble –'

He laughed, and either forgave or forgot.

'Will you come this way?' he invited, in a new tone of friendliness. 'We're rather in a mess here.'

'You're all alone, too,' she said, following him into his room,

'Sowter's out,' he answered laconically, waiting for her to precede him. He said nothing as to the office-boy, nor as to Mr Karkeek. Hilda was now sure that something strange had happened.

'So you've heard from Sarah, have you?' he began, when they were both seated in his own room. There were still a lot of papers, though fewer than of old, on the broad desk; but the bookcase was quite empty, and several of the shelves in it had slipped from the horizontal; the front part of the shelves was a pale yellow, and behind that, an irregular dark band of dust indicated the varying depths of the vanished tomes. The forlornness of the bookcase gave a stricken air to the whole room.

'She's not well.'

'Or she imagines she's not well.'

'Oh no!' said Hilda warmly. 'It isn't imagination. She really isn't well.'

'You think so?'

'I don't think – I know!' Hilda spoke proudly, but with the

restraint which absolute certainty permits. She crushed, rather than resented, George Cannon's easy insinuation, full of the unjustified superiority of the male. How could he judge – how could any man judge? She had never before felt so sure of herself, so adult and experienced, as she felt then.

'But it's nothing serious?' he suggested with deference.

'N – no – not what you'd call serious,' said Hilda judicially, mysteriously.

'Because she wants to give up the boarding-house business altogether – that's all!'

Having delivered this dramatic blow, George Cannon smiled, as it were, quizzically. And Hilda was reassured about him. She had been thinking: 'Is he ruined? If he is not ruined, what is the meaning of these puzzling changes here?' And she had remembered her shrewd mother's hints, and her own later fears, concerning the insecurity of his position: and had studied his tired and worn face for an equivocal sign. But this smile, self-confident and firm, was not the smile of a ruined man; and his flashing glance seemed to be an omen of definite success.

'Wants to give it up?' exclaimed Hilda.

He nodded.

'But why? I thought she was doing rather well.'

'So she is.'

'Then why?'

'Ah!' George Cannon lifted his head with a gesture signifying enigma. 'That's just what I wanted to ask you. Hasn't she said anything to you?'

'As to giving it up? No! . . . So it was this that you wanted to see me about?'

He nodded. 'She wrote me a few days after you came away, and suggested I should see you and ask you what you thought.'

'But why me?'

'Well, she thinks the world of you, Sarah does.'

Hilda thought: 'How strange! She did nothing but look after me, and wait on me hand and foot, and I never helped her in any way; and yet she turns to me!' And she was extremely flattered and gratified, and was aware of a delicious increase of self-respect.

'But supposing she does give it up?' Hilda said aloud. 'What will she do?'

'Exactly!' said George Cannon, and then, in a very confidential, ingratiating manner: 'I wish you'd write to her and put some reason into her. She mustn't give it up. With her help – and you know in the management she's simply wonderful – with her help, I think I shall be able to bring something about that'll startle folks. Only, she mustn't throw me over. And she mustn't get too crotchety with the boarders. I've had some difficulty in that line, as it is. In fact, I've had to be rather cross. You know about the Boutwoods, for instance! Well, I've smoothed that over. . . It's nothing, nothing – if she'll keep her head. If she'll keep her head it's a gold mine – you'll see! Only – she wants a bit of managing. If you'd write –'

'I shan't write,' said Hilda. 'I shall go and see her – at once. I should have gone in any case, after her letter this morning saying how unwell she is. She wants company. She was so kind to me I couldn't possibly leave her in the lurch. I can't very well get away today, but I shall go tomorrow, and I shall drop her a line tonight.'

'It's very good of you, I'm sure,' said George Cannon. Obviously he was much relieved.

'Not at all!' Hilda protested. She felt very content and happy.

'The fact is,' he went on, 'there's nobody but you can do it. Your mother was the only real friend she ever had. And this is the first time she's been left alone up there, you see. I'm quite sure you can save the situation.'

He was frankly depending on her for something which he admitted he could not accomplish himself. Those two people, George Cannon and Sarah Gailey, had both instinctively turned to her in a crisis. None could do what she could do. She, by the force of her individuality, could save the situation. She was no longer a girl, but a mature and influential being. Her ancient diffidence before George Cannon had completely gone; she had no qualms, no foreboding, no dubious sensation of weakness. Indeed, she felt herself in one respect his superior, for his confidence in Sarah Gailey's housewifely skill, his conviction that it was unique and would be irreplaceable, struck her as somewhat naïve, as being yet another example of the absurd family pride which she and her mother had often noticed in the Five Towns. She was not happy at the prospect of so abruptly quitting the delights of Lane End House and the vicinity of Edwin Clayhanger; she was not happy at the prospect of postponing the consideration of plans for her own existence; she was not happy at the prospect of Sarah Gailey's pessimistic complainings. She was above happiness. She was above even that thrill of sharp and intense vitality which in times past had ennobled trouble and misery. She had the most exquisite feeling of triumphant self-justification. She was splendidly conscious of power. She was indispensable.

And the dismantled desolation of the echoing office, and the mystery of George Cannon's personal position, somehow gave a strange poignancy to her mood.

They talked of indifferent matters: her property, the Orgreaves, even the defunct newspaper, as to which George Cannon shrugged his shoulders. Then the conversation drooped.

'I shall go up by the four train tomorrow,' she said, clinching the interview, and rising.

'I may go up by that train myself,' said George Cannon.

She started. 'Oh! are you going to Hornsey too?'

'No! Not Hornsey. I've other business.'

I

ON the following afternoon Hilda travelled alone by the local train from Bleakridge to Knype, the central station where all voyagers for London, Birmingham, and Manchester had to forgather in order to take the fast expresses that unwillingly halted there, and there only, in their skimming flights across the district. It was a custom of Five Towns hospitality that a departing guest should be accompanied as far as Knype and stowed with personal attentions into the big train. But on this occasion Hilda had wished otherwise. 'I should *prefer* nobody to go with me to Knype,' she had said, in a characteristic tone, to Janet. It was enough. The family had wondered; but it was enough. The family knew its singular, its mysterious Hilda. And instead of at Knype, the leave-takings had occurred at the little wayside station of Bleakridge, with wavy moorland behind, factory chimneys in front, and cinder and shard heaps all around. Hilda had told Janet: 'Mr Cannon may be meeting me at Knype. He's probably going to London too.' And the discreet Janet, comprehending Hilda, had not even mentioned this fact to the rest of the family.

George Cannon, in a light summer suit and straw hat, was already on the platform at Knype. Hilda had feared that at Bleakridge he might be looking out of the window of the local train, which started from Turnhill; she had desired not to meet him in the presence of any of the Orgreaves. But either he had caught the previous train to Knype, or he had driven down. Holding a Gladstone bag and a stick in one hand, he stood talking to another man of about his own age and height. The conversation was vivacious, at any rate on George Cannon's part. Hilda passed close by him amid the populous stir of the expectant platform. He saw her, turned, and raised his hat, but in a perfunctory, preoccupied manner; and instantly resumed the speech to his companion. Hilda recognized the latter. It was 'young

Lawton', son and successor to 'old Lawton', the most famous lawyer in the Five Towns. Young Lawton had a branch office at Turnhill, and lived in an important house half-way between Turnhill and Bursley, where, behind the Town Hall, was the historic principal office of the firm.

The express came loudly in, and Hilda, having climbed into a second-class compartment, leaned out from it, to descry her porter and bestow on him a threepenny bit. George Cannon and young Lawton were still in argument, and apparently quite indifferent to the train. Young Lawton's thin face had its usual faint, harsh smile; his limbs were moveless in an exasperating and obstinate calm; Hilda detested the man from his mere looks. But George Cannon was very obviously under excitement. His face was flushed; he moved his free arm violently – even the Gladstone bag swung to and fro; he punctuated his sentences with sharp, angry nods of the head, insisting and protesting and insisting, while the other, saying much less, maintained his damnable stupid disdainful grin.

Would he let the train go, in his feverish preoccupation? Hilda was seriously afraid that he would. The last trunks were flung into the front van, the stationmaster in his tall hat waved curtly to the glittering guard; the guard waved his flag, and whistled; a porter banged the door of Hilda's compartment, ignoring her gestures; the engine whistled. And at that moment George Cannon, throwing apparently a last malediction at young Lawton, sprang towards the train, and, seeing Hilda's face, rushed to the door which she strained to open again.

'I was afraid you'd be left behind,' she said, as he dropped his bag on the seat and the affronted stationmaster himself shut the door.

'Not quite!' ejaculated Cannon grimly.

The smooth, irresistible gliding of the train became apparent, establishing a sudden aloof calm. Hilda perceived that all her muscles were tense.

In the compartment was a middle-aged couple.

'What's this place?' asked the woman.

'Looks like Tamworth,' said the man sleepily.

'Knype, sir!' George Cannon corrected him very sharply. He was so wrought up that he had omitted even to shake hands with

Hilda. Making no effort to talk, and showing no curiosity about Hilda's welfare or doings, he moved uneasily on his seat, and from time to time opened and shut the Gladstone bag. Gradually the flush paled from his face.

At Lichfield the middle-aged couple took advice from a porter and stumbled out of the train.

II

'We're fairly out of the smoke now,' said Hilda, when the train began to move again. As a fact, they had been fairly out of the smoke of the Five Towns for more than half an hour; but Hilda spoke at random, timidly, nervously, for the sake of speaking. And she was as apologetic as though it was she herself who by some untimely discretion had annoyed George Cannon.

'Yes, thank God!' he replied fiercely, blowing with pleasure upon the embers of his resentment. 'And I'll take good care I never go into it again – to live, that is!'

'Really?' she murmured, struck into an extreme astonishment.

He produced a cigar and a match-box.

'May I?' he demanded carelessly, and accepted her affirmative as of course.

'You've heard about my little affair?' he asked, after lighting the cigar. And he gazed at her curiously.

'No.'

'Do you mean to say that none of the Orgreaves has said anything this last day or two?' He leaned forward. They were in opposite corners.

'No,' she repeated stiffly. Nevertheless, she remembered a peculiar glance of Tom's to his father on the previous day, when George Cannon's name had been mentioned.

'Well,' said he. 'You surprise me! That's all!'

'But –' She stopped, full of misgivings.

'Never head any gossip about me – never?' he persisted, as it were, menacing her.

She shook her head.

'Never heard that I'm not really a solicitor?'

'Oh! well – I think mother once did say something –'

'I thought so.'

'But I don't understand those things,' she said simply. 'Is anything the matter? Is –?'

'Nothing!' he replied, calm and convincing. 'Only I've been done! Done! You'll hear about it some day, I dare say . . . Shall I tell you? Would you like me to tell you?' He smiled rather boyishly and leaned back.

'Yes,' she nodded.

His attitude was very familiar, recalling their former relation of employer and employed. It seemed as natural to her as to him that he should not too ceremoniously conceal his feelings or disguise his mood.

'Well, you see, I expect I know as much about law as any of 'em, but I've never been admitted, and so –' He stopped, perceiving that she did not comprehend the significance of such a word as 'admitted'. 'If you want to practise as a solicitor you have to pass examinations, and I never have passed examinations. Very expensive, all that! And I couldn't afford when I was young. It isn't the exams that are difficult – you may tell that from the fellows that pass them. Lawton, for instance. But after a certain age exams become a nuisance. However, I could do everything else. I might have had half a dozen situations as managing clerk in the Five Towns if I'd wanted. Only I didn't want! I wanted to be on my own. I could get clients as quick as any of them. *And* quicker! So I found Karkeek – the excellent Mr Karkeek! Another of the bright ones that could pass the exams! Oh! He'd passed the exams all right! He'd spent five years and I don't know how many hundred pounds in passing the exams, and with it all he couldn't get above a couple of pounds a week. There are hundreds of real solicitors up and down the country who aren't earning more. And they aren't worth more. But I gave him more, and a lot more. Just to use his name on my door and my blinds. See? In theory I was his clerk, but in reality he was mine. It was all quite clear. He understood – I should think he did, by Jove!' George Cannon laughed shortly. 'Every one understood. I got a practice together in no time. *He* didn't do it. He wouldn't have got a practice together in a thousand years. I had the second-best practice in Turnhill, and I should soon have had the best – if I hadn't been done.'

'Yes?' said Hilda. The confidence flattered her.

'Well, Karkeek came into some money, – and he simply walked out of the office! Simply walked out! Didn't give me time to turn round. I'd always treated him properly. But he was jealous.'

'What a shame!' Hilda's scorn shrivelled up Mr Karkeek. There was nothing that she detested so much as disloyalty.

'Yes. I couldn't stop him, of course. No formal agreement between us. Couldn't be, in a case like ours! So he had me. He'd taken my wages quick enough as long as it suited him. Then he comes into money, and behaves like that. Jealousy! They were all jealous – always had been. I was doing too well. So I had the whole gang down on me instantly like a thousand of bricks. They knew I was helpless, and so they came on. Special meeting of the committee of the North Staffordshire Law Society, if you please! Rumours of prosecution – oh yes! I don't know what! ... All because I wouldn't take the trouble to pass their wretched exams ... Why, I could pass their exams on my head, if I hadn't anything better to do. But I have. At first I thought I'd retire for five years and pass their exams, and then come back and make 'em sit up. And wouldn't I have made 'em sit up! But then I said to myself, "No. It isn't good enough." '

Hilda frowned. 'What isn't?'

'What? The Five Towns isn't good enough! I can find something better than the law, and I can find something better than the Five Towns! ... And here young Lawton has the impudence to begin to preach to me on Knype platform, and to tell me I'm wise in going! He's the President of the local Law Society, you know! No end of a President! And hasn't even got gumption enough to keep his father's practice together! Stupid ass! Well, I let him have it, and straight! He's no worse than the rest. They've got no brains in this district. And they're so narrow – narrow isn't the word! Thick-headed's the word. Stupid! Mean! ... Mean! ... What did it matter to them? I kept to all their rules. There was a real solicitor on the premises, and there'd soon have been another, if I'd had time. No concern of theirs how the money was divided between me and the real solicitor. But they were jealous – there you are! They don't understand enterprise. They hate it. Nothing ever moves in the Five Towns. And they've got no manners – I do believe that's the worst. Look at

Lawton's manners! Nothing but a boor! They aren't civilized yet
– that's what's the matter with them! That's what my father used
to say. Barbarians, he used to say. "*Ce sont des barbares!*" . . *
Kids used to throw stones at him because of his neck-tie. The
grown-ups chuck a brick at anything they don't quite fancy.
That's their idea of wit.'

Hilda was afraid of his tempestuous mood. But she enjoyed
her fear, as she might have enjoyed exposure to a dangerous
storm. She enjoyed the sensation of her fragility and helplessness
there, cooped up with him in the close intimacy of the compartment. She was glad that he did not apologize to her for his lack
of restraint, nor foolishly pretend that he was boring her.

'It does seem a shame!' she murmured, her eyes candidly admitting that she felt enormously flattered.

He sighed and laughed. 'How often have I heard my father
say that – "*Ce sont des barbares!*" Peels only brought him over
because they could find nobody in the Five Towns civilized
enough to do the work that he did . . . I can imagine how he
must have felt when he first came here! . . . My God! . . . Environment! . . . I tell you what – it's only lately I've realized how I
loathe the provinces!'

The little interior in which they were, swept steadily and
smoothly across the central sunlit plain of England, passing
canals and brooks and cottages and churches – silent and stolid
in that English stupidity that he was criticizing. And Hilda saw
of George Cannon all that was French in him. She saw him quite
anew, as something rather exotic and entirely marvellous. She
thought: 'When I first met him, I said to myself he was a most
extraordinary man. And I was right. I was more right than I ever
imagined. No one down there has any idea of what he really is.
They're too stupid, as he says.'

He imposed on her his scorn of the provincial. She had to
share it. She had a vision of the Five Towns as a smoky blotch
on the remote horizon – negligible, crass, ridiculous in its heavy
self-complacency. The very Orgreaves themselves were tinged
with this odious English provincialism.

He smiled to himself, and then said, very quietly: 'It isn't of
the least importance, you know. In fact I'm rather glad. I've
never had any difficulty in making money, and when I've settled

up everything down there I shan't be precisely without. And I shall have no excuse for not branching out in a new line.'

She meekly encouraged him to continue.

'Oh yes!' he went on. 'The law isn't the only thing – not by a long way. And besides, I'm sick of it. Do you know what the great thing of the future is, I mean the really great thing – the smashing big thing?' He smiled, kindly and confidential.

She too smiled, shaking her head.

'Well, I'll tell you. Hotels!'

'Hotels?' She was perfectly nonplussed.

'Hotels! There'll be more money and more fun to be got out of hotels, soon, than out of any other kind of enterprise in the world. You should see those hotels that are going up in London! They'd give you a start, and no mistake! Yes, hotels! There aren't twenty people in England who know what a hotel is! But I know!' He paused, and added reflectively, in a comically naïve tone: 'Curious how these things come to you, bit by bit! Now, if it hadn't been for Sarah – and that boarding-house –'

He was using his straw hat as a fan. With an unexpected and almost childlike gesture he suddenly threw the hat up on to the rack above his head. 'How's that?'

'What a boy he is, after all!' thought Hilda sympathetically, wondering why in the midst of all her manifold astonishment she felt so light-hearted and gay.

'Funny parcel you've got up there!' he idly observed, glancing from one rack to the other.

The parcel contained Mrs Orgreave's generous conception of a repast proper to be eaten in a train in place of high tea. He helped her to eat it.

As the train approached London he resumed his manhood. And he was impeccably adult as he conducted her from Euston to King's Cross, and put her into a train in a corner of the station that the summer twilight had already taken possession of.

III

Late at night Hilda sat with Sarah Gailey in the landlady's small bedroom at the Cedars. It was lighted by a lamp, because the builder of the house, hating excess, had thought fit not to carry gas-pipes higher than the first floor. A large but old bedstead filled half the floor space. On the shabby dressing-table a pile of bills and various papers lay near the lamp. Clothes were hung behind the door, and a vague wisp of muslin moved slightly in the warm draught from the tiny open window. There were two small cane-chairs, enamelled, on which the women sat, close to each other, both incommoded by the unwholesome sultriness of the only chamber that could be spared for the private use of the house-mistress. This small bedroom was Sarah Gailey's home; its amenities were the ultimate nightly reward of her labours. If George Cannon had obtained possession of the Cedars as an occupation for Sarah, this room and Sarah's pleasure therein were the sole justification of the entire mansion.

As Hilda looked at Sarah Gailey's bowed head, but little greyed, beneath the ray of the lamp, and at her shrivelled, neurotic, plaintive face in shadow, and at her knotty hands loosely clasped, she contrasted her companion and the scene with the youthfulness and the spaciousness and the sturdy gay vigour of existence in the household of the Orgreaves. She thought, with a renewed sense of the mysterious strangeness of life: 'Last night I was there, far away – all those scores of miles of fields and towns are between! – and tonight I am here. Down there I was nothing but an idler. Here I am the strongest. I am indispensable. I am the one person on whom she depends. Without me everything will go to pieces.' And she thought of George Cannon's vast enigmatic projects concerning grand hotels. In passing the immense pile of St Pancras on the way from Euston to King's Cross, George Cannon had waved his hand and said: 'Look at that! Look at that! It's something after that style that I want for a toy! And I'll have it!' Yes, the lofty turrets of St Pancras had not intimidated him. He, fresh from little Turnhill and from defeats, could rise at once to the height of them, and by the force of imagination make them his own! He could turn abruptly from the law – to hotels! A disconcerting man! And the mere tone in which he mentioned his enterprise seemed, in a most surprising way, to dignify hotels, and even boarding-houses; to give romance to the perfectly unromantic business of lodging and catering! . . . And the seed from which he was to grow the magic plant sat in the room there with Hilda: that bowed head! The ambition and

the dream resembled St Pancras: the present reality was the
Cedars, and Sarah's poor, stuffy little bedroom in the Cedars.

Sarah began to cry, weakly.

'But what's the matter?' asked Hilda, the strong succourer.

'Nothing. Only it's such a relief to me you've come.'

Hilda deprecated lightly. 'I should have come sooner if I'd
known. You ought to have sent word before.'

'No, I couldn't. After all, what is it? I'm only silly. There's
nothing really the matter. The minute you come I can see that.
I can even stand those Boutwoods if you're here. You know
George made it up with them; and I won't say he wasn't right.
But I had to put my pride in my pocket. And yesterday it nearly
made me scream out to see Mrs Boutwood stir her tea.'

'But why?'

'I don't know. It's nerves, that's what it is ... Well, I've got
to go through these.' She fingered the papers on the dressing-
table with her left hand while drying her tears with the right.
'He's very wishful for proper accounts, George is. That's right
enough. But – well – I think I can make a shilling go as far as
anyone, and choose flesh-meat with anyone, too – that I will say
– but these accounts ...! George is always wanting to know
how much it costs a head a week for this that and the other ...
It's all very well for him, but if he had the servants to look after
and –'

'I'm going to keep your accounts for you,' Hilda soothed her.

'But –'

'I'm going to keep your accounts for you.' And she thought:
'How exactly like mother I was just then!'

It appeared to Hilda that she was making a promise, and
shouldering a responsibility, against her will, and perhaps
against her common sense. She might keep accounts at the Cedars
for a week, a fortnight, a month. But she could not keep accounts
there indefinitely. She was sowing complications for herself.
Freedom and change and luxury were what she deemed she
desired; not a desk in a boarding-house. And yet something
within her compelled her to say in a firm, sure, kindly voice:

'Now give me all those papers, Miss Gailey.'

And amid indefinite regret and foreboding, she was proud and
happy in her role of benefactor.

When Hilda at length rose to go to her own room, Sarah Gailey had to move her chair so that she might pass. At the door both hesitated for an instant, and then Hilda with a sudden gesture advanced her lips. It was the first time she and Sarah had ever kissed. The contact with that desiccated skin intensified to an extraordinary degree Hilda's emotional sympathy for the ageing woman. She thought, poignantly: 'Poor old thing!'

And when she was on the dark little square landing under the roof, Sarah, holding the lamp, called out in a whisper:

'Hilda!'

'Well?'

'Did he say anything to you about Brighton?'

'Brighton?' She perceived with certainty from Sarah's eager and yet apologetic tone, that the question had been waiting for utterance throughout the evening, and that Sarah had lacked courage for it until the kiss had enheartened her. And also she perceived that Sarah was suspecting her of being somehow in conspiracy with George Cannon.

'Yes,' said Sarah. 'He's got into his head that Brighton's the only place for this boarding-house business if it's to be properly done.'

'He never said a word to me about Brighton,' Hilda whispered positively.

'Oh!'

Hilda descended the stairs, groping. Brighton? What next?

CHAPTER 3
AT BRIGHTON

I

SHE thought vividly, one afternoon about three months later, of that final scrap of conversation. Just as she had sat opposite George Cannon in a second-class compartment, so now she was sitting opposite Sarah Gailey in a second-class compartment. The train, having passed Lewes, was within a few minutes of Brighton. And following behind them, somewhere at the tail of the train, were certain trunks containing all that she possessed and all that Sarah Gailey possessed of personal property – their sole chattels and paraphernalia on earth. George Cannon had willed it and brought it about. He was to receive them on the platform of Brighton Station. She had not seen very much of him in the interval, for he had been continually on the move between Brighton and Turnhill. 'In a moment we shall all be together again,' she reflected. 'This meeting also will happen, as everything else has happened, and a new period will definitely have begun.' And she sat and stared at the closed eyes of the desiccated Sarah Gailey, and waited for the instant of arrival apprehensively and as it were incredulously – not with fear, not with pleasure, but with the foreboding of adventure and a curious idea that the instant of arrival never would come.

For thirteen weeks, which had gone very quickly, she had devoted herself to Sarah Gailey, acting as George Cannon's precursor, prophet, and expounder. While the summer cooled into autumn, and the boarding-house season slackened and once more feebly brightened, she had daily conversed with Sarah about George's plans, making them palatable to her, softening the shocks of them, and voluntarily promising not to quit her until the crisis was past. She had had to discourse on the unique advantages of Brighton as a field for George's enterprise, and on George's common sense and on Sarah's common sense, and the interdependence of the two. When the news came that George had acquired down there a house in going order, she had had to prove that it was not the end of the world that was announced. When the news came that George had re-sold the Cedars to its original occupier, she had had to prove that the transaction did not signify a mysterious but mortal insult to Sarah. When the news came that the Cedars must be vacated before noon on a given Saturday, she had had to begin all her demonstrations afresh, and in addition attempt to persuade Sarah that George was not utterly mad – buying and selling boarding-house tenancies all over the South of England! – and that the exit from the Cedars would not be the ruin of dignity and peace, and the commencement of fatal disasters. In the hour when Sarah Gailey learnt the immutable Saturday of departure, the Cedars, which had been her hell, promised to become, on that very Saturday, a paradise.

On the whole, the three months had constituted a quarter of exceeding difficulty and delicacy. The first month had been rendered memorable by Sarah's astonishing behaviour when Hilda had desired to pay, as before, for her board and lodging. The mere offer of the money had made plain to Sarah – what she then said she had always suspected – that Hilda was her enemy in disguise and (like the rest) bent on humiliating her, and outraging her most sacred feelings. In that encounter, but in no other, Sarah had won. The opportune withdrawal of the Boutwoods from the boarding-house had assisted the establishment of peace. When the Boutwoods left, Miss Gailey seemed to breathe the drawing-room air as though it were ozone of the mountains. But her joy had been quickly dissipated, for to dissipate joy was her chief recreation. A fortnight before the migration to Brighton, Hilda, contemplating all that had to be done, had thought, aghast: 'I shall never be able to humour her into doing it all!' Closing of accounts, dismissals, inventories, bills, receipts, packing, decision concerning trains, reception of the former proprietor (especially that!), good-byes, superintending the stowage of luggage on the cab . . .! George Cannon had not once appeared in the last sensitive weeks, and he had therein been wise. And all that had to be done had been done – not by Hilda, but by Sarah Gailey the touchy and the competent. Hilda had done little but the humouring.

II

And there sat Sarah Gailey, deracinated and captive, to prove
how influential a person Hilda was! With the eyes shut, Sarah's
worn face under her black bonnet had precisely the aspect of a
corpse – and the corpse of somebody who had expired under the
weight of all the world's woe! Hilda thought: 'When she is dead
she will look just like that! . . . And one day, sooner or later, she
will be dead.' Strange that Sarah Gailey, with no malady except
her chronic rheumatism, and no material anxiety, and every
prospect of security in old age, could not be content, could not
at any rate refrain from being miserable! But she could not. She
was an exhaustless fount of worry and misery. 'I suppose I like
her,' thought Hilda. 'But why do I like her? She isn't agreeable.
She isn't amusing . . . She isn't pretty. She isn't even kind, now.
She's only depressing and tedious. As soon as she's fixed up
here, I shall go. I shall leave her. I've done enough, and I've had
enough. I must attend to my own affairs a bit. After all –' And
then Hilda's conscience interrupted: 'But can you leave her
altogether? Without you, what will happen to her? She's getting
older and worse every day. Perhaps in a few years she won't even
be competent. Already she isn't perhaps quite, quite as competent
as she was.' And Hilda said: 'Well, of course, I shall have to
keep an eye on her; come and see her sometimes – often.' And
she knew that as long as they both lived she could never be
free from a sense of responsibility towards Sarah Gailey. Useless
to argue: 'It's George Cannon's affair, not mine!' Useless to ask:
'*Why* should I feel responsible?' Only after she had laid Sarah
Gailey in the tomb would she be free. 'And that day too will
come!' she thought again. 'I shall have to go through it, and I
shall go through it!'

The poignant romance of existence enveloped her in its beautiful
veils. And through these veils she saw, vague and diminished, the
far vista of the hours which she had spent with the Orgreaves.
She saw the night of Edwin Clayhanger's visit, and herself and
him together in the porch; and she remembered the shock of his
words, 'There's no virtue in believing.' The vision was like that
of another and quite separate life. Would she ever go back to it?

Janet was her friend, in theory her one intimate friend; she had seen her once in London – beautiful, agreeable, affectionate, intelligent; all the Orgreaves were lovable. The glance of Edwin Clayhanger, and the sincerity of his smile, had affected her in a manner absolutely unique ... But would she ever go back? It seemed to her fantastic, impossible, that she should ever go back. It seemed to her that she was netted by destiny. In any case she knew that she could not, meanwhile, give to that group in Bursley even a part of herself. Hilda could never give a part of herself. Moreover, she was a bad letter-writer. And so, if among themselves the group at Bursley charged her with inconstancy, she must accept the accusation, to which she was inevitably exposed by the very ardour of her temperament.

The putting-on of brakes took her unawares. The train was in Brighton, sliding over the outskirts of the town. Miss Gailey opened her apprehensive eyes. Hilda saw steep streets of houses that sprawled on the hilly mounds of the great town like ladders: reminiscent of certain streets of her native district, yet quite different, a physiognomy utterly foreign to her. This, then, was Brighton. That which had been a postmark became suddenly a reality, shattering her preconceptions of it, and disappointing her she knew not why. She glanced forward, through the window, and saw the cavern of the station. In a few seconds they would have arrived, and her formal mission would be over. She was very agitated and very nervous. George Cannon had promised to meet them. Would he meet them?

The next instant she saw the platform. She saw George Cannon, conspicuous and debonair in a new suit, swinging his ebony stick. The train stopped. He descried them.

'There he is!' she said, bravely pretending to be gay. And she thought: 'I could not believe that this moment would come, but it has come.'

She had anticipated relief from this moment, but she was aware of no relief. On the contrary, she felt most uncomfortably apologetic to Sarah Gailey for George Cannon, and to George Cannon for Sarah Gailey. She had the constraint of a sinner. And, by the side of George Cannon on the platform, she was aware of her shabbiness and of her girlish fragility. Nevertheless, she put her shoulders back with a gesture like his own, thinking proudly, and trying to make her eyes speak: 'Well, here is Sarah Gailey – thanks to me!'

As Sarah greeted him, Hilda observed, with some dismay, a curious, very slight stiffening of her demeanour – familiar phenomenon, which denoted that Sarah was in the grip of a secret grievance: 'Poor old thing!' she thought ruefully. 'I'd imagined she'd forgiven him for bringing her here; but she hasn't.'

III

They drove down from the station in an open carriage, un-encumbered by the trunks, which George Cannon had separately disposed of. He sat with his back to the horse, opposite the two women, and talked at intervals about the weather, the prospects of the season, and the town. His familiarity with the town was apparently such that he seemed to be a native of it, and even in some mysterious way to have assisted in its creation and develop-ment; so that he took pride in its qualities and accepted responsi-bility for its defects. When he ceremoniously saluted two women who went by in another carriage, Hilda felt sharply the inferiority of an ignorant stranger in presence of one for whom the place had no secrets.

Her first disappointment changed slowly into expectant and hopeful curiosity. The quaint irregularities of the architecture, and the vastness of the thronged perspectives, made promises to her romantic sense. The town seemed to be endless as London. There were hotels, churches, chapels, libraries, and music-shops on every hand. The more ordinary features of main streets – the marts of jewellery, drapery, and tobacco – had an air of grandiose respectability; while the narrow alleys that curved enigmatically away between the lofty buildings of these fine thoroughfares beckoned darkly to the fancy. The multiplicity of beggars, louts, and organ-grinders was alone a proof of Brighton's success in the world; the organ-grinders, often a man and a woman yoked together, were extraordinarily English, genteel and prosperous as they trudged in their neat, middle-class raiment through the gritty mud of the macadam, stolidly ignoring the menace of high-stepping horses and disdainful glittering wheels. Brighton was evidently a city apart. Nevertheless, Hilda did not as yet understand why George Cannon should have considered it to be the sole field worthy of his enterprise.

Then the carriage rounded into King's Road, and suddenly she saw the incredible frontage of hotels, and *pensions*, and apartments, and she saw the broad and boundless promenade alive with all its processions of pleasure, and she saw the ocean. And everything that she had seen up to that moment fell to the insignificance of a background. She understood.

After a blusterous but mild autumn day the scarlet sun was setting calmly between a saffron sky and saffron water; it flashed upon waves and sails and flags, and upon the puddles in the road, and upon bow-windows and flowered balconies, giving glory to human pride. The carriage, merged in a phalanx of carriages, rolled past innumerable splendid houses, and every house without exception was a hostel and an invitation. Some were higher than any she had ever seen; and one terrific building, in course of construction, had already far overtopped the highest of its neighbours. She glanced at George Cannon, who, by a carefully casual demeanour, was trying not to take the credit of the entire spectacle; and she admitted that he was indeed wonderful.

'Of course, Sarah,' he said, as the carriage shortly afterwards turned up Preston Street, where the dying wind roughly caught them, 'we aren't beginning with anything as big as all that, so you needn't shiver in your shoes. You know what my notion is' – he included Hilda in his address – 'my notion is to get some experience first in a smaller house. We must pay for our experience, and my notion is to pay as little as possible. I can tell you there's quite a lot of things that have to be picked up before you've got the hang of a town like this – quite a lot.'

Sarah grimly nodded. She had scarcely spoken.

'We're beginning rather well. I've told you all about the Watchett sisters, haven't I? They're an income, a positive income! And then Boutwood and his wife have decided to come – did I tell you?'

'Bou –'

The syllable escaped explosively from Sarah Gailey's mouth, overcoming her stern guard. Instantly, by a tremendous effort, she checked the flow. But the violent shock of the news had convulsed her whole being. The look on her face was changed to desperation. Hilda trembled, and even the splendid and ever-resurgent George Cannon was discountenanced. Not till then had Hilda realized with what intense bitterness the souvenir of the Boutwoods festered in Sarah Gailey's unreasoning heart.

IV

'Here we are!' said George Cannon jauntily, as the carriage stopped in front of No. 59 Preston Street. But his jauntiness seemed factitious. The demeanour of all three was diffident and unnatural, for now had arrived the moment when George Cannon had to submit his going-concern to the ordeal of inspection by the women, and especially by Sarah Gailey. There the house stood, a physical fact, forcing George to justify it, and beseeching clemency from the two women. The occasion was critical; therefore everybody had to pretend that it was a perfectly ordinary occasion, well knowing the futility of the pretence. And the inevitable constraint was acutely aggravated by Sarah's silent and terrible reception of the news concerning the Boutwoods.

While George Cannon was paying the driver, Sarah and Hilda hesitated awkwardly on the pavement, their hands occupied with small belongings. They had the sensation of being foreigners to the house; they could not even mount the steps without his protection; scarcely might they in decency examine the frontage of the house. They could not, however, avoid seeing that a workman was fixing a new and splendid brass-plate at the entrance, and that this plate bore the words, 'Cannon's Boarding-house.' Hilda thought, startled: 'At last he is using his own name!'

He turned to them.

'You have a view of the sea from the bow-window of the drawing-room – on the first floor,' he remarked.

Neither Hilda nor Sarah responded.

'And of course from the other bow-window higher up,' he added, almost pitifully, in his careful casualness.

Hilda felt sorry for him, and she could not understand why she felt sorry, why it seemed a shame that he should be mysteriously compelled thus to defend the house before it had been attacked.

'Oh yes!' she murmured foolishly, almost fatuously.

The street and the house were disappointing. After the grandeur of the promenade, the street appeared shabby and third-rate; it had the characteristics of a side street; it was the retreat of those who could not afford anything better, and its base inhabitants walked out on to the promenade and swaggeringly feigned to be the equals of their superiors. The house also was shabby and third-rate – with its poor little glimpse of the sea. Although larger than the Cedars, it was noticeably smaller and meaner than any house on the promenade; and whereas the Cedars was detached, No. 59 was not even semi-detached, but one of a gaunt, tall row of stuccoed and single-fronted dwellings. It looked like a boarding-house (which the Cedars did not), and not all the style of George Cannon's suit and cane and manner, as he mounted the steps, nor the polish of his new brass-plate, could redeem it from the disgrace of being a very ordinary boarding-house.

George Cannon had made a serious mistake in bringing the carriage round by the promenade. True, he had exhibited the glory of Brighton, but he had done so to the detriment of his new enterprise. That No. 59 ought to be regarded as merely an inexpensive field for the acquiring of preliminary experience did not influence the judgement of the women in the slightest degree. For them it was a house that rightly apologized for itself, and whose apologetic air deserved only a condescending tolerance.

The front door stood open for the convenience of the artisan who was screwing at the brass-plate. He moved aside, with the servility that always characterizes the worker in a city of idlers, and the party passed into a long narrow hall, whose walls were papered to imitate impossible blocks of mustard-coloured marble. The party was now at home.

'Here we are!' said Hilda, with a gaiety that absolutely desolated herself, and in the same instant she remembered that George Cannon had preceded her in saying 'Here we are!' She looked from the awful glumness of Sarah Gailey to the equally awful alacrity of George Cannon, and felt as though she had committed some crime whose nature she could not guess.

A middle-aged maid appeared, like a suspicious scout, at the far end of the hall, beyond the stairs, having opened a door which showed a glimpse of a kitchen.

'That tea ready?' asked George Cannon.

'No, sir,' said the maid plumply.

'Well, let it be got ready.'

'Yes, sir.' The maid vanished, flouncing.

Sarah Gailey, with a heavy sigh, dropped her small belongings on to a narrow bare table that stood against the wall near the foot of the stairs. Daylight was fading.

'Well,' said George Cannon, balancing his hat on his cane, 'your luggage will be here directly. This is the dining-room.' He pushed at a yellow-grained door.

The women followed him into the dining-room, and stared at the dining-room in silence.

'There's a bedroom behind,' he said, as they came out, and he displayed the bedroom behind. 'That's the kitchen.' He pointed to the adjoining door.

'The drawing-room's larger,' he said. 'It includes the width of the hall.'

They climbed the narrow stairs after him wearily. The door of the drawing-room was ajar, and the chatter of thin feminine voices could be heard within. George Cannon gave a soundless warning whisper: 'The Watchetts.' And Sarah Gailey frowned back the information that she did not wish to meet the Watchetts just then. With every precaution against noise, George Cannon opened two other doors, showing bedrooms. And then, as it were, hypnotized by him, the women climbed another flight of narrow stairs, darkening, and saw more rooms, and then still another flight, and still more rooms, and finally the boasted view of the sea! After all, Hilda was obliged to admit to herself that the house was more impressive than she had at first supposed. Although single-fronted, it was deep, and there were two bed-rooms on the first floor, and four each – two large and two small – on the second and third. Eleven in all, they had seen, of which three were occupied by the Watchetts, and one, temporarily, by George Cannon. The rest were empty; but the season had scarcely begun, and the Boutwoods were coming. George Cannon had said grandly that Hilda must choose her room; she chose the smallest on the top floor. The furniture, if shabby and old-fashioned, was everywhere ample.

They descended, and not a word had been said about Sarah's room.

On the first floor landing, where indeed the danger was acutest, they were trapped by two of the Watchetts. These elderly ladies shot almost roguishly out of the drawing-room, and by their smiles struck the descending party into immobility.

'Oh! We saw you arrive, Mr Cannon!' said the elder, shaking her head. 'So this is Miss Gailey! Good afternoon, Miss Gailey! So pleased to make your acquaintance!'

There was handshaking. Then it was Hilda's turn.

'We're so sorry our eldest sister isn't here to welcome you to No. 59,' said the younger, 'She's had to go to London for the day. We're very fond of No. 59. There's no place quite like it, to our minds. And we're quite sure we shall be quite as comfortable with dear Miss Gailey as we were with dear Mrs Granville, poor thing. It was quite a wrench when we had to say good-bye to her last night. Do come into the drawing-room, please! There's a beautiful view of the sea!'

Sarah Gailey hesitated. A noise of bumping came from the hall below.

'I think that's the luggage,' she said. The smile with which she forced herself to respond to the fixed simper of the Watchetts seemed to cause her horrible torment. She motioned nervously to George Cannon, who was nearest the stairs.

'A little later, then! A little later, then!' said both the Watchetts, bowing the party away with the most singular grimaces.

In the hall, a lad, perspiring and breathing quickly, stood behind the trunks.

'Wait a moment,' George Cannon said to him, and murmured to Sarah: 'This is the basement, here.'

The middle-aged maid appeared at the kitchen door with a large loaded tray. 'Come along with that tea, Louisa,' he added pleasantly.

He went first, Sarah next, and Hilda last, cautiously down a short, dark flight of stone steps beneath the stairs; the servant followed. At the foot a gas-jet burned.

'Those Watchetts might be the landladies!' muttered Sarah, strangely ignoring the propinquity of the maid; and sniffed.

Hilda gave a short, uneasy laugh. She had a desire to laugh loudly and wildly, and by so doing to snap the nervous tension, which seemed to grow tighter and tighter every minute. Her wretchedness had become so exquisite that she could begin to enjoy it, to savour it like a pleasure.

And she thought, with conscious and satisfied grimness:

'So this is Brighton!'

CHAPTER 4
THE SEA

I

IN the evening Hilda, returning from a short solitary walk as far as the West Pier, found Sarah Gailey stooping over her open trunks in the bedroom which had been assigned to her. There were two quite excellent though low-ceiled rooms, of which this was one, in the basement; the other was to be used as a private parlour by the managers of the house. At night, with the gas lighted and the yellow blind drawn and the loose bundle of strips of silver paper gleaming in the grate, the bedroom seemed very cosy and habitable in its shabbiness; like the rest of the house it had an ample supply of furniture, and especially of those trifling articles, useful or useless, which collect only by slow degrees, and which are a proof of long humanizing habitation. In that room Sarah Gailey was indeed merely the successor of the regretted Mrs Granville, the landlady who had mysteriously receded into the unknown before the advent of Sarah and Hilda, but with whom George Cannon must have had many interviews. No doubt the room was an epitome of the character of Mrs Granville, presumably a fussy and precise celibate, with a place for everything and everything in its place, and an indiscriminating tendency to hoard.

Sarah Gailey was at that stage of unpacking when, trunks being nearly empty and drawers having scarcely begun to fill, bed, table, and chairs are encumbered with confused masses of goods apparently far exceeding the cubical content of the trunks.

'Can I do anything for you?' asked Hilda.

The new landlady raised her watery and dejected eyes. 'If you wouldn't mind taking every single one of those knick-knacks off the mantelpiece and putting them away on the top shelf of the cupboard –'

Hilda smiled. 'It's a bit crowded, isn't it?'

'Crowded!' By her intonation of this one word Sarah Gailey condemned Mrs Granville's whole life.

'Can I empty this chair? I shall want something to stand on,' said Hilda.

'Better see if the shelf's dusty,' Sarah gloomily warned her.

'Well,' murmured Hilda, on the chair, 'if my feather doesn't actually touch the ceiling!' Sarah Gailey made no response to this light-heartedness, and Hilda, with her hands full of vain gewgaws, tried again: 'I wonder what Mrs Granville would say if she saw me! . . . My word, it's quite hot up here!'

A resonant, very amiable voice came from beyond the door: 'Is she there?'

'Who?' demanded Sarah, grievous.

'Miss Lessways.' It was George Cannon.

'Yes.'

'I just want to speak to her if she's at liberty,' said George Cannon.

Hilda cried from the ceiling: 'I'll come as soon as I've –'

'Please go now,' Sarah interrupted in tense accents. Hilda glanced down at her, astonished, and saw in her eyes an almost childish appeal, weak and passionate, which gripped the heart painfully.

She jumped from the chair. Sarah Gailey was now sitting on the bed. Yes, in her worn face of a woman who has definitely passed the climacteric, and in the abandoned pose of those thin arms, there was the look and gesture of a young girl desperately beseeching. Hilda was puzzled and intimidated. She had meant to be jocular, and to insist on staying till the task was finished. But she kept silence and obeyed the supplication, from a motive of prudence.

'I wouldn't keep you from him for anything,' murmured Sarah Gailey tragically, as Hilda opened the door and left her sitting forlorn among all her skirts and linen.

II

'I'm here,' George Cannon called out from the parlour when he heard the sound of the door. He was looking from the window up at the street; the blind had not been drawn. He turned as Hilda entered.

'You've been out!' he said, observing that she was in street attire.

'What is it?' she asked nervously, fearing that some altercation had already occurred between brother and sister.

'It's about your private affairs – that's all,' he said easily, and half-humorously. 'If you'll just come in.'

'Oh!' she smiled her relief; but nevertheless she was still pre-occupied by the image of the woman in the next room.

'They've been dragging on quite long enough,' said George Cannon, as he stooped to poke the morsel of fire in the old-fashioned grate, which had a hob on either side. On one of these hobs was a glass of milk. Hilda had learnt that day for the first time that at a certain hour every evening George Cannon drank a glass of warm milk, and that this glass of warm milk was an important factor in his daily comfort. He now took the glass and drank it off. And Hilda had a peculiar sensation of being more intimate with him than she had ever been before.

They sat down to the square table in the middle of the room crowded with oddments of furniture, including a desk which George Cannon had appropriated to his own exclusive use. This desk was open and a portion of its contents were spread abroad on the crimson cloth of the table. Among them Hilda noticed, with her accustomed clerkly eye, two numbers of *The Hotel-Keeper and Boarding-House Review*, several sheets of advertisement-scales, and a many-paged document with the heading, 'Inventory of Furniture at No. 59 Preston Street'; also a large legal envelope inscribed, 'Lessways Estate'.

From the latter George Cannon drew forth an engraved and flourished paper, which he silently placed in front of her. It was a receipt signed by the manager of the Brighton branch of the Southern Counties Bank for the sum of three thousand four hundred and forty-five pounds deposited at call by Miss Hilda Lessways.

'Everything is now settled up,' he said. 'Here are all the figures,' and he handed her another paper showing the whole of the figures for the realization of her real property and of her furniture. 'It's in your name, and nobody can touch it but you.'

She glanced at the figures vaguely, not attempting to comprehend them. As for the receipt, it fascinated her. The fragile scrap represented her livelihood, her future, her salvation. It alone stood between her and unimagined terrors. And she was surprised to see it, surprised by its assurance that no accident had happened to her possessions during the process of transformation carried out by George Cannon. For, though he had throughout been almost worryingly meticulous in his business formalities and his promptitudes – never had any interest or rent been a day late! – she admitted to herself now that she had been afraid . . . that, in fact, she had not utterly trusted him.

'And what's got to be done with this?' she asked simply, fingering the receipt.

He smiled at her, with a touch of protective and yet sardonic condescension, without saying a word.

And suddenly it struck her that ages had elapsed since her first interview with him in the office over the ironmonger's at Turnhill, and that both of them were extraordinarily changed. (She was reminded of that interview not by his face and look, nor by their relative positions at the table, but by a very faint odour of gas-fumes, for at Turnhill also a gas-jet had been between them.) After an interval of anxiety and depression he had regained exactly the triumphant, self-sure air which was her earliest recollection of him. He was not appreciably older. But for her he was no longer the same man, because she saw him differently; knowing much more of him, she read in his features a thousand minor significances to which before she had been blind. The dominating impression was not now the impression of his masculinity; there was no clearly dominating impression. He had lost, for her, the romantic allurement of the strange and the unknown.

Still, she liked and admired him. And she felt an awe, which was agreeable to her, of his tremendous enterprise and his obstinate volition. That faculty which he possessed, of uprooting himself and uprooting others, put her in fear of him. He had willed to be established as a caterer in Brighton – he who but yesterday (as it seemed) was a lawyer in Turnhill – and on this very night, he was established in Brighton, and his sister with him, and she with his sister! The enormous affair had been accomplished. This thought had been obsessing Hilda all the afternoon and evening.

When she reflected upon the change in herself, the untravelled Hilda of Turnhill appeared a stranger to her, and a simpleton; no more!

As George Cannon offered no answer to her question, she said:

'I suppose it will have to be invested, all this?'

He nodded.

'Well, considering it's only been bringing in one per cent per annum for the last week . . . Of course I needn't have put it on deposit, but I always prefer that way. It's more satisfactory.'

Hilda could hear faintly, through the thin wooden partition, the movements of Sarah Gailey in the next room. And the image of the mournful woman returned to disquiet her. What could be the meaning of that hysteric appeal and glance? Then she heard the door of the bedroom open violently, and the figure of Sarah Gailey passed like a flash across the doorway of the parlour. And the footsteps of Sarah Gailey pattered up the stone stairs; and the front door banged; and the skirts and feet of Sarah Gailey intercepted for an instant the light of the street-lamp that shone on the basement-window of the parlour.

'Excuse me a minute,' muttered Hilda, frowning. By one of her swift and unreflecting impulses she abandoned George Cannon and her private affairs, and scurried by the area steps into the street.

III

Bareheaded, and with no jacket or mantle, Sarah Gailey was walking quickly down Preston Street towards the promenade, and Hilda, afraid but courageous, followed her at a distance of thirty or forty yards. Hilda could not decide why she was afraid, nor why it should be necessary, in so simple an undertaking as a walk down Preston Street, to call upon her courage. Assuming even that Sarah Gailey turned round and caught her – what then? The consequences could not be very terrible. But Sarah Gailey did not turn round. She went straight forward, as though on a definite errand in a town with which she was perfectly familiar, and, having arrived at the corner of Preston Street and the promenade, unhesitatingly crossed the muddy roadway of the promenade, and, after a moment's halt, vanished down the steps in the sea-wall to the left-hand of the pier. The pier, a double rope of twinkling lamps, hung magically over the invisible sea, and at the end of it, constant and grave, a red globe burned menacingly in the wind-haunted waste of the night. And Hilda thought, as she hastened with gathering terror across the promenade: 'Out there, at the end of the pier, the water is splashing and beating against the piles!'

She stopped at the parapet of the sea-wall, and looked behind her, like a thief. The wrought-iron entrance to the pier was highly illuminated, but except for a man's head and shoulders caged in the ticket-box of the turnstile, there was no life there; the man seemed to be waiting solitary with everlasting patience in the web of wavering flame beneath the huge dark sky. Scores of posters, large and small, showed that Robertson's *School* was being performed in the theatre away over the sea at the extremity of the pier. The promenade, save for one gigantic policeman and a few distant carriages, was apparently deserted, and the line of dimly lighted hotels, stretching vaguely east and west, had an air grim and forlorn at that hour.

Hilda ran down the steps; at the bottom another row of lamps defined the shore, and now she could hear the tide lapping ceaselessly amid the supporting ironwork of the pier. She at once descried the figure of Sarah Gailey in the gloom. The woman was moving towards the faintly white edge of the sea. Hilda started to run after her, first across smooth asphalt, and then over some sails stretched out to dry; and then her feet sank at each step into descending ridges of loose shingle, and she nearly fell. At length she came to firm sand, and stood still.

Sarah Gailey was now silhouetted against the pale shallows of foam that in ever-renewed curves divided the shore from the sea. After a time, she bent down, rose again, moved towards the water, and drew back. Hilda did not stir. She could not bring herself to approach the lonely figure. She felt that to go and accost Sarah Gailey would be indelicate and inexcusable. She felt as if she were basely spying. She was completely at a loss, and knew not how to act. But presently she discerned that the white foam was circling round Sarah's feet, and that Sarah was standing careless in the midst of it. And at last, timid and shaking with agitation, she ventured nearer and nearer. And Sarah heard her on the sand, and looked behind.

'Miss Gailey!' she appealed in a trembling voice.

Sarah made no response of any kind, and Hilda reached the edge of the foam.

'Please, please don't stand there! You'll catch a dreadful cold, and you've got nothing on your shoulders, either!'

'I want to make a hole in the water,' said Sarah miserably. 'I wanted to make a hole in the water!'

'Please do come back with me!' Hilda implored; but she spoke mechanically, as though saying something which she was bound to say, but which she did not feel.

The foam capriciously receded, and Hilda, still without any effort of her own will, stepped across the glistening, yielding sand and took Sarah Gailey's arm. There was no resistance.

'I wanted to make a hole in the water,' Sarah repeated. 'But I made a mistake. I ought to have gone to that groin over there. I knew there was a groin near here, only it's so long since I was here. I'd forgotten just the place.'

'But what's the matter?' Hilda asked, leading her away from the sea.

She was not extremely surprised. But she was shocked into a most solemn awe as she pressed the arm of the poor tragic woman who, but for an accident, might have plunged off the end of the groin into water deep enough for drowning. She did really feel humble before this creature who had deliberately invited death; she in no way criticized her; she did not even presume to condescend towards the hasty clumsiness of Sarah Gailey's scheme to die. She was overwhelmed by the woman's utterly unconscious impressiveness, which exceeded that of a criminal reprieved on the scaffold, for the woman had dared an experience that only the fierce and sublime courage of desperation can affront. She had a feeling that she ought to apologize profoundly to Sarah Gailey for all that Sarah must have suffered. And as she heard the ceaseless, cruel play of the water amid the dark jungle of ironwork under the pier, and the soft creeping of the foam-curves behind, and the vague stirrings of the night-wind round about – these phenomena combined mysteriously with the immensity of the dome above and with the baffling strangeness of the town, and with the grandeur of the beaten woman by her side; and communicated to Hilda a thrill that was divine in its unexampled poignancy.

The great figure of the policeman, suspicious, was descending from the promenade discreetly towards them. To avoid any encounter with him Hilda guided her companion towards the pier, and they sheltered there under the resounding floor of the pier. By the light of one of the lower lamps Hilda could now clearly see Sarah Gailey's face. It showed no sign of terror. It was calm enough in its worn, resigned woe. It had the girlish look again, beneath the marks of age. Hilda could distinguish the young girl that Sarah had once been.

'Come home, will you?' she entreated.

Sarah Gailey sighed terribly. 'I give it up,' she said, with weariness. 'I could never do it! I could never do it – now!'

Hilda pulled gently at her unwilling arm. She could not speak. She could not ask her again: 'What's the matter?'

'It isn't that the house is too large,' Sarah Gailey went on half meditatively; 'though just think of all those stairs, and not a tap on any of the upper floors! No! And it isn't that I'm not ready enough to oblige him. No! I know as well as anybody there's only him between me and starvation. No! It isn't that he doesn't consider me! No! But when he goes and settles behind my back with those Boutwoods –' She began to weep. 'And when I can hear you and him discussing me in the next room, and plotting against me – it's – it's more –' The tears gradually drowned her voice, and she ceased.

'I assure you, you're quite mistaken,' Hilda burst out, with passionate and indignant persuasiveness. 'We never mentioned you. He wanted to talk to me about my money. And if you feel like that over the Boutwoods, I'm certain he'll tell them they mustn't come.'

Sarah Gailey shook her head blankly.

'I'm certain he will!' Hilda persisted. 'Please –'

The other began to walk away, dragging Hilda with her. The policeman, inspecting them from a distance, coughed and withdrew. They climbed a flight of steps on the far side of the pier, crossed the promenade, and went up Preston Street in silence.

'I should prefer not to be seen going in with you,' said Sarah Gailey suddenly. 'It might –' she freed her arm.

'Go down the area steps,' said Hilda, 'and I'll wait a moment and then go in at the front door.'

Sarah Gailey hurried forward alone.

Hilda, watching her, and observing the wet footmarks which she left on the pavement, was appalled by the sense of her own responsibility as to the future of Sarah Gailey. Till this hour, even at her most conscientious, she had underestimated the seriousness of Sarah Gailey's case. Everybody had underestimated the seriousness of Sarah Gailey's case.

She became aware of some one hurrying cautiously up the street on the other side. It was George Cannon. As soon as Sarah had disappeared within the house he crossed over.

'What's the matter?' he inquired anxiously.

'Well –'

'She hasn't been trying to drown herself, has she?'

Hilda nodded, and, speechless, moved towards the house. He turned abruptly away.

The front door of No. 59 was still open. Hilda passed through the silent hall, and went timorously down the steps to the basement. The gas was still burning, and the clothes were still strewn about in Sarah Gailey's bedroom, just as though naught had happened. Sarah stood between her two trunks in the middle of the floor.

'Where's George?' she asked, in a harsh, perfectly ordinary voice.

'I don't think he's in the parlour,' Hilda prevaricated.

'Promise me you won't tell him!'

'Of course I won't!' said Hilda kindly. 'Do get into bed, and let me make you some tea.'

Sarah Gailey rushed at her and embraced her

'I know I'm all wrong! I know it's all my own fault!' she murmured, with plaintive, feeble contrition, crying again. 'But you've no idea how I try! If it wasn't for you –'

IV

That night Hilda, in her small bedroom at the top of the house, was listlessly arranging, at the back of the dressing-table, the few volumes which had clung to her, or to which she had clung, throughout the convulsive disturbances following her mother's death. Among them was one which she did not wish to keep, *The Girl's Week-day Book*, and also the whole set of Victor Hugo, which did not belong to her. George Cannon had lent her the latter in instalments, and she had omitted to return it. She was saying to herself that the opportunity to return it had at length arrived, when she heard a low, conspiratorial tapping at the door. All her skin crept as, after a second's startled hesitation, she moved to open the door.

George Cannon, holding a candle, stood on the landing. She had not seen him since the brief colloquy between them outside the house. Having satisfied herself that Sarah Gailey was safe, and to a certain extent tranquillized, for the night, she had awaited George Cannon's reappearance a long time in vain, and had then retired upstairs.

'You aren't gone to bed!' he whispered very cautiously. Within a few feet of them was an airless kennel where Louisa, the chambermaid, slept.

'No! I'm just – I stayed up for you I don't know how long.'

'Is she all right?'

'Well – she's in bed.'

'I wish you'd come to one of these other rooms,' he continued to whisper. All the sibilants in his words seemed to detach themselves, hissing, from the rest of the sounds.

She gave a gesture of assent. He tiptoed over the traitorous boards of the landing, and slowly turned the knob of a door in the end wall. The door exploded like the firing of a pistol; frowning, he grimly pushed it open. Hilda followed him, noiselessly creeping. He held the door for her. She entered, and he shut the door on the inside. They were in a small bedroom similar to Hilda's own; but the bed was stripped, the square of carpet rolled, the blind undrawn, and the curtains looped up from the floor. He put the candle on the tiny iron mantelpiece, and sat on the bed, his hands in his pockets.

'You don't mean to say she was wanting to commit suicide?'
he said, after a short reflective silence, with his head bent but
his eyes raised peeringly to Hilda's.

The crudity of the word, 'suicide', affected Hilda painfully.

'If you ask me,' said she, standing with her back rubbing
against the small wardrobe, 'she didn't know quite what she was
doing; but there's no doubt that was what she went out for.'

'You overtook her? I saw you coming up from the beach.'

Hilda related what had happened.

'But had you any notion – before –'

'Me? No! Why?'

'Nothing! Only the way you rushed out like that!'

'Well – it struck me all of a sudden! . . . You've not seen her
since you came in?'

He shook his head. 'I thought I'd better keep out of the way.
I thought I'd better leave it all to you. It's appalling, simply
appalling! . . . Just when everything was shaping so well!'

Hilda thought, bewildered: 'Shaping so well?' With her glance
she took in the little cheerless bedroom, and herself and George
Cannon within it, overwhelmed. In imagination she saw all the
other bedrooms, dark, forlorn, and inanimate, waiting through
long nights and empty days until some human creature as pathetic
as themselves should come and feebly vitalize them into a spurious
transient homeliness; and she saw George Cannon's bedroom –
the harsh bedroom of the bachelor who had never had a home;
and the bedrooms of those fearsome mummies, the Watchetts,
each bed with its grisly face on the pillow in the dark; and the
kennels of the unclean servants; and so, descending through the
floors, to Sarah Gailey's bedroom in the very earth, and the
sleepless form on that bed, beneath the whole! And the organism
of the boarding-house seemed absolutely tragic to her, compact
of the stuff of sorrow itself! And yet George Cannon had said,
'Shaping so well!'

'What's to be done?' he inquired plaintively.

'Nothing that I can see!' she said. She had a tremendous desire
to escape from the responsibility thrust on her by the situation;
but she knew that she could never escape from it; that she was
immovably pinned down by it.

'I can't see anything either,' said he, quietly responsive, and speaking now in a gentle voice. 'Supposing I tell her that she can go, and that I'll make her an allowance? What could she do, then? It would be madness for her to live alone any more. She's the very last person who ought to live alone. Moreover, she wouldn't accept the allowance. Well, then, she must stay with me – here. And if she stays here she must work, otherwise she'd never stay – not she! And she must be the mistress. She wouldn't stand having anyone above her, or even equal with her, that's a certainty! Besides, she's so good at her job. She hasn't got a great deal of system, so far as I can see, but she can get the work out of the servants without too much fuss, and she's so mighty economical in her catering! Of course she can't get on the right side of a boarder – but then I *can*! And that's the whole point! With me on the spot to *run* the place, she'd be perfect – perfect! Couldn't wish for anything better! And now she – I assure you I'm doing the best I can do for her. I do honestly assure you! If anybody can suggest to me anything else that I can do – I'll do it like a shot.' He threw up his arms.

Hilda was touched by the benevolence of his tone. Nevertheless, it only intensified her helpless perplexity. Sarah Gailey was inexpressibly to be pitied, but George Cannon was not to be blamed. She had a feeling that for any piteous disaster some one ought to be definitely blamable.

'Do you think she'll settle down?' George Cannon asked, in a new voice.

'Oh yes!' said Hilda. 'I think she will. It was just a sort of – attack she had, I think.'

'She's not vexed with me?'

Hilda could not find courage to say: 'She thinks you and I are plotting against her.' And yet she wondered why she should hesitate to say it. After a pause she murmured, as casually as possible: 'She doesn't like the Boutwoods coming back.'

'I knew you were going to say that!' he frowned.

'If you could manage to stop them –'

'No, no!' He interrupted – nervous, impatient. 'It wouldn't do, that wouldn't! It'd never do! A boarding-house can't be run on those lines. It isn't that I care so much as all that about losing a couple of boarders, and I'm not specially keen on the Boutwoods. But it wouldn't do! It's the wrong principle. You haven't got to let customers get on your nerves, so long as they pay and behave respectably. If I gave way, the very first thing Sarah would do would be to find a grievance against some other boarder, and there'd be no end to it. The fact is she wants a grievance, she must have a grievance – whether it's the Boutwoods or somebody else makes no matter! ... Oh no!' He repeated softly, gently, 'Oh no!'

She knew that his argument was unanswerable. She was perfectly aware that she ought to yield to it. Nevertheless, the one impulse of her being in that moment was to fight blindly and irrationally against it. Her instinct said: 'I don't care for arguments. The Boutwoods must be stopped from coming. If they aren't stopped, I don't know what I shall do! I can't bear to think of that poor woman meeting them again! I can't bear it.' She drew breath sharply. Startling hot tears came into her eyes; and she stepped forward on her left foot.

'Please!' she entreated, 'please don't let them come!'

There was a silence. In the agonizing silence she felt acutely her girlishness, her helplessness, her unreason, confronted by his strong and shrewd masculinity. At the bottom of her soul she knew how wrong she was. But she was ready to do anything to save Sarah Gailey from the distress of one particular humiliation. With the whole of her volition she wanted to win.

'Oh well!' he said. 'Of course, if you take it so much to heart –'

A peculiar bright glance shot from his eyes – the old glance that at once negligently asserted his power over her, and re-assured her against his power. Her being was suffused with gladness and pride. She had won. She had won in defiance of reason. She had appealed, and she had conquered. And she enjoyed his glance. She gloried in it. She blushed. A spasm of exquisite fear shot through her, and she savoured it deliciously. The deep organic sadness of the house presented itself to her in a new light. It was still sadness, but it was beautiful in the background. Her sympathy for Sarah Gailey was as keen as ever, but it had a different quality – an anguish less desolating. And the fact that a joint responsibility for Sarah Gailey's welfare bound herself and George Cannon together in spite of themselves – this fact seemed to her grandiose and romantic, no longer oppressive. To be alone with him in the secrecy of the small upper room seemed to endow her with a splendid worldly importance. And yet all the time a scarce-heard voice was saying clearly within her: 'This appeal and this abandonment are unworthy. No matter if this man is kind and sincere and admirable! This appeal and this abandonment are unworthy!' But she did not care. She ignored the voice.

'I'll tell Sarah in the morning,' he said.

'Please don't!' she begged. 'You might pretend later on that you've had a letter from the Boutwoods and they can't come. If you tell her tomorrow, she'll guess at once I've been talking to you; and you're not supposed to know anything at all about what happened tonight. She made me promise. But of course she didn't know that you'd found out for yourself, you see!'

George Cannon walked away to the window, and then to the mantelpiece, from which he took up the candle.

'I'm very much obliged to you,' he said simply, putting a faint emphasis on the last word. She knew that he meant it, without any reserves. But in his urbane tone there was a chill tranquillity that astonished and vaguely disappointed her.

BOOK IV

HER FALL

CHAPTER 1
THE GOING CONCERN

I

On a Saturday afternoon of the following August, Hilda was sitting at a book in the basement parlour of 'Cannon's Boarding-house' in Preston Street. She heard, through the open window, several pairs of feet mounting wearily to the front door, and then the long remote tinkling of the bell. Within the house there was no responsive sound: but from the porch came a clearing of throats, a muttering, impatient and yet resigned, and a vague shuffling. After a long pause the bell rang again; and then the gas globe over Hilda's head vibrated for a moment to footsteps in the hall, and the front door was unlatched. She could not catch the precise question; but the reply of Louisa, the chambermaid – haughty, scornful, and negligently pitying – was quite clear:

'Sorry, sir. We're full up. We've had to refuse several this very day . . . No! I couldn't rightly tell you where . . . You might try No. 51, "Homeleigh" as they call it; but we're full up. Good afternoon, sir, 'd afternoon 'm.'

The door banged arrogantly. The feet redescended to the pavement, and Hilda, throwing a careless glance at the window, saw two men and a woman pass melancholy down the hot street with their hand-luggage.

And although she condemned and despised the flunkey-souled Louisa, who would have abased herself with sickly smiles and sweet phrases before the applicants, if the house had needed custom; although in her mind she was saying curtly to the mature Louisa: 'It's a good thing Mr Cannon didn't hear you using that tone to customers, my girl'; nevertheless, she could not help feeling somewhat as Louisa felt. It was indubitably agreeable to hear a prosperous door closed on dusty and disappointed holiday-makers, and to realize, in her tranquil retreat, that she was part of a very thriving and successful concern.

II

George Cannon, in a light and elegant summer suit, passed slowly
in front of the window, and, looking for Hilda in her accustomed
place, saw her and nodded. Surprised by the unusual gesture, she
moved uneasily and blushed; and as she did so, she asked herself
resentfully: 'Why do I behave like this? I'm only his clerk, and
I shall never be anything else but his clerk; and yet I do believe
I'm getting worse instead of better.' George Cannon skipped
easily up to the porch; he had a latchkey, but before he could
put it into the keyhole Louisa had flown down the stairs and
opened the door to him; she must have been on the watch from
an upper floor. George Cannon would have been well served,
whatever his situation in the house, for he was one of those genial
bullies who are adored by the menials whom they alternately
cajole and terrorize. But his situation in the house was that of a
god, and like a god he was attended. He was the very creator of
the house; all its life flowed from him. Without him the organism
would have ceased to exist, and everybody in it was quite aware
of this. He had fully learnt his business. He had learnt it in the
fishmarket on the beach at seven o'clock in the morning, and in
the vegetable market at eight, and in the shops; he had learnt it
in the kitchen and on the stairs while the servants were cleaning;
and he had learnt it at the dinner-table surrounded by his
customers. There was nothing that he did not know and, except
actual cooking and mending, little that he could not do. He always
impressed his customers by the statement that he had slept in
every room in the house in order to understand personally its
qualities and defects; and he could and did in fact talk to each
boarder about his room with the intimate geographical knowledge of a native. The boarders were further flattered by the mien
and appearance of this practical housekeeper, who did not in the
least resemble his kind, but had rather the style of a slightly
doggish stockbroker. To be strolling on the King's Road in
converse with George Cannon was a matter of pride to boarders
male and female. And there was none with whom he could not
talk fluently, on any subject from cigars to ozone, according to
the needs of the particular case. Nor did he ever seem to be bored
by conversations. But sometimes, after benignantly speeding, for

instance, one of the Watchetts on her morning constitutional, he would slip down into the basement and ejaculate, 'Cursed hag!' with a calm and natural earnestness, which frightened Hilda, indicating as it did that he must be capable of astounding duplicities.

He came, now, directly to the underground parlour, hat on head and ebony stick in hand. Hilda did not even look up, but self-consciously bent a little lower over her volume. Her relation to George Cannon in the successful enterprise was anomalous, and yet the habit of ten months had in practice defined it. Neither paying board nor receiving wages, she had remained in the house apparently as Sarah Gailey's companion and moral support; she had remained because Sarah Gailey had never been in a condition to be left – and the months had passed very quickly. But her lack of occupation and her knowledge of shorthand, and George Cannon's obvious need of clerical aid, had made it inevitable that they should resume their former roles of principal and clerk. Hilda worked daily at letters, circularizing, advertisements, and – to a less extent – accounts and bills; the second finger of her right hand had nearly always an agreeable stain of ink at the base of the nail; and she often dreamed about letter-filing. In this prosperous month of August she had, on the whole, less work than usual, for both circularizing and advertisements were stopped.

George Cannon went to the desk in the dark corner between the window and the door, where all business papers were kept, but where neither he nor she actually wrote. When his back was turned she surreptitiously glanced at him without moving her head, and perceived that his hand was only moving idly about among the papers while he stared at the wall. She thought, half in alarm: 'What is the matter now?' Then he came over to the table and hesitated by her shoulder. Still, she would not look up. She could no longer decipher a single word on the page. Her being was somehow monopolized by the consciousness of his nearness.

'Interesting?' he inquired.

She turned her head at last and glanced at him with a friendly smile of affirmation, fingering the leaves of the book nervously. It was Cranswick's *History of Printing*. One day, a fortnight

earlier, while George Cannon, in company with her, was bargain-
ing for an old London Directory outside a bookseller's shop in
East Street, she had seen Cranswick's *History of Printing* (labelled
'Published at £1 1s, our price 6s. 6d') and had opened it curiously. George Cannon, who always kept an eye on her, had said
teasingly: 'I suppose it's your journalistic past that makes you
interested in that?' 'I suppose it is,' she had answered. Which
statement was an untruth, for the sole thought in her mind had
been that Edwin Clayhanger was a printer. A strange, idle
thought! She had laid the book down. The next day, however,
George Cannon had brought it home, saying carelessly: 'I bought
that book – five and six; the man seemed anxious to do business,
and it's a book to have.' He had not touched it since.

'Page 473!' he murmured, looking at the number of the page.
'If you keep on at this rate, you'll soon know more about printing
than young Clayhanger himself!'

She was thunderstruck. Never before had the name of Clayhanger been mentioned between them! Could he, then, penetrate
her thoughts? Could he guess that in truth she was reading
Cranswick solely because Edwin Clayhanger happened to be a
printer? No! It was impossible! The reason of her interest in
Cranswick, inexplicable even to herself, was too fantastic to be
divined. And yet was not his tone peculiar? Or was it only in her
fancy that his tone was peculiar? She blushed scarlet, and her
muscles grew rigid.

'I say,' George Cannon continued, in a tone that now was
unmistakably peculiar, 'I want you to come out with me. I want
to show you something on the front. Can you come?'

'At once?' she muttered glumly and painfully. What could be
the mystery beneath this most singular behaviour?

'Yes.'

'Florrie will be arriving at five,' said Hilda, after artificially
coughing. 'I ought to be here then, oughtn't I?'

'Oh!' he cried. 'We shall be back long before five.'

'Very well,' she agreed.

'I'll be ready in three minutes,' he said, going gaily towards
the door. From the door he gave her a glance. She met it,
courageously exposing her troubled features and nodded.

III

Hilda went into the bedroom behind the parlour, to get her hat and gloves. A consequence of the success of the boarding-house was that she was temporarily sharing this chamber with Sarah Gailey. She had insisted on making the sacrifice, and she enjoyed the personal discomfort which it involved. When she cautiously lay down on the narrow and lumpy truckle-bed that had been insinuated against an unoccupied wall, and when she turned over restlessly in the night and the rickety ironwork creaked and Sarah Gailey moaned, and when she searched vainly for a particular garment lost among garments that were hung pell-mell on insecure hooks and jutting corners of furniture – she was proud and glad because her own comfortable room was steadily adding thirty shillings or more per week to the gross receipts of the enterprise. The benefit was in no way hers, and yet she gloated on it, thinking pleasurably of George Cannon's great japanned cash-box, which seemed to be an exhaustless store of gold sovereigns and large silver, and of his mysterious – almost furtive – visits to the Bank. Her own capital, invested by George Cannon in railway stock, was bringing in four times as much as she disbursed; and she gloated also on her savings. The more money she amassed, the less willing was she to spend. This nascent avarice amused her, as a new trait in his character always amuses the individual. She said to herself: 'I am getting quite a miser,' with the assured reservation: 'Of course I can stop being a miser whenever I feel like stopping.'

Sarah Gailey was lulling herself in a rocking-chair when Hilda entered, and she neither regarded Hilda nor intermitted her see-saw. Her features were drawn into a preoccupied expression of martyrdom, and in fact she constantly suffered physical torture. She had three genuine complaints – rheumatism, sciatica, and neuritis; they were all painful. The latest and worst was the neuritis, which had attacked her in the wrist, producing swollen joints that had to be fomented with hot water. Sarah Gailey's life had indeed latterly developed into a continual fomentation and a continual rocking. She was so taken up with the elemental business of fomenting and of keeping warm, that she had no energy left for other remedial treatments, such as distraction in the open air. She sat for ever shawled, generally with heavy mittens on her arms and wrists, and either fomenting or rocking, in the eternal twilight of the basement bedroom. She eschewed aid – she could manage for herself – and she did not encourage company, apparently preferring to be alone with fate. In her easier hours, one hand resting on another and both hugged close to her breast, rocking to and fro with an astounding monotonous perseverance, she was like a mysterious Indian god in a subterranean temple. Above her, unseen by her, floor beyond floor, the life of the boarding-house functioned in the great holiday month of August.

'I quite forgot about the make-up bed for Florrie,' said Sarah Gailey plaintively as she rocked. 'Would you have time to see to it? Of course she will have to be with Louisa.'

'Very well,' said Hilda curtly, and not quite hiding exasperation.

There were three reasons for her exasperation. In the first place, the constant spectacle of Sarah Gailey's pain, and the effect of the pain on Sarah's character, was exasperating – to Hilda as well as to George Cannon. Both well knew that the watery-eyed, fretful spinster was a victim, utterly innocent and utterly helpless, of destiny, and that she merited nothing but patient sympathy; yet often the strain of relationship with Sarah produced in them such a profound feeling of annoyance that they positively resented Sarah's sufferings, and with a sad absence of logic blamed her in her misfortune, just as though she had wilfully brought the maladies upon herself in order to vex them. Then, further, it was necessary always to minister to Sarah's illusion that Sarah was the mainstay of the house, that she attended to everything and was responsible for everything, and that without her governance the machine would come to a disastrous standstill: the fact being that she had grown feeble and superfluous. Sarah had taught all she knew to two highly intelligent pupils, and had survived her usefulness. She had no right place on earth. But in her morose inefficiency she had developed into an unconscious tyrant – a tyrant whose power lay in the loyalty of her subjects and not at all in her own soul. She was indeed like a deity, immanent, brooding, and unaware of itself! ... Thus, the question of Florrie's bed had been discussed and settled long before Sarah Gailey had even thought of it; but Hilda might not tell her so. Lastly, this very question of Florrie's bed was exasperating to Hilda. Already Louisa's kennel was inadequate for Louisa, and now another couch had been crowded into it. Hilda was ashamed of the shift; but there was no alternative. Here, for Hilda, was the secret canker of George Cannon's brilliant success. The servants were kindly ill-treated. In the commercial triumph she lost the sense of the tragic forlornness of boarding-house existence, as it had struck her on the day of her arrival. But the image of the Indian god in the basement and of the prone forms of the servants in stifling black cupboards under the roof and under the stairs – these images embittered at intervals the instinctive and reflecting exultation of her moods.

She adjusted her small, close-fitting flowered hat, dropped her parasol across the bed, and began to draw on her cotton gloves.

'Where are you going, dear?' asked Sarah Gailey.

'Out with Mr Cannon.'

'But where?'

'I don't know.' In spite of herself there was a certain unnecessary defiance in Hilda's voice.

'You don't know, dear?' Sarah Gailey suddenly ceased rocking, and glanced at Hilda with the mournful expression of acute worry that was so terribly familiar on her features. Although it was notorious that baseless apprehensions were a part of Sarah's disease, nevertheless Hilda could never succeed in treating any given apprehension as quite baseless. And now Sarah's mere tone begot in Hilda's self-consciousness a vague alarm.

She continued busy with her gloves, silent.

'And on Saturday afternoon too, when everybody's abroad!' Sarah Gailey added gloomily, with her involuntary small movements of the head.

'He asked me if I could go out with him for a minute or two at once,' said Hilda, and picked up the parasol with a decisive gesture.

'There's a great deal too much talk about you and George as it is,' said Sarah, with an acrid firmness.

'Talk about me and –!' Hilda cried, absolutely astounded.

She had no feeling of guilt, but she knew that she was looking guilty, and this knowledge induced in her the actual sensations of a criminal.

'I'm sure I don't want –' Sarah Gailey began, and was interrupted by a quiet tap at the door.

George Cannon entered.

'Ready, miss?' he demanded, smiling, before he had caught sight of her face.

For the second time that afternoon he saw her scarlet, and now there were tears in her eyes, too.

She hesitated an instant.

'Yes,' she answered, with a painful gulp, and moved towards the door.

CHAPTER 2
THE UNKNOWN ADVENTURE

I

WHEN they were fairly out in the street Hilda felt like a mariner who has escaped from a lee shore, but who is beset by the vaguer and even more formidable perils of the open sea. She was in a state of extreme agitation, and much too self-conscious to be properly cognizant of her surroundings: she did not feel the pavement with her feet; she had no recollection of having passed out of the house. There she was walking along on nothing, by the side of a man who might or might not be George Cannon, amid tall objects that resembled houses! Her situation was in a high degree painful, but she could not have avoided it. She could not, in Sarah's bedroom, have fallen into sobs, or into a rage, or into the sulks, and told George Cannon that she would not go with him; she could not have dashed hysterically away and hidden herself on an upper floor, in the manner of a startled fawn. Her spirit was too high for such tricks. On the other hand, she was by no means sufficiently mistress of herself to be able to hide from him her shame. Hence she faced him and followed him, and let him see it. Their long familiarity had made this surrender somewhat easier for her. After all, in the countless daily contacts, they had grown accustomed to minor self-exposures – and Hilda more so than George Cannon; Hilda was too impatient and impulsive not to tear, at increasingly frequent intervals, the veil of conventional formality.

Her mood now, as she accompanied George Cannon on the unknown adventure, was one of abashed but still fierce resentment. She of course believed Sarah Gailey's statement that there had been 'talk' about herself and the landlord, and yet it was so utterly monstrous as to be almost incredible. She was absolutely sure that she had never by her behaviour furnished the slighest excuse for such 'talk'. No eavesdropper could ever have caught the least word or gesture to justify it. Could a malicious eaves-

dropper have assisted at the secret operations of her inmost mind,
even then he could scarcely have seen aught to justify it. Existence
at Brighton had been too strenuous and strange – and, with Sarah
Gailey in the house, too full of responsibilities – to favour dalli-
ance. Hilda, examining herself, could not say that she had not
once thought of George Cannon as a husband; because just as
a young solitary man will imagine himself the spouse of a dozen
different girls in a week, so will an unmated girl picture herself
united to every eligible and passably sympathetic male that
crosses her path. It is the everyday diversion of the fancy. But
she could say that she had not once thought seriously of George
Cannon as a husband. Why, he was not of her generation!
Although she did not know his age, she guessed that he must be
nearer forty than thirty. He was of the generation of Sarah Gailey,
and Sarah Gailey was the contemporary of her dead mother!
And he had never shown for her any sentiment but that of a
benevolently teasing kindliness. Moreover, she was afraid of
him, beyond question. And withal, he patently lacked certain
qualities which were to be found in her image of a perfect man.
No! She had more often thought of Edwin Clayhanger as a
husband. Indeed she had married Edwin Clayhanger several
times. The haunting youth would not leave her alone. And she
said to herself, hot and indignant: 'I shall have to leave Brighton!
I can see that! Sarah Gailey's brought it on herself!' Yes, she
was actually angry with Sarah Gailey, who however had only
informed her of a fact which she would have been sorry not to
know! And in leaving Brighton, that fancy of hers took her
straight to Bursley, to stay with Janet Orgreave in the house next
to the new house of the Clayhangers!

Whither was George Cannon leading her? He had not yet said
a word in explanation of the errand, nor shown in any way that
he had observed her extraordinary condition. He was silent,
swinging his stick. She also was silent. She could not have
spoken, not even to murmur: 'Where are you taking me to?'
They went forward as in an enchantment.

II

They were on the King's Road; and to the left were the high hotels and houses, stretching east and west under the glare of the sun into invisibility, and to the right was the shore, and the sea so bright that the eye could scarcely rest on it. Both the upper and the lower promenades were crowded with gay people surging in different directions. The dusty roadway was full of carriages, and of the glint of the sun on wheelspokes and horses' flanks, and of rolling, clear-cut shadows. The shore was bordered with flags and masts and white and brown sails; and in the white-and-green of billows harmlessly breaking could be seen the yellow bodies of the bathers. A dozen bare-legged men got hold of a yacht under sail with as many passengers on board, and pushed it forcibly right down into the sea, and then up sprang its nose and it heeled over and shot suddenly off, careering on the waves into the offing where other yachts were sliding to and fro between the piers, dominating errant fleets of row-boats. And the piers also were loaded with excited humanity and radiant colour. And all the windows of all the houses and hotels were open, and blowing with curtains and flowers and hats. The whole town was enfevered.

Hilda thought, her heart still beating, but less noisily, 'I scarcely ever come here. I don't come here often enough.' And she saw Sarah Gailey rocking and sighing and rocking and shaking her head in the mournful twilight of the basement in Preston Street. The contrasts of existence struck her as magnificent, as superb. The very misery and hopelessness of Sarah's isolation seemed romantic, splendid, touchingly beautiful. And she thought, inexplicably: 'Why am I here? Why am I not at home in Turnhill? Why am I so different from what mother was? What am I going to be and to do? This that I now am can't continue for ever.' She saw thousands of women with thousands of men. And, quite forgetting that to the view of the multitude she was just as much as any of them with a man (and a rather fine man, too!), she began to pity herself because she was not with a man! She dreamed, in her extreme excitation, of belonging absolutely to some man. And despite all her pride and independence, she dwelt with pleasure and longing on the vision of being his, of being at his disposal, of being under his might, of being helpless before him. She thought, desolated: 'I am nobody's. And so there is "talk"!' She scorned herself for being nobody's. To belong utterly to some male seemed to be the one tolerable fate for her in the world. And it was a glorious fate, whether it brought good or evil. Any other was ignobly futile, was despicable. And then she thought, savagely: 'And just see my clothes! Why don't I take the trouble to look nice?'

Suddenly George Cannon stopped on the edge of the pavement, and turned towards the houses across the street.

'You see that?' he said, pointing with his stick.

'What?'

'The Chichester.'

She saw, in gold letters over the front of a tall corner house: 'The Chichester Private Hotel.'

'Well?'

'I've taken it – from Christmas. I signed about an hour ago. I just had to tell some one.'

'Well, I never!' she exclaimed.

He was beyond question an extraordinary and an impressive man. He had said that, after experimenting in Preston Street, he should take a larger place and lo! in less than a year, he had fulfilled his word. He had experimented in Preston Street with immense success, and now he was coming out into the King's Road! (Only those who have lived in a side street can pronounce the fine words 'King's Road' with the proper accent of deference.) And every house in the King's Road, Hilda now newly perceived, was a house of price and distinction. Nothing could be common in the King's Road: the address and the view were incomparably precious. Being established there, George Cannon might, and no doubt would, ultimately acquire of the largest public hotels; indeed, dominate the promenade! It would be just like him to do so! A year ago he was a solicitor in Turnhill. Today he was so perfectly and entirely a landlord that no one could ever guess his first career. He was not merely extraordinary: he was astounding. There could not be many of his calibre in the whole world.

'How does it strike you?' he asked, with an eagerness that touched her.

'Oh! It's splendid!' she answered, trying to put more natural enthusiasm into her voice. But the fact was that the Chichester had not yet struck her at all. It was only the idea of being in the King's Road that had struck her – and with such an effect that her attention was happily diverted from her trouble, and her vexatious self-consciousness disappeared. She had from time to time remarked the Chichester, but never with any particularity; it had been for her just an establishment among innumerable others, and not one of the best – the reverse of imposing. It stood at the angle of King's Road and Ship Street, and a chemist's shop occupied the whole of the frontage, the hotel-entrance being in Ship Street; its architecture was flat and plain, and the place seemed neglected, perhaps unprosperous.

'Twenty bow-windows!' murmured George Cannon, and then smiled at himself, as if ashamed of his own naïvety.

And Hilda counted the windows. Yes, there were eight on King's Road and twelve at the side. The building was high, and it was deep, stretching far down Ship Street. In a moment it began to put on, for Hilda, quite special qualities. How high it was! How deep it was! And in what a situation! It possessed mysterious and fine characteristics which set it apart. Strange that hitherto she had been so blind to it! She and George Cannon were divided from the house by the confused and noisy traffic of the roadway, and by the streaming throngs on the opposite pavement. And none of these people riding or driving or walking, and none of the people pushing past them on the pavement behind, guessed that here on the kerb was the future master of the Chichester, an amazing man, and that she, Hilda Lessways, by his side, was the woman to whom he had chosen first to relate his triumph! This unrecognized secrecy in the great animated street was piquant and agreeable to Hilda, a source of pride.

'I suppose you've bought it?' she ventured. She had no notion of his financial resources, but her instinct was to consider them infinite.

'No! I've not exactly bought it,' he laughed. 'Not quite! I've got the lease, from Christmas. How much d'ye think the rent is?' He seemed to challenge her.

'Oh! Don't ask me!'

'Five hundred a year,' he said, and raised his chin. 'Five hundred a year! Ten pounds a week! Nearly thirty shillings a

day! You've got to pay that before you can even begin to think
of your own profits.'

'But it's enormous!' Hilda was staggered. All her mother's
houses put together had brought in scarcely a third of the rental
of that single house, which was nevertheless only a modest unit
in several miles of houses. 'But can you make it pay?'

'I fancy so! Else I shouldn't have taken it. The present man
can't. But then he's paying £550 for one thing, and he's old. And
he doesn't know his business ... Oh yes! I think I can see my
money back ... Wait till Christmas is turned and I make a
start!'

She knew that the future would justify his self-confidence. How
he succeeded she could not define. Why should he succeed where
another was failing? He could not go out and drag boarders by
physical force into his private hotel! Yet he would succeed. In
every gesture he was the successful man. She looked timidly up
at his eyes under the strong black eyelashes. His glance caught
hers. He smiled conqueringly.

'Haven't said a word to Sarah yet!' he almost whispered, so
low was his voice; and he put on a mock-rueful smile. Hilda
smiled in response.

'Shall you keep Preston Street?' she asked.

'Of course!' he said with pride – 'I shall run the two, naturally.' He put his shoulders back. 'One will help the other, don't
you see?'

She thought she saw, and nodded appreciatively. He meant to
run two establishments! At the same moment a young and stylish
man drove rather slowly by in a high dog-cart. He nodded
carelessly to George Cannon, and then, perceiving that George
Cannon was with a lady, raised his hat in haste. George
Cannon responded. The young man gazed for an instant hard
at Hilda, with a peculiar expression, and passed on. She did not
know who he was. Of George Cannon's relationships in the town
she was entirely ignorant, but that he had relationships was always
obvious.

She blushed, thinking of what Sarah Gailey had said about
'talk' concerning herself and George Cannon. In the young
man's glance there had been something to annoy and shame her.

'Come across and have a look at the place,' said George

Cannon, suddenly stepping down into the gutter, with a look first in one direction and then in the other for threatening traffic.

'I don't think I'll come now,' she replied.

'But why not? Are you in a hurry? You've plenty of time before five o'clock – heaps!'

'I'd prefer not to come,' she insisted, in an abashed and diffident voice.

'But what's up?' he demanded, stepping back to the pavement, and glancing directly into her eyes.

She blushed more and more, dropping her eyelids.

'I don't want to be talked about *too* much!' she muttered, mortified. Her inference was unmistakable. The whole of her mind seemed now to be occupied with an enormous grievance which she somehow had against the world in general. Her very soul, too, was bursting with this grievance.

'Talked about? But who –'

'Never mind! I know! I've been told!' she interrupted him.

'Oh! I see!' He was now understanding the cause of her trouble in Sarah Gailey's bedroom.

'Now look here!' he went on. 'I've just got to have a few words with you. You come across the road, please.' He was imperious.

She raised her glance for a timid moment to his face, and saw to her intense astonishment that he also was blushing. Never before had she seen him blush.

'Come along!' he urged.

She followed him obediently across the dangerous road. He waited for her at the opposite kerb, and then they went up Ship Street. He turned into the entrance of the Chichester, which was grandiose, with a flight of shallow steps, and then a porch with two basket-chairs, and then another flight of shallow steps ending in double doors which were noticeably higher than the street level. She still followed.

'Nobody in here, I expect,' said George Cannon, indicating a door on the right, to an old waiter who stood in the dark hall.

'No, sir.'

George Cannon opened the door as a master, ushered Hilda into a tiny room furnished with a desk and two chairs, and shut the door.

III

The small window was of ground glass and gave no prospect of
the outer world, from which it seemed to Hilda that she was as
completely cut off as in a prison. She was alone with George
Cannon, and beyond the narrow walls which caged them together, and close together, there was nothing! All Brighton, save
this room, had ceased to exist. Hilda was now more than ever
affrighted, shamed, perturbed, agonized. Yet at the same time
she had the desperate calm of the captain of a ship about to
founder with all hands. And she saw glimpses, beautiful and
compensatory, of the romantic quality of common life. She was
in a little office of a perfectly ordinary boarding-house – (she
could even detect the stale odours of cooking) – with a realistic
man of business, and they were about to discuss a perfectly
ordinary piece of scandal; and surely they might be called two
common-sense people! And withal, the ordinariness and the
midland gumption of the scene were shot through with the
bright exotic rays of romance! She thought: 'It is painful and
humiliating to be caught and fixed as I am. But it is wonderful
too!'

'The fact is,' said George Cannon, in an easy, reassuring
tone, 'we never get the chance of a bit of quiet chat. Upon my
soul we don't! Now I suppose it's Sarah who's been worrying
you?'

'Yes.'

'What did she say? ... You'd better sit down, don't you
think?' He swung round the pivoted arm-chair in front of the
closed desk and pointed her to it.

'Oh!' Hilda hesitated, and then sank onto the chair without
looking at it. 'She simply said there was a lot of talk about you
and me. Has she been saying anything to you?'

He shook his head, staring down at her. Hilda put her arms on
the arms of the chair, and, shirking the man's gaze, stared down
at the worn carpet and at his boots thereon. One instinct in her
desired that he should move away or that the room should be
larger, but another instinct wanted him to remain close, lest the
savour of life should lose its sharpness.

'It passes me how people can say such things!' she went on,

in a low, thrilled, meditative voice. 'I can't understand it!' She was quite sincere in her astonished indignation. Nevertheless, she experienced a positive pride at being brought into a scandal with George Cannon; she derived from it a certain feeling of importance; it proved that she was no longer a mere girlish miss.

George Cannon kept silence.

'I shall leave Brighton,' Hilda continued. 'That I've quite decided! I don't like leaving your sister, as ill as she is! But really –' And she thought how prudent she was, and how capable of taking care of herself – she all alone in the world!

'Where should you go to? Bursley? The Orgreaves?' George Cannon asked absently and carelessly.

'I don't know,' said Hilda, with curtness.

He stepped aside, in the direction of the window, and examined curiously the surface of the glass, as though in search of a concealed message which it might contain. In a new and much more animated voice he said to the window:

'Of course I know it's all my fault!'

Hilda glanced up at his back; he was still not more than three feet away from her.

'How is it your fault?' she asked, after a pause.

He made another pause.

'The way I look at you,' he said.

These apparently simple words made Hilda tremble, and deprived her of speech. They shifted the conversation to another plane. 'The way I look at you! The way I look at you!' What did he mean? How did he look at her? She could not imagine what he was driving at! Yes, she could! She knew quite well. All the time, while pretending to herself not to understand, she understood. It was staggering, but she perfectly understood. He had looked at her 'like that' on the very first day of their acquaintance, in his office at Turnhill, and again at the house in Lessways Street, and again in the newspaper office, and on other occasions, and again on the night of their arrival at Brighton. But surely not lately! Or did he look at her 'like that' behind her back? Was it possible that people noticed it? . . . Absurd! His explanation of the origin of the gossip did not convince her. She had, however, suddenly lost interest in the origin of the gossip. She was entirely occupied with George Cannon's tone, and his calm, audacious reference to a phenomenon which had hitherto seemed to her to be far beyond the region of words.

She was frightened. She was like some one walking secure in the night, who is stopped by the sound of rushing water and stands with all his senses astrain, afraid to move a step farther, too absorbed and intimidated to be aware of astonishment. The point was not whether or not she had known or guessed the existence of this unseen and formidable river; the point was that she was thrillingly on its brink, in the dark. Every instant she heard its swelling current plainer and plainer. She thought: 'Am I lost? How strange that this awful and exquisite thing should happen to just me!' She was quite fatalistic.

He turned his head suddenly and caught her guilty eyes for an instant before she could lower them.

'You don't mean to say you don't know what I mean?' he said.

She still could not speak. Her trouble was acute, her self-consciousness far keener than it had ever been before. She thought: 'But it's impossible that this awful and exquisite thing should happen in this fashion!' George Cannon moved a step towards her. She could not see his face, but she knew that he was looking at her with his expression at once tyrannic and benevolent. She could feel, beating upon her, the emanating waves of his personality. And she was as confused as though she had been sitting naked in front of him ... And he had brought all this about by simply putting something into words – by saying: 'It's the way I look at you!'

He went on:

'I can't help it, you know ... The very first minute I ever set eyes on you ... Of course I'm thirty-six. But there it is! ... I've never seen any one like you; and I've seen a few! The fact is, Hilda, I do believe you don't know how fine you are.' He spoke more quickly and with boyish enthusiasm; his voice became wonderfully persuasive. 'You are fine, you know! And you're beautiful! I didn't think so at first, but you are! You're being wasted. Why, a woman like you ...! You've no idea. You're so proud and stiff, when you want to be ... I'd trust you with anything. You're absolutely the only woman I ever met that I'd trust like a man! And that's a fact ... Now, nobody could ever think as much of you as I do. I'm quite certain of it. It couldn't be done. I *know* you, you see! I understand everything you do, and whatever you do, it's just fine for me. You couldn't be as happy with any one else! You couldn't! I feel that in my bones . . . Now – now, I must tell you something –'

The praise, the sympathy, the passion were astounding, marvellous, and delicious to her. Was it conceivable that this experienced and worldly man had been captivated by such a mere girl as herself? She had never guessed it! Or had she always guessed it? An intense pride warmed her blood like a powerful cordial. Life was even grander than she had thought! . . . She drooped into an intoxication. Among all that he had said, he had not said that he was not stronger than she. He had not relinquished his authority. She felt it, sitting almost beneath him in the slippery chair. She knew that she would yield to him. She desired to yield to him. Her mind was full of sensuous images based on the abdication of her will in favour of his.

'Now, look here, Hilda. I want to tell you –'

He perhaps did not intend that she should look up; but she looked up. And she was surprised to see that his face was full of troubled hesitations, showing almost dismay. He made the motion of swallowing. She smiled; and set her shoulders back – the very gesture that she had learned from him.

'What?' she questioned, in a whisper.

Her brief mood of courage was over. She sank before him again, and waited with bowed head.

Profoundly disturbed, he stood quite still for a few seconds, with shut lips, and then he made another step to approach.

'Your name's got to be Cannon,' she heard him say.

She thought, still waiting: 'If this goes on a moment longer I shall die of anticipation, in bliss.' And when she felt his hand on her shoulder, and the great shadow of him on part of her face, her body seemed to sigh, acquiescent and for the moment assuaged: 'This is a miracle, and life is miraculous!' She acknowledged that she had lacked faith in life.

She was now on the river, whirling. But at the same time she was in the small, hot room, and both George Cannon's hands were on her unresisting shoulders; and then they were round her, and she felt his physical nearness, the texture of his coat and of his skin; she could see in a mist the separate hairs of his tremendous moustache and the colours swimming in his eyes; her nostrils expanded in transient alarm to a faint, exciting masculine odour. She was disconcerted, if not panic-struck, by the violence of his first kiss; but her consternation was delectable to her.

And amid her fright and her joy, and the wonder of her extreme surprise, and the preoccupation of being whirled down the river, she calmly reflected, somewhere in her brain: 'The door is not locked. Supposing some one were to come in and see us!' And she reflected also, in an ecstasy of relief: 'My life will be quite simple now. I shall have nothing to worry about. And I can help him.' For during a year past she had never ceased to ask herself what she must do to arrange her life; her conscience had never ceased to tell her that she ought not to be content to remain in the narrow ideas of her mother, and that though she preferred marriage she ought to act independently of the hope of it. Throughout her long stay in Preston Street she had continually said: 'After this – what? This cannot last for ever. When it comes to an end what am I to do to satisfy my conscience?' And she had thought vaguely of magnificent activities and purposes – she knew not what . . . The problem existed no more. Her life was arranged. And now, far more sincerely than in the King's Road twenty minutes earlier, she regarded the career of a spinster with horror and with scorn. At best, she suddenly perceived with blinding clearness, it would have been pitiful – pitiful! Twenty minutes earlier, in the King's Road, she had dreamt of belonging absolutely to some man, of being at his disposal, of being under his might, of being helpless before him. And now! . . . Miracle thrice miraculous! Miracle unconceived, inconceivable! . . . No more "talk" now! . . .

She told herself how admirable was the man. She assured herself that he was entirely admirable. She reminded herself that she had always deemed him admirable, that only twenty minutes earlier, in the King's Road, when there was in her mind no dimmest, wildest notion of the real future, she had genuinely admired him. How clever, how tactful, how indomitable, how conquering, how generous, how kind he was. How kind to his half-sister! How forbearing with her! Indeed, she could not recall his faults. And he was inevitably destined to brilliant success.

She would be the wife of a great and a wealthy man. And in her own secret ways she could influence him, and thus be greater than the great.

Love? It is an absolute fact that the name of 'love' did not in the first eternal moments even occur to her. And when it did she gave it but little importance. She had to admit that she had not consciously thought of George Cannon with love – at any rate with love as she had imagined love to be. Indeed, her immediate experience would not fit any theory that she could formulate. But with the inexorable realism of her sex she easily dismissed inconvenient names and theories, and accommodated herself to the fact. And the fact was that she overwhelmingly wanted George Cannon, and, as she now recognized, had wanted him ever since she first saw him. The recognition afforded her intense pleasure. She abandoned herself candidly to this luxury of an unknown desire. It was incomparably the most splendid and dangerous experience that she had ever had. She did not reason, and she had no wish to reason. She was set above reason. Happy to the point of delicious pain, she yet yearned forward to a happiness far more excruciating. She was perfectly aware that her bliss would be torment until George Cannon had married her, until she had wholly surrendered to him.

Yet at intervals a voice said very clearly within her: 'All this is wrong. This is base and shameful. This is something to blush for, really!' She did blush. But her blushes were a part of the delight. And the voice was not persistent. She could silence it with scarcely an effort, despite its clarity.

'Kiss me!' George Cannon demanded of her, with eager masterfulness.

The request shocked her for an instant, and the young girl in her was about to revolt. But she kissed him – an act which combined the sweetness of submission with the glory of triumph! She looked at him steadily, confident in herself and in him. She felt that he knew how to love. His emotion filled her with superb pride. She seemed to be saying to him in a doomed rapture: 'Do you think I don't know what I am doing? I know! I know!'

The current of the river was tremendous. She foresaw the probability of disaster. She was aware that she had definitely challenged the hazard of fate. But she was not terrified in the dark, swirling night of her destiny. She straightened her shoulders. With all her innocence and ignorance and impulsiveness and weakness, she had behind her the unique and priceless force of her youth. She was young, and she put her trust in life.

CHAPTER 3
FLORRIE AGAIN

I

As they were walking home along the King's Road, Hilda suddenly stopped in front of a chemist's shop. 'I've got something to buy here,' she said diffidently, and then added: 'I'll follow you.'

'And what have you got to buy?' he asked, facing her, with his benevolent, ironical expression.

'Never mind!' she gently laughed. 'I shan't be many minutes after you.' She pretended to make a mystery. But her sole purpose was to avoid re-entering the house in his company; and she knew that he had divined this. Nevertheless, she found pleasure in the perfectly futile pretence of a mysterious purchase.

She was very self-conscious as they stood there on the dusty footpath amid the promenaders gay and gloomy, chattering and silent, who were taking the sun and the salt breeze. Despite her reason, she had a fear that numbers of people would perceive her to be newly affianced and remark upon the contrast between her girlishness and his maturity. But George Cannon was not in the slightest degree self-conscious. He played the lover with ease and said quite simply and convincingly just the things which she would have expected a lover to say. Indeed, the conversation, as carried on by him, between the moment of betrothal and the arrival at the chemist's shop, was the one phenomenon of the engagement which corresponded with her preconceived ideas concerning such an affair. It convinced her that she really was affianced.

'Well?' he murmured fondly and yet quizzically, as they remained wordless, deliciously hesitating to part. 'What are you thinking about?'

She replied with brave candour, appealing to him by a soft glance:

'I was only thinking how queer it is I should be engaged in

a room I'd never seen before in my life – going into it like that!'

He looked at her uncomprehending; for an instant his features were blank; then he smiled kindly.

'It's so strange!' she encouraged him.

'Yes. Isn't it?' he agreed, with charming, tranquil politeness.

'He doesn't see it!' she thought, as she watched the play of his face. 'He doesn't see how wonderful it is that I should go into a room that was absolutely unknown to me, and then this should happen at once. Why! I never knew there was such a room!' She could not define how she was affected by this fact, but she regarded the fact as tremendously romantic, and its effect on her was profound. And George saw in it no significance! She was disconcerted. She felt a tremor; it was as though the entire King's Road had quivered for a fraction of a second and then, feigning nonchalance, resumed its moveless solidity.

Inside the chemist's she demanded the first thing she set eyes on – a tooth-brush. All the while she was examining various shapes of tooth-brushes, she had a vision of George raising his hat to take leave of her, and she could see not only the curve of his hand and the whiteness of his cuff, but also the millions of tiny marks and creases on the coarse skin of his face, extraordinarily different from her own smooth, pure, delicate, silky complexion. And she remembered that less than three years ago she had regarded him as of another generation, as indefinitely older and infinitely more experienced than her childish and simple self. This reflection produced in her a consternation which was curiously blissful.

'No, madam,' the white-aproned chemist was saying. 'It's this size that we usually sell to ladies.'

She put on the serious judicial air of an authentic adult woman, and frowned at the chemist.

II

When, in Preston Street, she was reluctantly approaching the house, she saw a cab, coming downwards in the opposite direction, stop at No. 59.

'That must be Florrie!' she said, half-aloud.

The boarding-house being in need of another servant, young, strong and reliable, Hilda had suggested that Miss Florence Bagster might be invited to accept the situation. Sarah Gailey had agreed that it would be wise to have a servant from Turnhill; she mistrusted southern servants, and appeared to believe that there was no real honesty south of the Trent. Florence Bagster had accepted the situation with enthusiasm, writing that she longed to be again with her former mistress; she did not write that the mysterious and magnetic name of Brighton called her more loudly than the name of her former mistress. And now Florence was due.

But it was not Florence who emerged from the cab. It was a tall and full-bosomed young lady in a gay multi-coloured costume, and gloves and a sunshade and a striking hat. This young lady stood by the cab expectant and smiling while the cabman pulled a tin trunk off the roof of the vehicle, and then, when the cabman had climbed down and was dragging the trunk after him, she put out an arm and seized one handle of the trunk to help him, which act, so strange on the part of a young lady, made Hilda, coming nearer and nearer, look more carefully. She was astounded as she realized that the unknown young lady was not a young lady after all, but the familiar Florrie at the advanced age of sixteen.

The aged cabman had made no mistake. He left the tin trunk on the pavement and took timid Florrie's money without touching his hat for it. Florrie was laying her sunshade rather forlornly on the top of the tin trunk and preparing to lift the trunk un-aided, when Mr Boutwood, stout and all in black, came gallantly forth from the house to assist her. Sarah Gailey's opposition had not been persistent enough to keep the jovial Mr Boutwood out of No. 59. Shortly after Christmas his wife had died suddenly, and Mr Boutwood, with plenty of money and plenty of time on his hands, had found himself desolated. In his desolation he had sought his old acquaintance George Cannon, and the result had somehow been that bygones had become bygones and a new boarder had increased the prosperity of No. 59. Sarah Gailey could not object. Indeed, she had actually wept for the death of one enemy and the affliction of another. Moreover, she seldom had contact with the boarders now.

The rather peculiar circumstances of Florrie's arrival almost cured Hilda's self-consciousness, and she entered the house, in the wake of the trunk, with a certain forgetful ease. There was Mr Boutwood, still dallying with Florrie and the trunk, in the narrow hall! The shocking phenomenon of a boarder helping a domestic servant with her luggage had been rendered possible only by a series of accidents. The front door being left open on account of the weather, Mr Boutwood had had a direct view of the maiden, and the maiden had not been obliged to announce her arrival officially by ringing a bell. Hence the other servants had not had notice. And of the overseers of the house one was imprisoned in the basement and the other two had been out betrothing themselves! In the ordinary way the slightest un-usualness in the hall would instantly attract the attention of somebody in authority.

Mr Boutwood was not immediately aware of Hilda. His attitude towards Florrie was shocking to Hilda in a double sense; it shocked her as an overseer, but it shocked her quite as much as a young woman newly jealous for the pride of all her sex. Florrie was beyond question exceedingly pretty; in particular the chin pouted more deliciously than ever. Her complexion was even finer than Hilda's own. She had a simple, good-natured glance, a quick and extraordinarily seductive smile, and the unique bodily grace of her years. Her costume, though vulgar and very ill-made, was effective at a little distance; her form and movements gave it a fictitious worth. Indeed, she was an amazing blossom to have come off the dunghill of Calder Street. Domestic drudgery had not yet dehumanized nor disfigured her – it is true that her hands were concealed in gloves, and her feet beneath a flowing skirt. Now, Mr Boutwood's attitude showed very plainly that the girlish charms of Florrie had produced in him a definite and familiar effect. He would have been ready to commit follies for the young woman, and to deny that she was a drudge or any-thing but a beautiful creature.

Hilda objected. She objected because Mr Boutwood was a widower, holding that he had no right to joy, and that he ought to mourn practically for ever in solitude. She would make no allowance for his human instincts, his need of intimate com-panionship, his enormous unoccupied leisure. She would have condemned him utterly, on the score of his widowhood alone. But she objected far more strongly to his attitude because he was fat and looked somewhat coarse. She counted his obesity to him for a sin. And it was naught to her that he had been a martyr to idleness and wealth, which combination had prematurely aged him. Mr Boutwood was really younger than George Cannon, and Florence Bagster certainly seemed as old as Hilda. Yet the juxtaposition of the young, slim, and virginal Florrie and the large, earth-worn Mr Boutwood profoundly offended her.

It was Mr Boutwood who first discovered that Hilda was in the doorway. He was immediately abashed, and presented the most foolish appearance. Whereupon Hilda added scorn to her disgust. Florrie, however, easily kept her countenance, and with a pert smile took the hand which her former mistress graciously extended. By universal custom a servant retains some of the privileges of humanity for several minutes after entering upon a new servitude. Mr Boutwood vanished.

'Louisa will help you upstairs with the trunk,' said Hilda, when she had made inquiries about the wonderful journey which Florrie had accomplished alone, and about the health of Florrie's aunt and of her family. 'Louisa!' she called loudly up the stairs and down into the basement.

III

She followed the procession of the trunk upstairs, and, Louisa having descended again, showed Florrie into the kennel. This tiny apartment had in it two truckle-beds, and a wash-bowl on a chair, and little else. A very small square trap-window in the low ceiling procured a dusky light in the middle hours of the day. Florence seemed delighted with the room; she might have had to sleep under the stairs.

'Put on your afternoon apron, and then you can go down and see Miss Gailey,' said Hilda, and shut the door upon Florrie in her new home.

When she turned, there was George Cannon on the half-landing beneath the skylight! She knew not how he had come there, nor whether he had entered the house before or after herself.

'I'm glad he isn't fat!' she thought. And it was as though she had thought. 'If he were fat everything would be different.' Her features did not relax as she went down the five steps to the half-landing where he waited, smiling faintly. She thought: 'We must be very serious and circumspect in the house. There must never be the slightest –' But while she was yet on the last step, he firmly put his hands on her ears and, drawing her head towards him, kissed her full on the mouth, and she saw again, through her eye-lashes, all the details of his face. She yielded. All her ideas of circumspection melted magically away in an abandoned tenderness of which she was ashamed, but for which she would have unreflectingly made any sacrifice. The embrace was over in an instant. Besides being guiltless of obesity, George Cannon was free from the unpardonable fault of clumsiness. He was audacious, but he was not foolhardy, and he would never be abashed. True, she had seen dismay on his face at the moment of his declaration, but that moment was unique, and his dismay had ineffably flattered her. Now on the half-landing, she was drenched in bliss. And she felt dissolute; she felt even base. But she did not care. She thought, as it were, startled: 'This is love. This must be what love is. I must have been in love without knowing it. And as for a girl always knowing when a man's in love with her, and foreseeing the proposal, and all that sort of thing . . .' Her practical contempt for all that sort of thing could not be stated in words.

'Florrie's just come,' she whispered, and by a movement of the head indicated that Florrie was in the kennel.

They went together to the drawing-room on the first floor. It was empty, the entire population of the boarding-houses being still on the seashore. Hilda stood near the door, which she left open, and gave detailed news of Florrie in a tone very matter-of-fact. There was no reference to love, or to the new situation created, or to the vast enterprise of the Chichester. The topic was Florrie, and somehow it held the field despite efforts to dislodge it.

Then the stairs creaked. Already Florrie was coming down. In a trice she had made herself ready for work. She came down timidly, not daring to look to right nor left, but concentrating her attention on the stairs. She passed along the landing outside the drawing-room door, and Hilda, opening the door a little wider, had a full surreptitious view of her back; and George Cannon, farther within the room, also saw her. They watched her disappear on her way to find the basement and the formidable Sarah Gailey. Hilda was touched by the spectacle of this child disguised as a strapping woman, far removed from her family and her companions and her familiar haunts, and driven or drawn into exile at Brighton, where she would only see the sea once a week, except through windows, and where she would have to work from fourteen to sixteen hours a day for a living, and sleep in a kennel. The prettiness, the pertness, and the naïve contentedness of the child thus realizing an ambition touched her deeply.

'It does seem a shame, doesn't it?' she said.

'What?'

'Bringing her all the way up here, like this! She doesn't know a soul in Brighton. She's bound to be frightfully home-sick –'

'What about you?' George Cannon interrupted politely. 'Doesn't she know you?' He smiled with all his kindness.

'Yes – but –'

Hilda did not finish. It was not worth while. George Cannon had not understood. He did not feel as she felt, and her emotion was incommunicable to him. A tremendous misgiving seized her, and she had a physical feeling of emptiness in the stomach. It passed, swiftly as a hallucination. Just such a misgiving as visits nearly every normal person immediately before or immediately after marriage! She ignored it. She was engaged – that was the paramount fact! She was engaged, and joyously determined to prosecute the grand adventure to the end. The immensity of the risks forced her to accept them.

IV

That evening Sarah Gailey was in torment from the pain in her wrists. There was nothing to be done. She had had the doctor, and no article of the prescribed treatment had been neglected. With unaccustomed aid from Hilda she had accomplished the business of undressing and getting into bed, and now she sat up in bed, supported by her own pillows and one from Hilda's bed, and nursed her wrists, while Hilda poured drops of a narcotic for her into a glass of water. Apart from the serious local symptoms, her health was fairly good. She could eat, she could talk, she could walk, and her brain was clear. Hilda held the glass for her to drink, for it was prudent to keep her hands as much as possible in repose.

'There!' said Hilda, as if to a young child who had been querulous. 'I'm sure you'll sleep now!'

'I don't think I shall,' the sufferer whined.

'Oh yes, you will!' Hilda insisted firmly, although she was by no means sure. 'Let me take this extra pillow away, and then you can lie down properly.' She was thinking reproachfully: 'What a pity it is for all of us that the poor thing can't bear her pain with a little less fuss!' It was not Sarah alone who was embittered and fatigued by Sarah's pain.

'Where's George?' asked the invalid, when she was laid down.

'In the parlour. Why?'

'Oh, nothing!'

'By the way,' said Hilda, seized by a sudden impulse, which had its origin in Sarah's tone at once martyrized and accusing – 'by the way, who is it that's been talking scandal about me and George?'

'Scandal?' Sarah Gailey seemed weakly to protest against the word.

'Because, if you want to know,' Hilda continued, 'we're engaged to be married!' She reflected, contrite: 'This won't help her to sleep!' And then added, in a new, endearing accent, awaiting an outburst of some kind from Sarah: 'Of course it's a secret, dear. I'm telling no one but you.'

After a moment's silence, Sarah remarked casually, with shut-eyes: 'It'll be much the best not to tell anyone. And the shorter the engagement the better! Don't let anybody in the house know till you're married.' She sighed, put her cheek into the pillow, and moved her bound wrists for a few seconds, restlessly. 'If you turn the gas down,' she finished very wearily, 'I dare say I may get off. If only they'd stop that piano upstairs!'

She had displayed no surprise at the tremendous event, no sentimental interest in it. The fact was that Sarah Gailey's wrists

were infinitely more interesting to her than any conceivable project of marriage. Continuous and acute pain had withdrawn her
from worldly affairs, making her more than ever like a god.

Hilda was startled. But she was relieved. Now, for the first
time, she had the authentic sensation of being engaged. And it
appeared to her that she had been engaged for a very long
period, and that the engagement was a quite ordinary affair. She
was relieved; yet she was also grievously saddened. She lowered
the gas, and in the gloom gazed for a few seconds at the vague,
huddled, sheeted, faintly moaning figure on the bed; the untidy
grey hair against the pillow struck her as intolerably pathetic.

'Good night,' she said softly.

And the feeble, plaintive voice responded: 'Good night.'

She went out, leaving the door slightly ajar.

V

In the parlour adjoining, George Cannon was seated at the table.
When Hilda saw him and their eyes met, she was comforted; a
wave of tenderness seemed to agitate her. She realized that this
man was hers, and the realization was marvellously reassuring.
The sound of the piano descended delicately from the drawing
room as from a great distance. From the kitchen came the
muffled clatter of earthenware and occasionally a harsh, loud
voice; it was the hour of relaxed discipline in the kitchen, where,
amid the final washing-up and much free discussion and banter,
Florrie was recommencing her career on a grander basis. Hilda
closed the door very quietly. When she had closed it and was
shut in with George Cannon her emotion grew intenser.

'I think she'll get off now,' she whispered, standing near the
door.

'Have you told her?'

Hilda nodded.

'What does she say?'

Hilda raised her eyebrows: 'Oh! . . . Well, she says we'd better
keep it quiet, and make the engagement as short as possible.' She
blushed.

'Look here,' said George. 'Let's go out, eh?'

'But – what will people say?'

'What the devil does it matter what they say? I want you to come out with me.'

The whispered oath, and his defiant smile, enchanted her.

'We can go out by the area steps,' he continued. 'There's two of 'em sitting in the hall, but the front door's shut. Do go and get your hat.'

She left the room with an obedient smile. Pushing open Sarah's door very gently, she groped on the hooks behind it for her hat. 'It won't matter about gloves – in the dark,' she thought. 'Besides, I mustn't disturb her.' Before drawing-to the door she looked again at the bed. There was neither sound nor movement. Probably Sarah Gailey slept. The dim vision of the form on the bed and the blue spark of gas in the corner produced in Hilda a mood of poignant and yet delicious sorrow.

'Why, what's the matter?' George Cannon asked when she had returned to the parlour.

She knew that her eyes were humid with tears. Both her arms were raised above her head as she fixed the hat. This act of fixing the hat in George's presence gave her a new pleasure. She smiled at him.

'Nothing!' she said, whispering mysteriously. 'I think she's gone off. I'm so glad. You know she really does suffer dreadfully.'

His look was uncomprehending; but she did not care. The anticipation of going out with him was now utterly absorbing her.

He waited with his hand on the gas-tap till she was ready, and then he lowered the gas.

'Wait a moment,' she whispered at the door, and with a gesture called him back into the room from the flagged passage leading to the area steps.

On the desk was his evening glass of milk, which he drank cold in summer. She offered it to him in the twilit room like an enraptured handmaid. He had forgotten it. The fact that he had forgotten it and she had remembered it yet further increased her strange, mournful, ecstatic bliss.

'Have some,' he whispered, when he had drunk.

She finished the glass, trembling. They went forth, climbing the area steps with proper precautions and escaping as thieves escape, down the street. For an instant she glimpsed the wide-open windows of the drawing-room and the dining-room, from behind whose illuminated blinds came floating, as it were wistfully, the sound of song and chatter. She thought of Sarah Gailey prone and unconscious in the basement. And she felt the moisture of the milk on her lips. 'Am I happy or unhappy?' she questioned herself, and could not reply. She knew only that she was thrillingly, smartingly alive.

At the corner of Preston Street and King's Road a landau waited.

'This is ours,' said George casually.

'Ours?'

What a splendid masculine idea! How it proved that he too had been absorbed in the adventure! She admired him humbly, like a girl, like a little girl. With the most formal deference he helped her into the carriage.

'Drive towards Shoreham,' he commandingly directed the driver, and took his place by her side.

Yes! He was mature. He was a man of the world. He had had every experience. He knew how to love. That such a being was hers, that she without any effort had captured such a being, flattered her to an extreme degree. She was glorious with pride. She leaned back in the carriage negligently, affecting an absolute calm. She armed herself in her virginity. Not George Cannon himself could have guessed that only by a miracle of self-control did she prevent her hand from seeking his beneath the light rug that covered their knees! She intimidated George Cannon in that hour, and the while her heart burned with shame at the secret violence of her feelings. She thought: 'This must be love. This is love!' And yet her conscience inarticulately accused her of obliquity. But she did not care, and she would not reflect. She thought that she wilfully, perversely, refused to reflect; but in reality she was quite helpless.

Under the still and feverish night the landau rolled slowly along between the invisible murmuring sea and the lighted façades of Hove. Occasionally other carriages, containing other couples, approached, were plain for a moment, and dissolved away.

'So she thinks the engagement ought to be short?' said George Cannon.

'Yes.'

'So do I!' he pronounced with emphasis.

Hilda desired to ask him: 'How short?' But she could not. She could not bring herself to put the question. She was too proud. By a short engagement, did he mean six months, three months, a month? Dared she hope that he meant . . . a month? This was a thought buried in the deepest fastness of her soul, a thought that she would have perished in order not to expose; but it existed.

'I think I should like to go back now,' she breathed timidly, before they were beyond Hove. It was not a request to be ignored. The carriage turned. She felt relief. The sensation of being alive had been too acute to be borne, and it was now a little eased. She knew that her destiny was irrevocable, that nothing could prevent her from being George Cannon's. Whether the destiny was evil or good did not paramountly interest her. But she wanted to rush forward into the arms of fate, and to know her fate. She dreamed only of the union.

BOOK V

HER DELIVERANCE

CHAPTER 1
LOUISA UNCONTROLLED

I

HILDA, after a long railway journey, was bathing her face, arms, and neck at the large double washstand in the large double bedroom on the second floor of No. 59 Preston Street. At the back of the washstand was an unused door which gave into a small bedroom occupied by the youngest Miss Watchett. George Cannon came up quietly behind her. She pretended not to hear him. He put his hands lightly on her wet arms. Smiling with condescending indulgence, half to herself, she still pretended to ignore him, and continued her toilet.

The return from the honeymoon, which she had feared, had accomplished itself quite simply and easily. She had feared the return, because only upon the return was the marriage to be formally acknowledged and published. It had been obviously impossible to announce, during the strenuous summer season, the engagement of the landlord to a young woman who lived under the same roof with him. The consequences of such an indiscretion would have been in various ways embarrassing. Hence not a word was said. Nor were definite plans for the wedding made until George remarked one evening that he would like to be married at Chichester, Chichester being the name of his new private hotel. Which exhibition of sentimentality had both startled and touched Hilda. Chichester, however, had to be renounced, owing to the difficulty of residence. The subject having been thus fairly broached, George had pursued it, and one day somewhat casually stated that he had taken a room in Lewes and meant to sleep there every night for the term imposed by the law. Less than three weeks later, Hilda had unobtrusively departed from No. 59, the official account being that she was to take a holiday with friends after the fatigues of August and early September. She left the train at Lewes, and there, in the presence of strangers, was married to George Cannon, who had quitted

Brighton two days earlier and was supposed to be in London on business. Even Sarah Gailey, though her health had improved, did not assist at the wedding. Sarah, sole depositary of the secret, had to remain in charge of No. 59.

A strange wedding! Not a single wedding present, except those interchanged by the principals! Nor had any of the problems raised by the marriage been solved, or attacked. The future of Sarah Gailey, for example! Was Sarah to go on living with them? It was inconceivable, and yet the converse was also inconceivable. Sarah had said nothing, and nothing had been said to Sarah. Matters were to settle themselves. It had not even been decided which room Mr and Mrs Cannon should inhabit as man and wife. It was almost certain that, in the dead period between the popular summer season and the fashionable autumn season, there would be several bedrooms empty. Hilda, like George, did not want to bother with a lot of tedious details, important or unimportant. The attitude of each was: 'Let me get married first, and then I'll see to all that.'

Thus had the return been formidable to Hilda. All the way from Ireland she had been saying to herself: 'I shall have to go up the steps, and into the house, and be spoken to as Mrs Cannon! And then there'll be Sarah ... !' But the entry into the house had produced no terror. Everywhere George's adroitness had been wonderful, extraordinarily comforting and reassuring, and nowhere more so than in the vestibule of No. 59. The tone in which he had said to Louisa, 'Take Mrs Cannon's handbag, Louisa,' had been a marvel of ease. Louisa had incontestably blenched, for the bizarre Sarah, who conserved in Brighton the inmost spirit of the Five Towns, had thought fit to tell the servants nothing whatever. But the trained veteran in Louisa had instantly recovered, and she had replied 'Yes, sir,' with a simplicity which proved her to be the equal of George Cannon ... The worst was over for Hilda. And the next moments were made smooth by reason of a great piece of news which, forcing Sarah Gailey to communicate it at once, monopolized attention, and so entirely relieved the bride's self-consciousness.

Florence Bagster, having insolently quarrelled with her mistress, had left her service without notice. Mr Boutwood had also gone, and the connection between the two departures was only too apparent, not merely to Sarah, but also to the three Miss Watchetts, who had recently arrived. Florence, who could but whisper, had shouted at her mistress. Little, flushing, modest Florrie, who yesterday in the Five Towns was an infant, had compromised herself with a fat widower certainly old enough to be her father. And the widower, the friend of the house, had had so little regard for the feelings of the house that he had not hesitated to flaunt with Florrie in the town. It was known that they were more or less together, and that he stood between Florrie and the world.

II

'I suppose I'd better write at once to her mother – or perhaps her aunt; her aunt's got more sense,' said Hilda, as she dropped the sponge and groped for a towel, her eyes half blinded.

In moving she had escaped from his hands.

'What do you say?' she asked, having heard a vague murmur through the towel.

'I say you can write if you like.' George spoke with a careless smile.

Now, facing her, he put his hands on her damp shoulders. She looked up at him over the towel, leaning her head forward, and suspending action. Her nose was about a foot from his. She saw, as she had seen a hundred times, every detail of his large handsome, and yet time-worn face, every hair of his impressive moustache, all the melting shades of colour in his dark eyes. His charm was coarse and crude, but he was very skilful, and there was something about his experienced, weather-beaten, slightly depraved air, which excited her. She liked to feel young and girlish before him; she liked to feel that with him, alone of all men, her modesty availed nothing. She was beginning to realize her power over him, and the extent of it. It was a power miraculous and mysterious, never claimed by her, and never admitted by him save in glance and gesture. This power lay in the fact that she was indispensable to him. He was not her slave – she might indeed have been considered the human chattel – but he was the slave of his need of her. He loved her. In him she saw what love was; she had seen it more and more clearly ever since the day of their engagement. She was both proud and ashamed of her power. He did not possess a similar power over herself. She was fond of him, perhaps getting fonder; but his domination of her senses was already nearly at an end. She had passed through painful, shattering ecstasies of bliss, hours unforgettable, hours which she knew could never recur. And she was left sated and unsatisfied. So that by virtue of this not yet quite bitter disillusion, she was coming to regard herself as his superior, as being less naïve than he, as being even essentially older than he. And in speaking to him sometimes she would put on a grave and precociously sapient mien, as if to indicate that she had access to sources of wisdom for ever closed to him.

'But don't you think we *ought* to write?' she frowned.

'Certainly, if you like! It won't do any good. You don't suppose her aunt will come down here, do you? And even if she did . . . There it is, and there you are!'

'Just let me wipe my shoulders, will you?' she said.

He lifted his hands obediently, and as they were damp he rubbed them on the loose corner of the towel.

'Well,' he said, 'I must be off, I reckon.'

'Shall you see Mr Boutwood?'

'I might . . . I know where to catch him, I fancy.'

She seemed to have a glimpse of her husband's separate life in the town – masculine haunts and habits of which she knew nothing and would always know nothing. And the large existence of the male made her envious.

'Going to see him now?'

'Well, yes.' George smiled roguishly.

'What shall you say to him?'

'What can I say to him? No business of mine, you know, except that we've lost a decent servant. But I expect that's Sarah's fault. She's no use whatever with servants now, Sarah isn't.'

'*I* shall never speak to Mr Boutwood again!' Hilda exclaimed almost passionately.

'Oh, but –'

'His behaviour is simply scandalous. It's really wicked. A man like him!'

George put his lips out deprecatingly. 'You may depend she asked for it,' he said.

'What?'

'She asked for it,' he repeated with convinced firmness, and look at her steadily.

A flush slowly spread over her face and neck, and she lowered her gaze. In her breast pride and shame were again mingled.

'You keep your hair on, littl'un,' said George soothingly, and kissed her. Then he took his hat and stick, which were with a lot of other things on the broad white counterpane, and went off stylishly.

'You don't understand,' she threw at him with a delicious side-glance of reproof as he opened the door. She reproached herself for the deceiving coquetry of the glance.

'Don't I?' he returned airily.

He was quite sure that nothing escaped his intelligence. To Hilda, shocked by the coarseness and the obtuseness which evidently characterized his attitude, now as on other occasions, this self-confidence was desolating; it was ominously sinister.

III

She was alone with her image in the mirror, and the image was precisely the same that she had always seen; she could detect no change in it whatever. She liked the sensation of being alone and at home in this room which before she had only entered as an overseer and which she had never expected to occupy. She savoured the intimacy of the room – the necessaries on the washstand, the superb tortoiseshell brushes, bought by George in Dublin, on the dressing-table, the open trunks, George's clothes on a chair, and her own flimsy trifles on the bed. Through the glass she saw, behind her image, the image of the closed door; and then she turned round to look at the real door and to assure herself that it was closed. Childish! And yet . . .! George had shut the door. She remembered the noise of its shutting. And that noise, in her memory, seemed to have transformed itself into the sound of fate's deep bell. She could hear the clang, sharp, definite. She realized suddenly and with awe that her destiny was fixed hereafter. She had come to the end of her adventures and her vague dreams. For she had always dreamt vaguely of an en-larged liberty, of wide interests, and of original activities – such as no woman to her knowledge had ever had. She had always compared the life of men with the life of women, and admitted and resented the inferiority of the latter. She had had glimpses, once, of the male world; she had made herself the only woman shorthand-writer in the Five Towns, and one of the earliest in England – dizzy thought! But the glimpses had been vain and tantalizing. She had been in the male world, but not of it, as though encircled in a glass ball which neither she nor the males could shatter. She had had money, freedom, and ambition, and somehow, through ignorance or through lack of imagination or opportunity, had been unable to employ them. She had never known what she wanted. The vision had never been clear. And she reflected: 'I wonder if my daughter, supposing I had one, would be as different from me as I am from my mother?'

She could recall with intense vividness the moment when she had first really contemplated marriage. It was in the steam-tram after having seen Edwin Clayhanger at the door of Clayhanger's shop. And she could recall the sense of relief with which she had envisaged a union with some man stronger and more experienced than herself. In the relief was a certain secret shame, as though it implied cowardice, a shrinking away from the challenge of life and from the call of a proud instinct. In the steam-tram she had foreseen the time when she would belong utterly to some man, surrendering to him without reserve – the time when she would be a woman. And the thing had come about! Only yesterday she had been a little girl entering George Cannon's office with timid audacity to consult him. Only yesterday George Cannon had been a strange, formidable man, indefinitely older and infinitely cleverer than she. And now they were man and wife! Now she was his! Now she profoundly knew him, and he was no longer formidable, in spite of his force. She had a recondite dominion over him. She guessed herself to be his superior in certain qualities. He was revealed to her; she felt that she was not revealed to him, and that in spite of her whole-hearted surrender she had not given all because of his blindness to what she offered. She could not completely respect him. But she was his. She was naught apart from him. She was the wife. His existence went on mainly as before; hers was diverted, narrowed – funda-

mentally altered. Never now could she be enfranchised into the
male world!

IV

She slipped her arms into a new bodice purchased in London on
the second day of the marriage. Blushing, she had tried on that
bodice in a great shop in Oxford Street; then it was that she had
first said 'my husband' in public. All that day she had felt so
weak and shy and light and helpless and guilty that she had
positively not known what she was doing; she had moved in a
phantom world. Only, she had perceived quite steadily and practically that she must give more attention to her clothes. Her old
contempt for finery expired in the glory of her new condition.
And now, as she settled the elegant bodice on her shoulders, and
fastened it, and patted her hair, and picked up the skirt and poised
it over her head, she had a stern, preoccupied look, as of one who
said: 'This that I am doing is important. I must not be hurried
in doing it. It is vital that I should look well and that no detail of
my appearance should jar.' Already she could see herself standing before George when he returned for the meal – the first meal
which they would take together in the home. She could feel his
eyes on her: she could anticipate her own mood – in which would
be mingled pride, misgiving, pleasure, helplessness, abandonment – and the secret condescension towards him of her inmost
soul.

All alone in the room she could feel his hands again on her
shoulders: a mysterious excitation . . . She was a married woman.
She had the right to discuss Florrie's case with aloof disdain, if
she chose. Her respectability was unassailable. None might
penetrate beyond the fact of her marriage. And yet, far within
her, she was ashamed. She dimly admitted once more, as on
several occasions previous to her marriage, that she had dis-
honoured an ideal. Her conscience would not chime with the
conscience of society. She thought, as she prepared with pleasurable expectancy for her husband: 'This is not right. This cannot
lead to good. It must lead to evil. I am bound to suffer for it.
The whole thing is wrong. I know it, and I have always known it.'

Already she was disappointed with her marriage. Amid the fevers of bodily appetite she could clearly distinguish the beginning of lassitude; she no longer saw her husband as a romantic and baffling figure; she had explored and charted his soul, and not all his excellences could atone for his earthliness. She wondered grimly where and under what circumstances he had acquired the adroitness which had charmed and still did charm her. She saw in front of her a vista of days and years in which ennui would probably increase and joy diminish. And she put her shoulders back defiantly, and thought: 'Well, here I am anyhow! I wanted him, and I've got him. What I have to go through I shall go through!'

And all the time, floating like vapour over these depths was a sheeny mood of bright expectation and immediate naïve content. And she said gaily that she must write at once to Janet Orgreave to announce the marriage, and that her mother's uncle up in the North must also be informed.

V

Unusual phenomena made themselves apparent on the top staircase: raised voices which Hilda could hear more and more plainly, even through the shut door. At No. 59, in the off-seasons, nobody ever spoke in a loud tone, particularly on the staircase, except perhaps Florrie when, in conversation with Louisa, she thought she was out of all other hearing. Hilda's voice was very clear and penetrating, but not loud. George Cannon's voice in public places such as the staircase had an almost caressing softness. The Watchetts cooed like faint doves, thereby expressing the delicate refinement of their virginal natures. The cook's voice was unknown beyond the kitchen. And nobody was more grimly self-controlled in speech than Sarah Gailey and Louisa. These two – and especially Louisa – seemed generally to be restraining with ease tremendous secret forces of bitterness and contempt. And now it was just these two who were noisy, and becoming noisier, to the dismay of a scandalized house. Owing to some accident or negligence the secret forces had got loose.

Hilda shook her head. It was clear that the problem of Sarah Gailey would have to be tackled and settled very soon. The poor woman's physical sufferings had without doubt reacted detrimentally on her temperament and temper. She used to be quite extraordinarily adroit in the directing of servants, though her manner to them never approached geniality. But she had quarrelled with Florrie, and now she was breaking the peace with Louisa! It was preposterous and annoying, and it could not be allowed to continue. Hilda was not seriously alarmed, because she had the most perfect confidence in George's skill to restore order and calm, and to conquer every difficulty of management; and she also put a certain trust in herself; but the menacing and vicious accents of Louisa startled her, and she sympathized with Sarah Gailey, for whom humiliation was assuredly in store – if not immediately at the tongue of Louisa, then later when George would have to hint the truth to her about her decadence.

The dispute on the attic landing appeared to be concerning linen which Louisa had omitted to remove from Florrie's abandoned couch in her kennel.

'I ain't going to touch her sheets, not for nobody!' Louisa proclaimed savagely. And by that single phrase, with its implications, she laid unconsciously bare the sordid baseness of her ageing heart; she exposed by her mere intonation of the word 'sheets' all the foulness of jealousy and thwarted salacity that was usually concealed beneath her tight dress and neat apron, and beneath her prim gestures and deferential tones. Her undisciplined voice rang spinsterishly down the staircase, outraging it, defiling the whole interior.

Hilda as silently as possible unlatched the door of the bedroom, and stood with ear cocked. Should she issue forth and interfere, or should she remain discreetly where she was? Almost at the same instant she heard the cautious unlatching of the drawing-room door; two of the Watchetts were there listening also. And there came up from the ground floor a faint giggle. The cook, at the kitchen door, was enjoying herself and giggling moral support to her colleague. The giggle proved that the master was out, that the young mistress had not yet established a definite position, and that during recent weeks the old mistress must have been steadily dissipating her own authority. Hilda peered along the landing from her lair, and upstairs and downstairs; she could see nothing but senseless carpets and brass rods and steps and banisters; but she knew that the entire household – she had the sensation that the very house itself – was alert and eavesdropping.

There was a hesitating movement on the unseen stairs above, and then Hilda could see Sarah Gailey's felt slippers and the valance of her skirt. And she could hear Sarah's emotional breathing.

'Very well, Louisa, I've done!' Sarah's voice was quieter now. She was trying to control it, and to a limited extent was controlling its volume. It shook in spite of her. She spoke true. She had indeed done. She was at the end of her resources.

'I've been in houses,' Louisa conqueringly sneered, 'that I have! But I never been in a house afore where one as ought to have been a scullery-girl went off with a boarder, and nothing said, and him the friend of the master! And it isn't as if that was all! . . . Sheets, indeed!'

'I've nothing further to say,' Sarah returned unnecessarily, and descended the stair. 'I shall simply report to Mr Cannon. We shall see.'

'And what's this about *Mrs* Cannon?' Louisa shouted, beside herself.

The peculiarity of her tone arrested Sarah Gailey. Hilda flushed. The Watchetts were listening. The Watchetts had not yet been told of the marriage. The announcement was to be made to them formally, a little later. And now it was Louisa who was making the announcement, brutally, coarsely. The outrage of the episode was a hundredfold intensified; it grew into an inconceivable ghastly horror. Hilda's self-respect seemed to have a physical body, and Louisa to be hacking at it with a jagged knife.

'Mr Cannon has brought his wife home,' said Sarah Gailey shortly, with a dignity and courage that increased as her distance from the appalling, the incredible Louisa. Hilda could see her pale face now. The eyebrows and chin were lifted in scorn of the vile menial, but the poor head was trembling.

'And what about his other wife?'

'Louisa!' – Sarah Gailey looked again up the stairs – 'I know you're in a temper and not responsible for what you say. But you'd better be careful.' She spoke with elaborate haughty negligence.

'Had I?' Louisa shrilled. 'What I say is, What about his other wife? What about the old woman he married in Devonshire? Why, God bless me, Florrie was full of it – couldn't talk about anything else in bed of a night! Didn't you know the old woman'd been inquiring for her beautiful 'usband down your way?' She laughed loudly. 'Turnhill – what's-its-name? . . . And all of you lying low, and then making out all of a sudden as he's brought his wife home! A nice house! And I've been in a few, too!'

Hilda could feel her heart beating with terrific force against her bodice, but she was conscious of no other sensation. She heard a loud snort of shattering contempt from Louisa; and then a strange and terrific silence fell on the stairs. There was no sound even of a movement. The Watchetts did not stir; the cook did not stir; Sarah Gailey did not stir; Louisa's fury was sated. The empty landing lay, as it were, expectant at Hilda's door.

Then Sarah Gailey perceived Hilda half hidden in the doorway, and staggeringly rushed towards her. In an instant they were both in the bedroom and the door shut.

'When will George be back so that he can put her out of the house?' Sarah whispered frantically.

'Soon, I expect,' said Hilda, and felt intensely self-conscious.

They said no more. And it was as though the house were besieged and invested, and only in that room were they safe, and even in that room only for a few moments.

CHAPTER 2
SOME SECRET HISTORY

I

WITHOUT a word, Sarah had left the bedroom. Hilda waited, sitting on the bed, for George to come back from his haunts in the town. She both intensely desired and intensely feared his return. A phrase or two of an angry and vicious servant had almost destroyed her faith in her husband. It seemed very strange, even to her, that this should be so; and she wondered whether she had ever had a real faith in him, whether – passion apart – her feeling for him had ever been aught but admiration of his impressive adroitness. Was it possible that he had another wife alive? No, it was not possible! That is to say, it was not possible that such a catastrophe should have happened to just her, to Hilda Lessways, sitting there on the bed with her hands pressing on the rough surface of the damask counterpane. And yet – how could Louisa or Florrie have invented the story? ... Wicked, shocking, incredible, that Florrie, with her soft voice and timid, affectionate manner, should have been chattering in secret so scandalously during all these weeks! She remembered the look on Florrie's blushing face when the child had received the letter on the morning of their departure from the house in Lessways Street. Even then the attractively innocent and capable Florrie must have had her naughty secrets! ... An odious world! And Hilda, married, had seriously thought that she knew all about the world! She had to admit, bewildered: 'I'm only a girl after all, and a very simple one.' She compared her own heart in its simplicity with that of Louisa. Louisa horrified and frightened her ... Louisa and Florrie were mischievous liars. Florrie had seized some fragment of silly gossip – Turnhill was notorious for its silly gossip – and the two of them had embroidered it in the nastiness of their souls. She laughed shortly, disdainfully, to wither up silly gossip ... Preposterous!

And yet – when George had shown her the licence, in the name of Cannon, and she had ventured to say apologetically and caressingly: 'I always understood your real name was Canonges,' – how queerly he had looked as he answered: 'I changed it long ago – legally!' Yes, and she had persuaded herself that the queerness of his look was only in her fancy! But it was not only in her fancy. Suspicions, sinister trifling souvenirs, crowded into her mind. Had she not always doubted him? Had she not always said to herself that she was doing wrong in her marriage and that she would thereby suffer? Had she not abandoned the pursuit of religious truth in favour of light enjoyments? ... Foolish of course, old-fashioned of course, to put two and two together in this way! But she could not refrain.

'I am ruined!' she decided, in awe.

And the next instant she was saying: 'How absurd of me to be like this, merely because Louisa ...!'

She thought she heard a noise below. Her heart leapt again into violent activity. Trembling, she crept to the door, and gently unlatched it. No slightest sound in the whole house! Dusk was coming on swiftly. Then she could hear all the noises, accentuated beyond custom, of Louisa setting tea in the dining-room for the Watchetts, and then the tea-bell rang. Despite her fury, apparent in the noises, Louisa had not found courage to neglect the sacred boarders. She made a defiant fuss, but she had to yield, intimidated, to the force of habit and tradition. The Watchetts descended the staircase from the drawing-room, practising as usual elaborate small-talk among themselves. They had heard every infamous word of Louisa's tirade; which had engendered in them a truly dreadful and still delicious emotion; but they descended the staircase in good order, discussing the project for a new pier ... They reached the dining-room and shut the door on themselves.

Silence again! Louisa ought now to have set the tea in the basement parlour. But Louisa did not. Louisa was hidden in the kitchen, doubtless talking fourteen to the dozen with the cook. She had done all she meant to do. She knew that she would be compelled to leave at once, and not another stroke would she do of any kind! The master and the mistresses must manage as best they could. Louisa was already wondering where she would sleep that night, for she was alone on earth and owned one small trunk and a Post Office Savings Bank book . . . All this trouble on account of Florrie's sheets!

Sarah Gailey was in her bedroom, and did not dare to come out of it even to accuse Louisa of neglecting the basement tea. And Hilda continued to stand for ages at the bedroom door, while the dusk grew deeper and deeper. At last the front door opened, and George's step was in the hall. Hilda recognized it with a thrill of terror, turning pale. George ran down into the basement and stumbled. 'Hello!' she heard him call out. 'What about tea? Where are you all? Sarah!' No answer, no sound in response! He ran up the basement steps. Would he call in at the dining-room, or would he come to the bedroom in search of her? He did not stop at the dining-room. Hilda wanted to shut the bedroom door, but dared not because she could not do it noiselessly. Now he was on the first floor! She rushed to the bed, and sat on it, as she had been sitting previously, and waited in the most painful and irrational agony. She was astonished at the darkness of the room. Turning her head, she saw only a whitish blur instead of a face in the dressing-table mirror.

II

'What's up?' he demanded, bursting somewhat urgently into the bedroom with his hat on. 'What price the husband coming home to his tea? No tea! No light! I nearly broke my neck down the basement stairs.'

He put his hands against her elbows and kissed her, rather clumsily, owing to the gloom, between her nose and her mouth. She did not shrink back, but accepted the embrace quite insensibly. The contact of his moustache and of his lips, and his slight, pleasant masculine odour, produced no effect on her whatever.

'Why are you sitting here? Look here, I've signed the transfer of those Continental shares, and paid the cheque! So it's domino, now!'

Between the engagement and the marriage there had been an opportunity of purchasing three thousand pounds' worth of preference shares in the Brighton Hotel Continental Limited, which hotel was the latest and largest in the King's Road, a vast affair of eight stories, and bathrooms on every floor. The chance of such an investment had fascinated George. It helped his dreams and pointed to the time when he would be manager and part proprietor of a place like the Continental. Hilda being very willing, he had sold her railway shares and purchased the hotel shares, and he knew that he had done a good thing. Now he possessed an interest in three different establishments, he who had scarcely been in Brighton a year. The rapid progress, he felt, was characteristic of him.

Hilda kept silence, for the sole reason that she could think of no words to say. As for the matter of the investment, it appeared to her to be inexpressibly uninteresting. From under the lashes of lowered eyes she saw his form shadowily in front of her.

'You don't mean to say Sarah's been making herself disagreeable already!' he said. And his tone was affectionate and diplomatic, yet faintly ironical. He had perceived that something unusual had occurred, perhaps something serious, and he was anxious to soothe and to justify his wife. Hilda perfectly understood his mood and intention, and she was reassured.

'Hasn't Sarah told you?' she asked in a harsh, uncontrolled voice, though she knew that he had not seen Sarah.

'No; where is she?' he inquired patiently.

'It's Louisa,' Hilda went on, with the sick fright of a child compelled by intimidation to affront a danger. Her mouth was very dry.

'Oh!'

'She lost her temper and made a fearful scene with Sarah, on the stairs; she said the most awful things.'

George laughed low, and lightly. He guessed Louisa's gift for foul insolence and invective.

'For instance?' George encouraged. He was divining from Hilda's singular tone that tact would be needed.

'Well, she said you'd got a wife living in Devonshire.'

There was a pause.

'And who'd told her that?'

'Florrie.'

'*In*deed!' muttered George. Hilda could not decide whether his voice was natural or forced.

Then he stepped across to the door, and opened it.

'What are you going to do to her?' Hilda questioned, as it were despairingly.

He left the room and banged the door.

'It's not true,' Hilda was beginning to say to herself, but she seemed to derive no pleasure from the dawning hope of George's innocence.

Then George came into the room again, hesitated, and shut the door carefully.

'I suppose it's no good shilly-shallying about,' he said, in such a tone as he might have used had he been vexed and disgusted with Hilda. 'I have got a wife living, and she's in Devonshire! I expect she's been inquiring in Turnhill if I'm still in the land of the living. Probably wants to get married again herself.'

Hilda glanced at his form, and suddenly it was the form of a stranger, but a stranger who had loved her. And she thought: 'Why did I let this stranger love me?' It was scarce believable that she had ever seriously regarded him as a husband. And she found that tears were running down her cheeks; and she felt all her girlishness and fragility. 'Didn't I always know,' she asked herself, with weak resignation, 'that it was unreal? What am I to do now?' The catastrophe had indeed happened to her, and she could not deal with it! She did not even feel tragic. She did not feel particularly resentful against George. She had read of such catastrophes in the newspapers, but the reality of experience nonplussed her. 'I ought to do something,' she reflected. 'But what?'

'What's the use of me saying I'm sorry?' he asked savagely. 'I acted for the best. The chances were ten thousand to one against me being spotted. But there you are! You never know your luck.' He spoke meditatively, in a rather hoarse, indistinct voice. 'All owing to Florrie, of course! When it was suggested we should have that girl, I knew there was a danger. But I pooh-poohed it! I said nothing could possibly happen ... And just look at it now! ... I wanted to cut myself clear of the Five Towns, absolutely – absolutely! And then like a damnation fool I let Florrie come here! If she hadn't come, that woman might have inquired about me in Turnhill till all was blue, without you hearing about her! But there it is!' He snapped his fingers. 'It's my

fault for being found out! That's the only thing I'm guilty of . . .
And look at it! Look at it!'

Hilda could tell from the movements of the vague form in the
corner by the door, and by the quality of his voice, that George
Cannon was in a state of extreme emotion. She had never known
him half so moved. His emotion excited her and flattered her.
She thought how wonderful it was that she, the shaking little
girl who yesterday had run off with fourpence to buy a meal at a
tripe-shop, should be the cause of this emotion in such a man.
She thought: 'My life is marvellous.' She was dizzied by the conception of the capacity of her own body and soul for experience.
No factors save her own body and soul and his had been necessary to the bringing about of the situation. It was essential only
that the man and the woman should be together, and their com-
panionship would produce miracles of experience! She ceased
crying. Astounding that she had never, in George's eyes, suspected his past! It was as if he had swiftly opened a concealed
door in the house of their passion and disclosed a vista of which
she had not dreamed.

'But surely that must have been a long time ago!' she said in
an ordinary tone.

'Considering that I was twenty-two – yes!'

'Why did you leave her?'

'Why did I leave her? Because I had to! I'd gone as a clerk in a
solicitor's office in Torquay, and she was a client. She went mad
about me. I'm only telling you. She was a spinster. Had one of
those big houses high up on the hill behind the town!' He stopped;
and then his voice began to come again out of the deep shadow in
the corner. 'She wanted me, and she got me. And she didn't care
who knew! The wedding was in the *Torquay Directory*. I told her
I'd got no relations, and she was jolly glad.'

'But how old was she? Young?'

George sneered. 'She'd never see thirty-six again, the day she
was married. Good-looking. Well-dressed. Very stylish and all
that! Carried me off my feet. Of course there was the money . . . I
may as well out with it all while I'm about it! She made me an
absolute present of four thousand pounds. Insisted on doing it.
I never asked. Of course I know I married for money. It happens

to youths sometimes just as it does to girls. It may be disgusting, but not more disgusting for one than for the other. Besides, I didn't realize it was a sale and purchase, at the time! ... Oh! And it lasted about ten days. I couldn't stand it, so I told her so and chucked it. She began an action for restitution of conjugal rights, but she soon tired of that. She wouldn't have her four thousand back. Simply wouldn't! She was a terror, but I'll say that for her. Well, I kept it. Four thousand pounds is a lot of brass. That's how I started business in Turnhill, if you want to know!' He spoke defiantly. 'You may depend I never let on in the Five Towns about my beautiful marriage ... That's the tale. You've got to remember I was twenty-two!'

She thought of Edwin Clayhanger and Charlie Orgreave as being about twenty-two, and tried in her imagination to endow the mature George Cannon with their youth and their simplicity and their freshness. She was saddened and overawed; not wrathful, not obsessed by a sense of injury.

Then she heard a sob in the corner, and then another. The moment was terrible for her. She could only distinguish in the room the blur of a man's shape against the light-coloured wallpaper, and the whiteness of the counterpane, and the dark square of the window broken by the black silhouette of the mirror. She slipped off the bed, and going in the direction of the dressing-table groped for a match-box and lit the gas. Dazzled by the glare of the gas, she turned to look at the corner where stood George Cannon.

III

The whole aspect of the room was now altered. The window was blacker than anything else; light shone on the carved frame of the mirror and on the vessels of the washstand; the trunks each threw a sharply defined shadow; the bed was half in the shadow of its mahogany foot, and half a glittering white; all the array of requisites on the dressing-table lay stark under the close scrutiny of the gas; and high above the bed, partly on the wall and partly on the ceiling, was a bright oblong reflection from the up-turned mirror.

Hilda turned to George with a straightening of the shoulders, as if to say: 'It is I who have the courage to light the gas and face this situation!' But when she saw him her challenging pride seemed to die slowly away. Though there was no sign of a tear on his features, and though it was difficult to believe that it was he who had just sobbed, nevertheless, his figure was dismayingly tragic. Every feature was distorted by agitation. He was absorbed in himself, shameless and careless of appearances. He was no more concerned about appearances and manly shame than a sufferer dying in torment. He was beyond all that – in truth a new George Cannon! He left the corner, and sat down on the bed in the hollow made by Hilda, and stared at the wall, his hands in the pockets of his gay suit. His gestures as he moved, and his posture as he sat, made their unconscious appeal to her in their abandonment. He was caught; he was vanquished; he was despairing; but he instinctively, and without any wish to do so, kept his dignity. He was still, in his complete overthrow, the mature man of the world, the man to whom it was impossible to be ridiculous.

Hilda in a curious way grew proud of him. With an extra-ordinary inconsequence she dwelt upon the fact that, always grand – even as a caterer – he had caused to be printed, at the foot of the menu forms which he had instituted, the words: 'A second helping of all or any of the above dishes will willingly be served if so desired.' And in the general havoc of the shock she began to be proud also of herself, because it was the mysterious power of her individuality that had originated the disaster. The sense of their intimate withdrawn seclusion in the room, dis-ordered and littered by arrival, utterly alone save for the living flame of the gas, the sense of the tragedy, and of the responsibility for it, and especially her responsibility, the sense of an imposed burden to be grimly borne and of an unknown destiny to be worked out, the sense of pity, the sense of youth and force – these things gradually exalted her and ennobled her desolation.

'Why did you keep it from me?' she asked, in a very clear and precise tone, not aggrieved, but fatalistic and melancholy.

'Keep what from you?' At length he met her eyes, darkly.

'All this about your being married.'

'Why did I keep it from you?' he repeated harshly, and then his tone changed from defiance to a softened regret: 'I'll tell you

why I kept it from you! Because I knew if I told you I should have
no chance with a girl like you. I knew it'd be all up – if I so much
as breathed a hint of it! I don't suppose you've the slightest idea
how stand-offish you are!'

'Me stand-offish!' she protested.

'Look here!' he said persuasively. 'Supposing I'd told you I
wanted you, and then that I'd got a wife living – what would you
have said?'

'I don't know.'

'No! But *I* know! And suppose I'd told you I'd got a wife
living and then told you I wanted you – what then? No, Hilda!
Nobody could fool about with you!'

She was flattered, but she thought secretly: 'He could have won
me on any terms he liked! ... I wonder whether he *could* have
won me on any terms! ... That first night in this house, when we
were in the front attic – suppose he'd told me then – I wonder!
What should I have said?' But the severity of her countenance
was a perfect mask for such weak and uncertain ideas, and confirmed him deeply in his estimate of her.

He continued:

'Now that first night in this house, upstairs!' He jerked his
head towards the ceiling. She blushed, not from any shame, but
because his thought had surprised hers. 'I was as near as dammit
to letting out the whole thing and chancing it with you. But I
didn't – I saw it'd be no use. And that's not the only time either!'

She stood silent by the dressing-table, calmly looking at him
and she asked herself, eagerly curious: 'When were the other
times?'

'Of course it's all my fault!' he said.

'What is?'

'This! ... All my fault! I don't want to excuse myself. I've
nothing to say for myself.'

In her mind she secretly interrupted him: 'Yes, you have. You
couldn't do without me – isn't that enough?'

'I'm ashamed!' he said, without reserve, abasing himself. 'I'm
utterly ashamed. I'd give anything to be able to undo it.'

She was startled and offended. She had not expected that he
would kiss the dust. She hated to see him thus. She thought:
'It isn't all your fault. It's just as much mine as yours. But even if

I was ashamed I'd never confess it. Never would I grovel! And never would I want to undo anything! After all, you took the chances. You did what you thought best. Why be ashamed when things go wrong? You wouldn't have been ashamed if things had gone right.'

'Of course,' he said, after a pause, 'I'm completely done for!'

He spoke so solemnly, and with such intense conviction, that she was awed and appalled. She felt as one who, having alone escaped destruction in an earthquake, stands afar off and contemplates the silent, corpse-strewn ruin of a vast city.

And the thought ran through her mind like a squirrel through a tree: 'How *could* he refuse her four thousand pounds? And if she wouldn't have it back – well, what was he to do? She must be a horrible woman!'

IV

Both of them heard a heavy step pass up the staircase. It was Louisa's; she paused to strike a match and light the gas on the landing; and went on. But Sarah Gailey had given no sign, and the Watchetts were still shut in the dining-room. All these middle-aged women were preoccupied by the affair of George Cannon. All of them guessed now that Louisa's charge was not unfounded – otherwise, why the mysterious and interminable interview between George Cannon and Hilda in the bedroom? Hilda pictured them all. And she thought: 'But it is *I* who am in the bedroom with him! It is I who am living through it and facing it out! They are all far older than me, but they are outsiders. They don't know what life is!'

George rose, picked up a portmanteau, and threw it open on the bed.

'And what is to be done?' Hilda asked, trembling.

He turned and looked at her.

'I suppose I mustn't stay here?'

She shook her head, with lips pressed tight.

His voice was thick and obscure when he asked: 'You won't come with me?'

She shook her head again. She could not have spoken. She was in acute torture.

'Well,' he said, 'I suppose I can count on you not to give me up to the police?'

'The police?' she exclaimed. 'Why?'

'Well, you know – it's a three years' job – at least. Ever heard the word "bigamy"?' His voice was slightly ironical.

'Oh dear!' she breathed, already disconcerted. It had positively not occurred to her to consider the legal aspect of George's conduct.

'But what can you do?' she asked, with the innocent, ignorant helplessness of a girl.

'I can disappear,' he replied. 'That's all I can do! I don't see myself in prison. I went over Stafford Prison once. The Governor showed several of us over. And I don't see myself in prison.'

He began to cast things into the portmanteau, and as he did so he proceeded, without a single glance at Hilda:

'You'll be all right for money and so on. But I should advise you to leave here and not to come back any sooner than you can help. That's the best thing you can do. And be Hilda Lessways again! . . . Sarah will have to manage this place as best she can. Fortunately, her health's improved. She can make it pay very well if she likes. It's a handsome living for her. My deposit on the Chichester and so on will have to be forfeited.'

'And you?' she murmured.

His back was towards her. He turned his head, looked at her enigmatically for an instant, and resumed his packing.

She desired to help him with the packing; she desired to show him some tenderness; her heart was cleft in two with pity; but she could not move; some harshness of pride or vanity prevented her from moving.

When he had carelessly finished the portmanteau, he strode to the door, opened it wide, and called out in a loud, firm voice:

'Louisa!'

A reply came weakly from the top floor:

'Yes, sir.'

'I want you.' He had a short way with Louisa.

After a brief delay, she came to the bedroom door.

'Run down to the King's Road and get me a cab,' he said to her at the door, as it were confidentially.

'Yes, sir.' The woman was like a Christian slave.

'Here! Take the portmanteau down with you to the front door.'
He gave her the portmanteau.

'Yes, sir.'

She disappeared; and then there was the noise of the front door
opening.

George picked up his hat and abruptly left the room. Hilda
moved to and fro nervously, stiff with having stood still so long.
She wondered how he, and how she, would comport themselves
in the ordeal of adieu. In a few moments a cab drove up – Louisa
had probably encountered it on the way. Hilda waited, tense.
Then she heard the cab driving off again. She rushed aghast to the
window. She saw the roof of the disappearing cab, and the un-
wieldy portmanteau on it . . . He had gone! He had gone without
saying good-bye! That was his device for simplifying the situation. It was drastic, but it was magnificent. He had gone out of
the house and out of her life. As she gazed at the dim swaying
roof of the cab, magically the roof was taken off, and she could
see the ravaged and stricken figure within, sitting grimly in the
dark between the wheels that rolled him away from her. The
vision was intolerable. She moved aside and wept passionately.
How could he help doing all he had done? She had possessed
him – the memories of his embrace told her how utterly! All that
he had said was true; and this being so, who could blame his
conduct? He had only risked and lost.

Sarah Gailey suddenly appeared in the room, and shut the
door like a conspirator.

'Then – ?' she began, terror-struck.

And Hilda nodded, ceasing to cry.

'Oh! My poor dear!' Sarah Gailey moaned feebly, her head
bobbing with its unconscious nervous movements. The sight of
her worn, saddened features sharpened Hilda's appreciation of
her own girlishness and inexperience.

But despite the shock, despite her extreme misery, despite the
anguish and fear in her heart and the immense difficulty of the
new situation into which she was thus violently thrust, Hilda
was not without consolation. She felt none of the shame con-
ventionally proper to a girl deceived. On the contrary, deep
within herself, she knew that the catastrophe was a deliverance.
She knew that fate had favoured her by absolving her from the

consequences of a tragic weakness and error. These thoughts inflamed and rendered more beautiful the apprehensive pity for the real victim – now affronted by a new danger, the menace of the law.

BOOK VI

HER PUNISHMENT

CHAPTER 1
EVENING AT BLEAKRIDGE

I

WHEN Hilda's cab turned, perilously swaying, through the gate into the dark garden of the Orgreaves, Hilda saw another cab already at the open house door, and in the lighted porch stood figures distinguishable as Janet and Alicia, all enwrapped for a journey, and Martha holding more wraps. The long façade of the house was black, save for one window on the first floor, which threw a faint radiance on the leafless branches of elms, and thus intensified the upper mysteries of the nocturnal garden. The arrival of the second cab caused excitement in the porch; and Hilda, leaning out of the window into the November mist, shook with apprehension, as her vehicle came to a halt behind the other one. She was now to meet friends for the first time after her secret and unhappy adventure. She feared that Janet, by some magic insight of affection, would read at once in her face the whole history of the past year.

Janet had written to her, giving and asking for news, and urging a visit, on the very day after the scene in which George Cannon admitted his turpitude. Had the letter been sent a day or two sooner, reaching Hilda on her honeymoon, she would certainly have replied to it with the tremendous news of her marriage and, her marriage having been made public in the Five Towns, her shame also would necessarily be public. But chance had saved her from this humiliation. Nobody in the district was aware of the marriage. By a characteristic instinct, she had been determined not to announce it in any way until the honeymoon was over. In answer to Janet, she had written very briefly, as was usual with her, and said that she would come to Lane End House as soon as she could. 'Shall I tell her, or shan't I?' she had cogitated, and the decision had been for postponement. But she strongly desired, nevertheless, to pay the visit. She had had more than enough of Preston Street and of Brighton, and longed to leave at any price.

And at length, one dull morning, after George Cannon had sailed for America, and all affairs were somehow arranged or had arranged themselves, and Sarah Gailey was better and the autumn season smoothly running with new servants, she had suddenly said to Sarah: 'I have to go to Bursley today, for a few days.' And she had gone, upon the impulse, without having previously warned Janet. Changing at Knype, she had got into the wrong train, and had found herself at Shawport, at the far, lower end of Bursley, instead of up at Bleakridge, close by the Orgreaves! And there was, of course, no cab for her. But a cabman who had brought a fare to the station, and was driving his young woman back, had offered in a friendly way to take Hilda too. And she had sat in the cab with the young woman, who was a paintress at Peel's great manufactory at Shawport, and suffered from a weak chest; and they had talked about the potters' strike which was then upheaving the district, and the cab had overtaken a procession of thinly clad potters, wending in the bitter mist to a mass meeting at Hanbridge; and Hilda had been thereby much impressed and angered against all employers. And the young woman had left the cab, half-way up Trafalgar Road, with a delicious pink-and-white smile of adieu. And Hilda had thought how different all this was from Brighton, and how much better and more homely and understandable. And now she was in the garden of the Orgreaves.

Martha came peeping, to discover the explanation of this singular concourse of cabs in the garden, and she cried joyously:

'Oh, Miss Janet, it's Miss Hilda – Miss Lessways, I mean!'

Alicia shrieked. The first cab drew forward to make room for Hilda's, and Hilda stepped down into the glare of the porch, and was plainly beheld by all three girls.

'Will they notice anything?' she asked herself, self-conscious, almost trembling, as she thought of the terrific changes that had passed in her since her previous visit.

But nobody noticed anything. Nobody observed that this was not the same Hilda. Even in the intimacy of the affectionate kiss, for which she lifted her veil, Janet seemed to have no suspicion whatever.

'We were just off to Hillport,' said Janet. 'How splendid of you to come like this!'

'Don't let's go to Hillport!' said Alicia.

Janet hesitated, pulling down her veil.

'Of course you must go!' Hilda said positively.

'I'm afraid we shall have to go,' said Janet, with reluctance. 'You see, it's the Marrions – Edie's cousins – and Edie will be there!'

'Who's Edie?'

'Why! Tom's fiancée! Surely I told you!'

'Yes,' said Hilda; 'only I didn't just remember the name. How nice!'

(She thought: 'No sooner do I get here than I talk like they do! Fancy me saying, "How nice"!')

'Oh, it's all Edie nowadays!' said Alicia lightly. 'We have to be frightfully particular, or else Tom would cut our heads off. That's why we're going in a cab! We should have walked – shouldn't we, Janet? – only it would never do for us to *walk* to the Marrions' at night! "The Misses Orgreaves' carriage!"' she mimicked, and finicked about on her toes.

Janet was precisely the same as ever, but the pigtailed Alicia had developed. Her childishness was now shot through with gestures and tones of the young girl. She flushed and paled continuously, and was acutely self-conscious and somewhat vain, but not offensively vain.

'I say, Jan,' she exclaimed, 'why shouldn't Hilda come with us!'

'To the Marrions'? Oh no, thanks!' said Hilda.

'But do, Hilda! I'm sure they'd be delighted!' Janet urged. 'I never thought of it.'

Though she was flattered and, indeed, a little startled by the extraordinary seriousness of Janet's insistence, Hilda shook her head.

'Where's Tom?' she inquired, to change the subject.

'Oh!' Alicia burst out again. 'He's gone off *hours* ago to escort his ladylove from Hanbridge to Hillport.'

'You wait till you're engaged, Alicia!' Janet suggested. But Janet's eyes, too, twinkled the admission that Tom was just then providing much innocent amusement to the family.

'You'll sleep in my room tonight, anyhow, dear,' said Janet, when Martha and Hilda's cabman had brought a trunk into the hall, and Hilda had paid the cabman far more than his fare because he was such a friendly young cabman and because he possessed a pulmonary sweetheart. 'Come along, dear! ... Alicia, ask Swindells to wait a minute or two.'

'Swindells,' Alicia shouted to the original cabman, 'just wait a jiff!'

'Yes, miss.' The original cabman, being old and accustomed to evening-party work in the Five Towns, knew the length of a jiff, and got down from his seat to exercise both arms and legs. With sardonic pleasure he watched the young cabman cut a black streak in the sodden lawn with his near front-wheel as he clumsily turned to leave. Then Martha banged the front door, and another servant appeared in the hall to help the trunk on its way upstairs.

'No! I shall never be able to tell them!' thought Hilda, following the trunk.

Alicia had scampered on in front of the trunk, to inform her parents of the arrival. Mrs Orgreave, Hilda learnt, was laid up with an attack of asthma, and Osmond Orgreave was working in their bedroom.

II

Hilda stood in front of the fire in Janet's bedroom, and Janet was unlocking her trunk.

'Why! What a pretty bodice!' said Janet, opening the trunk. She stood up, and held forth the bodice to inspect it; and beneath Janet's cloak Hilda could see the splendour of her evening dress. 'Where did you get it?'

'In London,' Hilda was about to answer, but she took thought. 'Oh! Brighton.' It was a lie.

She had a longing to say:

'No, not Brighton! What am I thinking of? I got it in London on my honeymoon!'

What a unique sensation that one word would have caused! But she could not find courage to utter it.

Alicia came importantly in.

'Mother's love, and you are to go into her room as soon as you're ready. Martha will bring up a tray for you, and you'll eat there by the fire. It's all arranged.'

'And what about father's love?' Hilda demanded, with a sprightliness that astonished herself. And she thought: 'Why are these people so fond of me? They don't even ask how it was I didn't write to tell them I was coming. They just accept me and welcome me without questions ... No! I can never tell them! It simply couldn't be told, here! If they find out, so much the worse!'

'You must ask him!' Alicia answered, blushing.

'All right, Alicia. We'll be ready in a minute or two,' said Janet, in a peculiar voice.

It was a gentle command to Alicia to leave her elders alone to their adult confidences. And unwilling Alicia had to obey.

But there were no confidences. The talk, as it were, shivered on the brink of a confidence, but never plunged.

'Does she guess?' Hilda reflected.

The conversation so halted that at length Janet was driven to the banality of saying:

'I'm so sorry we have to go out!'

And Hilda protested with equal banality, and added: 'I suppose you're going out a lot just now?'

'Oh no!' said Janet. 'We go out less and less, and we get quieter and quieter. I mean *us*. The boys are always out, you know.' She seemed saddened. 'I did think Edwin Clayhanger would come in sometimes, now they're living next door –'

'They're in their new house, then!' said Hilda with casualness.

'Oh, long ago! And I'm sure it's ages since he was here. I like Maggie – his sister.'

Hilda knelt to her trunk.

'Did he ever inquire after me?' she demanded, with an air of archness, but hiding her face.

'As a matter of fact he *did* – once,' said Janet, imitating Hilda's manner.

'Well, that's something,' said Hilda.

There was a sharp knock at the door.

'Hot water, miss!' cried the voice of Martha.

The next instant Martha was arranging the ewer and the can and some clean towels on the washstand. Her face was full of joy in the unexpected arrival. She was as excited as if Hilda had been her own friend instead of Janet's.

'Well, dear, shall you be all right now?' said Janet. 'Perhaps I ought to be going. You may depend on it I shall get back as early as ever I can.'

The two girls kissed, with even more freedom than in the hall. It seemed astonishing to Hilda, as her face was close to Janet's, that Janet did not exclaim: 'Something has happened to you. What is it? You are not as you used to be! You are not like me!' She felt herself an imposter.

'Why should I tell?' Hilda reflected. 'What end will it serve? It's nobody's business but mine. *He* is gone. He'll never come back. Everything's over ... And if it does get about, well, they'll only praise me for my discretion. They can't do anything else.'

Still, she longed timorously to confide in Janet. And when Janet had departed she breathed relief because the danger of confiding in Janet was withdrawn for the moment.

III

Later, as the invalid had ordained, Hilda, having eaten, sat by the fire in the large, quiet bedroom of Mr and Mrs Orgreave. The latter was enjoying a period of ease, and lay, with head raised very high on pillows, in her own half of the broad bed. The quilt extended over her without a crease in its expanse; the sheet was turned down with precision, making a level white border to the quilt; and Mrs Orgreave did not stir; not one of her grey locks stirred; she spoke occasionally in a low voice. On the night-table stood a Godfrey's Chloride of Ammonia Inhaler, with its glass cylinder and triple arrangement of tubes. There was only this, and the dark lips and pale cheeks of the patient, to remind the beholder that not long since the bed had been a scene of agony. Mr Orgreave, in bright carpet slippers, and elegant wristbands blossoming out of the sleeves of his black house-jacket, stood bending above a huge board that was laid horizontally on trestles to the left of the fireplace. This board was covered by a wide length of bluish transparent paper which at intervals he pulled towards him, making billows of paper at his feet and gradually lessening a roll of it that lay on the floor beyond the table. A specially arranged gas-bracket with a green shade which threw a powerful light on the paper showed that Osmond Orgreave's habit was to work in that spot of an evening.

'Astonishing I have to do this myself, isn't it?' he observed, stooping to roll up the accumulated length of paper about his feet.

'What is it?' Hilda asked.

'It's a full-sized detail drawing. Simple! . . . But do you suppose I could trust either of my ingenious sons to get the curves of the mouldings right?'

'You'll never be able to trust them unless you begin to trust them,' said Mrs Orgreave sagely from the bed.

'Ha!' ejaculated Osmond Orgreave satirically. This remark was one of his most effective counters to argument.

'The fact is he thoroughly enjoys it, doesn't he, Mrs Orgreave?' said Hilda.

'You're quite right, my dear,' said Mrs Orgreave.

'Ah!' from Mr Orgreave.

He sketched with a pencil and rubbed out, vigorously. Then his eye caught Hilda's, and they both smiled, very content. 'They'd look nice if I took to drink instead of to work, for a change!' he murmured, pausing to caress his handsome hair.

There was a sharp knock at the door, and into this room also the watchful Martha entered.

'Here's the *Signal*, sir. The boy's only just brought it.'

'Give it to Miss Hilda,' said Mr Orgreave, without glancing up.

'Shall I take the tray away, 'm?' Martha inquired, looking towards the bed, the supreme centre of domestic order and authority.

'Perhaps Miss Hilda hasn't finished?'

'Oh yes, I have, thanks.'

Martha rearranged the vessels and cutlery upon the tray, with quick, expert movements of the wrists. Her gaze was carefully fixed on the tray. Endowed though she was with rare privileges, as a faithful retainer, she would have been shocked and shamed had her gaze, improperly wandering, encountered the gaze of the master or the guest. Then she picked up the tray, and, pushing the small table into its accustomed place with a deft twist of the foot, she sailed erect and prim out of the room, and the door primly clicked on her neat girded waist and flying white ribbons.

'And what am I to do with this *Signal*?' Hilda asked, fingering the white, damp paper.

'I should like you to read us about the strike,' said Mrs Orgreave. 'It's a dreadful thing.'

'I should think it was!' Hilda agreed fervently. 'Oh! Do you know, on the way from Shawport, I saw a procession of the men, and anything more terrible –'

'It's the children I think of!' said Mrs Orgreave softly.

'Pity the men don't!' Mr Orgreave murmured, without raising his head.

'Don't what?' Hilda asked defiantly.

'Think of the children.'

Bridling, but silent, Hilda opened the sheet, and searched round and about its columns with the embarrassed bewilderment of one unaccustomed to the perusal of newspapers.

'Look on page three – first column,' said Mr Orgreave.

'That's all about racing,' said Hilda.

'Oh dear, dear!' from the bed.

'Well, second column.'

'The Potters' Strike. The men's leaders,' she read the headlines. 'There isn't much of it.'

'How beautifully clearly you read!' said Mrs Orgreave, with mild enthusiasm, when Hilda had read the meagre half-column.

'Do I?' Hilda flushed.

'Is that all there is about it?'

'Yes. They don't seem to think it's very important that half the people are starving!' Hilda sneered.

'Whose fault is it if they do starve?' Osmond Orgreave glanced at her with lowered head.

'I think it's a shame!' she exclaimed.

'Do you know that the men broke the last award, not so very long since?' said Osmond Orgreave. 'What can you do with such people?'

'Broke the last award?' She was checked.

'Broke the last award! Wouldn't stick by their own agreement, their own words. I'll just tell you. A wise young woman like you oughtn't to be carried away by the sight of a procession on a cold night.'

He smiled; and she smiled, but awkwardly.

And then he told her something of the case for the employers.

'How hard you are on the men!' she protested, when he had done.

'Not at all! Not at all!' He stretched himself, and came round his trestles to poke the fire. 'You should hear Mr Clayhanger on the men, if you want to know what hard is.'

'Mr Clayhanger? You mean old Mr Clayhanger?'

'Yes.'

'But he isn't a manufacturer.'

'No. But he's an employer of labour.'

Hilda rose uneasily from her chair, and walked towards the distant, shadowed dressing-table.

'I should like to go over a printing-works,' she said abruptly.

'Very easy,' said Mr Orgreave, resuming his work with a great expulsion of breath.

Hilda thought: 'Why did I say that?' And, to cover her constraint, she cried out: 'Oh, what a lovely book!'

A small book, bound in full purple calf, lay half hidden in a nest of fine tissue paper on the dressing-table.

'Yes, isn't it?' said Mrs Orgreave. 'Tom brought it in to show me, before he went this afternoon. It's a birthday present for Edie. He's had it specially bound. I must write myself, and ask Edie to come over and meet you. I'm sure you'd like her. She's a dear girl. I think Tom's very fortunate.'

'No, you don't,' Osmond Orgreave contradicted her, with a great rustling of paper. 'You think Edie's very fortunate.'

Hilda looked round, and caught the architect's smile.

'I think they're both fortunate,' said Mrs Orgreave simply. She had almost no sense of humour. 'I'm sure she's a real good girl, and clever too.'

'Clever enough to get on the right side of her future mother-in-law, anyway!' growled Mr Orgreave.

'Anyone might think Osmond didn't like the girl,' said Mrs Orgreave, 'from the way he talks. And yet he adores her! And it's no use him pretending he doesn't!'

'I only adore you!' said Osmond.

'You needn't try to turn it off!' his wife murmured, beaming on Hilda.

Tears came strangely into Hilda's eyes, and she turned again to

the dressing-table. And through a blur, she saw all the objects
ranged in a long row on the white cloth that covered the rose-
wood; and she thought: 'All this is beautiful.' And she saw the
pale blinds drawn down behind the dressing-table, and the valance
at the top, and the draped curtains; and herself darkly in the
glass. And she could feel the vista of the large, calm, comfortable
room behind her, and could hear the coals falling together in the
grate, and the rustling of the architect's paper, and Mrs Orgreave's
slight cough. And, in her mind, she could see all the other rooms
in this spacious house, and the dim, misted garden beyond. She
thought: 'All this house is beautiful. It is the most beautiful thing
I have ever known, or ever shall know. I'm happy here!' And then
her imagination followed each of the children. She imagined
Marian, the eldest, and her babies, in London; and Charlie, also
in London, practising medicine; and Tom and Janet and Alicia
at the party at Hillport; and Jimmie and Johnnie seeing life at
Hanbridge; while the parents remained in tranquillity in their
bedroom. All these visions were beautiful; even the vision of
Jimmie and Johnnie flourishing billiard-cues and glasses and
pipes in the smoky atmosphere of a club – even this was beautiful; it was as simply touching as the other visions ... And she
was at home with the parents, and so extremely intimate with them
that she could nearly conceive herself a genuine member of the
house. She was in bliss. Her immediate past dropped away from
her like an illusion, and she became almost the old Hilda; she
was almost born again into innocence. Only the tragic figure of
George Cannon hung vague in the far distance of memory, and
the sight thereof constricted her heart. Utterly her passion for
him had expired: she was exquisitely sad for him; she felt towards him kindly and guiltily, as one feels towards an old error ...
And, withal, the spell of the home of the Orgreaves took away his
reality.

She was fingering the book. Its title-page ran: *The English
Poems of Richard Crashaw*. Now she had never even heard of
Richard Crashaw, and she wondered who he might be. Turning
the pages, she read:

> All thy old woes shall now smile on thee,
> And thy pains sit bright upon thee,

> All thy sorrows here shall shine,
> All thy sufferings be divine:
> Tears shall take comfort, and turn gems,
> And wrongs repent to diadems.

And she read again, as though the words had been too lovely to be real, and she must assure herself of them:

> Tears shall take comfort, and turn gems,
> And wrongs repent to diadems.

She turned back to the beginning of the poem, and read the title of it: 'A Hymn, to the name and honour of the admirable Saint Teresa – Foundress of the Reformation of the discalced Carmelites, both men and women: a woman for angelical height of speculation, for masculine courage of performance more than a woman: who yet a child outran maturity, and durst plot a martyrdom.'

The prose thrilled her even more intimately than the verse. She cried within herself: 'Why have I never heard of Richard Crashaw? Why did Tom never tell me?' She became upon the instant a devotee of this Saint Teresa. She thought inconsequently, with a pang that was also a reassurance: 'George Cannon would never have understood this. But every one here understands it.' And with hands enfevered she turned the pages again, and, after several disappointments, read:

> Oh, thou undaunted daughter of desires!
> By all thy dower of lights and fires;
> By all the eagle in thee, all the dove:
> By all thy lives and deaths of love:
> By thy large draughts of intellectual day,
> And by thy thirsts of love more large than they:
> By all thy brim-filled bowls of fierce desire,
> By this last morning's draught of liquid fire:
> By the full kingdom of that final kiss –

She ceased to read. It was as if her soul was crying out: 'I also am Teresa. This is I! This is I!'

And then the door opened, and Martha appeared once more: 'If you please, sir, Mr Edwin Clayhanger's called.'

'Oh ... well, I'm nearly finished. Where is he?'

'In the breakfast-room, sir.'

'Well, tell him I'll be down in a minute.'

'Hilda,' said Mrs Orgreave, 'will *you* mind going and telling him?'

Hilda had replaced the book in its nest, and gone quickly back to her chair. The entrance of the servant at that moment, to announce Edwin Clayhanger, seemed to her startlingly dramatic. 'What,' she thought, 'I am just reading that, and he comes! . . . He hasn't been here for ages, and, on the very night that I come, he comes!'

'Certainly,' she replied to Mrs Orgreave. And she thought: 'This is the second time she has sent me with a message to Edwin Clayhanger.'

Suddenly, she blushed in confusion before the mistress of the home. 'Is it possible,' she asked herself – 'is it possible that Mrs Orgreave doesn't guess what has happened to me? Is it possible she can't see that I'm different from what I used to be? If she knew . . . if they knew . . . here!'

She left the room like a criminal. When she was going down the stairs, she discovered that she held the *Signal* in her hand. She had no recollection of picking it up, and there was no object in taking it to the breakfast-room! She thought: 'What a state I must be in!'

CHAPTER 2
A RENDEZVOUS

I

'I SUPPOSE you've never thought about me once since I've left!'

She was sitting on the sofa in the small, shelved breakfast-room, and she shot these words at Edwin Clayhanger, who was standing near her. The singular words were certainly uttered out of bravado: they were a challenge to adventure. She thought: 'It is madness for me to say such a thing.' But such a thing had, nevertheless, come quite glibly out of her mouth, and she knew not why. If Edwin Clayhanger was startled, so was she startled.

'Oh yes, I have!' he stammered – of course, she had put him out of countenance.

She smiled, and said persuasively: 'But you've never inquired after me.'

'Yes, I have,' he answered, with a hint of defiance, after a pause.

'Only once.' She continued to smile.

'How do you know?' he demanded.

Then she told him very calmly, extinguishing the smile, that her source of information was Janet.

'That's nothing to go by!' he exclaimed, with sudden roughness. 'That's nothing to go by – the number of *times* I've inquired!'

II

She was silenced. She thought: 'If I am thus intimate with him, it must be because of the talk we had in the garden that night.' And it seemed to her that the scene in the garden had somehow bound them together for ever in intimacy, that, even if they pretended to be only acquaintances, they would constantly be breaking through the thin shell of formality into some unguessed deep of intimacy. She regarded – surreptitiously – his face, with a keen sense of pleasure. It was romantic, melancholy, wistful, enigmatic – and, above all, honest. She knew that he had desired to be an architect, and that his father had thwarted his desire, and this fact endowed him for her with the charm of a victim. The idea that all his life had been embittered and shadowed by the caprice of an old man was beautiful to her in its sadness: she contemplated it with vague bliss. At their last meeting, during the Sunday School Centenary, he had annoyed her; he had even drawn her disdain, by his lack of initiative, and male force in the incident of the senile Sunday School teacher. He had profoundly disappointed her. Now, she simply forgot this; the sinister impression vanished from her mind. She recalled her first vision of him in the lighted doorway of his father's shop. Her present vision confirmed that sympathetic vision. She liked the feel of his faithful hand, and the glance of his timid and yet bellicose eye. And she reposed on his very apparent honesty as on a bed. She knew, with the assurance of perfect faith, that he had nothing dubious to conceal, and that no test could strain his magnanimity. And, while she so reflected, she was thinking, too, of Janet's fine dress, and her elegance and jewels, and wishing that she had changed the old black frock in which she travelled. The perception that she could never be like Janet cast her down. But, the next moment, she was saying to herself proudly: 'What does it matter? Why should I be like Janet?' And, the next moment after that, she was saying, in another phase of her pride: 'I *will* be like Janet!'

They began to discuss the strike. It was a topic which, during those weeks, could not be avoided, either by the rich or by the poor.

'I suppose you're like all the rest – against the men?' she challenged him again, inviting battle.

He replied bluntly: 'What earthly right have you to suppose that I'm like all the rest?'

She bent her head lower, so that she could only see him through the veil of her eyelashes.

'I'm very sorry,' she said, in a low, smiling, meditative voice. 'I knew all the time you weren't.'

The thought shot through her mind like a lance; 'It is incredible, and horribly dangerous, that I should be sitting here with him, after all that has happened to me, and him without the slightest suspicion! . . . And yet what can stop it from coming out, sooner or later? Nothing can stop it.'

Edwin Clayhanger continued to talk of the strike, and she heard him saying: 'If you ask me, I'll tell you what I think – workmen on strike are always in the right . . . you've only got to look at them in a crowd together. They don't starve themselves for fun.'

What he said thrilled her. There was nothing in it, but there was everything in it. His generosity towards the oppressed was everything to her. His whole attitude was utterly and mysteriously different from that of any other man whom she had known . . . And with that simple, wistful expression of his!

They went on talking, and then, following in secret the train of her own thoughts, she suddenly burst out:

'I never met anybody like you before.' A pause ensued. 'No, never!' she added, with intense conviction.

'I might say the same of you,' he replied, moved.

'Oh no! I'm nothing!' she breathed.

She glanced up, exquisitely flattered. His face was crimson. Exquisite moment, in the familiarity of the breakfast-room, by the fire, she on the sofa, with him standing over her, a delicious peril! The crimson slowly paled.

III

Osmond Orgreave entered the room, quizzical, and at once began to tease Clayhanger about the infrequency of his visits.

Turning to Hilda, he said: 'He scarcely ever comes to see us, except when you're here.' It was just as if he had said: 'I heard every word you spoke before I came in, and I have read your hearts.' Both Hilda and Clayhanger were disconcerted – Clayhanger extremely so.

'Steady on!' he protested uncouthly. And then, with the most naïve ingenuousness: 'Mrs Orgreave better?'

But Osmond Orgreave was not in a merciful mood. A moment later he was saying:

'Has she told you she wants to go over a printing-works?'

'No,' Clayhanger answered, with interest. 'But I shall be very pleased to show her over ours, any time.'

Hilda, struck into silence, made no response, and instantly Clayhanger finished, in another tone: 'Look here, I must be off. I only slipped in for a minute – really.'

And he went, declining Mr Orgreave's request to give a date for his next call. The bang of the front door resounded through the house.

Mr Orgreave, having taken Clayhanger to the front door, did not return immediately into the breakfast-room. Hilda jumped up from the sofa, hesitant. She was disappointed; she was even resentful; assuredly she was humiliated. 'Oh no!' she thought. 'He's weak and afraid . . . I dare say he went off because Janet wasn't here.' She heard through the half-open door Mr Orgreave's slippers on the tiles of the passage leading to the stairs.

Martha came into the room with a delighted, curious smile.

'If you please, miss, could you come into the hall a minute? . . . Someone to speak to you.'

Hilda blushed silently, and obeyed. Clayhanger was standing in the chill hall, hat in hand. Her heart jumped.

'When will you come to look over our works?' he muttered rapidly and very nervously, and yet with a dictatorial gruffness. 'Tomorrow? I should like you to come.'

He had put an enchantment upon her by this marvellous return. And to conceal from him what he had done, she frowned and kept silent.

'What time?' she asked suddenly.

'Any time.' His eagerness was thrilling.

'Oh no! You must fix the time.'

'Say between half past six and a quarter to seven. That do?'

She nodded. Their hands met. He said adieu. He pulled open the heavy door. She saw his back for an instant against the pale gloom of the garden, in which vapour was curling. And then she had shut the door, and was standing alone in the confined hall. A miracle had occurred, and it intimidated her. And, amid her wondrous fears, she was steeped in the unique sense of adventure. 'This morning I was in Brighton,' she thought. 'Half an hour ago I had no notion of seeing him. And now! . . . And tomorrow?' The tragic sequel to one adventure had not impaired her instinct for experience. On the contrary, it had strengthened it. The very failure of the one excited her towards another. The zest of living was reborn in her. The morrow beckoned her, golden and miraculous. The faculty of men and women to create their own lives seemed divine, and the conception of it enfevered her.

CHAPTER 3
AT THE WORKS

I

THAT night, late, Hilda and Janet shut themselves up in the bedroom together. The door clicked softly under Janet's gentle push, and they were as safe from invasion as if the door had been of iron, and locked and double-locked and barred with bars of iron. Alicia alone might have disturbed them, but Alicia was asleep. Hilda had a sense of entire security in this room such as she had never had since she drove away from Lessways Street, Turnhill, early one morning, with Florrie Bagster in a cab. It was not that there had been the least real fear of any room of hers being attacked: it was that this room seemed to have been rendered mystically inviolate by long years of Janet's occupation. 'Janet's bedroom!' – the phrase had a sanction which could not possibly have attached itself to, for instance, 'Hilda's bedroom!' Nor even to 'mother's bedroom' – mother's bedroom being indeed at the mercy of any profane and marauding member of the family, a sort of market-place for the transaction of affairs.

And, further, Janet's bedroom was distinguished and made delicious by its fire. It happened to be one of the very few bedrooms in the Five Towns at that date with a fire as a regular feature of it. Mrs Orgreave had a fire in the parental bedroom, when she could not reasonably do without it, but Osmond Orgreave suffered the fire rather than enjoyed it. As for Tom, though of a shivery disposition, he would have dithered to death before admitting that a bedroom fire might increase his comfort. Johnnie and Jimmie genuinely liked to be cold in their bedroom. Alicia pined for a fire, but Mrs Orgreave, imitating the contrariety of fate, forbade a fire to Alicia, and one consequence of this was that Alicia sometimes undressed in Janet's bedroom, making afterwards a dash for the Pole. The idea of a bedroom was always, during nearly half the year, associated with the idea of discomfort in Hilda's mind. And now, in Janet's bedroom impressed as she was by the strangeness of the fact that the prime reason for hurrying at top-speed into bed had been abolished, she yet positively could not linger, the force of habit being too strong for her. And she was in bed, despite efforts to dawdle, while Janet was still brushing her hair.

As she lay and watched Janet's complex unrobing, she acquired knowledge. And once more, she found herself desiring to be like Janet – not only in appearance, but in soft manner and tone. She thought: 'How shall I dress tomorrow afternoon?' All the operations of her brain related themselves somehow to tomorrow afternoon. The anticipation of the visit to the printing-works burned in her heart like a steady lamp that shone through the brief, cloudy interests of the moment. And Edwin Clayhanger was precisely the topic which Janet seemed, as it were, expressly to avoid. Janet inquired concerning life at Brighton and the health of Sarah Gailey; Janet even mentioned George Cannon; Hilda steadied her voice in replying, though she was not really apprehensive, for Janet's questions, like the questions of the whole family, were invariably discreet and respectful of the individual's privacy. But of Edwin Clayhanger, whose visit nevertheless had been recounted to her in the drawing-room on her return, Janet said not a word.

And then, when she had extinguished the gas, and the oriental sleeve of her silk nightgown delicately brushed Hilda's face, as she got into bed, she remarked:

'Strange that Edwin Clayhanger should call just tonight!'

Hilda's cheek warmed.

'He asked me to go and look over their printing-works tomorrow,' said she quickly.

Janet was taken aback.

'Really!' she exclaimed, unmistakably startled. She spoke a second too soon. If she had delayed only one second, she might have concealed from Hilda that which Hilda had most plainly perceived, to wit, anxiety and jealousy. Yes, jealousy, in this adorably benevolent creature's tone. Hilda's interest in tomorrow afternoon was intensified.

'Shall you be able to come?' she asked.

'What time?'

'He said about half past six, or a quarter to seven.'

'I can't,' said Janet dreamily, 'because of that Musical Society meeting – you know – I told you, didn't I?'

In the faint light of the dying fire, Hilda made out little by little the mysterious, pale heaps of clothes, and all the details of the room strewn and disordered by reason of an additional occupant. The adventure was now of infinite complexity, and its complexity seemed to be symbolized by the suggestive feminine mysteriousness of what she saw and what she divined in the darkness of the chamber. She thought: 'I am here on false pretences. I ought to tell my secret. That would be fair – I have no right to intrude between her and him.' But she instinctively and powerfully resisted such ideas; with firmness she put them away and yielded herself with a more exquisite apprehension to the anticipation of tomorrow.

II

The order of meals at Lane End was somewhat peculiar even then, and would now be almost unique. It was partly the natural expression of an instinctive and justified feeling of superiority, and partly due to a discretion which forbade the family to scandalize the professional classes of the district by dining at night. Dinner occurred in the middle of the day, and about nine in the evening was an informal but copious supper. Between those two meals, there came a tea which was neither high nor low, and whose hour, six o'clock in theory, depended to a certain extent, in practice, on Mr Orgreave's arrival from the office. Not seldom Mr Orgreave was late; occasionally he was very late. The kitchen waited to infuse the tea until a command came from some woman, old or young, who attentively watched a window for a particular swinging of the long gate at the end of the garden, or listened, when it was dark, for the bang of the gate and a particular crunching of gravel.

On this Tuesday evening, Osmond Orgreave was very late, and the movement of the household was less smooth than usual, owing to Mrs Orgreave's illness and to the absence of Janet at Hillport in connection with the projected Hillport Choral Society. (Had Janet been warned of Hilda's visit, she would not have accepted an invitation to a tea at Hillport as a preliminary to the meeting of the provisional committee.) Hilda was in a state of acute distress. The appointment with Edwin Clayhanger seemed to be absolutely sacred to her: to be late for it would amount to a crime: to miss it altogether would be a calamity inconceivable. The fingers of all the clocks in the house were revolving with the most extraordinary rapidity – she was helpless.

She was helpless, because she had said nothing all day of her appointment, and because Janet had not mentioned it either. Janet might have said before leaving: 'Tea had better not wait too long – Hilda has to be down at Clayhanger's at half past six.' Janet's silence impressed Hilda: it was not merely strange – it was formidable: it affected the whole day. Hilda thought: 'Is she determined not to speak of it unless I do?' Immediately Janet was gone, Hilda had run up to the bedroom. She was minded to change the black frock which she had been wearing, and which she hated, and to put on another skirt and bodice that Janet had praised. She longed to beautify herself, and yet she was still hesitating about it at half past five in the evening as she had hesitated at eight o'clock in the morning. In the end she had decided not to change, on account of the rain. But the rain had naught to do with her decision. She would not change, because she was too proud to change. She would go just as she was! She could not accept the assistance of an attractive bodice! ... Unfeminine, perhaps, but womanly.

At twenty-five minutes to seven, she went into Mrs Orgreave's bedroom, rather like a child, and also rather like an adult creature in a distracting crisis. Tom Orgreave and Alicia were filling the entire house with the stormy noise of a piano duet based upon Rossini's *William Tell*.

'I think I'll miss tea, Mrs Orgreave,' she said. 'Edwin Clayhanger invited me to go over the printing-works at half past six, and it's twenty-five minutes to seven now.'

'Oh, but, my dear,' cried Mrs Orgreave, 'why ever didn't you tell them downstairs, or let me know earlier?'

And she pulled at the bell-rope that overhung the head of the bed. Not a trace of teasing archness in her manner! Hilda's appointment might have been of the most serious business interest, for anything Mrs Orgreave's demeanour indicated to the contrary. Hilda stood mute and constrained.

'You run down and tell them to make tea at once, dear. I can't let you go without anything at all. I wonder what can have kept Osmond.'

Almost at the same moment, Osmond Orgreave entered the bedroom. His arrival had been unnoticed amid the tremendous resounding of the duet.

'Oh, Osmond,' said his wife, 'wherever have you been so late? Hilda wants to go – Edwin Clayhanger has invited her to go over the works.'

Hilda, trembling at the door, more than half expected Mr Orgreave to say: 'You mean, she's invited herself.' But Osmond received the information with exactly the same polite, apologetic seriousness as his wife, and, reassured, Hilda departed from the room.

Ten minutes later, veiled and cloaked, she stepped out alone into the garden. And instantly her torment was assuaged, and she was happy. She waited at the corner of the street for the steam-car. But, when the car came thundering down, it was crammed to the step; with a melancholy gesture, the driver declined her signal. She set off down Trafalgar Road in the mist and rain, glad that she had been compelled to walk. It seemed to her that she was on a secret and mystic errand. This was not surprising. The remarkable thing was that all the hurrying people she met seemed also each of them to be on a secret and mystic errand. The shining wet pavement was dotted with dark figures, suggestive and enigmatic, who glided over a floor that was pierced by perpendicular reflections.

III

In the Clayhanger shop, agitated and scarcely aware of what she did, she could, nevertheless, hear her voice greeting Edwin Clayhanger in firm, calm tones; and she soon perceived very clearly that he was even more acutely nervous than herself: which perception helped to restore her confidence, while, at the same time, it filled her with bliss. The young, fair man, with his awkward and constrained movements, took possession of her umbrella, and then suggested that she should remove her mackintosh. She obeyed, timid and glad. She stripped off her mackintosh, as though she were stripping off her modesty, and stood before him revealed. To complete the sacrifice, she raised her veil, and smiled up at him, as it were, asking: 'What next?' Then a fat, untidy old man appeared in the doorway of a cubicle within the shop, and Edwin Clayhanger blushed.

'Father, this is Miss Lessways. Miss Lessways, my father ... She's – she's come to look over the place.'

'How-d'ye-do, miss?'

She shook hands with the tyrannic father, who was, however, despite his reputation, apparently just as nervous as the son. There followed a most sinister moment of silence. And, at last, the shop door opened, and the father turned to greet a customer. Hilda thought: 'Suppose this fat old man is one day my father-in-law? Is it possible to imagine him as a father-in-law?' And she had a transient gleam of curiosity concerning the characters of the two Clayhanger sisters, and recalled with satisfaction that Janet liked the elder one.

Edwin Clayhanger, muttering, pointed to an aperture in the counter, and immediately she was going through it with him, and through a door at the back of the shop. They were alone, facing a rain-soaked yard. Edwin Clayhanger sneezed violently.

'It keeps on raining,' Edwin murmured. 'Better to have kept umbrella! However –'

He glanced at her inquiringly and invitingly. They ran side by side across the yard to a roofed flight of steps that led to the printing-office. For a couple of seconds, the rain wet them, and then they were under cover again. It seemed to Hilda that they had escaped from the shop like fox-terriers – like two friendly dogs from the surveillance of an incalculable and dangerous old man. She felt a comfortable, friendly confidence in Edwin Clayhanger – a tranquil sentiment such as she had never experienced for George Cannon. After more than a year – and what a period of unforseen happenings! – she thought again: 'I *like him*.' Not love, she thought, but liking! She liked being with him. She liked the sensation of putting confidence in him. She liked his youth, and her own. She was sorry because he had a cold and was not taking care of it ... Now they were climbing a sombre creaking staircase towards a new and remote world that was separated from the common world just quitted by the adventurous passage

of the rainy yard ... And now they were amid oily odours in a
large raftered workshop, full of machines ... The printing-works!
... An enormous but very deferential man saluted them with
majestic solemnity. He was the foreman, and labelled by his white
apron as an artisan, but his gigantic bulk – he would have out-
weighed the pair of them – and his age set him somehow over
them, so that they were a couple of striplings in his vasty presence.
When Edwin Clayhanger employed, as it were, daringly, the
accents of a master to this intimidating fellow, Hilda thrilled with
pleasure at the piquancy of the spectacle, and she was admiringly
proud of Edwin. The foreman's immense voice, explaining
machines and tools, caused physical vibrations in her. But she
understood nothing of what he said – nothing whatever. She was
in a dream of oily odours and monstrous iron constructions,
dominated by the grand foreman: and Edwin was in the dream.
She began talking quite wildly of the four-hundredth anniversary
of the inventor of printing, of which she had read in Cranswick's
History ... at Brighton! Brighton had sunk away over the verge
of memory. Even Lane End House was lost somewhere in the
vague past. All her previous life had faded. She reflected guiltily:
'He's bound to think I've been reading about printing because I
was interested in *him*! I don't care! I hope he does think it!'
She heard a suggestion that, as it was too late that night to see the
largest machine in motion, she might call the next afternoon. She
at once promised to come ... She impatiently desired now to leave
the room where they were, and to see something else. And then
she feared lest this might be all there was to see ... Edwin
Clayhanger was edging towards the door ... They were alone on
the stairway again ... The foreman had bowed at the top like a
chamberlain ... She gathered, with delicious anticipation, that
other and still more recondite interiors awaited their visit.

IV

They were in an attic which was used for the storage of reams
upon reams of paper. By the light of a candle in a tin candlestick,
they had passed alone together through corridors and up flights of
stairs at the back of the shop. She had seen everything that
was connected with the enterprise of steam-printing, and now

they were at the top of the old house and at the end of the excursion.

'I used to work here,' said Edwin Clayhanger.

She inquired about the work.

'Well,' he drawled, 'reading and writing, you know – at that very table.'

In the aperture of the window, amid piles of paper, stood a rickety old table, covered with dust.

'But there's no fireplace,' she said, glancing round the room, and then directly at him.

'I know.'

'But how did you do in winter?' she eagerly appealed.

And he replied shortly, and with a slight charming affectation of pride: 'I did without.'

Her throat tightened, and she could feel the tears suddenly swim in her eyes. She was not touched by the vision of his hardships. It was the thought of all his youth that exquisitely saddened her – of all the years which were and would be for ever hidden from her. She knew that she alone of all human beings was gifted with the power to understand and fully sympathize with him. And so she grieved over the long wilderness of time during which he had been uncomprehended. She wanted, by some immense effort of tenderness, to recompense him for all that he had suffered. And she had a divine curiosity concerning the whole of his past life. She had never had this curiosity in relation to George Cannon – she had only wondered about his affairs with other women. Nor had George Cannon ever evoked the tenderness which sprang up in her from some secret and inexhaustible source at the mere sight of Edwin Clayhanger's wistful smile. Still, in that moment, standing close to Edwin in the high solitude of the shadowed attic, the souvenir of George Cannon gripped her painfully. She thought: 'He loves me, and he is ruined, and he will never see me again! And I am here, bursting with hope renewed, and dizzy with joy!' And she pictured Janet, too, wearying herself at a committee meeting. And she thought, 'And here am I . . .!' Her bliss was tragic.

'I think I ought to be going,' she said softly.

They re-threaded the corridors, and in each lower room, as they passed, Edwin Clayhanger extinguished the gas which he had lit there on the way up, and Hilda waited for him. And then they were back in the crude glare of the shop. The fat, untidy old man was not visible. Edwin helped her with the mackintosh, and she liked him for the awkwardness of his efforts in doing so.

At the door, she urged him not to come out, and referred to his cold.

'This isn't the end of winter, it's the beginning,' she warned him. Nobody else, she knew, would watch over him.

But he insisted on coming out.

They arranged a rendezvous for three o'clock on the morrow, and then they shook hands.

'Now, do go in,' she entreated, as she hurried away. The rain had ceased. She fled triumphantly up Trafalgar Road, with her secret, guarding it. 'He's in love with me!' If a scientific truth is a statement of which the contrary is inconceivable, then it was a scientific truth for her that she and Edwin must come together. She simply would not and could not conceive the future without him ... And this so soon, so precipitately soon, after her misfortune! But it was her very misfortune which pushed her violently forward. Her life had been convulsed and overthrown by the hazard of destiny, and she could have no peace now until she had repaired and re-established it. At no matter what risk, the thing must be accomplished quickly ... quickly.

CHAPTER 4
THE CALL FROM BRIGHTON

I

ON the next afternoon, at a quarter past two, Hilda and Janet were sitting together in the breakfast-room. The house was still. The men were either theoretically or practically at business. Alicia was at school. Mrs Orgreave lay upstairs. The servants had cleared away and washed up the dinner-things, and had dined themselves. The kitchen had been cleansed and put in order, and every fire replenished. Two of the servants were in their own chambers, enfranchised for an hour: one only remained on duty. All six women had the feeling, which comes to most women at a certain moment in each day, that life had, for a time, deteriorated into the purposeless and the futile; and that it waited, as in a trance, until some external masculine event, expected or unforeseen, should renew its virtue and its energy.

Hilda was in half a mind to tell Janet the history of the past year. She had wakened up in the night, and perceived with dreadful clearness that trouble lay in front of her. The relations between herself and Edwin Clayhanger were developing with the most dizzy rapidity, and in a direction which she desired; but it would be impossible for her, if she fostered the relations, to continue to keep Edwin in ignorance of the fact that, having been known for about a fortnight as Mrs George Cannon, she was not what he supposed her to be. With imagination on fire, she was anticipating the rendezvous at three o'clock. She reached forward to it in ecstasy; but she might not enjoy it, save at the price which her conscience exacted. She had to say to Edwin Clayhanger that she had been the victim of a bigamist. Could she say it to him? She had not been able to say it even to Janet Orgreave ... She would say it first to Janet. There, in the breakfast-room, she would say it. If it killed her to say it, she would say it. She must at any cost be able to respect herself, and, as matters stood, she could not respect herself.

Janet, on her knees, was idly arranging books on one of the lower bookshelves. In sheer nervousness, Hilda also dropped to her knees on the hearthrug, and began to worry the fire with the poker.

'I say, Janet,' she began.

'Yes?' Janet did not look up.

Hilda, her heart beating, thought, with affrighted swiftness: 'Why should I tell her? It is no business of anybody's except *his*. I will tell him, and him alone, and then act according to his wishes. After all, I am not to blame. I am quite innocent. But I won't tell him today. Not today! I must be more sure. It would be ridiculous to tell him today. If I told him it would be almost like inviting a proposal! But when the proper time comes – then I will tell him, and he will understand! He is bound to understand perfectly. He's in love with me.'

She dared not tell Janet. In that abode of joyful and successful propriety the words would not form themselves. And the argument that she was not to blame carried no weight whatever. She – she, Hilda – lacked courage to be candid . . . This was extremely disconcerting to her self-esteem . . . And even with Edwin Clayhanger she wished to temporize. She longed for nothing so much as to see him; and yet she feared to meet him.

'Yes?' Janet repeated.

A bell rang faintly in the distance of the house.

Hilda, suddenly choosing a course, said: 'I forgot to tell you. I'm supposed to be going down to Clayhanger's at three to see a machine at work – it was too late last night. Do come with me. I hate going by myself.' It was true: in that instant she did hate going by herself. She thought, knowing Janet to be at liberty and never dreaming that she would refuse: 'I am saved – for the present.'

But Janet answered self-consciously:

'I don't think I must leave mother. You'll be perfectly all right by yourself.'

Hilda impetuously turned her head; their glances met for an instant, in suspicion, challenge, animosity. They had an immense mutual admiration the one for the other, these two; and yet now they were estranged. Esteem was nullified by instinct. Hilda thought with positive savagery: 'It's all fiddlesticks about not leaving her mother! She's simply on her high horse!' The whole colour of existence was changed.

II

Martha entered the room. Neither of the girls moved. Beneath the deferential servant in Martha was a human girl, making a third in the room, who familiarly divined the moods of the other two and judged them as an equal; and the other two knew it, and therefore did not trouble to be spectacular in front of her.

'A letter, miss,' said Martha, approaching Hilda. 'The old postman says it was insufficiently addressed, or it 'ud ha' been here by first post.'

'Was that the postman who rang just now?' asked Janet.

'Yes, miss.'

Hilda took the letter with apprehension, as she recognized the down-slating calligraphy of Sarah Gailey. Yes, the address was imperfect – 'Miss Lessways, c/o Osmond Orgreave, Esq., Lane End House, Knype-on-Trent', instead of 'Bursley, Knype-on-Trent'. On the back of the envelope had been written in pencil by an official, 'Try Bursley'. Sarah Gailey could not now be trusted to address an envelope correctly. The mere handwriting seemed to announce misfortune.

'From poor Sarah,' Hilda murmured, with false, good-tempered tranquillity. 'I wonder what sort of trouble she thinks she's got into.'

She thought: 'If only I was married, I should be free of responsibility about Sarah. I should have to think of my husband first. But nothing else can free me. Unless I marry, I'm tied to Sarah Gailey as long as she lives . . . And why? . . . I should like to know!' The answer was simple: habit had shackled her to Sarah Gailey.

She opened the letter by the flickering firelight, which was stronger on the hearthrug than the light of the dim November day. It began: 'Dearest Hilda, I write at once to tell you that a lawyer called here this afternoon to inquire about your Hotel Continental shares. He told me there was going to be some difficulty with the Company, and, unless the independent share-holders formed a strong local committee to look after things, the

trouble might be serious. He wanted to know if you would support a committee at the meeting. I gave him your address, and
he's going to write to you. But I thought I would write to you as
well. His name is Eustace Broughton, 124 East Street, in case. I
do hope nothing will go wrong. It is like what must be, I am sure!
It has been impossible for me to keep the charwoman. So I sent
her off this morning. Can you remember the address of that Mrs
Catkin? . . .' Sarah Gailey continued to discuss boarding-house
affairs, until she arrived at the end of the fourth page, and then, in
a few cramped words, she finished with expressions of love.

'Oh dear!' Hilda exclaimed, rising, 'I must write some letters
at once.' She sighed, as if in tedium. The fact that her fortune was
vaguely threatened did not cause her anxiety: she scarcely
realized it. What she saw was an opportunity to evade the immediate meeting with Edwin – the meeting which, a few minutes
earlier, she had desired beyond everything.

'When? Now?'

Hilda nodded.

'But what about Master Edwin?' Janet asked, trying to be gay.

'I shan't be able to go,' said Hilda carelessly, at the door. 'It's
of no consequence.'

'Martha has to go down town. If you like, she could call in
there, and just tell him.'

It was a reproof, from the young woman who always so
thoughtfully studied the feelings of everybody.

'I'll just write a little note, then, thanks!' Hilda returned
calmly, triumphing after all over Janet's superiority, and thinking,
'Janet can be very peculiar, Janet can!'

III

For more than twenty hours, Hilda was profoundly miserable.
Towards the evening of the same day, she had made herself quite
sure that Edwin Clayhanger would call that night. Her hope
persisted until half past nine: it then began to fade, and, at ten
o'clock, was extinct. His name had been mentioned by nobody.
She went to bed. Having now a room of her own, which overlooked the Clayhanger garden and house, she gazed forth, and, in
the dark, beheld, with the most anxious sensations, the building

in which Edwin existed and was concealed. 'He is there,' she said. 'He is active about something at this very instant – perhaps he is reading. He is close by. If I shouted, he might hear . . .' And yet she was utterly cut off from him. Again, in the late dawn, she saw the same building, pale and clear, but just as secretive and enigmatic as in the night. 'He is asleep yet,' she thought. 'Why did he not call? Is he hurt? Is he proud?'

She despaired, because she could devise no means of resuming communication with him.

Immediately after dinner on the next day, she went with Janet to Janet's room, to examine a new winter cloak which had been delivered. And, while Janet was trying it on, and posing coquettishly and yet without affectation in front of the glass, and while Hilda was reflecting jealously, 'Why am I not like her? I know infinitely more than she knows. I am a woman, and she is a girl, and yet she seems far more a woman than I –' Alicia, contrary to all rules, took the room by storm. Alicia's excuse and salvation lay in a telegram, which she held in her hand.

'For you, Hilda!' cried the child, excited. 'I'm just off to school.'

Hilda reached to take the offered telegram, but her hand wavered around it instead of seizing it. Her eye fastened on a circular portion of the wall-paper pattern, and she felt that the whole room was revolving about her. Then she saw Janet's face transformed by an expression of alarm.

'Are you ill, Hilda?' Janet demanded. 'Sit down.'

'You're frightfully pale,' said Alicia eagerly.

Hilda sat down.

'No, no,' she said. 'It was the pattern of the wall-paper that made me feel dizzy.' And, for the moment, she did honestly believe that the pattern of the wall-paper had, in some inexplicable manner, upset her. 'I'm all right now.'

The dizziness passed as suddenly as it had supervened. Janet held some ineffectual salts to her nose.

'I'm perfectly well,' insisted Hilda.

'How funny!' Alicia grinned.

Calmly Hilda opened the telegram, which read: 'Please come at once. – Gailey.'

She gave the telegram to Janet in silence.

'What can be the matter?' Janet asked, with unreserved, loving solicitude. The cloud which had hung between the two enthusiastic friends was dissipated in a flash.

'I haven't an idea,' said Hilda, touched. 'Unless it's those shares!' She had briefly told Janet about the Hotel Continental Limited.

'Shall you go?'

Hilda nodded. Never again would she ignore an urgent telegram, though she did not believe that this telegram had any real importance. She attributed it to Sarah's increasing incompetence and hysterical foolishness.

'I wonder whether I can get on to Brighton tonight if I take the six train?' Hilda asked; and to herself: 'Can it have anything to do with George?'

Alicia, endowed with authority, went in search of a Bradshaw. But the quest was fruitless. In the Five Towns the local time-table, showing the connections with London, suffices for the citizen, and the breast-pocket of no citizen is complete without it.

'Clayhangers are bound to have a Bradshaw,' cried Alicia, breathless with running about the house.

'Of course they are,' Janet agreed.

'I'll walk down there now,' said Hilda, with extraordinary promptitude. 'It won't take five minutes.'

'I'd go,' said Alicia, 'only I should be late for school.'

'Shall I send someone down?' Janet suggested. 'You might be taken dizzy again.'

'No, thanks,' Hilda replied deliberately. 'I'll go – myself. There's nothing wrong with me at all.'

'You'll have to be sharp over it,' said Alicia pertly. 'Don't forget it's Thursday. They shut up at two, and it's not far off two now.'

'I'm going this very minute,' said Hilda.

'And I'm going this very second!' Alicia retorted.

They all three left Janet's bedroom; the new cloak, cast over a chair-back, was degraded into a tedious banality – and ignored.

In less than a minute Hilda, hatted and jacketed and partially gloved, was crossing the garden. She felt most miraculously happy and hopeful, and she was full of irrational gratitude to Alicia, as though Alicia were a benefactor! The change in her mood seemed magic in its swiftness. If Janet, with calm, cryptic face, had not been watching her from the doorway, she might have danced on the gravel.

CHAPTER 5
THURSDAY AFTERNOON

I

SHE was walking with Edwin Clayhanger up Duck Bank on the
way to Bursley railway station. A simple errand and promenade –
and yet she felt herself to be steeped in the romance of an adventure! The adventure had surprisingly followed upon the
discovery that Alicia had been quite wrong. 'Clayhangers are
bound to have a Bradshaw,' the confident Alicia had said. But
Clayhangers happened not to have a Bradshaw. Edwin was alone
in the stationery shop, save for the assistant. He said that his
father was indisposed. And whereas the news that Clayhangers
had no Bradshaw left Hilda perfectly indifferent, the news that
old Darius Clayhanger was indisposed and absent produced in
her a definite feeling of gladness. Edwin had decided that the most
likely place to search for a Bradshaw was the station, and he had
offered to escort her to the station. Nothing could have been more
natural, and at the same time more miraculous.

The sun was palely shining upon dry, clean pavements and
upon roads juicy with black mud. And in the sunshine Hilda was
very happy. It was nothing to her that she was in quest of a
Bradshaw because she had just received an ominous telegram
urgently summoning her to Brighton. She was obliviously happy.
Every phenomenon that attracted her notice contributed to her
felicity. Thus she took an eager joy in the sun. And a marked
improvement in Edwin's cold really delighted her. She was
dominated by the intimate conviction: 'He loves me!' Which
conviction excited her dormant pride, and made her straighten
her shoulders. She benevolently condescended towards Janet.
After all Janet, with every circumstance in her favour, had not
known how to conquer Edwin Clayhanger. After all she, Hilda,
possessed some mysterious characteristic more potent than the
elegance and the goodness of Janet Orgreave. She scorned her
former self-depreciations, and reproached her own lack of faith:

'I am I!' That was the summary of her mood. As for her attitude
to Edwin Clayhanger, she could not explain it. Why did she like
him and like being with him? He was not brilliant, nor masterful, nor handsome, nor well dressed, nor in any manner imposing.
On the contrary, he was awkward and apologetic, and not a bit
spectacular. Only the wistful gaze of his eyes, and his honest
smile, and the appeal of his gestures . . .! A puzzling affair, an
affair perfectly incomprehensible and enchanting.

They walked side by side in silence.

When they had turned into Moorthorne Road, half-way up
whose slope lies the station, she asked a question about a large
wooden building from whose interior came wild sounds of
shouting and cheering, and learnt that the potters on strike were
holding a meeting in the town theatre. At the open outer doors
was a crowd of starving, shivering, dirty, ragged children, who
romped and cursed, or stood unnaturally meditative in the rich
mud, like fakirs fulfilling a vow. Hilda's throat was constricted
by the sight. Pain and joy ran together in her, burning exquisitely;
and she had a glimpse, obscure, of the mystical beauty of the
children's suffering.

'I'd no idea there was a theatre in Bursley,' she remarked idly,
driven into a banality by the press of her sensations.

'They used to call it the Blood Tub,' he replied. 'Melodrama
and murder and gore – you know.'

She exclaimed in horror. 'Why are people like that in the Five
Towns?'

'It's our form of poetry, I suppose,' said he.

She started, sensitively. It seemed to her that she had never
understood the secret inner spirit of the Five Towns, and that by
a single phrase he had made her understand it . . . 'Our form of
poetry'! Who but he could have said a thing at once so illumi-
nating and so simple?

Apparently perplexed by the obvious effect on her of his
remark, he said:

'But you belong to the Five Towns, don't you?'

She answered quietly that she did. But her heart was saying:
'I do *now*. You have initiated me. I never felt the Five Towns
before. You have made me feel them.'

II

At the station the head porter received their inquiry for a Bradshaw with a dull stare and a shake of the head. No such thing had ever been asked for at Bursley Station before, and the man's imagination could not go beyond the soiled time-tables loosely pinned and pasted up on the walls of the booking-office. Hilda suggested that the ticket-clerk should be interrogated, but the aperture of communication with him was shut. She saw Edwin Clayhanger brace himself and rap on the wood; and instead of deploring his diffidence she liked it and found it full of charm. The partition clicked aside, and the ticket-clerk's peering suspicious head showed in its place mutely demanding a reason for this extraordinary disturbance of the dream in which the station slumbered between two half-hourly trains. With a characteristic peculiar slanting motion Edwin nodded.

'Oh, how-d'ye-do, Mr Brooks?' said Edwin hastily, as if startled by the sudden inexplicable apparition of the head.

But the ticket-clerk had no Bradshaw either. He considered it probable, however, that the stationmaster would have a Bradshaw. Edwin had to brace himself again, for an assault upon the fastness of the stationmaster.

And in the incredibly small and incredibly dirty fastness of the stationmaster, they indeed found a Bradshaw. Hilda precipitately took it and opened it on the stationmaster's table. She looked for Brighton in it as she might have looked for a particular individual in a city. Then Edwin was bending over it, with his ear close to her ear, and the sleeve of his overcoat touching her sleeve. She was physically aware of him, for the first time. She thought, disconcerted: 'But he is an utter stranger to me! What do I know of him?' And then she thought: 'For more than a year he must have carried my image in his heart!'

'Here,' said Edwin brusquely, and with a certain superiority, 'you might just let me have a look at it myself.'

She yielded, tacitly admitting that a woman was no match for Bradshaw.

After a few moments' frowning Edwin said:

'Yes, there's a train to Brighton at eleven-thirty tonight!'

'May I look?'

'Certainly,' said he, subtly condescending.

She examined the page, with a serious deliberation.

'But what does this "*f*" mean?' she asked. 'Did you notice this "*f*"?'

'Yes. It means Thursdays and Saturdays only,' said Edwin, his eyes twinkling. It was as if he had said: 'You think yourself very clever, but do you suppose that I can't read the notes in a time-table?'

'Well –' She hesitated.

'Today's Thursday, you see,' he remarked curtly.

She was ravished by his tone and his manner. And she became humble before him, for in the space of a few seconds he had grown mysteriously and powerfully masculine to her. But with all his masculinity there remained the same wistful, honest, boyish look in his eyes. And she thought: 'If I marry him it will be for the look in his eyes.'

'I'm all right, then,' she said aloud, and smiled.

With hands nervously working within her muff, she suddenly missed the handkerchief which she had placed there.

'I believe I must have dropped my handkerchief in your shop!' she was about to say. The phrase was actually on her tongue; but by a strange instinctive, defensive discretion she shut her mouth on it and kept silence. She thought: 'Perhaps I had better not go into his shop again today.'

III

They descended the hill from the station. Hilda was very ill at ease. She kept saying to herself: 'This adventure is over now. I cannot prolong it. There is nothing to do but to go back to the Orgreaves, and pack my things and depart to Brighton, and face whatever annoyance is awaiting me at Brighton.' The prospect desolated her. She could not bear to leave Edwin Clayhanger without some definition of their relations, and yet she knew that it was hopeless and absurd to expect to arrive immediately at any such definition: she knew that the impetuosity of her temperament could not be justified. Also, she feared horribly the risk of being caught again in the net of Brighton. As they got lower and lower down the hill, her wretchedness and disquiet became acute,

to the point of a wild despair. Merely to temporize, she said, as
they drew opposite the wooden theatre:

'Couldn't we just go and look in? I've got plenty of time.'

A strange request – to penetrate into a meeting of artisans on
strike! She felt its strangeness: she felt that Edwin Clayhanger
objected, but she was driven to an extremity. She had to do
something, and she did what she could.

They crossed the road, and entered the huge shanty, and stood
apologetically near the door. The contrast between the open
street and the enclosed stuffiness of the dim and crowded interior
was overwhelming. Hundreds of ragged and shabby men sat in
serried rows, leaning forward with elbows out and heads pro-
truding as they listened to a speech from the gimcrack stage. They
seemed to be waiting to spring, like famished and ferocious tigers.
Interrupting, they growled, snarled, yapped, and swore with
appalling sincerity. Imprecations burst forth in volleys and in
running fires. The arousing of the fundamental instincts of these
human beings had, indeed, enormously emphasized the animal
in them. They had swung back a hundred centuries towards
original crude life. The sophistication which embroiders the will-
to-live had been stripped clean off. These men helped you to
understand the state of mind which puts a city to the sack, and
makes victims especially of the innocent and the defenceless.
Hilda was strangely excited. She was afraid, and enjoyed being
afraid. And it was as if she, too, had been returned to savagery
and to the primeval. In the midst of peril, she was a female
under the protection of a male, and nothing but that. And she was
far closer, emotionally, to her male than she had ever been before.

Suddenly, the meeting came to an end. In an instant, the mass of
humanity was afoot and rounding upon them, an active menace.
Hilda and Edwin rushed fleeing into the street, violently urged by
a common impulse. The stream of embittered men pursued them
like an inundation. When they were safe, and breathing the free
air, Hilda was drenched with a sense of pity. The tragedy of
existence presented itself in its true aspect, as noble and majestic
and intimidating.

'It's terrible!' she breathed.

She thought: 'No! In this mood, it is impossible for me to leave
him! I cannot do it! I cannot!' The danger of re-entering the

shop, which would be closed now, utterly fascinated her. Supposing that she re-entered the shop with him, would she have the courage to tell him that she was in his society under false pretences? Could she bring herself to relate her misfortune? She recoiled before the mere idea of telling him. And yet the danger of the shop glittered in front of her like a lure.

The future might be depending solely on her own act. If she told him of the lost handkerchief, the future might be one thing: if she did not tell him, it might be another.

The dread of choosing seized her, and put her into a tremble of apprehension. And then, as it were mechanically, she murmured (but very clearly), tacking the words without a pause on to a sentence about the strikes: 'Oh, I've lost my handkerchief, unless I've left it in your shop! It must have dropped out of my muff.'

She sighed in relief, because she had chosen. But her agitation was intensified.

IV

In search of a lost handkerchief, they regained the Clayhanger premises by an unfamiliar side door. She preceded him along a passage and then, taking a door on the left, found herself surprisingly in the shop, behind a counter. The shop was lighted only by a few diamond-shaped holes in the central shutters, and it had a troubling aspect of portent, with its merchandise mysteriously enveloped in pale sheets, and its chairs wrong side up, and its deep-shadowed corners. Destiny might have been lurking in one of those baffling corners. From above, through the ceiling, came the vibration of some machine at work, and the machine might have been the loom of time. Hilda was exquisitely apprehensive. She thought. 'I am here. The moment of my departure will come. When it comes, shall I have told him my misfortune? What will have happened?' She waited, nervous, restless, shaking like a victim who can do naught but wait.

'Here's my handkerchief!' she cried, in a tone of unnatural childish glee, that was one of the effects of her secret panic.

The handkerchief glimmered on the counter, more white than anything else in that grey dusk. She guessed that the shop-assistant must have found it, and placed it conspicuously on the counter.

They were alone: they were their own prisoners, secure from the street and from all interruption. Hilda, once more and in a higher degree, realized the miraculous human power to make experience out of nothing. They had nothing but themselves, and they could, if they chose, create all the future by a single gesture.

Suddenly, there came a tremendous shouting from Duck Square, in front of the shop. The strikers had poured down from Moorthorne Road into Duck Bank and Duck Square.

Edwin, who was in the middle of the shop, went to the glazed inner doors, and, passing through into the porch, lifted the letter-flap in a shutter, and, stooping, looked forth. He called to her, without moving his face from the aperture, that a fight was in progress. Hilda gazed at his back, through the glass, and then, coming round the end of the counter, approached quietly, and stood immediately behind him, between the glazed doors and the shutters. The two were in a space so small that they could scarcely have moved without touching.

'Let me look,' she stammered, unable any longer to tolerate the inaction.

Edwin Clayhanger stepped aside, and held up the letter-flap for her with his finger. She bent her head to the oblong glimpse of the street, and saw the strikers engaged in the final internecine folly of strikers: they had turned their exasperated wrath upon each other. Within a public-house at the top of the little Square, other strikers were drinking. One policeman regarded them.

'What a shame!' she cried angrily, dropping the flap, and then withdrew quickly into the shop, whither Edwin had gone. As she came near him, her mood changed. She smiled gently. She summoned all her charm; and she knew that she charmed him.

'Do you know,' she said, 'you've quite altered my notion of poetry – what you said as we were going up to the station!'

'Really?' He flushed.

Yes, she had enchanted and entranced him. She had only to smile and to use a particular tone, soft and breaking . . . She knew that.

'But you *do* alter my notions,' she continued, and her clear voice was poured out like a liquid. 'I don't know how it is . . .' She stopped. And then, in half-playful accents: 'So this is your little office!'

Her hand was on the knob of the open door of the cubicle, a black erection within the shop, where Edwin and his father kept the accounts and wrote letters.

'Yes. Go in and have a look at it.'

She murmured kindly: 'Shall I?' and went in. He followed.

For a moment, she was extremely afraid, and she whispered, scared: 'I must hurry off now.'

He ignored this remark.

'Shall you be at Brighton long?' he demanded.

And he was so friendly and simple and timorous and honest-eyed, and his features had such an extraordinary anxious expression that her own fear seemed to leave her. She thought, as if surprised by the discovery: 'He is a good friend.'

'Oh, I can't tell,' she answered him. 'It depends.'

'How soon shall you be down our way again?' His voice was thickening. She shook her head, speechless. She was afraid again now. His face altered. He was standing almost over her. She thought: 'I am lost! I have let it come to this!' He was no longer a good friend.

He began to speak, in detached bits of phrases:

'I say – you know –'

'Good-bye, good-bye,' she murmured anxiously. 'I must go. Thanks very much.'

And foolishly she held out her hand, which he seized. He bent passionately, and kissed her like a fresh boy, like a schoolboy. And she gave back the kiss strongly, with all the profound sincerity of her nature. His agitation appeared to be extreme; but she was calm; she was divinely calm. She savoured the moment as though she had been a watcher, and not an actor in the scene. She thought, with a secret sigh of bliss: 'Yes, it is real, this moment! And I have had it. Am I astonished that it has come so soon, or did I know it was coming?' Her eyes drank up the face and the hands and the gestures of her lover. She felt tired, and sat down in the office chair, and he leaned on the desk, and the walls of the cubicle folded them in, even from the inanimate scrutiny of the shop.

V

They were talking together, half-fearfully, and yet with the
confidence of deep mutual trust, in the quick-gathering darkness of
the cubicle. And while they were talking, Hilda, in her head, was
writing a fervent letter to him: '. . . You see it was so sudden. I
had had no chance to tell you. I did so want to tell you, but how
could I? And I hadn't told anybody! I'm sure you will agree
with me that it is best to tell some things as little as possible.
And when you had kissed me, how could I tell you then – at
once? I could not. It would have spoilt everything. Surely you
understand. I know you do, because you understand everything.
If I was wrong, tell me where. You don't guess how humble I
am! When I think of you, I am the humblest girl you can imagine.
Forgive me, if there is anything to forgive. I don't need to tell
you that I have suffered.'

And she kept writing the letter again and again, slightly al-
tering the phrases so as to improve them, so as to express herself
better and more honestly and more appealingly.

'I shall send you the address tomorrow,' she was saying to
him. 'I shall write you before I go to bed, whether it's tonight or
tomorrow morning.' She put the fire of her love into the assurance. She smiled to entrance him, and saw on his face that he
was beside himself with joy in her. She was a queen, surpassing
in her prerogative a thousand elegant Janets. She smiled; she
proudly straightened her shoulders (she the humblest!), and her
boy was enslaved.

'I wonder what people will say,' he murmured.

She said, with a pang of misgiving about his reception of her
letter:

'Please tell no one!' She pleaded that for the present he should
tell no one. 'Later on, it won't seem so sudden,' she added
plausibly. 'People are so silly.'

The sound of another battle in Duck Square awoke them. The
shop was very chilly, and quite dark. Their faces were only pale
ovals in the blackness. She shivered.

'I must go! I have to pack.'

He clasped her: and she was innocently content: she was a
young girl again.

'I'll walk up with you,' he said protectively.

But she would not allow him to walk up with her, and he yielded. He struck a match. They stumbled out, and, in the midnight of the passage, he took leave of her.

Walking up Trafalgar Road, alone, she was so happy, so amazed, so relieved, so sure of him and of his fineness and of the future, that she could scarcely bear her felicity. It was too intense ... At last her life was settled and mapped out. Destiny had been kind, and she meant to be worthy of her fate. She could have swooned, so intoxicant was her wonder and her solemn joy and her yearning after righteousness in love.

CHAPTER 6

MISCHANCE

I

TWELVE days later, in the evening, Hilda stood by the bedside of Sarah Gailey in the basement room of No. 59 Preston Street. There was a bright fire in the grate, and in front of the fire a middle-aged doctor was cleansing the instrument which he had just employed to inject morphia into Sarah's exhausted body. Hilda's assumption that the ageing woman had telegraphed for her on inadequate grounds had proved to be quite wrong.

Upon entering the house on that Thursday night, Hilda, despite the anxious pale face of the new servant who had waited up for her and who entreated her to see Sarah Gailey instantly, had gone first to her own room and scrawled passionately a note to Edwin, which ran: 'DEAREST, – This is my address. I love you. Every bit of me is absolutely yours. Write me. – H. L.' She gave the letter to the servant to post at once. And as she gave it she had a vision of it travelling in post-office railway vans, and being sorted, and sealed up in a bag, and recovered from the bag, and scanned by the postman at Bursley, and borne up Trafalgar Road by the postman, and dropped into the letter-box at Edwin's house, and finally seized by Edwin; and of it pleasing him intensely – for it was a good letter, and she was proud of it because she knew that it was characteristic.

And then, with her mind freed, she had opened the door of Sarah's bedroom. Sarah was unquestionably very ill. Sarah had been quite right in telegraphing so peremptorily to Hilda; and if she had not so telegraphed she would have been quite wrong. On the previous day she had been sitting on the cold new oilcloth of the topmost stairs, minutely instructing a maid in the craft of polishing banisters. And the next morning an attack of acute sciatica had supervened. For a trifling indiscretion Sarah was thus condemned to extreme physical torture. Hilda had found her rigid on the bed. She suffered the severest pain in the small of the

back and all down the left leg. Her left knee was supported on
pillows, and the bed-clothes were raised away from it, for it
could tolerate no weight whatever. The doctor, who had been
and gone, had arranged a system of fomentation and hot-water
bottles surpassing anything in even Sarah's experience. And there
Sarah lay, not feverish but sweating with agony, terrified to move,
terrified to take a deep breath, lest the disturbance of the muscles
might produce consequences beyond her strength to endure. She
was in no danger of death. She could talk. She could eat and drink.
Her pulse was scarcely quickened. But she was degraded and
humiliated by mere physical anguish to the condition of a brute.
This was her lot in life. All through that first night Hilda stayed
with her, trying to pretend that Sarah was a woman, and in the
morning she had assumed control of the house.

She had her secret to console her. It remained a secret because
there was no one to whom she could relate it. Sarah had no ear
for news unconnected with her malady. And indeed to tell Sarah,
as Sarah was, would have been to carry callousness to the point
of insult. And so Hilda, amid her enormous labours and fatigue,
had lived with the secret, which, from being a perfumed delight,
turned in two days to something subtly horrible, to something
that by its horror prevented her from writing to Edwin aught but
the briefest missives. She had existed from hour to hour, from
one minute apprehensively to the next, day and night, hardly
sleeping, devoured inwardly by a fear at once monstrous and
simple, at once convincing and incredible. As for the letter which
mentally she had composed a hundred times to Edwin, and which
she owed to him, it had become fantastic and then inconceivable
to her.

II

One of the new servants entered the room and handed a letter to
Hilda, and left the room and shut the door. The envelope was
addressed 'Miss Lessways, 59 Preston Street, Brighton', in
Edwin Clayhanger's beautiful handwriting. Every evening came
thus a letter, which he had posted in Bursley on the previous day.
Hilda thought: 'Will this contain another reproach at my irregularity? I can't bear it, if it does.' And she gazed at the hand-

writing, and in particular at her own name, and her own name
seemed to be the name of somebody else, of some strange young
woman. She felt dizzy ... The door of Sarah's wardrobe was
ajar, and, in the mirror of it, Hilda could see herself obscurely, a
black-robed strange young woman, with untidy hair and white
cheeks and huge dark, staring heavy eyes, with pouches beneath
them. The image wavered in the mirror. She thought: 'Here it is
again, this awful feeling! Surely I am not going to faint!' She
could hear Sarah's sighing breath: she could hear the singing of
the shaded gas-flame. She turned her gaze away from the mirror,
and saw Sarah's grey head inadvertently nodding, as it always
nodded. Then the letter slipped out of her hand. She glanced
down at the floor, in pursuit of it: the floor was darkly revolving.
She thought: 'Am I really fainting this time? I mustn't faint. I've
got to arrange about that bacon tonight and – oh, lots of things!
Sarah is not a bit better. And I must sit with her until she gets off
to sleep.' Her legs trembled, and she was terrorized by extraordinary novel sensations of insecurity. 'Oh!' she murmured
weakly.

III

'You've only fainted,' said the doctor in a low voice.

She perceived, little by little, that she was lying flat on the floor
at the foot of Sarah's bed, and that he was kneeling beside her.
The bed threw a shadow on them both, but she could see his
benevolent face, anxious and yet reassuring, rather clearly.

'What?' she whispered, in feeble despair. She felt that her
resistance was definitely broken.

From higher up, at the level of the hidden bed, came the regular
plaintive respiration of Sarah Gailey.

'You must take care of yourself better than this,' said the
doctor. 'Perhaps this is a day when you ought to be resting.'

She answered, resigned:

'No, it's not that. I believe I'm going to have a child. You
must ...' She stopped.

'Oh!' said the doctor, with discretion. 'Is that it?'

Strange, how the direct words would create a new situation!
She had not told the doctor that she had been through the

ceremony of marriage, and had been victimized. She had told
him nothing but the central and final thought in her mind. And
lo! the new situation was brought into being, and the doctor was
accepting it! He was not emitting astounded 'buts –!' Her direct-
ness had made all possible 'buts' seem ridiculous and futile, and
had made the expression of curiosity seem offensive.

She lay on the floor, impassive. She was no longer horrified by
expectancy.

'Well,' said the doctor, 'we must see. I think you can sit up
now, can't you?'

Three-quarters of an hour afterwards, she went into Sarah's
room alone. She was aware of no emotion whatever. She merely
desired, as a professional nurse might have desired, to see if
Sarah slept. Sarah was not sleeping. She moaned, as she moaned
continually when awake. Hilda bent over her trembling head,
whose right side pressed upon the pillow.

'How queer,' thought Hilda, 'how awful, that she didn't even
hear what I said to him! It will almost kill her when she does
know.'

Sarah's eyes blinked. Without stirring, without shifting her
horizontal, preoccupied gaze from the wall, she muttered
peevishly:

'What's that you were saying about going to have a child?'

Startled, Hilda moved back a little from the bed.

'The doctor says there's no doubt I am,' Hilda answered
coldly.

'How queer!' Sarah said. 'I quite thought – but of course, a
girl like you are couldn't be sure. I should like another biscuit.
But I don't want the Osbornes – the others.' She resumed her
moaning.

IV

On the following Saturday morning – rather more than a fortnight after her engagement to Edwin Clayhanger – Hilda came
out of the kitchen of No. 59 Preston Street, and shut the door on a
nauseating, malodorous mess of broken food and greasy plates,
in the midst of which two servants were noisily gobbling down
their late breakfast, and disputing. With a frown of disgust on

her face, she looked into Sarah Gailey's bedroom. Sarah, though vaguely better, was still in constant acute pain, and her knee still reposed on a pillow, and was protected from the upper bed-clothes, and she still could not move. Hilda put on a smile for Sarah Gailey, who nodded morosely, and then, extinguishing the smile, as if it had been expensive gas burning to no purpose, she passed into the basement sitting-room, and slaked the fire there. With a gesture of irresolution, she lifted the lid of the desk in the corner, and gazed first at a little pile of four unopened letters addressed to her in Edwin's handwriting, and then at a volume of Crashaw, which the enthusiastic Tom Orgreave had sent to her as a reward for her appreciation of Crashaw's poems. She re-leased the lid suddenly, and went upstairs to her bedroom, chatting sugarily for an instant on the way with the second Miss Watchett. In the bedroom, she donned her street-things, and then she descended. She had to go to the Registry Office in North Street about a new cook. She stopped at the front door, and then surprisingly went down once more into the basement sitting-room. Standing up at the desk, she wrote this letter: 'DARLING JANET, – I am now married to George Cannon. The marriage is not quite public, but I tell you before anybody, and you might tell Edwin Clayhanger. – Your loving H. L.' Least said soonest mended! And the conciseness would discourage questioning. She inserted the letter into an envelope, which she addressed and stamped, and then she fled with it from the house, and in two minutes it was in a letter-box, and she was walking slowly along the King's Road past the shops.

The letter was the swift and desperate sequel to several days' absolutely sterile reflection. It said enough for the moment. Later, she could explain that her husband had left her. She could not write to Edwin. She could not bring herself to write anything to him. She could not confess, nor beg for forgiveness nor even for sympathetic understanding. She could not admit the uninstructed rashness which had led her to assume positively, on inadequate grounds, that her union with George Cannon had been fruitless. She must suffer, and he also must suffer. Rather than let him know, in any conceivable manner, that, all unwitting, she was bearing the child of another at the moment of her betrothal to himself, she preferred to be regarded as a jilt of the very worst kind. Strange that she should choose the role of deceiver instead of the role of victim! Strange that she would sooner be hated and scorned than pitied! Strange that she would not even give Edwin the opportunity of treating her as a widow! But so it was! For her, the one possible attitude towards Edwin was the attitude of silence. In the silence of the grave her love for him existed.

As she walked along the chill promenade she looked with discreet curiosity at every woman she met, to see her condition. This matter, which before she had never thought of, now obsessed her; and all women were divided for her into two classes, the expectant and the others. Also her self-consciousness was extreme, more so even than it had been after her mother's death. She was not frightened – yet. She was assuredly not panic-stricken. Rather her mood was grim, harsh, and calmly bitter. She thought: 'I suppose George must be informed.' It affected her queerly that if she took it into her head she need never go back to Preston Street. She was free. She owed nothing to anybody. And yet she would go back. She would require a home, soon. And she would require a livelihood, for the shares of the Brighton Hotel Continental Limited promised to be sterile and were already unsaleable. But apart from these considerations, she would have gone back for Sarah Gailey – because Sarah Gailey was entirely dependent on her. She detested Sarah, despite Sarah's sufferings, and yet by her conscience she was for ever bound to her.

The future loomed appalling. Sarah's career was finished. She could not be anything but a burden and a torment; her last years would probably be dreadful, both for herself and for others. The prospects of the boarding-house were not radiant. Hilda could direct the enterprise, but not well. She could work, but she had not the art of making others work. Already the place was slightly at sixes and sevens. And she loathed it. She loathed the whole business of catering. Along the entire length of the King's Road, the smells of basement kitchens ascended to the pavement and offended the nose. And Hilda saw all Brighton as a colossal and disgusting enlargement of the kitchen at No. 59. She saw the background and the pits of Brighton – that which underlies and hides behind, and is not seen. The grandeur of the King's Road was naught to her. Her glance pierced it and it faded to an hallucination. Beyond it she envisaged the years to come, the

messy and endless struggle, the necessary avarice and trickeries
incidental to it – and perhaps the ultimate failure. She would
never make money – she felt that! She was not born to make
money – especially by dodges and false politeness, out of idle,
empty-noddled boarders. She would lose it and lose it. And she
pictured what she would be in ten years: the hard-driven landlady, up to every subterfuge – with a child to feed and educate,
and perhaps a bedridden, querulous invalid to support. And
there was no alternative to the tableau.

She went by the Chichester, which towered with all its stories
above her head. Who would take it now? George Cannon would
have made it pay. He would have made anything pay. How? ...
She was definitely cut off from the magnificence of the King's
Road. The side street was her destiny; the side street and shabbiness. And it was all George's fault – and hers! The poverty, if
it came, would be George's fault alone. For he had squandered
her money in a speculation. It astounded her that George, so
shrewd and well balanced, should have made an investment so
foolish. She did not realize that a passion for a business enterprise,
as for a woman, is capable of destroying the balance of any man.
And George Cannon had had both passions.

And then she saw Florrie Bagster, on the other side of the
street, walking leisurely by the sea-wall, alone. If Mr Boutwood
had had a more generous and wild disposition he might have
allowed Florrie to ruin him in six months of furs and carriages
and champagne. But Mr Boutwood, though a dog, was a careful
dog, especially at those moments when the conventional dog can
refuse nothing. Florrie was well and warmly dressed – no more;
and she was on foot. Hilda's gaze fastened on her, and immediately divined from the cut and fall of the coat that Florrie
had something to conceal from every one but her Mr Boutwood.
And whereas Florrie trod the pavement with a charming little
air that wavered between impudence and modesty, between timid
meekness and conceit, Hilda blushed with shame and pity. She
on one footpath, and Florrie on the other!

'Soon,' she thought, 'I shall not be able to walk along this
road!'

She had sinned. She admitted that she had sinned against some
quality in herself. But how innocently and how ignorantly!

And what a tremendous punishment for so transient a weakness! And new consequences, still more disastrous than any she had foreseen, presented themselves one after another. George had escaped, but a word of open scandal, a single whisper in the ear of the old creature down at Torquay, might actuate machinery that would reach out after him and drag him back, and plant him in jail. George, the father of her child, in jail! It was all a matter of chance – sheer chance! She began to perceive what life really was, and the immense importance of hazard therein. Nevertheless, without frailty, without defection, what could chance have done? She began to perceive that this that she was living through was life. She bit her lips. Grief! Shame! Disillusion! Hardship! Peril! Catastrophe! Exile! Above all, exile! These had to be faced, and they would be faced. She recalled the fireiest verse of Crashaw, and she set her shoulders back. There was the stuff of a woman in her ... Only a little while, and she had seen before her a beloved boy entranced by her charm. She had now no charm. Where now was the soft virgin? ... And yet, somehow, magically, miraculously, the soft virgin was still there! And the invincible vague hope of youth, and the irrepressible consciousness of power, were almost ready to flame up afresh, contrary to all reason, and irradiate her starless soul.

MORE ABOUT PENGUINS
AND PELICANS

Penguinews, which appears every month, contains details of all the new books issued by Penguins as they are published. From time to time it is supplemented by *Penguins in Print*, which is a complete list of all titles available. (There are some five thousand of these.)

A specimen copy of *Penguinews* will be sent to you free on request. For a year's issues (including the complete lists) please send 50p if you live in the British Isles, or 75p if you live elsewhere. Just write to Dept EP, Penguin Books Ltd, Harmondsworth, Middlesex, enclosing a cheque or postal order, and your name will be added to the mailing list.

In the U.S.A.: For a complete list of books available from Penguin in the United States write to Dept CS, Penguin Books Inc., 7110 Ambassador Road, Baltimore, Maryland 21207.

In Canada: For a complete list of books available from Penguin in Canada write to Penguin Books Canada Ltd, 41 Steelcase Road West, Markham, Ontario

Penguin Modern Classics

THE GRAND BABYLON HOTEL

Arnold Bennett

Arnold Bennett's reputation has revived suddenly and re-markably over recent years. His status as a 'Penguin Modern Classics' author is assured, though not all his work reaches the high standard of such novels as *Anna of the Five Towns*.

The Grand Babylon Hotel is in this category. Written 'for a lark' and sold as a serial for £100, the novel was intended by its author to be 'absolutely sublime in those qualities that should characterize a sensational serial'. And it is.

As action crowds on action (with cliff-hangers to close every chapter) crowned heads, petty princelings and pluto-crats jostle with international conspirators and murderers in the public rooms and corridors of the greatest hotel in Europe.

When Theodore Racksole, New York railroad millionaire, buys the Grand Babylon on a whim, he is warned by the vendor, M. Felix Babylon: 'You will regret the purchase.' Returning to his table in the *salle à manger*, he imparts the news to his beautiful daughter, Nella.

And now read on.

Penguin Modern Classics

ANNA OF THE FIVE TOWNS

Arnold Bennett

This is one of the finest of Arnold Bennett's novels, a brilliantly detailed picture of life in the potteries; a tightly knit story of the destructive forces of evangelism and industrial expansion at work in a small community.

'Bennett at his best . . . In *Anna of the Five Towns* Bennett was writing more nearly at a tragic level than ever he was to do later'—Walter Allen.

NOT FOR SALE IN THE U.S.A.

Penguin Modern Classics

CLAYHANGER

Arnold Bennett

Arnold Bennett's careful evocation of a boy growing to manhood during the last quarter of the nineteenth century, with its superb portrait of an autocratic father, stands on a literary level with *The Old Wives' Tale*. Set, like its successful predecessor, in the Five Towns, *Clayhanger* was destined to be the first novel in a trilogy.

Of the book and its hero Walter Allen has written in *The English Novel:* 'He is one of the most attractive heroes in twentieth-century fiction,' Bennett, who believed inordinately in the 'interestingness' of ordinary things and ordinary people, was never more successful in revealing the 'interestingness' of an apparently ordinary man than in Edwin Clayhanger.

Penguin Modern Classics

THE GRIM SMILE
OF THE FIVE TOWNS

Arnold Bennett

In the short stories which make up *The Grim Smile of the Five Towns*, Arnold Bennett caught some of the manner of Maupassant, one of the French writers on whom he modelled his writing. The redolent tale of the coffin and the cheese, 'In a New Bottle', and 'The Silent Brothers' (who have not addressed one another for ten years) possess the true ring.

The pride, pretensions and provincial snobbery of the Potteries are handled by Arnold Bennett with amused tolerance. Most of his stories, like the four linked adventures of Vera Cheswardine, set the home life of middle-class manufacturers of earthenware and porcelain against a 'singular scenery of coaldust, potsherds, flame and steam'. But Bennett never ignores the less successful members of families in a region where 'clogs to clogs is only three generations'.

Penguin Modern Classics

THE JOURNALS OF
ARNOLD BENNETT

Financially and socially Arnold Bennett was successful in a way few writers have emulated in this century: envy characterized him as a kind of literary mogul, provincial, swaggering and vulgar. Men who knew him, however, found him essentially modest, simple, and of exceptional integrity.

From 1896 (when he finished his first novel, *A Man From the North*, at the age of twenty-nine) to the end of his life in 1931 (when Baker Street was 'strawed' to hush the traffic) he kept a diary. Here he recorded what he had done, or seen, or been told, whether in England, France, America or elsewhere, whether at home, in hotels, aboard liners or yachts. His journals are of interest not only for his impressions of well-known writers and political figures, but also for their record of an author's life, of books planned, words written, pounds earned.

In this edition *The Florentine Journal* and new journals recently discovered at Keele University have been added to the condensed text prepared for Penguins by Frank Swinnerton. The whole provides a clear self-portrait of a writer whose reputation is now poised to surmount old prejudice.

NOT FOR SALE IN THE U.S.A.